MICKY TARGETT'S RUN

DC Taplin

Amazon

THR

Central

9010000106055L

With heartfelt thanks to Rhiannon Chandler and everyone on the hill who has made that place really feel like home to me.

They'll never find me up there.

And thanks to Steve Stewart for making my life infinitely easier.

Also by this author

ONE WAY FLIGHT

This book is dedicated to Ted Taplin

1927 – 2011.

The toughest man I ever knew.

INTRODUCTION

CHIANG RAI, THAILAND - FEBRUARY 2008

Hiding.

There are a lot of places to hide in this world – should a man feel the need and circumstances demand. And there's a man who certainly did feel the need, and has laboured under some very demanding circumstances.

The place this man chose to hide has suited him well. Agreeable climate, delightful people, cold beers and great food. Better than Essex anyway.

Out of Chiang Rai town heading north east on the 4013. Less than five miles and you're in hilly, tranquil emptiness. Then a right at Nit's guest house, past the little temple and then follow the road to the end. There's an interesting place where they don't want any I.D. and they never check your surname.

There are lots of stray dogs in Chiang Rai and a while ago a couple of concerned Brits started up a sanctuary to look after them. The ravaged, the beaten, the pregnant and the invalided. All are welcome. Soi dogs. Soi means 'street' in Thai and anyone so inclined can go there to volunteer, help look after the mutts. There's no money in it but it's a good place to hide, should a man feel the need. Palm trees *and* dog shit, yeah, Thailand's got it all.

And that's where this man works. Works and hides. Been taking care of run A4 for a while. The months turned into years and he truly can't remember how many of those there have been. He keeps himself to himself, doesn't mingle so much with the gap year kids and trustafarians, the divorced Aussie women ticking off their bucket lists. Stays in his room most of the time. Reads a lot. Loves the work though. Loves the dogs and they seem to love him back. You know where you are with a dog. No lying or cheating. No treachery.

That's why the organisers gave him A4 because that's where the nutters end up. The amputees with nothing left to lose. The fighting dogs bred into insanity. Somehow they leave the man alone. Yeah he's got a few chunks out of his forearms, but he loves the mad bastards and now they look on him like he's their mascot or something.

Mid-afternoon Friday, and the volunteers knock off early, zipping away on their little Japanese scooters like happy, excited bees ready to pollinate whatever they can find in the local bars. The permanent Burmese workers don't look so lively. Soaked in sweat, wearing ill-fitting Wellingtons, they clomp to their cheaply built, no AC accommodation block. Room and board and a few Baht to send home.

The man hangs back in A4, sits on a crude bench. He closes his eyes, breathes. He's wearing a T-shirt that must be as old as he is. There's the image of a gangster on the front. Al Capone? A machine gun underneath with the legend – 'Bugsys. No.1 in Santa Ponsa'.

He has a look about him that tells you he's been on the wrong end of a lot of things in his life, but he also looks like he can handle it. And that he is past caring either way. The deepness of his tan accentuates the scar on his temple. No dog did this though, it's too thin. A knife or probably a razor.

His long hair is greying, and he's one of those blokes that could be any age. Early-thirties, done way too much, all the way through to well preserved late-forties. Impossible to tell unless you know about some of the things he's been into.

A flame-eyed part Mastiff - part Manticore the size of a small horse sways over to him. It manoeuvres awkwardly, like a lorry parking, and sits on his foot. The man smiles, scratches the back of the thing's tufted head.

'Made it through another day didn't we, Pittsy?'

A bass-heavy growl that could indicate either agreement or contentment or possibly both, rumbles towards the fierce Thai sun.

A bearded man passes along the walkway separating A4 from the rest of the compound. He stops, hangs his fingers through the wire fencing, slugs from a bottle of water. He wears a sweat-stained 'Soi Dogs' vest and talks in a beer-stained Auckland accent.

'Coming for a cold one, Phil?'

The man thinks that he should. The man *knows* that he should. A recluse can attract as much attention as a flamboyant loudmouth. But he just can't be arsed. Prefers it with the dogs.

'Maybe next week, mate. Got to watch the pennies.'

The beard eyes him through the fence, nods and the man gets an odd feeling that he can't quite place. If it's not paranoia then it's a close relative. Eyes on him again?

Left alone he slides off the bench, sits on the rough concrete and wraps his arms and legs around the great, mad hound. He leans forward, rests his head upon the back of its neck. He closes his eyes and ruminates, not for the first time, upon a few of life's recent and significant imponderables. Why does he feel so tired all the sodding time? Why, when he drinks say, two litres of fluid, does he need to get up several times during the night to piss three? Why, even in sodding Thailand, does he have so much trouble getting laid? And most weirdly of all, why, after all this time and in spite of all the above concerns, does he enjoy the best, most profound sleep of his whole life? But he thinks he knows the answer to the last one.

He falls into a soothing rhythm of breathing in time with the dog, even dallies at the peripheries of an afternoon drowse. Then he is jolted to alertness by the sudden tensing of the massive bundle of cable-like sinews he holds in his arms. Then the fearsome detonation in the throat of this thing, the blazing of the hackles into his face. He clamps his hands tight at the dog's bulging chest but it breaks out like a sprinter through the winner's tape. In seconds it is across the run and standing tall against the fence.

'Pittsy! Oi! Get over here!'

The dog ceases barking immediately, now just conjuring a noise like a truck thrashing its gears. Its eyes blaze and when the man is standing next to it, no taller than the animal, he sees someone approaching.

'Down, Pitts. Get back.'

He heaves on two full hands of the dog's neck hackles, pulls him down onto all fours and pushes him away from the fence. The dog stares back up at him, barks indignantly once then flinches as the man feigns to beat him with his hand. It takes a defiant nip at his shin and backs off.

He ignores the sting and the trickle of blood and turns to face the cause of the alarm, sees a *farang* walking, almost ambling towards the run. Another dog barks.

'Shut it.'

The visitor nears and the man sees he isn't dressed for the weather. Heavy jeans, smart shirt and decent shoes. Then, the dropped penny. The wash of recognition. His heart thumps up the panic but then calms. He's nothing if not a realist and after everything he's been through he knows nothing lasts forever. Knows this day is overdue.

The visitor nears the fence, stops and takes in the scene. His handsome face creases into something that could be a smile. Except it isn't, it's just a rictus of smug satisfaction.

'Well well, Mr. Targett I presume. Same old story, eh? Living in shit and chasing mangy bitches around. How you been, Micky boy?'

PART ONE. REBIRTH   RELOAD   RE UP

CHAPTER ONE

Micky Targett lives in a beach hut except it's not on the beach. Which really makes it just a hut. He doesn't care because it's both cheap and clean and that'll do. His needs are simple and he's not much of a one for entertaining these days.

He can survive on next to nothing here which is just as well because that's pretty much all he has. That doesn't stop him being generous. He knows that, even though he's up against it, the life that he was born into was infinitely easier and more privileged than his Asian friends could ever dream about. They all call him kun Phillip and he likes that. Some get it wrong and it turns into Phirrip but he likes that even more. He feels guilty that he's deceiving them but he can't deny it's good being someone else.

On the whole he is as content as a man in his position can be. His life is mapped out for him and, whilst he occasionally refers back to the excitement of his previous existences, he is happy with what he does. What he has brought upon himself to do.

His life has been so full that he has a thousand memories to call upon. Many are bad but some make him smile. Many is the time he thinks about 'clean' sausages, or a girl with emeralds for eyes. Or a Waterford woman, kind and brave, who gave him a shot at grabbing back what was left of his life.

But when the man came to see him he knew it was all over. He felt the clutching fingers of the old life on his shoulders, clawing at him.

Reminding him.

He showers, gets the stink of the dogs off him. He cleans the bite on his shin but that's all he does. No plasters in the shack and as for a tetanus shot – he can't be arsed. He pulls on a pair of shorts, grabs a Leo lek from the wheezing fridge and sits on the terrace with a clear view of wide, green fields. Feet up on the rickety fence, he looks at the old buffalo down towards the far tree line. There's a brown bird sitting on his spine but he doesn't seem to mind.

He takes a long pull on the cold beer which he sluices around onto his upper west side. He does this to see if he still has a toothache and, in his madly upside down world, is almost relieved to appreciate that he does. Being reminded of normality has its uses.

He closes his eyes and waits. Waits for the sweeping purple whirls, the scudding, fluffy, white clouds and the echoes of his former lives.

Micky Targett wonders where he'll be transported to, wonders what's frying live tonight in the skillet of his memory bank. He takes a deep breath and thinks back to what happened.

SANTA PONSA, MALLORCA, SPAIN - MAY 1992

The problem, when you're someone with Micky's history and appetites, is separating what's real from what isn't. Way back when, that wasn't a problem at all, far from it. Back in the old days that was the *aim*. Walking that line into confused, merry oblivion was the holy grail, and he was very good at it. But that was in prehistoric times.

Then everything turned to shit and Micky was a dead man and then everything turned to Ambrosia and Nectar and Micky was golden again. He was suddenly a protected species holding a suitcase full of cash. Okay so he needed it explained to him just how the heck that had happened but that wasn't the point. The point was he was both loaded and in the A team. But at a price.

Connie Chetkins had used Micky in a play of such awesome complexity and panache that it made Micky's head swim with wonder and admiration. But they'd all come out on top. Micky had unwittingly opened up a new route of cocaine into England from the continent and Connie was so far in front of the game on that already it was ridiculous. Not only that but Micky had helped Connie put together a Deutschmark forgery scam that would also reap massive dividends.

Perhaps the biggest coup though was Micky had, again without his own knowledge, helped identify the threat of a takeover bid from Pete Chalmers and Denny Masters, a threat that had been dealt with accordingly. Whatever that meant. So now Micky was living under Connie's considerable wing and to show his gratitude Connie had paid him handsomely for his not inconsiderable trouble.

Now ordinarily, Micky would attempt to blaze through that folding, two hundred and twenty untraceable large ones if you please, with both alacrity and determination. But no, those were not ordinary circumstances and Connie was laying down the rules; no drugs, moderate drinking only and no scams outside the firm. At first he was tempted to tell Connie what to do with his rules but he knew that his position had all the hallmarks of a last chance because, even if he wasn't bunging it up his rancid schnozz at a terrifying rate of knots, two twenty k wasn't *that* much. He had opportunities but he also had commitments and wrongs still to right.

The iron lady had been deposed two years previously and in April ninety-two her replacement, John 'Mr. Grey' Major, lead the Tories to a decisive, fourth consecutive election victory. The next day the IRA welcomed him into office by detonating a one ton bomb at London's Baltic Exchange building.

The UK was stuck in a recession and in September of that year, Chancellor Norman Lamont would hike interest rates from ten percent to twelve percent and then to a sodomising fifteen percent – in a single *day*. But nobody was buying, the strategy or Sterling. George Soros shorted the shit out of everything making a billion dollars for himself in the process, as the country crashed out of the ERM.

All of that passed Micky by. Back in the spring of that year he was still struggling with the how and why of merely being alive. And of being relatively rich. And on occasion he would look down at his kneecaps, those sad, unbalanced yet still functional parts of his body and a pleasant wonderment would settle over him. Because there they still were, between his shins and his thighs. Go figure.

But there were also temptations, and Santa Ponsa in Mallorca in the early summer of ninety-two was not the ideal place for a messed up balloon-head holding two twenty large in cash. Not if he was trying to behave himself it wasn't. For a start Spain had always been cocaine's first European landing point on its way over from South America. Secondly British tourist destinations hadn't been slow in replying to the ever increasing demand for Ecstasy. Just when he needed to keep it tight, he bumped into an old friend.

The unlikely strains of Deeply Dippy by Right Said Fred float from the radio in Captain Francis' sensational apartment perched on a hill overlooking the bay. Micky peers out of the lounge window down to the shimmering pool two stories below. A few years before, slaughtered on drink and drugs, he had taken on the dive without even being able to remember it. Made it by inches apparently.

'Excuse me?' The good Captain enquires.

It did actually sound like a bad joke, thinks Micky, not at all sure what to say or do. 'I'm err, yeah . . I'm off the gear.'

The Captain smiles, waits patiently for the inevitable punch line.

Captain Tony Francis was one of Mick's first customers in the legendary Bugsy's Bar. A career oil-rigger, he had made Santa Ponsa his home for his down time off the rig. Twenty-eight days on some stinking pile of dangerous and remote metal in the North Sea or the Egyptian desert, then twenty-eight days off, living the sun-splashed dream by Med.

After the demise of Bugsy's Micky had stayed in touch and had visited many times, on ordinary holidays and, later on, during his criminal career. And now here they were, a fortuitous rendezvous in the street and, oh dear, it looks like it might be party time.

'What does that mean exactly?'

Micky watches him select a CD, Achtung Baby, from a rack on the counter top. But he knows they won't be listening to it. He watches his friend pull a credit card from his wallet. But he knows he won't be spending any money. Then Franny rummages around in a cupboard, but there will be no cooking done this night. The big bag of white powder he retrieves is upended on the CD case and two huge lines are hacked from it. He rolls up a thousand Peseta note.

'Mate,' whimpers Micky.

'No seriously, I want to know. Have a line and tell me all about it.'

CHAPTER TWO

CHIANG RAI, THAILAND - OCTOBER 1995

Priow, tall and skinny as a bamboo shoot, looks after his parents and his two younger sisters who live west of Chiang Rai town in little more than a two-room hut. The one with he blue door. The children were born in Thailand but his father is Burmese and his mother is possibly Laotian, although she's not entirely sure. It wasn't that long ago that no one in Chiang Rai and the neighbouring provinces paid any attention to nationality and several languages and cultures bled into each other. But now borders feature very much in Priow's life. It's how he takes care of the family.

He remembers well only a few years back how big and strong his father was and how good they all had things. His dad worked hard on local farms and saved to buy a small boat to fish from. Priow went to the local school with the other kids and everyone was happy. Then his father had enough money to buy a long-tail and made good money from the booming tourist trade, zipping through the lush landscape on the local rivers. They lived in a proper house in Chiang Rai town.

Then the change came.

Priow's father had always smoked opium, it was normal among the locals and the hill tribes. He liked it on occasion but could equally leave it alone. Then one of his friends gave him a Yaba pill. The change was as immediate as it was irreversible. The drug possessed him and altered his character so completely he was unrecognizable. So affected by it was he, he couldn't look after the family. Along with taking the pills he would drink all the time. He didn't eat, lost weight, his teeth started to fall out and he looked old beyond his years. Work was impossible.

The house went first. They had to move out of town into the little wooden place. Then, because he needed money, he sold the long-tail. Priow remembers one night an argument between his parents in the next room, The walls so tatty he could actually *see* into the room.

'Now you can't work. You have to stop taking this stuff.'

'Shut the fuck up, woman. All you ever do is moan.'

'We have no money for the school. We have no money to eat!'

Priow's two sisters, Mayuree and Nok, started to cry and cuddled up to him on their bed. He wrapped an arm around each and tried to be brave. His heart pounded in his bony chest.

'Is there anything to drink around here?'

'You useless loser.'

'Stop *talking*, woman.'

The slap and the sound of their mother falling to the floor resounded around the shack.

One day, Priow said to himself. *One day I'll be strong enough and I'll be out from under all this.*

The beatings of his mother became a regular thing that she could calmly anticipate. With a stoicism that chilled Priow she would hold her hand up to her husband. 'Do you have no decency left?' And he would wait.

'Take your sisters,' she said to Priow. 'Take them to play by the stream.'

Priow's eyes bored into his father who would simply turn his back. But Priow could do nothing other than tend his mother's wounds when he came back.

By that time Priow's father was in debt, and the man he owed money to was not a man who liked being owed money. But he was a businessman and businessmen think of solutions.

'You.' Priow's father was standing with him one day. 'You think you're tough. You think you want to be the man. Now's your chance.'

Priow walked over to them, ignored his father and stared up at the other man.

'Go with him. He will show you what to do.'

The family still possessed the old, eight foot fishing dinghy that Priow's dad used to use. In no time, and at no cost to them, it was patched up and a small Suzuki outboard put in place. One night the man and Priow climbed in it and chugged up the Mae Nam Kok towards the border. Priow had no idea what was going to happen. About three hours later the man steered towards the bank where, miraculously thought Priow, there was a tying up point.

'Watch and remember everything. You will not get a second chance, and if you make a mistake it will be very bad for your family.' The man led the way through long grass, past massive stands of bamboo.

Priow was becoming more terrified with each step through the immense dark. After about ten minutes he heard the sound of traffic.

'All you need to know is don't get seen. Wait for the traffic to stop and then run. Okay GO!'

Priow was fast and easily kept up with the man. Over the road and into the trees on the other side.

'Look back and look around. Remember the way you've come.'

On they trekked, over hills, through copses of dark teak trees and fields of long grass until the man held up a finger. He looked around, almost sniffing the air. 'This is Burma. Not long now.'

On heavy legs and with his brain spinning Priow followed, and pretty soon he wasn't feeling so fast or so strong. Then the track they'd been following widened into a gravel road and on the road was a car. The man whistled, the car's lights flashed.

Their footsteps scrunched on the gravel. 'Everything ok?'

Priow observed as a young man got out of the car and walked around to the rear. 'Yeah, no trouble.'

He dragged a rucksack out of the boot and brought it to the man.

'This is Priow,' the man said. 'You and him will be working this from now on.'

Priow only understood a little of what they were saying but he looked at the rucksack and hoped it wasn't his job to carry it. It was half the size he was.

'This is Wunna,' the man told Priow. 'You will meet him here whenever you are told to and whatever he gives you has to be brought back to Chiang Rai. Understand?'

Priow nodded mournfully.

'Ok, off you go.'

The young man shoved the rucksack at Priow.

'What?' Priow blurted involuntarily.

The two men glared down at him and Priow genuinely thought he would never see another sunrise. Then they both laughed.

'Only joking, kid. I'll be going back with you. Just this once. And keep your whiney voice down. Now put that on.'

The bag was so big and heavy the others had to help him to strap it on. Then they went all the way back. When they finally arrived and tied up, Priow was so exhausted he could barely move. The man had the rucksack and then pulled Priow close to him by his shirt front.

'Remember what I said. No mistakes. You lose anything, you take anything, you even *look* in the bag, your family will pay.'

So Priow was a drug courier. He was thirteen years old.

CHAPTER THREE

SANTA PONSA, MALLORCA - MAY 1992

I'm a creep, I'm a weirdo
What the hell am I doing here?

A cab drops Micky off at big Connie's faux Essex mansion sometime in the mid-morning. The scar in the middle of his forehead is all but healed, he's looking bright-eyed and bushy-tailed and is ready for what comes next. The fact that he is two and a half days late weighs on his mind but if there are any questions, which there will be, he has answers.

The doorbell chimes all the way through Land Of Hope and Glory before the massive lump of Beech swings open revealing the equally massive lump of looming and very unsmiling gangster known as Connie Chetkins.

Connie is a tad pissed off that Micky has been on the missing list for this amount of time, but has to admit the kid looks pretty good. He was expecting a call from the local hospital/cops/refuse collectors telling him a wreck of an individual had been found in a ditch somewhere and could he please come along and take possession.

'Morning, Con. Alright?' breezes Micky.

Connie stands aside. ''Ello, boy. Was wondering when I'd see you. Perhaps I should buy you a diary. And a pen. Then you could make a note of when someone has kindly invited you to dinner.'

The door closes and they stand in the cavernous entrance hall.

Micky looks around, thinks he's been in smaller rave venues. He holds his hands up in mock surrender, although it's it actually not too far away from the real kind.

'I know, Con. Sorry. I should have got in touch. Rude of me. But you see . . .'

'This sounds like it might be entertaining,' Connie interjects. 'Let's have a seat.'

Micky trails him through the preposterously large lounge and out to the kitchen where Connie opens his fridge and grabs two cans. Five percent Fosters Export, Mick notes.

'Not for me,' he says.

'What's up? It's nearly eleven.'

The sarcasm isn't lost on Micky. 'You know what, I think I'm off the booze as well.'

'As well as what?' Connie asks, jabbing his chin towards the terrace.

'As well as the gear,' Micky tells him, walking outside, once again taking in the fabulous one-eighty. *Jesus,* he thinks, *it was only a couple of days ago I thought I was going to be killed here.*

Connie pops his can and sits under the parasol, as does Micky. 'I think I've had a revelation.'

Connie gags on his beer. 'Oh really? A revelation. Wow, life around you is never dull, is it? And what form, pray tell, did this revelation take?'

'Nothing heavy, Con. Met a mate, we took a drive up to Alcudia, just hung out and talked. And I realized that I have to change. I'm thirty-two and, thanks to you I've been given a second chance. I've had some shit come my way, as you know, but a lot of my pain is self-inflicted. If I stay healthy I could achieve a lot.'

Connie looks at him. Does that thing he can do of looking *into* a man. Searching. Makes Micky squirm.

'Plus I got responsibilities. Me pop and all that. When I got here a few days ago I was all over the place. I was in no kind of shape to break bread and talk with real people. Thought I'd best keep out of the way and get meself together properly.'

Connie drinks and looks. Then looks some more.

'So apologies once again for the no-show but I thought it for the best.'

The parasol flutters in the sweet morning air. Nothing else moves including Connie.

'Is everyone still around? Georgie? Your other guests? We were going to talk about a possible bar or restaurant.'

Connie smiles like he has just made a decision that pleases him. 'No, son. George has nipped back to London and the Mayor has a busy schedule. But don't worry about business out here. We had a fruitful evening and everyone is happy about everything. Lots of time.'

'Good because I think I need to get busy back home.'

'Oh yeah?'

'Yeah. I got a lot to do. Me dad's bungalow. That's a real investment and something I can be doing for him right away.'

'That's a solid move, boy. Run me those number again.'

It still shreds Micky's guts to think about it. His widowed father's retirement home was worth about two hundred thousand. His eldest son Nigel defrauded him out of title to it and then mortgaged it for one hundred and sixty and didn't meet any of the repayments. This led to the defrauded bank sending the bailiffs around to evict the old guy from his own home. Micky managed to regain possession, then hired a solicitor who put together a case for Eddie Targett to remain in the house pending investigation. The bank, doubtless guilty of negligence in okaying the iffy mortgage application was on very thin ice and is simply sitting back, waiting for Mick's dad to die before re-taking possession.

Micky's scumbag brother had legally got away with it because it was down to the bank to push charges and no way were they going to do that and risk losing the only investment they had. But he didn't get away with it. Neither did his piece of shit wife who was also complicit. Steps were taken. Upon Connie's suggestion, along with Micky's acquiescence, a couple of chaps were sent round.

'Yeah, given what you tell me I'm sure they would be happy with a hundred large to just get rid. Their legal bills will be colossal. You got a brief?'

'Yeah.'

'There you go. That'll put that to bed and you can concentrate your mind on getting back in front of the game. Meantime I'll be working on the restaurant over here. I meant what I said the other day, I could use you front of house. People like you. Fuck knows why but hey . . .'

'So I just walk a suitcase full of cash through UK customs?'

'It's no biggie. I've done it. There's a casino down the road and I know the *jefe*. We'll get proof from them of this ridiculous night of luck you've had.'

'Right.'

'Don't take all of it, though. Take say, 'undred and fifty. Leave the rest here. The casino man will no doubt need a taste. You treat your dad, get yourself set. You shouldn't need any more than that.'

Micky eyes his man, suspects there's something unsaid. 'Don't trust me, Con?'

'Insurance, son. Make sure you come back. Now you keep it tight.' A meaty paw slams onto Micky's shoulder, big grins all round.

'Give it a couple of days, though. Sandra and James are in tonight.'

Micky smiles and warmly thinks of his former lover and, for the millionth time, tries to take himself back to the night he will never remember. Dragging Connie's daughter out of a beating at the hands of her Spanish boyfriend. Saving the life of the unborn son she didn't even know she was carrying. Altruism at its most pure. Shame he was so pissed he can't recall a thing about it but a hero is a hero, right?

That evening a cab purrs to a halt in the drive and there they are. Christ, thinks Micky, she looks good, and they embrace. A ready made family?

Micky crouches to get close to the boy and the whole house hears the resounding crack of his knee. Big laughs all round.

'Say hello to Micky, James,' Sandra prompts the gorgeous kid.

'Hello Micky.'

'Hi, son. How you doing?'

'I'm okay thank you.'

The boy suddenly gets shy, ducks behind his mother and Micky is in pieces with the beauty of it all. It's almost too much for him. A good life. A good, decent, normal life. He can't distance himself from the terrible possibilities that it's both within his reach but also that he is not worthy of it and never will be.

There is small talk and there is dinner and Micky takes it easy on the wine. But he's itchy. He wants to get back into town. Wants to get back on it with the good Captain. He owes him money for one thing. But Micky Targett sits and smiles and sips the Rioja. Keeps it tight.

The next day he wakes up so rested and feeling so healthy he can't help but think there's something wrong with him. He pads to the roomy en suite, brushes his teeth and checks himself out. So far so good.

It isn't exactly hot but a dazzling late-April Mallorcan sun has told Connie what's going to happen.

'Out on the boat,' pronounces the big man over eggs and coffee.

'Boat?'

'Yeah, the Sunseeker.'

Micky is doubtful. He used to get seasick on the ferries doing the booze runs to Calais.

But Sandra and the young one are up for it and Micky knows you don't argue with one Chetkins, much less three.

So then the four of them are tottering down the steps cut into the cliff face, arms full of toys, food, drink and fishing rods and all kinds of crap. Under instruction Micky is then on the jetty untying. He jumps back on as Connie hits the start button and the engines gurgle into life. Clear of the dinky harbor Connie gives it some welly.

Micky takes a seat at the side of the rear deck, throws back his head and grins his arse off. Despite his recent upturn he still feels weak. Not necessarily in the physical sense, but weak emotionally, from all the beatings and the drugs, from the fear of dying and the unrelenting crush of not being in control. But he is also warmed and nourished by the lifeblood of redemption, and by the knowledge that some people thought he'd really been a cause worth fighting for after all.

There is not a single cloud in the sky.

James, impossibly cute and well behaved, plays with his toys, and Micky knows that when he looks at this kid what he is feeling is nothing less than pure love.

Sandra gets down to her bikini and, not unnaturally, Micky can't help but look. He tries to remember the last time he had sex. And with whom. Asking him to explain Einstein's theory of relativity would have been easier. Whoever, whenever, wherever, he knows he is on the way back to some strength or other because he knows he's staring and he has to look away.

Connie, if possible, appears more solid than the omnipotent rock Mick always thought him to be. Not too far out he cuts the engines and rigs up the fishing rods, one off the back and one each off the sides. Spanish guitar floats from the stereo.

Nothing happens at all. Micky wants to talk business with Connie but thinks he can't because Sandra and the boy are there. Sandra doesn't want to talk family stuff with her dad because it will bore Micky. Less comes out of the water than goes in because the boy manages to drop a toy over the side. One of those Transformer things. Slowly it sinks out of sight and he gets really upset about it.

'Never mind, darling, we'll get you another one.'

Eager to repay some faith, or at least make an impression, Micky lurches forward, rips off his T-shirt and clambers up onto the side of the boat. The other three look at him like there's no way anyone would be that stupid.

He's airborne before they can do anything.

'Mick don't, it's too dee …..'

Connie's words are lost in the echo chamber of the Mediterranean sea, and the metallic rush into Micky's ears focuses his remaining senses so completely he is able to see the bright blues and reds of the toy wheeling downwards only a few metres below. What a coup if he could save it for the lad. And down and down. But as the pressure increases and the sunlight begins to fade, the panic comes as he knew it would. Slowing, he thrashes on.

He pops his ears but suddenly it's darker and now cold. One more stroke. One more. One more. Gotcha, ya bastard. But then rather than striking upwards with everything he has for the hero's welcome he fully deserves, he stops. Neutral buoyancy now, hanging free, in the ocean and in time. And the panic leaves him and he isn't scared. And he knows what to do. Just stay here. Let go. Be free.

Peace.

An accident. No one to blame. Not even him.

He's sure he's not going to change his mind but then something changes it for him. The knowing that he has to go back and right his family's wrong.

Also, fuck drowning. He's read that it's not the drifting off to sleep some people will have you believe. More like having your lungs blow-torched, your blood vessels ruptured, your eyes forced from their sockets. No, not this tme. And anyway, there's hope now. And if there is hope then there is a foothold in this life and sometimes that is all you can ask for. So he keeps calm and forces his way back up. Back to the warmth and the sunlight. Back to life.

With the almighty expulsion of air that greets his return to sea level out comes everything he's eaten and drunk for breakfast and dinner the night before. He may be a hero but there is very little glamour to go with it. He treads water until he stabilises, barely hearing the panicked instructions Connie barks at him. He looks up at the looming hulk of the boat and flaps his way weakly to the stern, grabs at the chrome ladder.

On trembling legs he hauls himself up onto the deck. Just as he is about to present the prize to young James, just as he readies himself for some serious thanks and adulation, he slips on the sodden fibreglass, trips to the side of the boat and reaches out to brace himself. As he does so his arm jolts, and the poxy thing slips from his numbed fingers and plops into the water once again.

*

The up-market Spanair scheduled flight back to the UK two days later is a troublesome one for Micky. Not as bad as the trip on the way out obviously but, despite Connie's assurances and the casino paperwork in his pocket, one hundred and fifty grand in cash will make the average customs officer cum in his pants. That's before Micky gets thrown in the airport brig to answer all manner of incriminating questions. To steady his nerves he grabs a gin and tonic from the hot stewardess and thinks back to all the madness with the Captain.

'I mean it. I want to know. You're giving up drugs?'
'Yes.'

Twelve and a half seconds later the top of Micky Targett's head lifts off, able no longer to accommodate the riot of pleasure going on inside. It's been forever since he touched cocaine and Franny's stuff is well primo. Fuck yeah! He makes an immediate mental note, while he is still able, to get Franny's dealer's number.

The good Captain grabs the rolled up thousand that is hanging limply from Micky's jittering fingers.

'So that's what abstention looks like. I'd often wondered.' He smashes a line himself.

So then the beers come out and then the gin and the rum and the music is on and they're both bombing around the flat and it's just like the old days. Except Micky knows. He knows he can't be doing this. When Connie Chetkins tells you to do something that thing needs to get done and, more importantly, *stay* done. The road back to the real world riding on it. So then he starts getting the horrors because he begins to wonder if he really *wants* to go back to the real world. Why can't he just stay where he is? Bouncing up and down with his best mate in this amazing place, epic tunes blaring and a headful of bugle.

'So what happened to you?'

Head down and halfway through some mega air-guitar work, Micky doesn't hear. He just plays on and on, picking the notes. Working the fret.

The Captain totters to the area of the kitchen worktop that doubles as a bar. Pours himself another large one. Bacardi and lemonade, like the old days.

'Mick,' he shouts.

'You got me on my knees! Layla, I'm begging darling please . . .'

'Oi, Eric!'

Micky grins and looks across, jumps down from the sofa. He actually removes the imaginary Strat from his shoulders and hands it to the imaginary guitar tech. Joins Franny at the bar.

''Sup, nigger?'

'Your face, what's that all about? You look like you've been through a mincer.'

The mincer indeed. That's what life had become, one long process of being ground down and spat out the other side.

'Should see the other bloke.' He tops up the G.T. and snorts loudly.

'Seriously, I heard something back from my brother. That bloke he used to see, Jim Titmus. Jim the printer. I heard some weird things back from all of that.'

Micky slugs half a tumbler. Thinks back. Fuck, did all that really happen?

'Yeah well, things got a bit frilly for a while there. Can't make an omelette without . . . rolling a few stones.' He frowns in concentration, looks over his shoulder, looks at the door. Was that someone outside?

'Turned out alright though.'

'Yeah, you said. So what's the plan? How long you here for?'

'Aah not too sure. Zip a dee doo dah zip . . . Me dad innit?'

'What?'

Micky eyes him with both confusion and suspicion and wonders, not for the first time, who is this person? But then a distant memory overtakes him, his body relaxes, flows, eases itself into an arching expression of joy and harmony. Then he says, 'In the wilds of Borneeoooo.'

Franny takes a step back.

'Je t'adore, ich liebe dich. Mmm m mmm m mmm m mmm.'

'The fuck are you talking about?'

Even though Layla has slowed and morphed into the piano section Micky moves away from the bar into the open space of the lounge, heading bobbing, jerking his limbs every which way, moving and grooving to whatever it is he can hear in sparse cupboards of his addled brain. The Captain grins.

'Eskimo – Arapaho.'

At that precise moment the sounds of raised voices and footsteps on concrete are plainly audible from down below near the pool. They both freeze.

'The fuck izzat?' The Captain hisses.

Leaping into action Micky slides to the side lounge window, opens it a fraction and leans out to look down onto the communal patio area. To his horror, and there is no mistake, he clearly sees the dark uniform, the polished shoes, the shiny peak of the cap. And they're coming up the stairs.

'It's the cops! Fuck!'

The Captain turns as white as the pile of cocaine at his elbow. 'Fuck off is it!'

'I'm telling ya.'

'Shit!'

' . . . Flush it.'

'Fuck off!'

'Mate, we're gonna get busted. Move!'

It is in that moment, that nanosecond that Micky tells himself that he will never get in this position again. What had Connie said? Just what had Connie said only a couple of hours previously? He got his very life handed back to him on one proviso; No more drugs! Now here he is, about to get dragged off to the cells by the fucking Guardia.

'Chuck it down the sink now. I'll stall them.'

He slithers to the door and flicks the lock, stands with his legs splayed and his back braced against it, glaring at his panic-stricken friend who is genuinely overcome with inertia. Until a mighty fist thumps on the door.

'Do it!' Micky squeals.

Franny finally leaps into action. He turns on the tap and the smothered Achtung Baby goes in the sink. He picks up the bag and holds it open under the gushing water. A good twenty grams of Mallorca's finest boils and fizzes and disappears before their disbelieving eyes. Franny even has the foresight to grab the rolled-up thousand note, smooth it out and stuff it into is jeans pocket.

'Open the door please.' They hear from outside in stern English.

'We good?' Micky asks.

Franny, smooths his hand around the sink, shoves the sodden, empty plastic bag down the waste disposal, turns off the tap. He appears illogically calm. 'Good.'

Micky snorts one last time, unlocks and opens the door. Instead of the massed ranks of Guardia Civil they are expecting they see only one short and rotund man smiling benignly. He wears a smart, dark blue uniform with a tie and a neat peaked hat. On his left shoulder is small, embroidered patch that proclaims SEGURIDAD. He looks past Micky and sees The Captain.

'Hola, Mr. Tony.' He announces gayly, his Mallorquin accent as strong and flavoursome as a punchy Sangria. Staring at him from three feet away Micky's face is ruptured by both shock and confusion. From across the room by the sink Franny ticks and twitches.

'Sorry to bother you, my friend. Mrs. Sanchez downstairs, she has asked me to ask you to turn the music down please. She is trying to sleep.'

Layla comes to its twittering conclusion and silence descends, a silence so horrible and heavy and so laden with unpleasantness that it threatens to obliterate all three of them under its terrible weight.

Micky can't work out what is happening but Franny can. Finally and with a dreadful finality to his voice he speaks.

'Mrs. Sanchez is trying to sleep. Right. Okay. Thank you, Antonio. Please apologise to Mrs. Sanchez for me. I think the evening is over now anyway.'

The security guard for the apartment block affects a pleased little bow and removes himself from the scene as quickly as he had arrived. Micky stares after him until the footsteps recede into the dark night. He slowly closes the door and looks at his friend.

Franny is leaning back against the kitchen counter. He seems relaxed but his head begins to move from side to side. He sighs wearily, closes his eyes. He speaks softly, to himself. Across the room, the trembling and deeply traumatized Micky is unable to hear what he says. But what Franny, unable to give vent to his upset and indignation in any other way says is, 'Fuck. My. Old. Boots.'

Then Micky, finally, feels able to speak and what *he* says surprises even him. 'Right,' he begins. 'Please don't tell me, right . . . please don't tell me that you just flushed all our gear down the plughole.'

Micky sinks his gin and tonic and then hits up the stewardess for another.

'Actually, miss, could you leave me with a couple of those little bottles and another tin of Schweppes. Save me bothering you again.'

Her dimpled smile and chestnut eyes all but break his heart.

'And have you got Gordon's and not Larios?'

He looks out the window. Now he can smile about it. He can smile about it *now*. But he thought Franny was seriously going to kill him. It took at least half an hour of placation and promises to bring his friend around and keep him away from the knife drawer.

After that they were both still so freaked out they actually *did* go to Alcudia because they both felt that was the only way to calm the fuck down from it all. In that state there was no way that Micky could have gone back to Connie's to pick up any cash. So Franny had to fund the whole thing.

'Whatever this costs I'll pay and then I'll give you the same amount again. Plus I'll replace the coke. That's how sorry I am.'

And they had a great time. It was a bonkers ride up there in

Franny's Jeep and by the time they got there the sun was coming up but they scored a nice hotel and shot the shit and got to know each other again.

'You ever think you're in too deep?' Franny asked that evening as they sipped on huge bowls of Margaritas.

'I know I am, mate, that's why I'm stopping.'

'You didn't stop very well last night.'

'That was your fault, I'm easily led.'

'Seriously.'

'It's all worked out. Seriously. Look I know I can trust you with this but I have a lot of money back at my boss's place. With that I can go again. It's safe.'

Franny smiled but he wasn't convinced. Worried was what he was.

Two days later they drove home to Santa Ponsa and Micky went round to Connie's, squared things with him then grabbed a wad of Sterling from his stash and gave it to Franny. They embraced and Micky told him he'd be back as soon as he could.

And now, two days after *that*, as they wing in towards Luton, Micky slugs his gin and tonic and thinks about his suitcase in the hold of the plane that might just as well be a fucking great bomb it's that ridiculous a thing.

ESSEX, ENGLAND - MAY 1992

At the exact same moment Micky is whacking the G&T and stressing about getting through customs, a man is walking towards the phone ringing upon his cluttered desk. The man is well-built, prematurely balding/shaven headed and in his mid-thirties. He sits down and picks up the receiver.

'Romford CID, DS Pitts speaking.'

'Hello, mate, it's me,' says the phone.

'Hey, there he is. In fact where he is? You back?'

'Yeah. Got in last night.'

'How was it?'

'Warm. And rainy. Florida doing what Florida does.'

'Kirsty and the kids like it?'

'Loved it, boss. If I ever see another rollercoaster again though.'

'Listen to the grumpy old git.'

'Nah it was good. Felt like I needed it.'

'Good for you. And now?'

'Yeah, fine.'

'As in fine and ready?'

'Yeah why not? If you and good old uncle Met can keep funding my lifestyle I'm sure I can keep running down villains for you.'

'That's what we like to hear. The powers that be are very grateful for your help in putting away that team of fuckwits in Chingford.'

'All part of the service. Anything in particular you want looking at?'

'Yeah well, it's this connection between Essex and the City types. You know, the traders and the dealers.'

'Oh yeah?'

'Yeah, it's like we're stuck in the eighties with this. All over the news still. Making us look bad.'

'Ok, I gotcha.'

'These overpaid, lairy wankers. Brentwood, Upminster, Billericay. You know the kind of thing.'

'Tell me about it. Bollinger chunder is something I have to deal with on a regular basis.'

'You always did have a way with words.'

'Part of the schtick innit? Alright guv'. I'll rank up over there. See what I can pick up.'

'Right.'

'You still able to supply the Charlie, should I need to go that way?'

'Yeah, 'course.'

'Sweet. Let you know when I've got something.'

'Go careful.'

DURHAM, ENGLAND - MAY 1992

At the exact moment DS Raymond Pitts of the Metropolitan police force is going about his daily business, at the other end of the country irritable voices echo along dank Victorian corridors. Metal doors clang shut. Keys, so many keys, jangle and turn and deprive men of their liberty. Another grim afternoon in Durham jail.

Terry 'The Harmer' Farmer lies on his bed, stares at the ceiling. The all-consuming fury has finally cleared and he can do some proper thinking. But try as he may he still can't work it out. A screw, Barnesy, leans against the door frame. He's one of the decent ones, affable, working his time up to retirement. But he's a screw and that's reason enough for Terry to loathe him.

'Visit, Farmer. Move yourself.'

Jimmy Mulroney feels like he's been travelling for a week. He's all for visiting his mates and family when they go away but Durham? He doesn't know where that is but it *feels* like it's at the end of the known universe. The bus to Black Horse Road station then the tube all the way across to Victoria. Then around the corner and down the hill to the coach station. Then it's up the M11 and onto the A1 and it takes *forever*. But that was okay because it gave him time and space away from London and time and space from what had happened.

And what had happened was . . . Well, that was what he needed to speak to Terry about but it was all a bit coincidental. All just a little bit wonky. He knew the half of it and figured Terry would know the rest.

Finally off that sodding bus, then more shoe leather into the town to the gate to show ID and to book in. Then it's the usual horse shit queueing up and getting treated like scum. Then the pat down, the wait, leave the phone in a locker. More waiting. He's been there for over half an hour when he gets the nod. Follow the screw, through another door and into the main visiting room. Spots Terry over the far side.

Because of his charges, Terry is under proper eyeball so he's told Jimmy not to bring any gear in. They shake hands but there are no smiles. Terry is looking at some nasty time, seven years and eight months, and no one seems to know how it happened. Jimmy has news for him that will shed light, but it's not something Terry is going to like. Situation he's in though, he's not really going to like anything anyone tells him.

'Alright, son. What's the scam?'

''Ello, Tel.'

They sit and look at each other and Jimmy can see Tel has lost both weight, colour and any remnant of the humour he had when he went in. He knows Terry is a proper face, prison not the kind of thing to put him out of his stride at all. Never has been. But seven – eight? That's a shedload of Saturday nights whichever way you dice it. Even with good behaviour he . . Jimmy smiles when he considers the possibility of Terry behaving in a place like this.

'So what do you know, Jim?'

'Something ain't right, Tel.'

'You come all this way to tell me that? You should have put that priceless snippet in a letter and saved the journey.'

'I got a name for you.'

'Oh yeah?'

'Yeah. Micky fucking Targett.'

At the exact moment Terry Farmer feels a certain red mist descend upon him, Micky grabs his case and heads towards customs. Wasn't all this bollocks supposed to be in the past? He's had the reprieve to end them all, cashed in the score of a lifetime and this is the best way they can think of to move the folding around? What about these wire transfers he's heard about? Where's the early-nineties technology? Single man on his own as well.

Walking just in front of him are the two girls he saw across the aisle from him on the plane. Maybe . . .

'Oh hi, you were on my flight, yeah? Just come back from Mallorca with Spanair.'

One is keen, well unwilling to fuck him off immediately. The other one looks at her shoes. Micky slots in alongside them.

'Yeah. We had a week, cheap as chips. Shame about the weather.'

'Better than Margate though. Listen do you fancy splitting a cab? I can't be arsed training it all the way into London.'

They look at each other. Not keen.

'Not really. Bit expensive. We've spent soooo much money.'

'It won't be that much and those cases look heavy. Where you going?'

'Bromley.'

'Look, tell you what. I've just had a right result over there. Mate of mine took me to the casino one night and what happens? He loses a bundle and I couldn't stop winning. I'll pay. Charing Cross is it?'

'London Bridge.'

Micky smiles. After all, he's not worried about some piddling cab fare, he's got a hundred and fifty large at the end of his arm. He's just got to get it through.

'Whatevs. That's not out of my way. I can't go to Bromley but I'll drop you at London Bridge. On me.'

They swap glances. He seems like a nice bloke.

By this time they're approaching the entrance to the green channel. Micky looks through and sees customs officers on duty. Got to look like a couple and her mate.

He grins broadly. 'Blimey, I heard you Kent girls were hard to please but I had no idea. Now if an attractive young female had made *me* an offer like that . . .'

Halfway through. One of the women officers checks them out. The girl closest to him laughs. Even the moody one is smiling.

Micky smiles and shrugs. 'Hey, just 'cos a bloke's from Essex doesn't mean he's *all* bad.'

They both giggle aaaaaaand, we're through. Out into the arrivals area, Micky is swooning with relief. Then there's this voice.

'So how much did you win?'

He exhales noisily. Looks around. 'Sorry?'

'At the casino?'

'Oh er, coupla grand.'

It's only when they are in the cab that Micky ponders how much money he has and, more than that, what it means he can do. With that kind of dosh well, he can basically do anything.

On the way into the city he actually thinks of running the girls - the reticent one has loosened up and is the cuter of the two - all the way home but just being back in London brings him square on to a weird reality. He is both alive and rich, impossibilities a week ago, but he has a hell of a lot to do and doesn't really know how to go about it. Keep it tight.

They get out at London Bridge and Micky comes away with the warm glow of doing a pleasant thing, along with two phone numbers. Then, for old time's sake he runs the cab to Fenchurch Street and jumps on the Shoebury train. He's tired but knows he won't be catching the night flight down to there this day. He's out at Upminster and in a cab down the hill to the bungalow.

As he stands in front of the property the confliction and the distress are on him like the cold rain which chooses that precise moment to start falling. Is this his home? How can it be when it is the source of so much pain? Whatever he feels about the house and his family, he knows he has to get it together and keep it together. He has the guts and now the resources to bring his whole world back to sanity and prosperity.

He reaches to his pocket but in the bedlam of his departure the week before he didn't bother taking his keys with him, or if he did he has no idea where they are now. The lights are on inside. He breathes deeply and rings the bell.

Terry Farmer reaches out slowly and grabs onto the formica-topped table in front of him. The table is, by necessity, bolted to the floor, but that doesn't mean Tony can't and won't rip it up and use it as a weapon or some kind of bargaining tool should he deem it useful so to do. His eyes swivel in their sockets. Rasping exhalations leave his nose. Jimmy has seen this only a few times in the past and what normally happens afterwards is something he doesn't particularly care to remember.

'Tel,' he ventures cautiously.

Farmer holds up a flat palm as if to silence Jimmy, and all Jimmy can do is sit there and hope for the best. Hope for the passing of the storm. Jimmy thinks it might be an idea to let Terry have a couple of minutes, nip to the loo maybe, but then he also thinks it would be quite a laugh to see what Terry might do with the heads of a few of the screws should events take that particular course. But as things stand, the Durham prison visitor's centre isn't going to make it onto the local evening news. Although Jimmy hasn't told Terry what he knows yet.

'What might *he* have to do with anything? In fact give me the rundown again of your little encounter with him.'

'Right. So I goes into the Yaksak, get me takeaway. Friday night innit? Place me order and I'm sitting out the front waiting. I glance down into the restaurant bit and who do I see? Our boy Micky.'

'But you told my brief he was with Dixie, yeah?'

'Yeah.'

'And what, the pair of them are like, on a date kind of thing?'

'Looked like it. Had their heads together, chatting. Looked well loved up.'

'So you let him have it.'

'Too right. Bastard's quick though. Got his arm up to block me but I still slashed him on the side of his swede. Gonna scar that is.'

Farmer nods his grizzly head in fiendish glee.

'But before I can have another go, Dixie's up with a bottle of vino which she lumps over me nut. Next person I see is a fucking paramedic shining a torch in me eyes.'

Framer tries to imagine the scene then tries not to. Juliette 'Dixie' Dixon is the sweetest piece of arse he has ever clamped his maulers on and the thought of her being wasted on that dipshit wannabe gets him in a way he never expected.

'And?'

'And this is not long after you've come out the last time, right? And then Dixie don't want to work with you no more, and you said Denny and Pete wouldn't front you any gear.'

'Correct.'

'And you told me you were putting the squeeze on this bloke.'

'Yeah. He had tax to pay.'

'And then what happens? You get fitted up.'

Farmer relaxes. It's a line of thought that has of course occurred to him more than once.

'Yeah yeah, I know. The bloke had all the reason to have a pop back, but he's a nobody. No way in the world does he have the clout to make something like that happen. The gun, the gear, access to my car. No, Jim. Not in a million years.'

'Pete and Denny?'

'No no, that's wide of the mark as well. Alright they weren't doing me any favours by denying me a bit of chop and keeping Dixie to themselves, but I was straight out the boob. They couldn't take a chance on me and they knew I'd be back on me feet soon enough anyway. Besides, we got too much history.'

'Anyone who *has* got the clout you don't have good history with?'

'Probably yeah, but no one that junkie twat knows.'

Then Jimmy drops the bomb. Drops it and even feels the need to lean back out of arm's reach. Just in case.

'What about Georgie Harper?'

Jimmy has seen his cousin lose his cool a few times. Seen him not look himself. Normally it's when the old bill are in the process of kicking his door in, but he's never seen him look like this. If he didn't know him so well he might call it fear.

'What do you mean?'

Jimmy scans the room, edges forward. He even lowers his voice. 'I got warned off.'

Feathers of doubt and shock tickle Tel's subconscious. His normally gymnastically capable brain suddenly can't find purchase on anything except locked doors, dead ends and unanswered questions. There is so much he doesn't understand about why he is sitting in a prison for something he didn't do, and that is fucking terrifying.

'You got warned off. You got warned off hurting Micky Targett . . .'

' . . By Georgie Harper. He came down the pub.'

Big Tel thinks he is going to faint. If you told him the Pope had appeared on *Wogan* dressed as a Nazi with his knob out he would have gladly believed it in front of this. *The* Georgie Harper. What the actual fuck?

'Jim . . .'

'I'm telling ya.'

'You know what he looks like, yeah?'

''Course I do.'

'Down the pub? Down the 'Cod? The Duke Of Marlborough's Codpiece? Our local?'

'You don't have to keep on like this. . .'

'In fucking Walfamstowe?'

'Tel, I'm aware of how important this is because he threatened *me*. Knows where *my* mum lives. Knows where *my* sister lives. So how the fuck can that be, cuz?'

That right there was the question to end them all. Georgie Harper, the last throwback to the glory days of east London gangsterism. Consigliere to the twins. Nipper Read's nemesis.

'Things ain't bad enough with you in here I've got him on me arse. Anything you want to tell me then please go right ahead.'

Terry looks across at his younger cousin, looks at his mad eyes, like two bloodshot pickled onions. He loves him and he cherishes him but as he sits there he knows there is precisely zero he can think of to tell him. How the hell would a know-nothing, skinny, grammar school, Essex nonce like Micky Targett be able to call upon an underworld legend like Georgie Harper to help him out in his time of need? But maybe it wasn't so much the why as the where. Essex. Micky lived in Essex. Maybe it wasn't Georgie. Maybe it went even higher. Because he knows that Georgie Harper provides 'security arrangements' for another well own Essex man; Connie Chetkins. Who also has a place in Mallorca, and wasn't that where Targett boy had some bar a few years ago?

'Tel,' Jimmy is saying, but Terry doesn't hear. Terry doesn't hear because he now knows this whole calamity is so far above his pay grade there's nothing he can do. Nothing, that is, apart from keep his head down and get his time done. Good behavior. What would that be like, he wonders.

'Tel?'

But Terry also knows that if he does slip, if he does behave *badly* while doing his time, then it's probably best if he does that at the start of his sentence than at any other point. That way his rehabilitation, along with the diminishing likelihood of his recidivism, will be seen to take place as that sentence progresses. Get it out the way now.

Jimmy is babbling on about something but that is now completely immaterial because Terry sees the screw Barnesy across the room. Sees him smiling and joking with another one of the bastards. So he's up and he's over there, and before anyone knows what's what he's whaling on the pair of them. Jimmy stands and stares. A woman screams. Screws appear out of the woodwork and pile into the melee. An alarm wails. Despite half a dozen blokes on his back Terry's right arm can clearly be seen hammering away onto its chosen target.

'Out! Everybody out,' yells a screw. 'Visiting over!'

His back to the wall Jimmy edges around the room. 'I'll catch you later, Tel,' he calls as he heads for the door.

Incredibly he gets an answer. 'Okay, boy,' calls out Terry with an innocuous and quite blithe avuncularity. 'Go easy. You're in charge.'

Jimmy ducks out of there. It's going to be a long journey home.

*

Micky Targett lies back on his bed. No, he lies back on his mum's bed. It was on this spot that his mother drew her last breath and that's why he chooses to sleep there. He appreciates that Connie Chetkins laid an entire Encyclopedia Britannica of answers on his sorry arse only a few days ago, but Micky knows, as sure as he knows there is a hundred and fifty thousand pounds in cash in his wardrobe, that the real answers to the *real* questions will come from her and only her.

So he lies back and he thinks about what has been and what might yet be.

'Seems like it all turned out okay, Mum,' he murmurs, sure to get his words right and certainly sure not to swear. 'But it's all so tough. I don't know who I can trust. And it's fucking danger - . . . shit, sorry. I mean it's dangerous. There are bad people around. I get hurt.'

He waits. Waits for something. He knows he won't be afraid.

'I know I've done bad things but I've got another chance. We'll get your lovely house back and I'll look after the old man. He growls a lot but that's only because he misses you. And because of what Nigel and Nicky did.'

He feels himself breaking up, feels the tears rinse his tired eyes.

'Everything is rubbish without you. I'll try to be good. And I'm sorry what I did to Nigel.'

The reunion with his dad went better than he thought it would. That was mainly because Micky's dad hadn't noticed he was missing. He'd rung the bell a couple of times and the door was opened. The man before him looked so small and so frail Micky wondered what must have happened to him in the week they'd been apart.

'Alright, boy. Nice trip?'

That was it.

As Micky walked in, closed the door behind him and followed his dad into the kitchen for a cup of tea, he realized that it was all down to perspective. The week that had just passed, and indeed the build up to it, was so different from the points of view of the two men, it was like looking at an object through opposite ends of the same telescope.

Micky had recently lost a fifty kilo load of Connie's in a service station on the M2. Then he'd been relieved of a suitcase full of cash, the proceeds of the forged currency scam, at the side of the road over in Surrey. He'd been bashed over the head with the blunt end of a sawn-off shotgun in an adjacent field and left for dead. Then he'd woken up in intensive care and then Connie had presented him with a one way ticket to his own funeral. *Then*, once he showed up for said funeral, Connie told him what had really happened and, by the way, here's two hundred and twenty thousand untraceable English pounds. That was Micky's end of things.

Micky's dad, of course, didn't know any of that. He just thought his son was going away for a week and he was under that impression because that was all Micky could think of by way of a farewell. Understanding this, he didn't take his dad's apparent indifference to heart.

As the pair of them sipped their tea and munched on chocolate Hobnobs, Micky gave some thought to the fact that the old boy had been a bit of a lad in the old days. A career Stevedore in the Royals and then Tilbury docks, he was never averse to driving a few bottles of Scotch and the occasional side of beef out through the dock gates in the back of his car under his sheepskin. On top of that he was a tasty amateur middleweight, a skillset he, according to Micky's aunt and uncles, was always ready to employ, as the need arose, in an impressive array of pubs and other locations around the East End of London.

So Micky felt quite relaxed about showing his dad what he'd brought home from his holidays. Obviously he couldn't tell him the whole story. The drugs, the scams, the guns. No, That might be a bit much, even for Rock Steady Eddie Targett. But Connie's ruse about the casino winnings. He'd been confident customs would wear that, what with the documented proof, and now Micky saw no reason the same thing won't slide it past the old man. Deep breath.

'Listen, this thing with the house.'

'What thing?'

Micky looked back, thinks he's taking the piss.

'Dad, do you not remember going to court a little while ago? We got kicked out of here because . . .'

Blank stares. Micky panics, worries he has forgotten.

'Nigel and Nicolette stole the house, dad. We had to get a lawyer round here.'

It was like a reminder he didn't need. Perhaps he'd been trying to forget about it while Micky had been away, and perhaps he'd managed to do just that.

'What about it?' He winced as his arthritic hip punished him once again.

'Something unbelievable happened when I was in Spain.' He couldn't hide his grin.

'Did it now?'

'I've got a way to get the house back.'

Eddie Targett's shoulders, already weighted by time and worry and betrayal, visibly sagged even more. His eyes closed. A man, so used to winning just about every fight he ever got into, had been cowed and broken by the worst defeat he'd ever had to face. It chilled Micky to see it.

'Let it go, boy.'

'No. No I ain't going to let it go. This is your house.'

'I'm safe, the lawyer woman said so.'

'Oi, that ain't the point. This house is not going out of the family in that way. Me mum wanted to retire here. We're going to get it back, we're going to tell that bank to fuck off, and then when you peg out this house will stay in our family. That's what is going to happen.'

The old guy let the words, and Micky's indignation, sit with him for a moment.

'I don't understand a lot of it, Mick. What can we do?'

So Micky slipped off his kitchen stool, cleared a space on the counter top and slung his case up where he unzipped it. He cleared away a towel and a few of his clothes.

'Our luck's turned, pop. We're rolling downhill again.'

Despite being shattered on a cosmic scale Micky finds he can sleep only for a few disturbed hours. It's a total head-job for him anyway, being back in Essex, back in the house. Being alive *anywhere* is incomprehensible. Sketchy stuff in his head. Mad dreams. The usual scene is in there, being chased but he can't run. His legs weigh a ton and his shoes keep falling off, so he has to stop to put them back on. Then the shape, the thing chasing him catches up so he's off again. Then the only way he can get away is to turn and try to leg it backwards. But then he keeps smacking into things because he can't see where he's going, but at least he can see what's chasing him. But is that a good thing? The big black shape. But just what is that?

So when it gets light he gives up and drags his jeans on. His dad is already sitting in the kitchen with his mug of tea and for a man who's just been thrown a much needed lifebelt, he ain't looking too happy.

'Listen,' Eddie begins as Micky snaps on the kettle. 'Did you say you've got some money?'

Micky is seriously starting to get worried by the old guy.

'Yeah.'

'Well I don't care where it came from.'

'I told you where it came from. Where else do you think I got it?' Christ, Micky thinks, who'd have thought that a free tickle to the tune of one fifty large would be such a problem?

Eddie waves a dismissive hand between them. 'I don't care. But are you sure we're doing the right thing?'

'Of course. We straightened that out last night.'

Eddie thinks it's a lot of money to give to a bunch of bankers. Especially when he's safely back in the house. But the boy is insistent. And it is his money, wherever the shifty little fucker got it.

'Principal, pop. This house stays in the family until one of us makes the free choice to do something with it.'

'You might want to think about getting us a new car, that old thing outside died last week.'

As a testament to his thoroughness, Connie had taken Micky to the casino in Mallorca and introduced him to the owner. They'd had a laugh, a couple of beers, a spot of lunch and talked through the whole scam. Strictly roulette. Doubling. Micky hadn't known what that was but by the end of that afternoon he was clued up to the eyeballs. It cost five grand. It cost Micky five grand for a piece of paper. He'd also chucked a couple of thou at Captain Francis and banked the other sixty-odd with Connie. Wasn't money supposed to attract money?

But now that he's back the practicalities of it all must be faced. He proposes to offer the bank holding the charge against the bungalow a flat one hundred thousand pounds to lift it. Fine, but that means he has to walk into his local Barclays and dump that amount of cash on the counter. Maybe that's why he hadn't slept so well.

When all the eviction shit was hitting the fan, Micky, not wishing to leave the bungalow unoccupied, had called a local law firm and one of their partners, Mrs. Yardley, had made a house call. Mick had explained what had happened, the lawyer yelled fraud! And a judge had ruled against the eviction pending further investigation. That investigation would not take place because the victim of the fraud was not Eddie Targett, but the bank which had lent Nigel and his wife the money they borrowed against the property. Stalemate.

So he calls the law firm and makes an appointment with Mrs. Yardley for that afternoon.

Later that day, before he leaves the house, he slides into his old bedroom, checks in with his heroes. The posters on the wall; Sheene, Blackmore and Mackay. All still there, still keeping guard. They've never let him down and now he can feel like he's making things up to them.

Without the use of the old Fiesta, stricken terminally in the drive, Micky has no choice but to hoof it to the station. This is a pain, literally, because despite enjoying a night on his own mattress his back and knee aren't doing him any favours.

Essex, when you're broke and you think you're going to die, is not a pleasant place. That goes without saying. But flush once again and with prospects a-plenty, he's keen to take the air and re-acquaint himself with his surroundings. Essex, yeah, engine room of the country. Crucible of culcha.

But something's not right. Over the previous year he was so wrapped up in his own struggles, and so consumed by the extremes of his drug indulgences and failing mental health that he hadn't noticed. Hadn't noticed the gloom, the chronic comedown. Hadn't noticed that the once indomitable good lady Essex was bent over an alley wall and taking it hard from whoever happened by.

Where was the swagger? Where was the confidence? Where was all the dosh? It's spring ninety-two and Essex is dead. Deader than disco. Deader than Freddie.

Micky hoofs it up Corbets Tey Road and sees not one but two boards in gardens advertising the sale of the properties by way of auction. Foreclosure has become a normal way of homes changing hands. He's also taken with the number of boarded up shops, the lack of people out and about and the rancid demeanour of those that are. How the mighty have fallen, he thinks as he heads up the hill towards the station, towards the Yeoman. And is if to emphasise the pervading gloom, it starts raining as he gets there. Ah, the Essex Yeoman. The greatest and the worst pub in the world

He can't remember the last time he was in there. That's nothing new because when he was going in there every night he still couldn't remember the last time he was in there. He cups his hands to the glass, looks inside and thinks, yeah, still a shithole.

Maybe now he's minted again he can go in and hold his head up, stand a few rounds for the lads. But then he thinks about the time he was so wrecked he was lying down in the khazi among all the normal Friday night human effluvia. If that wasn't enough a few of the locals, including some his so-called friends, were having a real laugh pissing all over him.

He also has time to think of Connie and his conditions, and about how close he came to blowing it with that last mega twist off with the Captain a few days ago.

Keep it tight.

On the Romford train he thinks about drugs. Christ, he misses it all so much. But even if he wanted to get slaughtered who does he know? Ishy is living up north somewhere. Farmer is living in jail. Masters and Chalmers have removed themselves from public life completely. Romanov is overseas dying. Little Jen is already dead. Jesus, all that wedge back at the house and sod all to spend it on.

But he knows he can't think like that because he has got something to spend it on. He's got a house to buy and a slinky way to go about it. He thinks.

He wonders how it might have been for his brother that time, getting an eye gouged out? He was fine with it when it happened because it was no more than justice. An outrageous kind of justice but hey, making his own father homeless and broke was a pretty outrageous move on Nigel's part. But more and more Micky is troubled by what he did.

And now he has to move and dodge and pay to set the whole fiasco straight. But that's okay, he reckons. Get the house back in pop's name, then everything'll be right with the world again. Micky can then hook up with Connie back over in Santa P, learn from the master and make a fortune there. Then, in time, the Upminster bungalow will be worth an absolute bundle, Rock Steady Eddie will do what comes naturally to oldsters and Micky will inherit.

All he has to do is stay sober, keep off the gear and stop having bad luck. Shouldn't be too difficult.

Then, as the train drags away from Emerson Park station, Micky, for the first time in an eon, thinks seriously about women.

There was this girl he knew once who had two mouths. One was around his dick and the other was smothering his own lips. Then licking his tongue and his balls at the same time. Where the hell had he met her? Where was she *from*? Then he remembers. Back when he was someone. The warehouse loft overlooking the silver snake of the Thames. Julie and Jade sharing his drugs and sharing him. The wonder of it. The ecstasy of it. One day, he thinks as a middle-aged woman in young woman's clothes sits across from him. One day he'll be back there.

Okay so there was Sandra over in Mallorca but he isn't likely to see her again for months. And even if that does progress it's not without its complications. Is he man enough to take on the boy as well? And if he's going to be working with Connie . . .

So there really is sod all in the diary for him.

Yet there was a time.

His ex-girlfriend Julie? He'd seen her about a year before on a cross channel ferry. Successful and happy, hooked up with some bloke. Jade? Julie's best mate and a secret affair he couldn't resist, chasing her dream man over in the States.

Kerry Pattison. An old flame from his first tour of duty in Mallorca back in the mid-eighties. She was with his former mdma/coke partner Ishy Zamaan. He'd done two years because of mistakes Micky had made and Christ alone knew where they were now.

Juliette 'Dixie' Dixon. Queen of the carder and kiters. Crack cocaine and heroin. Betrayer of souls and breaker of hearts. Looks fading and bang out of allies.

Then he thought about Jennifer Baddows. Little Jen, who had died in agony and terror in police custody. Boiling alive on the drugs she was selling for him.

Yeah, right old charmer was Micky Targett. Proper lady's man.

He exits Romford station and turns left into the precinct and immediately wishes he had worn an asbestos suit. How had he not noticed his fellow Essex dwellers had become so scummy? So fucking medieval? When had all this happened? Who were these caterwauling, scabrous serfs? And was it all down to the money? Down to the recession? Unpleasant children were suddenly spawning unpleasant children of their own.

A spotty, tatty youth wearing a grey tracksuit, a white baseball cap back to front, sporting a tattoo of a spider on his cheek and what looks like a corkscrew through his eyebrow, is attacking an ATM machine. While he does this his mid-teen 'partner', in regulation black lycra trousers and proudly displayed, flowing belly, hangs back tending to their wailing and equally uncouth looking progeny.

'Says we ain't got no money.'

'Well don't look at me. Wot you done wiv it?'

'Oi fuck off, there was twenty quid in here yesterday.'

'Well then you must have taken it out then. Now wot we gonna feed him wiv?'

And so on and so forth.

Micky makes a mental note; get the business done and get the fuck out of Dodge sharpish.

In the waiting room at the solicitor's Micky is somewhat alarmed to note that the standard of the firm's clientele is broadly on a par with what he'd seen outside in the street.

This is the first time he's been to the offices of Magee and Cobham and, in all frankness, he is less than impressed.

Mrs. Yardley, their erstwhile saviour and heroine, works in a shit box of about ten by eight. Every conceivable surface is laden with brown files tied up with red string. The carpet is stained, the windows streaked with grime. The seat he is not even invited to sit on has a wobbly leg.

The woman herself is pasty and unkempt. Her greasy hair is pulled tightly back into a classic Croydon facelift. With her huge eyes and fuzzy down, she suggests the appearance of a vaguely disinterested cow. She rises to limply shake his hand as he walks in and Micky notices she is pregnant.

Christ, he thinks, *someone had to have done that.*

He tries to shake himself of his concern because this should be a time of positivity and vim. He is, after all, there with good news.

'How can I help?' she asks somewhat breathlessly. 'You said in your phone call that something good has happened.'

'Indeed,' says Micky, keen to impart the news with a mischievous sense of drama. 'You could say there has been . . . a development.'

He was kind of hoping there might be a cup of tea and a digestive but evidently it's not that kind of firm. He watches as she opens a notepad and grabs a biro. One of those cheap plastic ones.

'I'm all ears.'

'I came into some money.'

She looks up, unimpressed. 'Okay.'

'I, that is me and me dad, would like you to look at buying the house back from the bank.'

'I see. Mr. Targett I don't have the figures to hand. Do you happen to recall what the debt on the house is?'

'A hundred and sixty thousand pounds.'

'I remember now.'

Micky watches her scribble.

'And you have some money, you say.'

'Yeah, I won some money in a casino in Spain. A hundred and fifty thousand pounds.'

Finally he has the attention he was looking for. He wasn't after a hot, fawning secretary and a conference with the partners in the boardroom, but a little respect is always nice.

'You *won* a hundred and fifty thousand pounds?'

Micky shrugs. 'Happy days eh?'

'In a casino?'

'In Spain. I have proof. All above board.'

'Right.'

'Thing is though, we'd obviously like to part with as little as possible. So we were thinking, round numbers and all that, we'd offer them a hundred thousand. Square the debt. Dad gets the house back in his name, the bank do one.'

'Do one? Do one what?'

'No, I mean, they go away.'

She makes a couple of notes. Stops. Thinks.

'Mr. Targett where is this money now?'

'It's . . . safe.'

'In a bank?'

'No.'

'You say it was won in Spain.'

'Yes.'

'Was it not transferred through the banking system?'

Micky starts to feel uncomfortable. Since when was a bundle of folding bad news?

'No. We thought it would be simpler to not do that.'

'So it's still in Spain?'

Jesus, he thinks, *she's worse than the cops. And the bitch is on my side.*

'No. The cash was brought into the country.'

'Physically?'

'Yup.'

'Did you do that?'

'Yes. Is that illegal do you think?'

'I really don't know but I will have to find that out before we go any further with this.'

'I have proof of the legitimacy of the money.'

'As you say and that's all well and good, but that might not be the only issue at hand here.'

More scribbling.

'So you brought one hundred and fifty thousand pounds . . . In Sterling?'

'Yes.'

'You brought that amount of money into the country but you haven't put it in a bank.'

'That was something else I wanted to talk to you about.'

'Oh yes?'

'Yes. Obviously it's a lot of cash, what do you think their attitude would be when I hand it over the counter?'

'They will ask a lot of questions.'

'And I'll answer them.'

She stares at him and he stares back but he finds he can't intimidate her.

'So this money is yours, not your father's?'

'That's right.'

'Even so this may affect the status of his claim for Legal Aid.'

'Oh yeah?'

'Of course. Your father has a legitimate claim because he has no money and very little income. Now he has a hundred thousand pounds or so at his disposal.'

Micky thinks, sod it, forgot about that. Still, who needs Legal Aid now he's rich?

'Okay but if the bank go for it then the rest of the process will be just tying up loose ends, right? Even if we don't have Legal Aid then I can afford to pay the bills.'

'Perhaps. *If* they go for it.'

They face each other and Micky can't help but feel both uncomfortable and a little worried. This wasn't the party atmosphere he was anticipating.

Mrs. Yardley draws a breath and lays down her pen. Micky waits, watches this woman hold up a V sign.

'Two things; I'm going to need to speak to my superior about this whole thing, specifically your taking this money to a high street bank. You don't need me to tell you to keep the money safe until you hear back from me.'

Micky doesn't like this, doesn't like it at all.

'Secondly there is something I don't think you've considered.'

'And what's that?'

'Even if the bank agrees to relinquish their charge against the house in consideration for a sum of money, whatever that sum may be, even if they do that that is only half of what needs to be done.'

Micky squints in confusion. Connie Chetkins, his sage and guru, told him this was going to be a cakewalk.

'Don't you see? The bank don't own the property. Even if they want to do a deal they can't. They would need the owner to agree to that. Your brother has to be involved in this too. And he needs to do what you ask him.'

Head down and deep in thought, his emotions boiling to the surface, Micky slaloms past the flotsam of human detritus in the precinct and goes back to the station. But he doesn't head home. He jumps a London-bound train and gets off at Seven Kings. He has business to do and a man to do it with.

In his previous life Micky bought his cars from Prime Motors on the strip, and Prime was run by a top chap called Chrissie Jarvis. Chris never did Micky any particular favours with the cars that he bought but Micky didn't give a rat's arse about that because he had so much money. And one of the reasons he was loaded was because he used to sell Chris humongous amounts of cocaine.

Now Micky is back and, despite once again having a *lot* of money he is looking for a bargain. Him and his dad need transport and he's not about to be extravagant or taken for a run of the mill punter in any way, shape or whatever.

He walks from Seven Kings station and into the middle of second-hand car heaven, Essex style. He gets to the showroom and shimmies his way between the Granadas and the lower-end Mercs towards the office. Seated at a desk, typing on a keyboard whilst cramming a Curly Wurly into his fat, bald head is Chris Jarvis. Old style grey metal filing cabinets occupy half the space. The upper section of one wall is covered in car keys on hooks.

Casually, Micky leans on the frame of the door and waits. Eyes meet and it's as good as he thought it would be because it's a bit like when the Coyote chases the Roadrunner off a cliff and he peddles madly in clean air, staying where he is. There's a blank look on his face while he tries to work it out.

The Curly Wurly is discarded onto the desk and a meaty palm whacks down hard right after it. Big Chris stands up.

'Mother*fuck*er!'

''Ello, mate.'

They embrace and there is much slapping of backs, cheesy grins and bonhomie.

'Jesus, you look well.'

'You seem surprised.'

'I am.'

'Why?'

Serious suddenly. 'I heard you was dead.'

Even by Micky's wayward standards, this is a tad leftfield.

'Really? Who told you that?'

Chris's several chins rest upon his chest as he thinks. 'Not sure. Down the pub. Can't remember exactly . . . Walthamstow maybe.'

Micky says nothing.

'No, that wasn't it. I didn't hear you was dead.'

'Pleased to hear it.'

'No, I heard you was *gonna* be dead.'

This, not unnaturally, strikes Micky as being even worse.

'Well who the fuck said that? And when?'

'Christ, mate, how do I know? It wasn't said *to* me. I was with some people and I overheard.' He shakes his flabby head. 'Not sure who. And it was a mumfs back.'

No surprise really, Micky thinks. Over the last year or so a veritable Burke's Peerage of Essex and East London shitheads had wanted him damaged. But now things are different. He's back, he's healthy, he's got cash and he has his arse covered. Fuck 'em all.

'Anyway,' he sings. 'Reports of my demise have been greatly . . .' He can't help but think on it. Is he out of the woods? Jimmy Mulroney? Pete and Den? Walthamstow?

'So where you been? How long since I seen you?'

Micky shivers himself back into the room, back into the present.

'Dunno, mate. I do remember you *horrendously* kicking me in the nuts when you bought the 308 back from me. When was that?'

Chris howls with laughter. 'Mate when that thing left here it was in A1 nick. When it came back it looked like you'd been rallying up mountains in it.'

Micky nods sheepishly. It's a fair point. Back then, with his income, who cared about anything?

'Got to be two years, maybe longer,'

Micky nods again. Two years. Two lost years. Anger. Hate. Humiliation. Depression. Drug addiction. Resignation. Re-birth.

Chris seems to sense that whatever scary woods Micky may have wandered into, he isn't out of them yet.

'Sit down, son. Grab that chair.'

Micky does so, and, on Chris's desk, notices the keyboard, a beige plastic box with a television screen type thing sitting on it. He juts his chin towards it. 'Wassat?'

'Computer, innit.'

'Really?'

'That is an Amstrad PC4386SX. State of the art. Shugsy's finest.'

'Very nice. What's it for?'

'Got all me stock on it. Receipts and exes. Everything. No one writes anything down anymore. Future, mate.'

Chris taps his fingertips affectionately on the keys. 'Very hi-tech. I got one at home like it for my kid. *He* shows *me* how it works. He's thirteen and he can handle computers. Christ, when I was thirteen I couldn't even handle me knob.'

Micky looks at the thing like it's a box of writhing cobras.

'Jesus, where you *been*? 'Ere, you ain't been away have you?'

'Had a week in Mallorca.'

'No, I mean *away* away.'

Micky grins and shakes his head. 'That's probably the one place I haven't been.'

'Result. You want a cup of tea?'

'No ta.'

Chris eases his breadth back into his chair, sucks chocolate from his teeth.

'You still doing the booze runs?'

'No, mate. Not for a while. I've had . . . I've had a lot on. Distractions. But things are coming around and I wouldn't mind doing that again. If I do I'll let you know.'

'Would appreciate it. Loads of people doing it now but if it's you then I'll buy from you.'

Micky knows the question is coming and Chrissie doesn't disappoint.

'You still get the . . .' His eyebrows do a neat little dance.

'Nah, mate. Had a bit of grief. Keeping away from it for a while.'

Chris Jarvis nods, saves what he wants to say for a minute.

'Anyway, thing is I actually won a few quid in a casino.'

'Get the fuck out.'

'Seriously. Not a lot but I need a car.'

Chris holds his hands out palms up and smiles. 'I'm touched you thought of me. Got a fully-loaded Cosworth coming in at the weekend. Look proper with you in it.'

Micky already has the 'slow down' palm in Chris's face.

'Not that kind of car, bruv. It's for me dad. Nothing fancy. He goes to the golf club and Tescos and that's it.'

'I see.'

'In fact I'll take the best thing you've got in the place for two grand.'

'I see.'

'Escort I saw over there as I walked in?'

Chris heaves himself off the grumbling swivel chair. 'Let's have a stroll around and see what we got.'

As they exit the office and step out in the covered forecourt rammed with vehicles Micky feels a light tug on his arm. Then he is staring into the hilly acreage of Chris's pale, fleshy face. His earnestness is palpable.

'Also, maybe *I* can help *you*,' he drawls as he closes one nostril with the end of a sausage-like finger. He does not, obviously, need to say anything else.

The next day, as Micky drives away in a nice, shiny VW Scirocco, he can't help thinking that five thousand pounds is a little more than he should be shelling out on something he was meant to do cheaply. Not only that but he's going to have to buy a ton of CDs because there's no bastard tape deck in the thing.

Chrissie though, he's got Micky's back. He's got service history for the car, well he has now, a brand new MOT and he assures him there was only one careful owner.

'A nervous nun by all accounts but you don't want to hear about that do you?'

Couple of things though; one, his dad will love the car. Two, he knows Chrissie Jarvis knows a lot of people. A lot of the *right* people. And the coke is therefore likely to be good.

CHAPTER FOUR

CHIANG RAI, THAILAND - DECEMBER 1995

Priow hears a noise and stands as still as the hot night that surrounds him. He knows that failure and its repercussions cannot be contemplated. He closes his eyes and listens to his own heartbeat, terrified that it is thumping so loudly they can hear it as well. They? Who?

It's been two months since he began his new job. It still terrifies him. The forest, the river, the night and the whole world pulsate with menace and danger.

His boss, kun Paithoon, never smiles. Never tells him he has done good.

Priow has had to give up school because he can only work at night. There is no choice. He works at night and sleeps all day, exhausted by effort and by fear.

His useless father owes kun Paithoon money and this helps him pay that debt, but when will all this be over?

His father still lives on the Yaba pills and consumes practically nothing else. He is either incoherent or comatose. All day and every night. Frighteningly skeletal, he looks like he's dead already.

Priow realizes that his own effort and risk pay for his father's drugs but he knows that what he does is very valuable to kun Paithoon too. Yes, they get food provided and some clothes so the family is protected and won't go hungry, but there should be more.

And he now knows what is in the bag.

The first time he looked inside the rucksack he thought his heart was going to explode. Under the light of a flawless crescent moon, his shaking hands undid the buckles and straps and there they were. Ten big clear plastic bags containing thousands of little red pills. There were so many Priow wasn't even sure there was a number big enough to count all of them.

And he knew what they were because he had seen his father taking them.

Then he asked his friends if they knew anything about it. One of them talked to his brother and a few days later the bigger, older boy came to see Priow.

'I'm Thanawat. What do you want to know?'

'The red pills.'

'Yeah, what about them?'

'What are they? What do they do?'

The big boy smirked. 'What is all this? You're just a kid. You shouldn't be taking them. Leave all that to your dirty old man.'

'Don't call him that. He's not well.'

'I know he's not well, everybody does and everybody knows why. Don't touch that shit if that's what you're thinking.'

Priow chews his lip. He doesn't know if he should tell anyone what he does. But he wants to get money to help his mother and sisters.

'How much do they cost?'

'Why, you going to steal some of your dad's?'

'You're an arsehole you know that?'

'Hey, watch yourself.'

'Maybe I can get some. Can you buy them from me?'

'Maybe. How many can you get. The price changes if there are a lot.'

Priow thinks. He hates what's happening to him. He needs to sleep and he wants to go back to school. Wants to be normal again.

'I'll find out,' he tells the boy.

But Priow doesn't know how he can do it. The plastic bags are sealed shut so he can't just take one or two. If he takes one of the big bags then kun Paithoon will surely know.

He doesn't go every night, only when kun Paithoon tells him to. But everything always happens the way it is supposed to. Priow always ties up at the same spot, Wunna is always there on time and the bag is always heavy

And he is always scared.

One night he gets back to the boat but he hears something. He squats down in the long grass on the riverbank and waits. Doesn't move, doesn't even breathe.

The straps of the bag bite into his shoulders and the weight of it tears at his back muscles until the pain makes him dizzy. Eventually he stands and looks around. Nothing. He slithers down the bank and clambers into the boat. Pulls on the rope but the engine only coughs. He pulls again and again.

Not now, not tonight.

The engine judders into life and Priow opens up the throttle, heads back to Chiang Rai. The sweat pours into his already tearful eyes.

He cools as he heads downstream, the four or five knots he makes provide a breeze of a sort. Two hours later he is back at the outskirts of Chiang Rai town.

He kills the engine and ties up. He heaves the rucksack onto his back, tightens the straps and heads towards the road. He takes just a few more steps before he hears something. An instant after that, he feels a sensation he has never felt before either. Oddly and horribly, he is able to identify the feeling. He knows, as sure as he knows that his life is over, that he has been hit over the back of the head with something hard and heavy. He is unconscious before he hits the ground.

Priow is out of the drugs business. He is still only thirteen.

Thanawat is *in* the drugs business. He is fifteen.

He has no idea how long it takes him to come to but he instantly wishes he hadn't. His head feels like it isn't a part of him anymore. He struggles to his knees and begins to cry. He cries because of the crippling pain, but he also cries because he is in trouble. *Bad* trouble. He looks around for the rucksack but knows he won't find it.

The walk back to his house is agonizing. With every step the pain worsens. He touches the back of his head, feels the gash and the lump that grows by the minute, sees the blood on his fingertips.

As he approaches his family shack he sees the pick-up truck parked outside.

He staggers in and his mother runs to him, embraces him, screams when she sees his blood soaked hair and shirt. She sits him down, pours water onto his head, dabs at the gaping lesion. Everybody is there; his sisters, his spaced out father and kun Paithoon who looks on coldly and disdainfully.

'Where is it?' Is all he says.

'Gone,' sniffles Priow, terrified of what the sneering man will do. 'They hurt me.'

Paithoon thinks, stands and reaches into the front pocket of his neatly pressed trousers. He walks to Priow's father and tips twenty Yaba pills into his outstretched palm. The old man grins, his eyes dance. Paithoon addresses the room but no one in particular.

'I tried to help you people. I was kind and this is how you repay me.'

'It wasn't his fault,' pleads Priow's mother. 'Please leave us alone.'

Paithoon nods. 'Yes. Yes I will do that. You will not see me again and I don't expect to see any of you again.'

He turns to look at the Priow's two sisters sitting dumbstruck against the far wall. He points.

'That one. She will repay your debt.'

He strides across the dirt floor, picks up Mayuree and throws her over his shoulder. Priow stands and challenges Paithoon but his legs can't hold him. He can't even focus. Without breaking stride Paithoon lifts his right foot and powers it into Priow's chest. He is all but airborne, flying backwards and slamming into the wall. He collapses like a sack of rags. Priow's mother wails, turns to her husband.

'Do something! Stop him. Our girl!'

Priow's father reaches for a bottle of Samsong rum, chucks three pills into his mouth and washes them down. The sound of the truck's engine and the scrabble of the tyres on the dirt road drown out the rest of the screams.

Mayuree is now part of the South East Asian human trafficking trade. She is ten years old.

CHAPTER FIVE

UPMINSTER, ESSEX - MAY 1992

I was blind now I can see
You made a believer out of me

On his toes on a footstool Micky reaches upwards to grab the handle of the hatch to the loft space and lowers the folding ladder. Taking care not to stress his dodgy knee he climbs up, snaps on the light and lets his eyes settle.

He sees a ton of junk, his mother's stuff mainly. An old Singer sewing machine. A Kenwood Chef food mixer. It's all tut and none of it will ever be used, but the old man can't bring himself to part with any of it. It's been six years and Micky knows his dad is still in bits. Knows he always will be.

Along with the clutter is a certain suitcase and in the suitcase is a certain bundle of good news. Cash in the attic. But it's getting smaller by the day.

Of the seventy grand in Mallorca five went to the casino owner and a couple went to Captain Francis. Expensive night that was. Of the one-fifty he brought back, five have already gone to Chrissie Jarvis for the Scirocco, which had to be insured. That got Micky thinking and then he realized the house wasn't insured either. Another monkey.

Micky then thought that if he wanted to be active, contactable and indeed, 'back in the game', whatever that meant, then he needed to be mobiled up. Great advances had been made in the development of cell phones since he last had one and the classy little Nokia 101 slipped into his pocket nicely. Two hundred quid.

One day he was checking up on his dad and noticed the shiny arse to his trousers, the holes in his socks, even a sole hanging off a shoe. He was suddenly aware of his scraggy hair and thought the old guy probably hadn't spent a dime on himself, apart from beer, since before his mother had died. And when he checked in the mirror Micky saw he wasn't looking too suave either. So out they went over to Lakeside in Thurrock for some new clobber and a freshen up. Four hundred quid. Each.

It was actually fun spending the money. His money. The money he had sweated and suffered for. But he knows it isn't real. He knows he has fights and confrontations ahead.

So he sits there staring at one hundred and forty odd thousand pounds in cash and hopes there is never a fire in the house. Okay so they are insured now, but he can't see Legal and General wearing a claim like that.

He counts out some money, not even sure he should be doing what he *thinks* he intends to do. He doubts any good will come of it but the tradition of it is part of his psyche, part of who and what he actually is. It is Friday night.

So maybe two hundred quid ought to do it. And then he grabs another oner just in case.

Micky Targett is going to the Essex Yeoman.

It's a warm, early summer night but he opts for his new leather jacket, smart shirt and brand new black jeans. He feels it important to look sharp.

His dad spins him up there in the Scirocco and then, deep breath as he pauses at the doors, he's in. Immediately he winces as he wades through the smokey atmosphere, then he scopes to the left and the right as he makes his usual shortest possible route to the bar. A few suits are anchored to the ramp, two hollow-eyed bozos feed a fruit machine. He orders his usual from the bored teenager masquerading as a bargirl.

''Scuse me?'

'Pint of Holsten please.'

'We don't do that.'

If she had told Micky the Queen of England had been caught doing acid during trooping the colour he would not have been anymore shocked. He scans the ranked taps. What is the world coming to?

'Stella then, darling.'

He has no idea when slow motion became an integral part of the service industry but then he has been out of circulation for some time.

'Does Arthur still run this place?'

'Who?'

'Sugar Ray. Arthur Robinson.'

'Never heard of them.'

Eventually his beer comes. He pays (how much?) and considers the tradition. Okay so it's not Holsten but Stella is still a quality drop. Up to the lips, tilt the head back, then let's have you right now, Mister Weekend. Five, six large swallows until it begins to bite. Aaaaaand relax. Yeah, good to know he's still got it.

Elbow on the counter he scans what used to be his domain. He's not sure but it looks like he doesn't know a single soul in the place. But why would that surprise him? He hasn't been in there since . . .

Jesus. As he ponders he realizes that the time-line of the last half a dozen or so years of his life are completely lost to him. When did he lose the Metropolitan Wharf apartment? When was he doing the booze runs? When was he running the Ferrari? When was he undergoing mental health care?

For a moment Micky genuinely struggles to remember how old he is. Then, once he remembers, he is alarmed by such an unpleasant reality. So he tries to forget about it, but by then it is obviously too late. Jesus indeed. When the fuck had it all happened? And where had he been when it was going on? He's not sure but he reckons it's about ten years since Andy Thompson was on that very spot looking to talk to him. Talk to him about some mad scheme of buying a bar in Mallorca. And the rest, as they say . . .

Feeling discombobulated and a tad out of place, Micky does what he's never done in the Yeoman, or maybe even in any boozer he's ever been in. He sits down. Back to the wall. Check the place out. He takes another pull on the Stella.

On the table is a discarded copy of that week's Romford Recorder. The headline blares; Drug Related Crimes Soar – Police Concerned.

Alongside is a photograph of a shaven-headed, plain clothes officer holding up several plastic bags of white powder.

Micky hears the street door of the pub flap open and the big man strolls in like he'd been born in there. No nonsense. He knows what he wants and what he wants is his beer. Micky is grinning as he calls across. 'Oi, you only putting in half a shift these days?'

The Stomach doesn't slow, he's too busy for that, but he turns so Micky can see his face, his reaction. Surprise of course, then shock. Then he sees what he hoped for, what he longed for. Gladness and a real affection swelling his eyes.

'Jesus H. Christ. I heard you was dead.'

'I'm hearing that a lot lately.'

'Hang on.'

Steven Waverley gets his business of the moment done at the bar and strides to join Micky at the table. He waves a bunch of muscular savaloys towards his old friend and Micky shakes.

'Where the fuck you been hiding then?'

'I've just been to Mallorca for a week but other than that . . .'

He lets the sentence go unfinished because, in effect, he actually doesn't know where he's been hiding. Okay he was at his dad's most of the time wallowing in depression, his mind raddled by demonic drugs, but that's not really pub chit-chat is it?

'I've been around. Had some agro. Family issues. Money got a bit tight.'

'And now? You look well.'

'Cheers. I feel rested. And yeah, I'm back in front of the game. Get this, I won a chunk of money at the casino in Mallorca.'

Instead of the pleased grin and the 'good on yers' that he got from Chrissie Jarvis, he is surprised at the Stomach's reaction. As in there isn't one. Only a look that says – spare me the bullshit, this is why we haven't spoken since god knows when.

Micky is momentarily scuppered. 'Not a lot. You know, not going to change anyone's life, but more than welcome.'

The Stomach disappears half his Stella, has his attention drawn to the door as a fat, mustachioed man wearing ludicrous khaki shorts staggers into the pub.

'Oi. PC. Over here.'

'Geeeezah!' hollers the man as he thumps The Stomach on the

back. 'Hold up, son. Need to syphon the python. Jack Dash here we come.' He's straight off into the latrines.

'Lively bloke,' observes Micky. 'PC?'

'He's a funny bastard. Cabbie. PC stands for Professional Cockney. Wait 'til you hear him speak. That sometimes gets shortened to Pro Cock. And that sometimes gets shortened to just the Cock. But he don't know that. He answers to PC but his name's Bill something.'

Micky nods. Drains his glass. 'So how's you? Markets treating you alright?'

'Yeah same old. Drives me nuts but the money's good. Moved to Brentwood about a year ago.'

'Did you?'

'Yeah, mate.' He sends over another look that Micky can't quite decipher. Something like – If you weren't such a waster you'd know all this shit, and Micky starts to wonder if he needs to defend his corner.

'You missed my wedding too.'

Micky feels himself flush and knows there is no possible defence to this. The pair of them go back to their early-teens at school. Inseparable. Micky knows that the invite was sent. Or made orally in person and there is only one reason he didn't go. He was too fucked up. He had no idea how far out he had drifted. Now though, at least he knows how far back he has to come.

The Stomach finishes his beer and momentarily, they both stare into their empty glasses as if expecting them to magically refill of their own accord.

The Pro Cock powers from the toilets. 'What we having then, lads?'

'I'll go a Stella please, mate. PC I don't suppose you know my old mucker from way back. Mick this is PC, PC meet Micky Targett.'

A while ago, a less capable, less observant Micky would not have noticed what happened to the man's face in that fraction of a second between alarm and recovery. And it really was less than a second. A tremor of acknowledgement, of recognition. The Stomach didn't see it but Micky did. Not the face, the name. They shake hands and PC is all smiles.

'Cool name, mate. Wouldn't miss it for the world. Ha! What's your poison, Geez?'

'Stella for me too please, PC.'

Micky watches him lumber to the bar. 'How did you meet him?'

'He picked me up in his cab one time. Got chatting. He lives in Romford but he floats around. Sometimes ranks up outside here at the station. He talks a lot and he talks a lot of bollocks but he's alright, especially when he's working because it's a guaranteed lift home.'

'So if you live in Brentwood what are you doing here?'

'Friday night, mate.'

'I'm very impressed you haven't been down to Shoebury already tonight.'

'Ha! Been a while since I made the old night flight. How's your pop?'

'He's okay. Driving me nuts.'

'So you still living back home?'

Yeah well, here we are. Micky knew it was coming, it being one of the reasons he was reluctant to retake his place in uncivilized Essex society. How do you square that? All that flash, all that front. The warehouse apartment, the Jag then the Ferrari, the string of hot girls and here we are, thirty-two years of age, living with your dad.

Fuck it, thinks Micky, I got nothing to be ashamed of.

'Yeah.' He shrugs, feeling the freedom of the honesty. 'He's had a rough time of it so I don't mind being around. Still figuring out what I want to do when I grow up.'

As the pints go down the familiar tickle at the back of Micky's brain asks him a familiar question; how are we going to get out of it tonight? He's feeling good with the beer but so what?

A few of the lads show up. Breezer Deller hasn't changed a bit, but to say things are as they were is like is like saying England still has a decent football team. Micky does the rounds, makes some small talk, buys a few beers but it's all very low key compared to the way it was.

Davey Watkins is looking well-turned out and content with life, if a little on the bald and plump side. The plumbing business he started with his cousin a few years back rode the wave all the way through the eighties, then grew into property management. Five vans, eight employees. Micky asks himself, not for the first time in his life and almost certainly not for the last, why aren't I normal?

Davey stands from the table, holds out a hand which Micky takes.

'Micky boy, good to see you and good to see you looking well. You go easy.'

'Cheers, mate. And yourself. Where you going?'

'Family life, son. Missus at home and a young 'un won't go to sleep unless I'm there.'

'You got a kid?'

'Two. One of each.'

'Jesus.'

'A man I often feel in need of. Where did it all go, eh?'

Micky smiles warmly. 'Sounds like you're in the better place, Daveyboy. I've got to stay here with all these ugly fuckers.'

Dave throws his head back and lets go his raucous honk of a laugh but then suddenly is serious. Serious with some eyeball and Micky knows that when this man is looking at you, it's best to look right back. 'I mean it, mate, you go easy.'

Micky watches him go, suddenly feeling very sad for himself. He leans back, taps his fingers on the sticky table. Feels like getting properly wrecked is now *not* a good idea. Maybe he should slide out too? He reaches for his glass only to see a full one appear right next to it.

'Not the time to slow down, geez'. Cheers.'

The Pro Cock weighs heavily onto the chair next to Micky who raises his eyebrows in both surprise and appreciation.

'Cheers . . . PC?'

'I've been called worse.'

'Me and you both.' They clink glasses and drink hard. Micky is starting to feel quite pissed, but not in a good way. Not in a 'there's no other place I'd rather be' way. More of a 'all I'm doing now is bolstering the hangover' thing. But someone's just bought him a pint.

'So the Stomach tells me you and him were tight at school, Mick.'

'Yeah. We used to compete for the class dunce hat.'

'Ha! Is there a picture of you two in short strides somewhere?'

'Probably. If that gets into the papers were both done for.'

'So where you been for the last year or so? Big man says you've been around but you ain't been around.'

Micky wants to tell him. Wants to tell all of them. About his insane, scumbag brother wrecking his family, about his erstwhile friends and colleagues beating the crap out of him, slashing him with a razor, poisoning him. Wants to tell them about his mum who died young and in agony, leaving him shorn of hope, adrift from reason. About the fact that a couple of weeks ago he thought he was on his way to Spain to be killed.

Then he wants to tell them about how wrong he was. Murder was never on the agenda. Not only that but a man gave him a case full of money instead. What Micky most wants is simply someone to talk to. He drinks some more. Doesn't answer.

'Dat righ' you 'ad a bar in Spain?'

'Yeah.'

'Sweeet. Sweet as, bro'. Christ. Bet that was jumping.'

'You could say that.'

'I like Mallorca. Magalluf innit. Fuckin' tarts are gagging for it.'

'I was in Santa Ponsa, next town along. Little bit more upmarket but just as wild.'

'What was the record numbuh o' slappers you boffed in a season?'

Micky takes a good look at this caricature sitting next to him. This sweaty mound of anti-culture could be anything between twenty and forty-five. He's wearing shorts and tennis shoes. With black socks. He has a mustache, for fuck's sake. And the speech. Is this all an act? Is there a reason for this? Micky marvels at the yodeled dipthongs, the slobbering esses, the aggressive percussion of the glottal stops. No wonder Essex people suffer derision.

'I was never one to count, mate. Safe to say we ain't never going to see that time again.'

'You go' that right, bruv'. So where you from? Roun' 'ere?'

'Mile End in the beginning. Then we moved out when I was a kid.'

'No shit! Proper area.'

No it's not, thinks Micky. It was a slum then and it's an overpriced ghetto now.

'So wiv de wind going the righ' way you woz born wivin the sound. You're a proper Cockney.'

'As opposed to . . .?'

The gale of laughter rocks that whole side of the pub. 'Haaa! Nice one, son. So you'd be West Ham then?'

Christ, thinks Micky, now we're onto the sodding football.

'Nah mate, I don't get involved. I got plenty of other things to get upset about.'

'Yeah but, West Ham innit?'

'Well you know what they say about the 'Ammers?'

'Wassat?'

'Life gives us West Ham so that death won't seem so bad.'

Micky gets a look back that makes him think he's pushed it too far. Not that he particularly cares. But then the table is slammed upon and the laughter is thrashing through the air. They both drink.

'So you a Romford boy, yeah?'

'Yeah well, Chadwell 'eaf.'

'How long you been cabbing?'

'Free years. Money's good but it's a lot of work and a real 'andbrake on the fun.'

'I can imagine.'

'Yup, married with two sprogs but I'm still one for a party. Love a Jack and Jill, me.'

'Ah yeah? I was known to set a dance floor alight myself back in the old days. Where do you go?'

'I like the heavy stuff. Techno. 'ard 'ouse. There's a once a mumfer called Lost. Usually in Brixton but they wander.'

Micky eyes him doubtfully. 'Really?'

'Mate, don't le' this cuddly exterior fool you. I'm a goddam *ninja* on the dance floor. Just don't ge' in the fuckin' way.'

And now Micky laughs. Maybe the bloke's alright after all. It was a conversation that was happily continued in the Kusum Bugh Indian restaurant later on.

Four or five of them rolled down the hill and by the time they were being seated the Professional Cockney was acting like he was Micky's best mate. This was okay with Micky because they had a lot in common. Mainly drug experiences. PC crammed in next to him on the bench seat.

'So what's your fave then? I'm a Mitsubishi man meself.'

'Hey I'm well off the scene. All in the past for me.'

'Nah nah nah. Not 'avin' that. You're still a pup.'

Cobras all round.

'So back in the day, then?'

Micky thinks, do I want to dig all this up? Bloke's harmless but he feels the need to lower his voice. Doesn't want the Stomach to hear.

'I like the mdma. The crystal, you know.'

'Well yeah,' chuffs PC. 'I mean wouldn't we all. Common as Unicorn shit though innit?'

'Depends on who you know.'

Chicken Tikka Masalas all round.

'So what you saying?'

'I ain't saying anything. You ever hear of Midnights and Stingers?'

This pulls the Pro Cock up. Shuts him up too and Micky feels this is not a bad thing. Talking business, *old* business, *nasty* business at dinner. Bit undignified.

It's a good night, proper old school evening and Micky is happy to realise he still knows how to enjoy one of those. Cold lager and a hot curry. There's a moment when he chews slowly and solemnly, appreciating the taste of not just the food and the beer but of everything. This life. This normal life. No drugs, no fights, no cops, no hookers, no dramas of any kind. *Wow*, he thinks, *so this is how the world is. I can get with that.*

Then, when the owner, the oft lugubriously drunk Atam, starts handing out free drinks from his own bottle of Punjabi brandy, that's when you know it's time to get gone.

Outside, the Stomach and Breezer get in the cab they have ordered. Micky offers his hand but the Stomach steps past it and gives Micky the bear hug. A proper one, from the heart. They stand apart and the big man eyes Micky in much the same way as Watkins did in the pub.

'Good to have you back, mate. Good to have *you* back.' The point of the massive index finger leaves a mark, an emotional mark, in Micky's chest.

This leaves Micky and PC to walk it up to the lights where they will go their separate ways.

'Listen,' says PC.

Micky isn't sure he wants to. When someone asks you to listen to what they are saying, when they know full well you already are means, in Micky's experience, that it's rarely something you want to hear. In Micky's experience.

'What you were saying in there? Midnights and Stingers . . .'

'Oh yeah?'

'That was you, wasn't it?'

In truth Micky is flattered by the notoriety. The reputation. See, he *was* good at something. Not anything you'd want to cheer your granny up with but still.

'Yeah well, long time ago.'

'Fuck. That was *you*? Fuck, man, I can understand you keeping your head down. Didn't some girl die in jail?'

Christ, this is all I need. 'I don't think so.'

'So are you Frosty too?'

'What?'

'You know, Frosty? The Snowman? Can you get coke?'

Micky chuckles to himself as they near the traffic lights in the middle of Upminster. This bloke is a riot.

'Frosty. Nice one.'

'Seriously, geez'. I'm always up for a line. Got a bunch of lively mates as well. Be worth your while.'

Micky thinks back to the offer big Chrissie made to him at the car showroom. Those two matching halves of the perfect whole.

Then he thinks back to the man he owes it all to, Connie Chetkins. His advice. No, his instructions. Keep it tight.

He knows what he has to do.

Yeah, Micky Targett is back in the drug business. He is thirty-two years old.

CHAPTER SIX

CHIANG RAI, THAILAND - FEBRUARY 2008

Micky opens his eyes, releases himself from the swirling, hypnotising vortex of memories. He looks out at the field now swaddled in the dark blue Thai night. He can't see the buffalo but, as per his usual meanderings, he can hear him up closer to the shack. The cicadas will be kicking off soon but for the moment the only sounds are the tramping and the munching of the old beast.

He reaches down and rubs his right knee. It seems intrusive surgical procedures agree with him no more than did the original biking injury itself all those years ago.

As he hauls himself up from the squeaking bamboo chair he feels an even worse jolt from his arthritic left hip. It needs a replacement, he knows that for sure. He knows this because he remembers the same procedure he bought for his dad and he knows that he is his father's son. But medical care isn't free and the little money he has left will be needed for more pressing things.

He shuffles inside and grabs another Leo from the fridge, noticing he has forgotten to buy food again. There is a half-eaten pack of peanuts on a shelf in the kitchen and that's dinner for this evening.

He reaches for his anti-mosquito spray, shakes the bottle only to find it empty.

He looks at the three wall posters, and then at the framed picture of his two greatest heroes.

Back out on his seat on the ramshackle terrace he props his legs back up onto the crude wooden fence. He turns on his little radio already set to his favourite station. Music and news.

All this time in Thailand has left him with a decent if rudimentary grasp of the language and he enjoys practicing, enjoys testing himself. Weird that he was never able to make serious headway with French or Spanish but the bizarre nuances, tones and inflections of Thai seem to make sense to him. He can even read a little.

He thinks about the man who came to visit. Thinks about what he said and what he offered. The new technology, the new opportunities. Damn, says Micky to himself, if that shifty old bastard came all this way then he must be sure. And it's true, it doesn't get any more epicentral than this.

Micky thinks about filling the pipe but holds off. When he rolls the film of what's happened to him over the years he usually prefers no interference. No fogginess. He closes his eyes again, sips his beer which he manages to force down past the sudden lump in his throat.

His thoughts have become more and more dominated by two figures from his past; his dad and Tik, and all these years later it still breaks him up when they both appear to him. Fuck it, he thinks, and stuffs his pipe with the finest opium money can buy.

The odd thing is, since he came north to Chiang Rai and made his commitments, his bad dreams have eased. He knows what that was now. The shape. The threat. The terror in the night. He knows that what he is doing in Chiang Rai is a kind of penance for sins committed throughout his adult life. His devotion to Tik and her family have relieved him of the haunting load he was carrying.

Then the Pattaya days are in his head. Things were rolling back then. That year or however long it was.

Walking Street they call it. A few other things besides but that's the name the main, furred-up artery of the place is known by the world over.

Walking Street. That festering gash of disease-sodden fun. Hobbling Street more like. Every libidinous fucker, jacked on Viagra or Cialis hustling their prearranged hard-ons along, looking for a Thai holster for their farang gun. A pocket full of rubber and a head full of grubby ideas cadged from cheap porn films.

Some allowing themselves to be slowed and seduced by the girls hanging around on door duty outside the clubs. Others already decided where they're going, head down, remorseless in their pursuit of what they came here for. Pattaya, fuck yeah.

Half a dozen Indians might be spread out across the street, arms around each other. Smiling and laughing, the sub-continent's chosen ones, away from the daily thresh of Indian life. Part of the new breed of tourists.

And the Chinese. Groups fifty strong and more, following a squawking tour guide. Nobody speaks or smiles. No one even blinks. They just stare. Stare at the girls, stare at the lights. Do nothing, say nothing, spend nothing. Go home.

Less obtrusive are the Russians. There's even a grin here and there on the faces of those new-century Cossacks. They look so normal they might even pass for regular sex tourists. The male scum of this entire earth is indeed washed along this putrid gutter.

Here in Asia you can do what you want. *Be* what you want.

And Micky had the whole motherfucking cesspit *down*. He was rolling like it was late-eighties Balearics. He kept it mainstream though. Walking Street and the sois off that. Twelve and Diamond. Kept it in the light.

Because, as he well knows, there is darkness in that place. Back out of the glare with the one-eyed gimps and the amputees. The slaves, the grannies, the children. Away from the neon and the tour groups. *Anyone* can get what they want back there.

But while Micky kept it above board he still went at it hard. It's what he does best.

They say Pattaya lived at that kind of pace can only be done for two or three days at a stretch. They say that if you push the gear and the girls any harder than that then you're free-falling your way to permanent psychosis, and Thailand is most def not the kind of place where you want to be found climbing a lamp post barking at the moon. They don't even like *sane* foreigners here.

But then Micky is not a normal foreigner with normal issues. He nursed his own home grown psychosis for many years and carries it with him everywhere he goes so he has no need of any cut price, half-arsed Asian version. Oh no, he's got the real thing. He's from Essex and he is Micky Targett.

Then one night . . .

Just gone midnight and he was starting to come up. One of each to get things moving. Normal. Not only that but he had a couple of days holiday to come down in. So he was all set to rock the casbah.

Fatefully he was back at the dive shop, not sure if he'd set the alarm at the end of the working day. And he'd left the door open while he was inside.

He'd just seen that he actually *had* set the alarm (early stage dementia on the way, Micky boy) and was making his way out when a tiny ball of sound and movement flew into the darkened shop. The door slammed shut and the lock catch was thrown. The intruder pelted along the length of the place and ducked breathlessly behind the serving counter at the far end.

And Micky Targett looked down into the soulless, lifeless eyes of a terrified child.

And that right there was how he came to be living in a shack up north sitting on his wobbling, creaking verandah, smoking opium, covered in mosquito bites. His obligation-filled life laid out before him like a lit path through a dark forest.

And that is absolutely fine by him.

He puffs and he drifts and the smoke makes things simpler. The smoke softens the hurt he feels. It eases his . . Yes, it eases his burden.

In and out of time he goes again. He is everywhere and nowhere. He is a time traveler. A quantum bronco rider.

Suddenly he is cold. So very cold. He's in a car with a friend and it's the middle of the night and they are miles from anywhere. Starry starry night, and even though they are running the heaters he can see his breath inside the car.

Then the headlights strafing across the rural blackness. And in that car are three men. It's a big car but the men seem to fill it. The car stops grill to grill and the lights are killed. So quiet and *so* cold.

Now he's at the big house. He's nervous. Don't make a fool of yourself, son.

And there is this girl. Not a girl, a real woman. Older than him. Smarter than him. *Much* prettier than him, and her eyes are *so* beautiful. And she's asking questions. They're all asking questions. It's a game and he's at the centre.

And then she's kissing him and it's beautiful. And then there's a man and he kisses Micky too. And everything is alright. It's fun. He is with friends.

Answer the question - hit the line - take the shot.

Answer the question - hit the line - take the shot.

And it's okay and they love him and he is in love. Everything is okay because he is among friends and he knows he can trust them. And the woman. Lisa. She's the answer to everything. Damn. He's finally found the answer.

Or so he thought. Micky thinks a lot of things that usually turn out to have no meaning, no substance. That woman, she was the one for him. They both knew it and they shone together for a brief while, bathed in each other's aura.

She offered him not just his chance of redemption, but a chance of normality, but his old life wasn't having any of that. His past wasn't about to let him get away that easily.

His longed for normality wasn't snatched from him, though. It wasn't so much that. He himself was snatched *from* normality and dragged back into the murk of his other world. Denied his chance of love by the life he was never meant for.

DONCASTER, ENGLAND - JUNE 1994

Ishmael Zamaan looks at the paperwork on his dining table. Checks it and checks it again. It has to be right. Satisfied he folds it perfectly in half and then over to the quarter. Before he leans into the crease he lines up the edges of the sheets once again. Precision is everything in his chosen business.

He gingerly slips the application form into the pre-addressed envelope which he seals. First class stamp. Satisfied with what he has done and the way he has done it, he pulls a beer from the fridge.

He's come a long way and things seem to be working out. High and lows. You need the one to appreciate the other. He thinks back to how it all happened and knows that whichever way he crunches the numbers of his eventful life, all the arrows invariably line up and point towards one person; Micky Targett.

He and Micky made a fortune together in the late-eighties. Micky had the cocaine and Ishy had the mdma and the acid. Great times and happy days. But then Micky fell out with his partners and his main salesperson for the mdma died. That lead to two things; first off, he lost the source of the coke and the main market for the mdma. That was bad enough. But what happened after that screwed Ishy's life in an unimaginable way. Micky's disgruntled ex-partners put a tail on him which led to Ishy who was then grassed to the police. He copped four years and did just over two.

But inside he found out he had a talent for computers and he spent his time keeping his head down and his eyes and ears open. And it *was* grim in there. Unbearable at times but he made the most of it and got himself some of that old time rehabilitation.

On the outside he made the unlikely move from Brighton to Doncaster where his brother was going great guns running his own I.T. start up. His girlfriend Kerry went with him.

Kerry Pattison knew Micky Targett from a previous life. Mallorca. Then she met Ishy in Brighton, kept in touch with Micky and introduced them.

A few years learning his trade properly with his brother gave him all the grounding he needed. But what neither Ishy's brother nor his life up north could give him was what he craved most, being back in the action. Have you *been* to Doncaster?

So the time to make his move is upon him. He hadn't heard of the brokerage he is applying to before it was brought to his attention. But he did his research and knows he could find his way around their systems, knows he could help develop them. Most of all he knows about what they would pay, to start and in the future, and it is all about the future.

 Yeah, time to make his move.

The problem, he knows, will be his criminal record. One bust back in the early days for possession and then the big one, possession with intent to supply class As. Only time will tell him what the attitude of the company will be to that but he knows he has to try.

And this web thing. There's something in this. How would it be if you could sell things, could sell something and no one knew where you were? Or even *who* you were? The anonymity. Got to be something in this.

He also knows the move back south, to London will bring other opportunities and other challenges. No way can Ishy afford to get nicked *again*. He'll be looking at serious time if that ever happens but he'd loved being a drug dealer, had a talent for it. His Dutch connection has long gone but he is heading for the big smoke where all things are possible. Who knows what fun and games might come his way? He feels like a modern day Dick Whittington.

And Kerry will be with him. She has a friend in Redhill where they can land which is close enough to town to commute.

Long way to go, Ishy knows, but he is more than excited. And who knows, if the mad fucker is still alive, and be careful what you wish for, he could bump into Micky Targett.

CHAPTER SEVEN

ESSEX – SPRING 1992

His friends call him 'Eezzer and he is the main geezer
And he'll vibe up the place like no other man could

Micky wakes. Wakes but takes his time.

He is alive.

Saturday morning. Essex. But is it morning? Time was a Friday skinful and a curry would have seen him sparko all the way through until kick-off time the next day.

He reaches for his phone. Nine-twelve. No wonder his head hurts.

As he relieves his screaming bladder he looks down at the carpet. Then thinks, *carpet?* Whoever thought it was a good idea to carpet a bathroom? Has that always been here?

He glumly regards the avocado suite, the plastic taps. Jeezus, the place is grim. Might have to take a look at this.

No sign of the old boy and no sign of the car, so Micky takes his coffee into the lounge and thinks about what he needs to do.

He has a hundred and forty-two grand in cash in a case above his head that is feeling more and more like a liability. It's not safe to bank it and, according to his brief, it might not even be viable to use. He thinks the simplest thing might be to just resort to type and bung it up his nose.

This gets him thinking about cocaine and big Chrissie Jarvis over at the car lot. Source sourced. Then he thinks about the night before.

That bloke. What did The Stomach call him? PC? The Pro Cock. Bit of a wanker but so what? All the chop he can handle the man said. Interesting. Nothing wrong with getting a little business done while he sorts the house out.

Thinking about money, he slips into his dad's bedroom to check something.

Halfway to the far wall he pulls up as he feels some kind of rank stickiness on the soles of his bare feet, sees that the carpet in the bedroom is in a similar state to that in the bathroom. Fuck *me*.

He grabs the brief case that contains not only all the documents relating to the theft of the house but his dad's bank statements. He sees the balance in the account is in the low four hundreds. There is a weekly credit of sixty-seven pounds a week. The PLA payor tells Micky this is his pension from the docks.

He flicks back to the time when the old guy was in credit to the tune of many many thousands of pounds. Over the last year or so this balance was reduced to next to nothing by a few large cheque withdrawals. Micky knows how this happened. He also knows that going over it again will inflame him to the point of murder, but he can't stop himself. He has seen all this before but he wasn't entirely in control of his wits and faculties at the time.

He reaches for his dad's cheque book, flicks through the stubs, all made out to cash, the numbers corresponding to the numbers on the statement. £1,000. £1,500. £3,000. On each stub Micky sees written in his dad's child-like hand the one word; Nigel.

One eye wasn't enough, Micky thinks, because the fat, useless obscenity didn't even need to forge the signature. He just asked his own father to sign the cheques knowing he would do so without question.

In the kitchen Micky grabs a bowlful of cereal and makes another coffee. He feels his head begin to clear. He looks out of the kitchen window into the garden, at the old wooden bench where his dad used to sit with his mum when she was alive. Then later where he sits alone. Sometimes dozing, sometimes talking. Talking to her.

Micky needs to make good. Needs to do something outstanding with his life, and he knows what it is.

He turns on the radio and smiles, sings along, does his jig. "Ezer Goode 'Ezer Goode. He's Ebeneezer Goode!'

80

That's a bit more like it. He thinks about getting off on one. Christ, he needs to get wrecked and bad. Then his phone rings. Saturday morning? Local number but he doesn't know it.

'Hello?'

'Is this Mr. Targett?'

'Yes it is. Who's that?'

'Mr. Targett this is Ben Yardley. I got a call last night from your father's solicitor Emily Yardley at Magee and Cobham. I understand she told you I might be calling.'

'Right. She said she'd need to run things past her boss first.'

'Indeed and that she did. She is due to call you on Monday to talk about this. She's asked me to tell you that Magee and Cobham don't feel comfortable continuing working for you and your dad.'

'I see.'

'But she took the liberty of discussing your case with me and . . .'

'Is she allowed to do that? Client confidentiality?'

'Well it was more like a discussion between colleagues. I do consultancy work and occasionally freelance for her firm. Among others.'

'Oh okay.'

'She told me where you are with your current situation and we agreed that I might be in a more favourable position to help than she is.'

Micky is immediately suspicious. Yeah, the woman was obviously not keen on half of what they discussed, and in truth he was never that taken with her superior attitude. If she'd been a looker then maybe. But now some bloke is calling out of the blue. On a Saturday.

'You're presumably related.'

'She's my cousin.'

If her side of the family got the good looks then this bloke, Micky tells himself, is some kind of gargoyle.

'Alright then. Well if my father no longer has legal representation with his current firm then I guess we are in the market.'

'Very good. What she tells me about your situation sounds interesting. Obviously I need to know more. Do you have your diary there?'

'They only confuse me. What you doing this afternoon?'

Setting aside his initial reservations, Micky feels the bloke sounds sufficiently wide to warrant a sit down, and as he strolls into the Beedle and Bastard pub just off the A127 near Romford he's feeling quite psyched about it. A lawyer you can talk to, he muses. About anything?

Micky drifts along the bar and scopes the room. He sees a tall, casually but well-dressed man in his late-thirties rise from his table against the far wall. Their eyes meet.

'Mr. Targett?'

'Mr. Yardley.'

'Please, call me Ben.' The man offers his hand which Micky can't help noticing is incredibly smooth. He spots the uniformally shaped and nourished fingernails.

'Sure. I'm Micky.'

A few minutes later the two men face each other over soft drinks. Micky is surprised by how Ben Yardley opens.

'Can I ask you how your dad is, Micky?'

A brief with a heart? Or just sycophantic?

'He's okay thanks. Tough bloke.'

'We can learn a lot from that generation.'

'For real.'

'Quite a story, what happened.'

'Yeah well, someone has to be related to the arseholes of this world. Sadly me and my dad are.'

'Have you seen your brother? Any contact?'

A ripple through Micky's consciousness. The warm plastic bags on his thighs. The pale eye.

'No.'

'And the case. You're at an impasse, right?'

'Yup. The bank won't pursue my brother even though he defrauded them. They'll just sit on their hands, monitor the situation and wait for my dad to die. Then they'll take the house.'

'Which bank? Amro?'

'Yeah. My brother borrowed initially from a small lender called Paragon Loans but they got bought out by ABN.'

'Well, I can see their logic. The country's coming out of recession. The value of your father's house is going to fly over the coming years. They wouldn't mind some of that.'

'Well I'm kind of hoping they'll be tempted to cut their losses.'

82

'Maybe.'

'Particularly if we sue them. Or at least threaten to.'

'Could be good leverage.'

'Maybe drum up some adverse publicity.'

Micky watches him sip as he thinks. Looks at the diamond rings, one on each hand. Sees the discreet Breitling.

'I understand you've come into some money.'

'Yeah. Got lucky at the tables in Mallorca. Never really gambled before. Mug's game.'

Ben Yardley gives him some eye and likes what he sees. Sure, Micky Targett (is that really his name?) comes across as a yob. Probably worked at it. Is there a class in cheeky, small-time villainy at a college somewhere? But he can see this man has a sense of humour. Enjoys the game. Has substance to him. - Got lucky at the tables - Yeah right.

'How much? A hundred and fifty thousand?'

'Actually it was a lot more than that.'

'Oh really?'

'Yeah. I left some there. Possible business opportunity.'

Ben grins, sips his lemonade. *Fucking love it,* he thinks.

'Here's a question about that. What would have happened if I'd been stopped?'

'By customs?'

'Yeah. I had proof of the win.'

'They would have given you a hard time. Probably contacted the casino, although they may or may not have given them any information. They may even have seized the money pending enquiries. But if it's your money you would have got it back.'

'I see.'

'London is wide open at the moment. Since the Wall came down there has been an influx of dodgy cash into the country. Into London. Eastern European and Russian mainly but no one's fussy. The government is keen to keep that flow healthy and uninterrupted. The UK banking system is one of the oldest, loosest and one of the most corruptible in the world.'

'Happy days. Next question, what would the cashier of my local Barclays do as and when I pass a hundred thousand across the counter?'

'That I couldn't say but similarly if the money is provably yours there's ultimately nothing they can do. They'd probably take it and then involve the police afterwards.'

'I see.'

'But if you are going to do that then I would advise doing it quickly because there are changes coming. That crooked system I just mentioned? Even the Tories know they can't keep getting away with it. It's all going to happen next year.'

'You know about changes to the law coming next year?'

'Pays to be well-informed. Money laundering. All that iffy cash flooding in. Questions are being asked and efforts, even if they are superficial, will be made to mollify. This time next year you'll only be able to dump ten grand in a bank account without setting off alarm bells.'

'But they'll take it now?'

'They'll take it and you'll get away with it. But, as I say, you might end up talking to the police.'

Micky knows there are things he doesn't want to talk to the police about. Quite a lot of things.

'That a problem?'

Micky shrugs. 'No one *likes* talking to the police.'

'And they might mention it to the revenue.'

'Right.'

'There is another way.'

'I'm pleased you said that.'

'You pass it to me. It becomes legitimate straight away.'

'I give you a hundred thousand pounds?'

'It would go into my company's client's account. I don't have to justify it to anyone.'

Micky gives him the eyeball. Is he serious?

'I give you a hundred thousand pounds?'

Ben Yardley smiles a big handsome smile. Swirls his lemonade and ice around in his glass. 'Don't worry. I'll give you a receipt.'

'Your cousin mentioned this may affect our Legal Aid claim.'

'Your father has one hundred thousand pounds. Of course he can't claim Legal Aid.'

'It's not his money. It's mine.'

'Doesn't matter. If it's being used for his case it's his money. But you have funds, right?'

'How much do you reckon this will cost to chase through if Amros agree to take the one hundred?'

'It's really difficult to say. We might get away with five thousand. But it's not the bank I'd be worrying about.'

'Oh no?'

'My cousin told me she mentioned this also. The bank may *agree* to remove their charge over the property. But it's not theirs to sign over to you. Or your father. They don't own it.'

Micky sighs as the odious truth is brought home to him again. He'd hoped that he'd seen the last of his brother's vile, fat, ugly incomplete visage. His merest mention makes him feel unwell, and the idea of him being back in his world was an invasion of and a disruption to the newly established life of calmness he was hoping to enjoy.

'Do you know where he lives?'

'No. Well, I have the last address for him but he told me that place was being repossessed.'

'Let me have that. I'll be able to run him down without too much trouble. I know an ex-detective who does private work.'

Ben leans his frame over to one side, plucks a card from his wallet.

'My numbers are on here,' he tells Micky.

Classic embossed black ink on white. Benjamin J. Yardley Associates BA (hons). LLB. Plus the numbers. No address.

'Where's your office?'

'I don't have one because I don't need one. I work from home.'

'Where do you live?'

'Emerson Park.'

Micky runs his thumb along the edge of the card. Thinks it through. Ben Yardley runs his own show so he has direct access to the boss. Plus Micky likes him, realizes that he can have a 'conversation' with him. About lots of things.

'One thing I will stress about the house,' says Micky, his mind made up already. Ben raises his eyebrows.

'I don't want you to think I'm some kind of crazy person but that house will not go out of my family. If I don't get it back this is what will happen; When the old man dies I will, in the run up to my eviction, dismantle the place, brick by brick. Then I'm going to sell the bricks so that by the time they take possession they won't even be able to rebuild it. They'll have to start again. Whilst I'm doing that I will dig under the plot of the house and pour as much pollutant into the soil as I can. The entire area will become toxic.'

Ben notices that Micky's eyes have misted with a far off, demented scintilla. Understands what he is dealing with.

'My point is I'm hoping that in some way you can communicate to them that it's my offer or nothing.'

So a few days later Micky gave Ben Yardley a hundred thousand pounds in cash and Ben Yardley did indeed give Micky a receipt. Which he keeps.

Less than a week after that Ben calls Micky with some news. The unpleasantness of his past is closer than he thought.

'Found your brother.'

What he says next makes things infinitely more uncomfortable.

'You should write to him.'

'What? Me? Why?'

'Appeal to his sense of fairness.'

'You're joking, right? You know what he did.'

'Of course I do. Perhaps he's wishing to make amends. He's clearly lacking in decent morals but if you can appeal to him it will save us a lot of trouble and you a lot of money.'

'Have you been in touch with Amros?'

'I've written to them but received no reply. I have a mortgage number from the documents I got from Magee and Cobham but my letter will not very likely find its way onto the desk of anyone who knows about this case. ABN Amro is a large organization and this mortgage does not originate from their lending department. This could take some time. While we're waiting you need to get your brother onside.'

The thought of any contact whatsoever nauseates Micky.

'I know your relationship with him is broken, Mick but is there any other reason why you shouldn't reach out?'

Micky can think of six. One eyeball and five of his sister-in-law's toes.

'If we take him to court, it will be difficult and expensive. We have to try this first.'

Micky replaces the receiver on the lounge phone, looks out through the French windows onto the garden where his dad is down on his knees digging with a trowel. He looks at the old black and white picture on the china cabinet. The pair of them, young and handsome and hopeful. Knows what he has to do.

In solidarity with Ben Yardley, Micky had ignored his request for one thousand five hundred pounds on account and given him a straight five. Show of faith.

'Let's hope that gets us across the finishing line.'

Ben had taken it with a nod but no further comment. He knew that unless Nigel Targett was willing to play ball he'd be receiving a lot more than five grand over the coming months. Or even years.

So Micky writes a letter to the brother he had deliberately disfigured a couple of years previously. Unsurprisingly he keeps it to a minimum, and of course he is safe in the knowledge that Nigel had no idea where the assault came from. He had, Micky is aware, quite a few enemies.

'You seem to have made a concerted effort to fuck up the old man's life. Mine too as it now falls upon me to look after him. I am trying to get the house back in his name. You'll be contacted by our solicitor. Do what he says. Micky.'

He also feels reasonably safe in the knowledge that he will get no response. Or not one that will do him any good.

It is in this period that Micky garners an understanding of how frustrating the laboring wheels of English litigation can be. As in fuck all ever seems to happen yet it is still bowel-quakingly expensive. Several times a week he considers the diminishing stash in the loft of the house that now looks quite pathetic sat in the case it once so proudly filled. Okay, he still has sixty something grand safe with Connie in Mallorca, but suddenly that doesn't seem like too much at all.

He takes time to look around the house, and can see how it has been neglected since his mother died. Mainly because since then, albeit for different reasons, neither his dad nor himself were in any kind of condition to notice.

So Micky shells out to spruce the place up. New carpets, new white goods. Proper combi-boiler to replace the toxic, fire-breathing monstrosity that sat on the kitchen floor like a poor man's Bophal power station.

Another five grand.

Even without a financially draining legal case to run, Micky is staggered by how expensive nineties Essex life is. When you don't have an income.

He fears that his brother won't sign over the house, unless he is made to. He suspects that the bank won't wipe the debt, unless it is made to. He knows Ben Yardley will cost bundles more to do what they've set out to do. And he knows there is zero point in him getting any form of nine to five because, for him, there's no sodding money in it.

So he thinks more and more about dealing drugs.

He thinks about The Stomach's mate. That bloke from the Yeoman. PC.

He thinks about how easy it would be. Collect from Chrissie Jarvis, sell to PC. But so what? Okay, he said he had mates but all it will probably add up to is a few grams at the weekend. That's if he doesn't turn out to be full of shit. And Micky knows he'll end up hoovering any spare.

He thinks back to the old days, the golden years. Double run. Ounces down to Ishy in Brighton and collecting ounces of mdma to bring back. Nothing ground breaking. Nothing you'd hear about on the news. But making *bundles*. And all his other contacts. Rafa in Mallorca, his friends in Essex. Chrissie Jarvis himself was a happy and lucrative customer. All the people he met ripping it up in London with Romanov.

He's getting nostalgic thinking about how good things were, and he's getting depressed about how stifled and boring things are now.

Then, as if to regain some of the former chutzpah that once illuminated his life on a daily basis, weird shit starts happening.

The first thing was a phone call. From that bloke.

''Ullo?'

'Izzat Mick?'

'Yup. Who's that?'

'Mick it's PC.'

'Sorry say again.'

'Big Steve's mate. PC. The Pro Cock, geez.'

'Oh yeah. Yeah gotcha. How goes it?'

'Alright mate. Yourself?'

'Yeah so so. Got a lot on and getting nowhere fast with it.'

'Ain't that the way, son. Always us grafters getting stiffed. Listen, bruv. I hope you don't mind me belling you like this. Got your number from the big fella . . .'

'Yeah, thought so.' From experience Micky knows what is coming. He remembers calls like this from before.

'Thing is is . . . The thing is is I was wondering if you'd . . .'

'Hang on PC. Don't do it on the phone. I haven't spoken to anyone.'

'Ah, okay.'

'Not saying I won't but I really have got a ton of shit on my plate right now.'

'Alright. No worries. Think you will anytime soon?'

'Well . . .'

'Shit, was hoping to hook up soonish. Summer's here and the time is right. Know what I mean? I got my boys screaming at me. I'm sure a regular half an oz a week is just for starters.'

Micky thinks about the diminishing stash in the loft. Thinks about the buzz he used to get from knocking out gear. Counting the greens, everyone always pleased to see him.

Decides against it.

The summer of nineteen ninety-two rolls past. The Barcelona Olympics. Rhythm Is A Dancer by Snap livens up the country as dance music seizes more and more footholds in the consciousness of youthful minds. Micky gets caught up in the lives of a new BBC soap opera called Eldorado. Obviously it's complete bollocks, but it makes Micky think back to Santa Ponsa and the life he had when he was young. When he was someone else.

Then, as summer turns into autumn, news finally comes back from ABN Amro bank. As Ben Yardley had predicted it had been a trial in itself to get the case on the desk of someone who might be able to make a decision.

In that time Nigel Targett had still refrained from replying to Micky's initial approach and the two subsequent letters he had dispatched.

''Ullo.'

'Micky Targett – Ben Yardley. How are you?'

'Hi, Ben. Well, when watching Gladiators on telly is the highlight of your week you know things can only improve.'

Ben laughs his loud, blokey laugh, the one that really shouldn't come from a cultured man such as himself, and not for the first time, Micky thinks it would probably be a real giggle to hang out with him. Get a little rat-arsed.

'Well maybe I can cheer you up. Good news and, I think, workable news. The bank want to play.'

'Okay, but I feel this may come with a qualifier.'

'They do realise they need to deal with you, and they should tread carefully as they do so.'

'Okay.'

'That said, Amros is a massive multi-national. A couple of hundred grand either way is nothing to them. But they want one-thirty.'

'Shit.'

'It's actually not that bad.'

'One thirty out of one sixty?'

'Except it's not one-sixty. We've still got double digit interest rates and that clock hasn't stopped ticking. On one-sixty that's thirteen hundred pounds a month. Three years or so is getting on for fifty grand. And that's compound.'

Micky isn't sure what that is but he keeps forgetting about all the mortgage payments that haven't been made.

'So the debt is well over two hundred now. By the time this gets settled one-thirty could be around half of what they are owed. But they are prepared to agree to a fixed sum right now.'

No way out of this, Micky reckons. Fighting with a bank over money?

'So?'

'So if you were in my boots?'

'If it was me I'd go for it. Get that half of the deal agreed, then we work on the other half. Don't forget, the value of *your* house is going up every day.'

Micky knows he's right. 'Yeah.'

'Good boy.'

'Thing is they can't expect me to shell that out until we get the other half together.'

'No no no. They understand the situation. I've explained we need to get your brother to the table as well. We'll do everything at the same time.'

'Right. So we good?'

'Yup, on we go, my boy.'

'Right. I'll make that happen. Two other things; we need to get your dad to make a will. Talk to him about things. The simpler the better. If you are his sole beneficiary that would be good.'

'Sure.'

'Also, couple of weeks. October twenty-fifth. Saturday. You free?'

'I rarely know what I'm doing later in the day. What's happening?'

'My birthday. Having a bunch of friends round. Thought you might like to join us.'

'Mingling with the clients? Isn't that frowned upon?'

'Well technically you're not my client, your dad is.'

'Okay then, sounds good. Where you at?'

'I'll text you the address. Coolie. Still no word from your brother?'

'No.'

'Well, now we have to move this along. Maybe time to get over there. Give him a knock.'

Micky's heart surges into his throat. The thought of seeing him. The thought of *appealing* to him. Fuck. That. Shit.

The very next day things become clearer when Eddie plops an envelope in front of Micky as he glugs his morning coffee. He'd recognise that ignorant scrawl anywhere.

He takes the envelope into his room, shaking hands rip it open. There is no Dear Micky.

'My life is very different now to the way it was. I'm not with Nicky anymore. Martin is growing up fast, he's almost as tall as you. How is dad?'

Micky checks the envelope for the rest of it. But *that* is it. He stomps around his room for a while then gets straight back on to Ben Yardley.

'He's taking the piss.'

'It would seem so.'

Micky sweats and seethes, fumes and farts.

91

'And that was it?' Ben has heard of and seen some things. The Targett's are something else.

'Yeah. Just a few lines. No mention of anything. He's just blanked me.'

'What does he mean, his life is very different?'

Lawyer – client confidentiality. Micky wonders what it would be like to tell Ben what happened, what Micky *made* happen. Then ditches that idea completely.

'Christ knows. I haven't spoken to him in years. He's going to make this as difficult as he can.'

'Well, we've tried nice. I'll draw up a letter saying we'll take him and his wife to court. Private prosecution. I'll take advice from a barrister, get a case together and explain he either does what we ask or else.'

'Like it.'

'He'll either fold or he'll be looking at legal fees of his own. Then we'll get him in court, win and he'll pay for everything.'

Micky is delighted but knows he's getting in deeper.

'Okay. Barrister though. You know the right one?'

'Sure do.'

'I feel you burning through my five thou', Ben. Go easy on me where you can will you?'

'Don't worry. It's all shelling out at the beginning. See you on the twenty-fifth, yeah?'

'Yeah. Yeah I'll be there. Feels like I need a good twist off after this.'

'Great. See you then.'

Ben Yardley puts down his phone and makes a note in his case log. Makes a note to charge Micky Targett another ninety pounds for that particular phone call. Along with all the others.

Micky knows he's going to need to get back to Mallorca for more money. He looks forward to the trip, but knows there is no point in any of it f he can't get his brother to sign over the house.

Thinking about money he remembers to ask his dad about his state pension.

'Where do you get it?'

'From the bloke.'

'What?'

'The Paki in the shop.'

Micky cringes. He knows his dad has a warm heart, knows he's not like that.

'Which shop?'

'You know, they sell stamps.'

'The Post Office?'

'Yeah.'

The next day, being a Thursday and with a reinvigorated interest in the family finances, Micky accompanies Eddie to the Post Office. Eddie takes a brown paper bag with him.

Once again Micky is amazed at how much of his father's life, how much of *life*, he knows nothing about. For a start he is astonished to see his father greeted like some kind of heroic family member.

'Edward!' Calls an Indian guy in his mid-twenties running the confectionery and cigarette counter. Eddie leans across the counter to shake hands.

'Morning, son. You okay?'

'Very good, boss.'

''Ere, listen.' He points over his shoulder in Micky's direction. 'This is my son. I don't suppose you can get him a job can you?'

The young man, amused yet embarrassed, lifts his eyebrows in Mick's direction.

They progress through the shop towards the Post Office. Micky watches his dad's worsening limp and makes a serious mental note to get him to a doctor to look at that hip.

Halfway along the shop an elderly Indian man is on his knees stacking a shelf with bottles of bleach. He sees Eddie walking towards him and is immediately compelled to struggle to his feet.

'Here he is,' beams Eddie.' 'Here's my mate.'

Micky is gob-smacked to see the two men embrace like twins separated at birth.

'How are you, Sir? How are you, dear friend?'

Eddie offers the man the bag he has brought with him. 'For you and your wife,' he says.

The old man waggles his head and beams with delight. 'Thank you so much, Mister Edward. My wife always loves your baking.'

'Anytime, brother.'

At the Post Office counter another grinning Indian sees Eddie approaching.

'Mister Targett, Sir. Thursdays are our favourite day.'

'Mine too, Joe because that's when you give me money.'

'You're welcome, old friend. How are you?'

'Very well, Joe,' Eddie says, digging his wallet from his back pocket. From there he fishes out a plastic card which he hands over. The man hands it straight back.

'The machine, Edward. You know what to do.'

Micky watches fascinated as Eddie shoves the plastic into what looks like an ordinary credit or debit card reader. Eddie readies his finger. Silence descends save for Joe flicking through the pages of a cheap notepad.

'Ready, Edward?'

The intensity of concentration displayed on Eddie's face looks like it would test the sanity of a normal human being. He can't even bring himself to speak, only capable of a single, pronounced nod of his head.

'Six.'

Eddie's gnarled forefinger circles the keypad, finds its target with jolting impact. Micky sees Joe grinning massively.

'Two.'

And so on. Micky cannot believe what he is seeing. In time Joe is counting out fifty-four pounds and fifteen pence, Eddie's weekly state pension. He can't not say something.

'Joe, right?'

'Yes, my friend.'

'I'm his son. Why is it you have his PIN number?'

'Your father is a fine man but sometimes he is forgetful. He can't memorize the number and when he writes it down he always loses the piece of paper. We thought this would be easier.'

'How long you been doing this?' he asks with a smile, unable to fault the logic.

'Two years or so.'

Another weird thing that happens is Ben Yardley's birthday party. As he is getting ready to go out Micky gets a call from The Stomach inviting him to *his* birthday party.

'Cool, man. When is it?'

'Tonight.'

'Ah Jesus, mate.'

'What?'

'A bit of notice would have been good.'

'What, you busy?'

'Yeah. I'm just about to go to another bash.'

'Blow it out.'

Micky thinks. Can I swing that? Could I? Should I?

'Who's this then?'

'My lawyer?'

'Your *lawyer*?'

It does sound a bit crap.

'What do you need a lawyer for?'

Micky doesn't know why he still can't talk about what happened. It's no one's fault. So why the shame?

'I'll tell you when I see you. But I got to go. Been lined up for a few weeks. Sorry.'

'Down to me. Should have thought of it sooner. Ain't seen you down the Yeoman lately.'

'Yeah I know. Maybe next week. Still Fridays, yeah?'

'Yeah sure. Listen that bloke asked me to give you a shake. The Pro Cock. Wants you to call him.'

'Okay. Alright, mate. Well, have a good one.'

'Yeah, you too. Catch you next week maybe.'

Micky hangs up knowing his old friend really didn't want him at his party at all. In a few brief hours that sting of rejection would be his last consideration.

In lieu of any gear Micky gets on it by way of a couple of tins of Holsten with his dad. Suitably fortified he accepts Eddie's kind offer of a lift. Less than a hundred yards into the fifteen minute journey he bitterly regrets going anywhere near the car because Eddie is a fucking maniac. It has been a long time since Micky was a passenger with him and he makes a solemn vow, as Eddie inadvertently guides the Scirocco onto the pavement towards a group of youngsters, to leave it at least as long before he does anything quite so rash again. Red lights go unheeded. Signalling is clearly optional. They get there.

Micky doesn't know Emerson Park well but knows it's an upmarket area of Hornchurch. And where Ben lives is quite clearly the upmarket end of Emerson Park.

He feels suddenly shy when Eddie screams away leaving him looking up at the imposing detached house set in generous gardens. He's never been too comfortable in the company of professionals, always worried about making a fool of himself. Getting found out. Then again, he reckons, as he opens the gate and walks to the dark, oak door, he can always do what he used to do; get slaughtered and find out what happened in the morning.

Ben Yardley greets him with his ebullient charm and handsome grin and relieves him of the eight tins of Stella and bottle of Gordon's gin he's brought over in a plastic bag.

'You didn't need to do that, Mick but thank you. Come through, my friend.'

'Call that your birthday present because at the rates you charge me that's all you're getting.'

Micky gets the raucous laughter, the hearty slap on the back. 'We're in the kitchen.'

He wasn't sure what to expect from a solicitor's fortieth birthday party so he isn't overly concerned when, at just before nine in the evening, he sees there are only four other people there. There is no music playing. And everyone looks at him.

He's never thought of himself as lacking in confidence but under the searching gaze of those people he really wishes he'd gone to the Stomach's bash instead.

That said, two of them are quite doable.

Micky slips out of his leather jacket as Ben does the intros.

'Everyone, this is Micky Targett, client of mine and all round solid chap. Micky, from the left this is Cathy, Lisa, John and Moira.'

Micky grins, effects a modest nod. 'Hi everyone.'

A chorus of greetings.

He wishes he could disappear into the incredibly expensive wallpaper, but opts for grabbing a Stella from Ben before he even has a chance to load them in the fridge. He gets at it, no glass.

There is a table loaded with enough cold cuts, cheeses, dips, olives, vol au vents and all manner of delicious nibbly things to feed an army. On Ben's invitation Micky helps himself, only then realizing he hasn't eaten a thing all day. Makes a note to look after himself a bit more. Keep off the booze. To help him out with the cheese, Ben pours him a small, glass bucket of Burgundy.

'Nice place,' Micky tells his host as they look out through the French windows onto the illuminated and neatly clipped and bordered lawn.

'Thanks. I've been here for five years now. Can't imagine living anywhere else.'

'You an Essex man then?'

'Yeah, Woodford.'

'I always thought you were posh.'

'Yeah yeah. You? Upminster boy?'

'Proper Eastender, mate. Third generation Cockney.'

'A dying breed. How is your dad?'

'He's ok thanks. He just dropped me off.'

'You should have brought him in.'

'Nah, he's even shyer than I am.'

The big friendly laugh again. Nice guy, thinks Micky.

'You? Shy? Yeah okay. So you said there was no one you wanted to bring tonight. You single?'

Micky lugs heavy on the grape. Damn that shit is good. 'Yeah, just me. I think I've annoyed enough women in the world for the time being. They probably need a rest.'

'And how did you manage that?'

Micky senses the hovering succulence, the luscious change in air pressure, even before she arrives at his elbow. He looks across to see Ben smiling, then back to see her looking directly into him.

Micky shrugs. 'Nothing conscious. I suppose I just have a gift for it.'

Ben chuckles. 'You know what, Lisa, something tells me this man has more secrets than the rest of us put together. Excuse me.'

With a wry smile he ambles across the expanse of the dining area back to the kitchen where the others are still gathered.

Micky is grateful Ben has addressed her by her name as he'd already forgotten what this one is called. This one, the really pretty one with the dark skin and the incredible eyes. Now his mind is racing. Think of something funny, you knob.

She takes a slow lap around behind him, picks out an olive. Stares at him.

'You have a gift for annoying women?' She's interested in what he says. Hopes he doesn't disappoint. *That scar on his temple is fucking sexy,* is what she's thinking.

'I've been noted for it in the past. I'm determined to have a night off.'

'Don't change a thing on my account.'

He checks her out and can't find a thing to quibble about. Not that he wouldn't, quibble that is. If he got a good enough drunk on. Caramel skin and jade green eyes. Five four with a great, curvy body. Big, fat, sexy lips. He's going half Jamaican – half Swedish.

'How do you know Ben?'

'I was at Uni with him.'

'You a lawyer?'

'No. I'm a teacher.'

'Oh yeah? What?'

'English. A-level mostly.'

Micky finishes what he is eating, washes it away by emptying his glass.

'Good on you. I used to like English.'

'What do you do?'

He's been at the place five minutes and it's already getting embarrassing. He really needs to work out some patter for all this bollocks. Goes for safety.

'I'm kind of between jobs at the moment.'

'What did you used to do?'

'I ran a motorcycle courier company.'

'Oh yeah. What happened to that?'

'I had a bad accident. I wrecked my knee, we got bought out and I went to work for the company that bought us. Sales.'

She nods and Micky senses she's getting bored already. She carefully places the olive stone in a napkin which she holds onto. Sips a white wine. He can't help staring at her lips. And that top is really tight.

'At the moment I'm back living with my father.' Doesn't feel right saying the word father instead of dad but he's anxious not to have her think . . . What? That he's in his thirties and he's still living at home with his dad.

She nods. Fuck.

'This is how I know Ben. He's running a case for us. Regarding the house. And my dad seems to be going downhill at the moment.'

'How do you mean?'

Good question. How does he mean?

'Well he's starting to show his age. He'll outlive us all, but he's getting a bit erratic. I moved back in to keep an eye on him.'

'Hmm, you worried it's dementia?'

The word hits Micky hard. He can't even contemplate what that might be like.

'I know how tough that is. My grandmother is hanging on but she's been struggling for the last ten years.'

'How old is she?'

'Eighty-four.'

'How old are you? If you don't mind.'

She shakes her head and her tangle of black curls fans and writhes hypnotically.

'Thirty-seven. You?'

'Jesus, I figured you for my age. I'm thirty-two.'

'Jesus, I figured you for my age.'

They both laugh and Micky feels he needs to look at every part of her at the same time. The dancing green eyes, the delectable dimples, the ridiculously white teeth. The whole deal.

'How did you get that scar?'

Secretly Micky quite likes having his scar. He got over the fact of it soon after it happened. Now he just enjoys the air of toughness, the hint of danger that comes with it.

'It's a dueling scar.'

Her brow wrinkles, she thinks she's misheard 'What?'

'I wanted pistols but it makes too much noise. You know, at dawn out on the heath.'

She closes her eyes and opens them *ever* so slowly. She sees his kindly face break into a genuine, warm smile. Good looking bloke, she tells herself.

'Seriously. You get caught shagging someone's wife?'

'Shagging? That the kind of vernacular you working on with the kids?'

'Vernacular? Well, get you and your fancy vocab. Didn't figure you for the literary sort.'

'Oh yeah, man of mystery, me. As Ben says, I've got secrets up the wazoo.'

'That where you keep them?'

'Mick! Micky!'

Mick looks across to see Ben beckoning him back to the kitchen.

'Moira reckons she was in Mallorca back in the eighties. Didn't you have a bar over there?'

Micky looks at Lisa. *She said the word 'shagging' so off to a good start,* he thinks.

Lisa looks at Micky. *Cocky fucker but cute,* she thinks.

'Before this evening is over I'm going to know about the scar and a hell of a lot else.'

Micky smiles then heads across to the others hoping no one spots the raging hard-on.

It's a cool gathering and Micky likes everyone and everyone seems to like him. He finds it a little unnerving that no one else shows up but only because he doesn't want the evening to be a flop for Ben's sake.

He's keeping a lid on the drinking. At one point he goes upstairs to take a leak. Admires the immaculate bathroom and can't help but compare it to his own. Every surface glistens. The floor warms his shoeless feet. As he drills into the porcelain he checks out something he's never seen before; an electric toothbrush. Two of them. Who's he knocking off? Lisa? Then he sees the lotions, the potions, the products, the Braun electric razor. Hair brushes, nail clippers. Soon enough, he thinks. Get the house back, get over to Mallorca, get at it with Connie. Soon I'll be living like this.

He finishes up and glances at the mirror. He's looking alright but knows he needs to do more. The hair, the skin. It wasn't that long ago he was a bedraggled, drug-fucked suicide candidate needing psychological counselling and anti-depressants just to stay alive, so he knows he's doing okay. Knows he can thrive. He just needs weird shit to stop happening to him.

As he exits the bathroom he looks through an open door across the spacious landing to see Lisa in one of the bedrooms.

'Hey.'

'Hey, there you are,' she says.

Side on Micky spots the hinted swell of her belly along with the enticing cling of her skirt to her generous behind. She's looking up at something on the wall. He slides into the room then sees the massed ranks of floor to ceiling books.

'Whoa. Now that's a collection. Man must love a read.'

'That's about as axiomatic as it gets.'

Micky wonders if there is a dictionary he can grab without her noticing.

In front of the window there is a desk with a sleek computer set up on it. Not the joke plastic lumps he saw at Chrissie Jarvis' place. In a cabinet next to the desk is a printer and fax machine. Every square inch of every other wall is obscured by a book. Apart from a gap on one wall where hangs a picture frame. Instead of a picture there is text.

I said there was a society of men among us, bred up from their youth in the art of proving by words multiplied for the purpose, that white is black, and black is white, according as they are paid. To this society all the rest of the people are as slaves.

Micky thinks he knows it but can't recall from where.

'I love coming in here. He reads so much there's always something new to look at.'

One area is covered with austere looking law text books. Company law, Precedents, Criminal law, Civil law and so on. But the rest is a little easier on the eye and, thinks Micky, on the brain. He stands beside but a fraction behind her, near enough to name her scent. If he knew anything about that kind of girlie shit. He deliberately leans *against* her. She doesn't move.

'I like checking out people's books,' he tells her. 'If there isn't at least one I've read I'm disappointed.'

'Oh yeah? Show me one here, and I'll be testing you on it.'

Bollocks, there better be one, he thinks.

His eyes laser across the spines. Yes!

'I got a book voucher prize at school for scoring a bunch of O-levels and I bought that with it. It changed everything for me. Up until I read that I thought literature was something you had to do at school, not something that would make me laugh, make me asks questions, make me cry. Make me wonder.'

She looks up at him with fresh eyes. 'That's some catch, that catch-22'

He grins as he remembers. 'It's the best there is.'

'Extra points if you can name that character.'

'Doc Daneeka.'

She is obviously impressed. 'Anything else?'

He scopes the massed ranks again. 'The Plague by Camus.'

'Very high brow.'

'I wouldn't have chosen to read it. Did it in French. La Peste. L'Etranger too.'

'So you speak French?'

'Not so's you'd notice. I did the A-level but I didn't really do anything with it. Whoa. Money by Martin Amis. John Self is a hero to us all.'

'I've not read that. What about the classics?'

'I could never get on with Shakespeare or the Brontes or even Dickens. That's basically why I didn't carry on with English.'

'What are you, nuts? So you read Voltaire and Balzac instead?'

A bolt of memory hits him as if it was pure lightening.

'But it was the best of all possible worlds.'

She laughs again and recalibrates her initial impressions, which were positive enough to begin with. He senses this. Emboldened he says, 'So, you and Ben?'

She trains her stunning eyes onto him. 'What?'

'Old friends from the way back. Stayed in touch . . .'

'Yes?'

'Good looking, successful bloke. Was there ever a 'you and him'?'

Her face eases into another fabulous smile. Micky is smitten.

'You're so cute. We should get back down. They'll be starting soon.'

'Starting what?'

'He didn't tell you?'

'Tell me what?'

She smiles again, shakes the curls. Then she links arms with him and leads him out of the room onto the landing. 'You're so cute.'

Downstairs there has been a seismic shift in mood. The other four are all seated around the mahogany dining table. Music is playing, Wish You Were Here by Pink Floyd. There is a place mat in front of the six chairs but not plates and no cutlery. In the middle of the table is a bowl of sugar but there are no cups. Then Micky understands.

'There they are,' says Ben.

'I had to drag him away from your library, Ben. Did you know how well read this man is?'

'A man of secrets indeed.' This was John who is so similar in manner to Ben he thinks they may have been related. The perfect, immovable hair, designer shirt, ironed black jeans. His neatly trimmed beard is so immaculate it looks like it has been painted on. But Micky is staring at the bowl of sugar. Except it ain't sugar.

'Let's see if we can get him to share a few.'

Lisa sits Micky down and settles in next to him. Only then does Micky notice the straw at the side of his table mat in place of the cutlery. And one of Ben's business cards. Oh dear. Oh dearie dearie dear.

Cathy and the other one are wearing beaming smiles. Micky Targett, on the outside looking in once again. Ben has the floor.

'Micky you are here for two reasons. One, I like you and think of you fondly enough to ask you to my birthday party. Two, I think I know you well enough to say you'll be a great contributor to the occasional evenings we have.'

He lets the words ring around the room. Micky stares at him, then stares at the bowl.

'Great deal of trust involved though. We're all professional people. Everyone has a career and therefore a lot to lose. I've invited you into that circle because I feel, I mean I *know* I can trust you.'

'That's very good of you Ben.'

'I'm sure you'll be good for us, Mick. What happens here, stays here. Actions. Words. Complete freedom. But it stays here. Every. Single. Thing.'

Micky looks around the table at the five responsible alpha adults who are all staring back at him and he knows that whatever happens, what*ever* happens, he'll be a match for all of them. He's just about on the right side of fairly pissed to handle anything.

'Sounds like fun.'

'Rules,' Ben continues. 'Someone will ask you a question. It can be about anything. You either answer it or you don't. If you answer it, and you *will* answer it truthfully, you get a line. Keep it to three inches. If you choose not to answer then you don't get a line and you forfeit your chance to ask your question next time around. You in?'

Micky smiles, thinks back to the Friday afternoon Charlie sessions with Romanov, Masters and Chalmers that often finished around ten on Saturday morning. Then he considers the work he put in down in the trenches of Bugsy's bar in Mallorca. Drinking games. Four or five hardened nutters hunched together. Captain Francis, Randy Schnipper, Brad. Forty, maybe fifty nominated down-in-ones between them in an evening. Pint of Lager and Crème Du Menthe, glass of Bacardi and Sherry mix.

'Oh I am *so* in.'

'As you're the newbie don't be surprised if you get more than your fair share of questions.' Says the one who isn't Lisa or Cathy. Mick can't help it but he's zoning her out already.

'I'd be disappointed if it was any other way.'

They all laugh and Micky gets the feeling he used to get when he was in the company of civilians back in the old days. He was never a real face. Never a tough guy, but people knew there was something. Knew he was a villain. An outlier.

That's how it is with this lot. Fuck client confidentiality because Micky knows that Ben has told them all about him already. Bloke shows up with a hundred and fifty grand in cash he says he won in a Mallorcan casino. Yeah right.

So Micky is comfortable. Jesus, Micky is *flying*. There's Floyd on the stereo, he's with a bunch of interesting, good looking people (apart from one) and the hot one seems to like him. Yeah this'll do. Lisa actually raises her hand to ask a question.

'Can I go first?'

Even before MC Ben gives her the nod Micky knows what she's going to say.

'On you go, Lease.'

'I'd like to ask Micky something.' She smiles through her radiating eyes.

'I told you I'd be finding this out didn't I? How did you get that scar on your face?'

He's right back there in the Yaksak. Dinner with Dixie, then the movement in the aisle. The blur of attack as Jimmy Mulroney drew his blade.

Micky thinks it funny there's currency in this. He's in with a bunch of suburban upwardly types. Let them have it.

'A man slashed me with a razor.'

The silence tells him all he needs to know. He can handle this lot but already they're not sure they can handle him. It's like they've invited the fox into the hen house.

'Why did he do that?'

'That's two questions.'

'Loose rules, Mick. Humour us,' Ben says.

'Long one short – there was bad blood between me and his family. He thought he'd pay me back for that. I was sitting in a restaurant at the time. But hey, probably my fault for going to Walthamstow in the first place.'

'Oh my God.' Cathy says. Mick looks at her, then at John who smiles thinly.

'Thanks, Mick. Help yourself.' Ben tells him.

Micky twirls the business card, dips into the bowl (got to be a good two ounces) and shows them how it's done. 'Nice party, man.'

'In fact why don't you ask away, Mick. You're in the chair.'

Micky hammers his line and immediately thinks this shindig isn't all it's cracked up to be because the Charlie, frankly, isn't very good. But then he reckons he'll just have to answer a lot of questions.

'Cathy,' he says sniffing loudly. The woman immediately snaps to attention.

'You ever do the gay thing? Specifically with either of these two?'

Standard schoolboy stuff but Ben and John are roaring with laughter. Lisa coyly face-palms, as much to hide a smile as anything else. Micky has clearly hit a nerve straight away.

'Moira and I have just split up,' Cathy tells him.

Moira! That was it. Brilliant. Lisa, Cathy, Moira, John and Ben. Goddit.

'Sorry to be personal,' Micky offers.

Cathy smiles pleasantly enough as she dips into the bowl. 'I suppose that's what we're here for.'

'What about you?' This is John. '*You* ever do the gay thing?'

Five sets of eyes are on him like headlamps.

Micky knows this will be a long night. He's their new plaything but he's ready.

'Damn, I'm going to be wrecked before midnight. Nah. Few snogs in the clubs and at after-parties when I was a raver a few years back. I got a lot of gay friends. If you go for someone, why not? But I'm not wired that way.'

He looks across at Lisa and makes it as obvious as he can. 'I like girls.'

Lisa stares right back. Micky dips in again as Ben explains.

'The thing about the game, Micky is that you can be . . . strategic. From now on we all ask a question in turn but we can ask it of whomever. So you can target someone or help him or her out if they are looking groggy by not asking them. Let's give it an hour and then we'll start drinking as well. All good fun.'

All good fun is right. Micky, suddenly all teeth and charm, is having a whale of a time with his new found chums. Ben is in his imperious element as he knows he has scored a sensational, social, net-busting goal inviting Micky. He is the perfect combination of Essex rough, tempered with both a working brain and a self-deprecating sense of humour. And he has lived a life none of them could have imagined for themselves. Most of them aim questions at him, especially when they see he can handle the powder.

'Have you ever killed anyone?'

'No.' He thinks of little Jen.

'You ever been married?'

'No.' He thinks of his Julie

'Are you a gangster?'

'Not anymore.' He thinks of Connie Chetkins, of Denny Masters, of Pete Chalmers.

It's all good-natured stuff and he fields it with eloquent bonhomie. Fires back.

'You two ever get laid with blokes?' He asks Moira and Cathy.

'Once.'

'Never. Eww.'

Then he looks at Ben and he looks at John sitting next to him and he finally gets it. It's not that sex is always on Micky's mind, he struggles to remember when he was last near a woman, but this penny has finally dropped. His next question comes around. Takes a chance.

'You two,' he nods at the pair of them, confidently adventurous on the booze and the coke. 'You ever get with the girls?'

'You're a very perceptive person, Micky.' This is John.

'Not really, John. You two are too good-looking to be straight.

And I've seen Ben's shoe collection.'

Laughter all round again. It's all going well. They take a break. Mick scans the endless ranks of Ben's vinyl *and* CDs. Puts on the new Love Symbol album by Prince. Even sings along with Sexy Motherfucker. He loads up on water. Hydrates. Lisa joins him in the kitchen. She is unsteady on her feet but her smile is radiant. Micky can't believe that's down to him. Can he?

'You're an interesting chap.'

'Thank you. I've done a few things.'

'Clearly. So you're not a gangster anymore? So that means . . ?'

'I thought we were taking a break.'

'We are. Now we're having a conversation.'

'It's a long story. I don't like the idea this is the last time I'll see you.'

'It won't be.'

'That makes me happy. I wouldn't want to hog the big chair all night.'

'Are you uncomfortable here?'

'I'm not used to sharing so much with strangers, but I am having a great time.'

'You really used to be a criminal?'

'Yeah.'

'I'd like to hear about that.'

'I ain't saying nuffink 'til my brief gets here.'

Lisa guffaws again. 'That's no excuse, he's sitting right over there.'

They both laugh, she drinks wine, he glugs back more water.

'You got a criminal record?'

'Yeah, nothing worth bragging about.'

She grins, shakes the curls and he feels it. He feels himself falling again. A thirty-seven year old teacher. And she's half black. He knows, much as he loves his mates, that she wouldn't be welcome in their orbit. Fuck 'em.

'Where are your parents from?'

'Mum's Nigerian, dad's English.'

'Ah okay. You have the most gorgeous eyes.'

She's heard it before but likes it from him. 'Thank you.'

Just then Ben sways into the kitchen. He's sufficiently out of it to take a chance. But he figures he's got it right thus far so what the fuck? He's always been good with people. He slips his arm around Lisa's waist and kisses her cheek.

'Nice party, Ben,' she tells him.

Then he steps to Micky, places a warm palm on his shoulder and kisses him in the same way.

It's not a problem for Micky. He did it all with his mates; Love Muscle at The Fridge, Trade at Turnmills. The music was hard and heavy and there were always loads of single straight girls out for a night of not having to deal with idiot straight blokes. Except him. His gay friends occasionally tried it on but they respected the slap on the wrist. It was all cool.

But Ben doesn't know any of that. Micky stares him down and Ben starts to thinking his party is about to come to an unfortunate and premature end.

'Next time you kiss me, Ben, try to leave a couple of days stubble will you? I like my men a little rougher than that.'

There follows the most tantalizing hiatus. Then Ben and Lisa erupt with laughter, Lisa even needs to cling onto the granite counter top.

'What did I tell you?' Ben asks her. 'Didn't I tell you this man was the bomb?'

Beaming with delight Lisa strides to Micky, wraps herself around him and smothers him in a luscious kiss. Micky says a silent prayer of thanks to whoever is listening that he didn't end up at The Stomach's party.

*

Micky strolls into an elegant bar, the sort where all of the women are in floor length dresses and all the men wear suits. It's not normally his kind of place but he knows he's on enough of a roll to have a good time. Outside in the street is that black thing that keeps chasing him but he's ahead of it now. Way out in front, in clean air.

He saunters through the interior, his knee feels good, like before the accident. His hip and back too. People give him room, a blonde checks him out. By the time he makes it to the bar he's ready for something long and cold.

The barman has his back turned, busy working on something on the rear counter. Micky does that thing of coughing politely. Nothing.

'Excuse me?'

The barman turns, he is holding a long drink crammed with crushed ice and verdant finery that flowers and flows over the edge of the glass. But it isn't the elegance of the beverage which catches Micky's eye. The barman.

'Keith?'

'Hello Mick.'

'What you doing here?'

'Getting this ready or you.'

'Very kind but . . .'

'Not full time, I still work with the boys.'

'Good to hear.' Micky takes the drink, sips. It is heaven in a glass.

'One thing though,' Keith Richards wants to know. 'Why do you have an axe in your head?'

*

Micky wakes to familiar sensations, the most apparent being that he feels like someone has indeed cleaved his head in half with an axe. And left it there.

He can't breathe through his nose. His mouth feels like a cactus farm. His senses scramble and he thinks about his dad. Hopes he's okay. Then he realizes he's not in his bed. Not in his house. But he can't fucking remember a*nything!*

With no time to focus he senses a presence. Hears soft footsteps. Then he looks up and sees a man enter the room.

'Hey, sleepy head. How you feeling?'

Ben Yardley, wearing a dressing gown, holding two coffees. *Fuck!*

He sits on the edge of the bed, places a mug on the night table next to Micky. He notices there is a heart shape on the mug with the motto; 'I love everyone'.

'I guessed black lots of sugar.'

'Close enough,' Micky says and hauls himself up. Drinks. Flushes. Tries to remember.

'Quite a night.'

Micky doesn't answer. His head whirls. Surely not. Surely not.

Please, no. He actually concentrates on his rectum, his penis, tries to think back as both panic and nausea sweep over him.

'Gets a little wild when you add a shot with each line doesn't it?' Ben says.

'What's the time, Ben?'

'Just gone eleven. You need to be somewhere?'

'Er yeah, probably.'

The coffee is strong and tastes good.

'What time did we finish?'

'About four. You don't remember?'

'Actually not too much at the moment but it'll come back.'

'You must remember the dancing?'

Micky flexes his knee. 'Oh bollocks.'

Ben chuckles, sips his coffee, places a hand on Micky's thigh. 'That was the best one we've had so far. It went perfectly, thanks to you.'

Micky nods solemnly. 'That's good to know. One thing though, Ben. . .'

'Yeah?'

'I'm in your bed.'

'Uh huh?'

They stare at each other. Ben thinks, *Oh my God! He can't remember if me and him got it on or not.*

Please don't tell me you shagged a bloke, Micky beseeches himself.

Ben feels the devil in him wanting to drag this one out but he likes Micky too much.

'Let's put it like this, there's good news and, as always, there's bad news.'

'I glad I'm already lying down for this.'

'The good news, for *you* I'm guessing, is that you didn't fuck me last night.'

Micky is so relieved his hangover practically clears in that instant.

'The bad news is that Lisa is a bit pissed off you didn't fuck her either.'

'What?'

'Yeah. She was in here with you. She left about twenty minutes ago. You totally zonked on her so she says.'

Micky smiles. Back in the saddle. Kind of.

CHAPTER EIGHT

So if you think the going gets tough just remember
What time is love?

Mid-morning on Monday, secure and content in the knowledge that he is not a gay man, Micky gets to work. First port of call is big Chrissie Jarvis over on the car strip in Seven Kings where he places an order for three ounces of what Chrissie describes as 'primo rocket fuel'.

'Normally eleven hundred on the oz, son but I'll do that for you at a flat three.'

Once that order is placed Micky drives to Romford and parks up. From there he calls Ben Yardley. He doesn't go into details over the phone because he doesn't have to. Downstairs and fully dressed the previous Sunday Micky broached the subject.

'If you're a regular then I can get you stuff much better than what you're getting.'

'I was kind of hoping you'd say something like that. My guy is a bit of a peasant and the quality is sketchy.'

'I'll step in. How much how often?'

'Well last night was a special occasion, we only do that a few times a year. But all of us do coke plus a few others I could introduce you to. I'll take a couple of grams a week but I'm not being in the middle for the others. You'll have to deal straight with them.'

'That's fine. I was needing to get Lisa's number anyway.'

Ben nods knowingly. 'I thought you would.'

So on the phone Micky tells Ben he'll have whatever he needs by the end of the week. Asks him how the case is going.

'Waiting for the barrister's opinion. Once we get that we can file the case. On the evidence we have from all the old correspondence your brother left lying around he won't be able to answer it.'

'Time frame?'

'I wish you wouldn't ask me things like that. Christmas and all that nonsense coming up so we'll file by start of business January. He'll be given thirty days in which to defend it or fold. So by the first week of February latest you should be looking good.'

'Okay. I'll get over to Spain and bring some more money back.'

'Ah yeah. You won it at a casino right? When you going to call her?'

'This evening.'

'Good luck, lover boy.'

After that Micky calls the Pro Cock.

'Geeeeeeeeeezah!'

''Ello, mate.'

'Long time no wotsit. How's tricks?'

'Yeah ok thanks. Listen, seems I may have come across a little something to liven your day.'

Micky can hear the silence.

'Far fucking out, man.'

'I'll have in two days, maybe tomorrow. I'll bell you. Lucky number?'

'Say, five for starters.'

'Shall be done.'

'Ledge.'

Micky hangs up and wonders why he didn't ask the price. He puts it down to the fact the bloke is a dick-brained, loud-mouthed, Sun reading, Tory voting gutter-ponce with too much money.

Then he starts calling Connie Chetkins. This is invariably an exasperatingly drawn out procedure because he rarely answers his phone. Micky has 'a' number for him in the UK but he clearly doesn't have 'the' number. Which means he always ends up calling the Mallorca house which is where he knows he'll at least get to talk to someone. Usually Barbara. He is surprised when Connie picks up.

'Afternoon, boy. How goes it?'

'Alright, Con. Yourself.'

Micky experiences a frisson of guilt. Keep it tight, Connie had said when he warned him to stay out of the game.

'Yeah, mustn't grumble. What can I do for you?'

'Con I need to pop over and grab some more cash. This house thing is getting drawn out. The bank'll have a deal but it's not the one I wanted.'

'I see. Ah well, at least you're getting on with it. When you thinking?'

'Up to you.'

'I'm off to South Africa on Wednesday, not sure for how long. No worries. What will you need?'

'Better make it forty.'

'Okay, if you can't get here before then I'll make sure it's in the house. Barbara will sort it for you.'

'Okay that's great, cheers. When you back over here?'

'Not sure, son.'

Micky wants to prolong the conversation. Wants to be close, but knows he can't push the man.

Then he calls Sandra Chetkins.

The last time he'd seen her was back in Mallorca, seven or eight months ago. He'd made a fool of himself nearly drowning off the back of Connie's boat but they had got on well for the brief time they'd had together. But he doesn't know how he feels about her. Less how she feels about him.

And now there's Lisa.

'Hey hot stuff. How you doing?'

'Mister Targett in person, well we are honoured. What's going on?'

'Wondered if you fancied a meet up.'

'It'll have to be soon. I'm going over to see mum at the weekend.'

'Well howzabout that? That's where I wanted to meet you.'

Again Micky thinks he hears something in the silence. The hesitation. Less than a second but it could mean . . . What?

'Well that'll be fab. What's the occasion?'

'I need to pick up something from your dad. He says he's going away but it'll be there for me. How long you there for?'

'Two weeks.'

'Great. I'll bob over for a couple of days in that time.'

Micky then does the kind of shopping he likes. Set of digital scales, kilo of glucose, a thick-paged magazine and a pack of plastic bags. Fuck yeah.

Then he hits the bucket shop travel agent he uses. Scores flights and three nights at the Rey Don Jaime in old Santa P.

Two days later he is pulling away from big Chrissie's showroom in a *tremendously* good mood. A quick sampling reveals the stuff is indeed *muy* primo. Three ounces rammed down the front of his trousers does nothing for his comfort levels but it's always been safety first.

Back at the Upminster house he weighs out twenty grams and adds three of glucose to that. Knows it's a favourable Essex street mix. Then he wraps up twenty-five point nines and one half a gram. He doesn't touch any of it. He calls PC.

''Ello?'

''Ello, mate. It's Mick. Anytime you like.'

'Epic. The Yeoman? Half an hour?'

'Gets a bit lively in there. The Huntsman? In the garden.'

'Safe.'

Before he leaves he washes the cereal bowl in which he ground the mix. He finds his dad prowling around.

'You seen my wallet?'

'Nope. Where did you leave it?'

'Well if I knew *that*.'

He watches the old guy pat himself down, rummage in the kitchen draws. He follows him as he limps through into the lounge and sees him lift the seat cushion of the appalling nineteen-sixties chair he can't bring himself to throw away. All along the window sill, the coffee table.

'Look I've just got to pop out. I won't be long. We'll find it when I get back.'

Micky sits at a wooden table in the garden of the Huntsman and Hounds sipping a beer wishing he'd worn a proper jacket. Getting on for November. Still, get over to Mallorca for a couple of days. That'll be good. Maybe it's better Connie isn't there, that way him and Sandra might . . . His muse is disturbed by the clattering holler of a diesel.

The Pro Cock windmills across the lawn wearing his horrible

khaki shorts and dirty Converse trainers. His jowls flap with each stride. In fact, Micky notices, he carries with him several chins but not the one made of bone he should be wearing front and centre.

He comes on like a brother from the trenches he hasn't seen for twenty years. Handshakes, fist-bumps, geezahs. He sits opposite.

'Star. Knew you wouldn't let me down, bruv. You had a dip?'

'Yeah, mate. It's fine.'

'Sweet as. You want another drink?'

'Nah I'm alright. In fact I've got to get somewhere really.'

'Fair enough.'

'Under the table.'

Micky passes the bag of wraps across into PC's grasping hand.

'What we got here.'

'Five grams as per.'

'Ledge. What I owe you?'

'Fifty a pop but call it two-twenty.'

'You're a nice man to work with.'

He eases his bulk to one side to retrieve his wallet from his back pocket, the twenties come to Micky under the table.

'Ain't seen you out much?'

'Yeah I'm a bit tied up. Me dad is getting to be a bit of a handful.'

'Always time for Friday night though.'

Micky thinks the bloke's not wrong. 'Yeah, I should be able to make it this week.'

'Pukka. Alright, Geez I'll get back at it. Plenty more where that came from?'

'Yup.'

'Nice one. Be lucky.'

Micky watches him go and doesn't know what to make of him. Maybe he's just full of himself. Then he remembers something, sends a text - 'Best not to let the other Yeoman lads know about this'.

A minute later he gets the reply – 'no worries m8'.

Back at his house Eddie Targett is all but ripping the wallpaper down looking for his wallet. It's dinner time anyway and Micky pulls two microwaveable meals from the fridge. He opens the door to the ancient Morphy Richards.

In the lounge his dad has dragged the sofa into the middle of the room.

'Dad.'

'What?'

'Come in the kitchen.'

Micky leans casually against the counter top and Micky points into the microwave. Eddie can't believe it.

'How did it get in there?'

'At a guess I'd say that someone who lives in this house put it in there. And I'll give you a clue, it wasn't me.'

A fantastic grin overtakes Eddie's face. 'Well done, boy.'

'I suppose it's safe there,' says Micky. 'Unless some bastard breaks in and nicks the microwave obviously.'

Later that evening Micky lies on his bed and calls Lisa. He's not sure how to play it on account of the complete memory blank he suffered from about eleven o'clock onwards on the night in question. They wound up in bed together but he couldn't seal the deal? Hardly flattering but the circumstances were exceptional. Still, she's obviously keen.

'Hello?'

'Lisa?'

'Well well. Sleeping beauty. How are you?'

'Out of practice, clearly.'

'Ha! You drank sooooo much.'

'He's a bugger that Ben. I felt like a mouse walking into a room full of cats.'

The seductive, girlie laugh. 'Ah no, don't try to give me any of that innocent crap. You were actually the last one on your feet. We couldn't get you to sit down.'

'Yeah, I heard I was the evening's cabaret.'

'Yeah well, you got some moves, boy.'

'So there is an upside to memory loss after all.'

'You can't remember?'

'Nope. I don't get on it like I used to. Like I say, out of practice.'

'Moira, Cathy and John all crashed out too they were so mangled. Me, you and Ben carried on but you had so much more than the rest of us so you did rather well actually.'

'Pleased I didn't let anyone down.'

'Well, I wouldn't say that.'

'Ah.'

The giggle again. Micky has a raging hard on *now.* But it's no fucking good to him *now* is it?

'How was the rest of your weekend?' He ventures.

'Slow, calm and restful.'

'Me too.'

'I'm not a kid anymore. Recovery time isn't what it was.'

'There's the truth.'

Then silence. Micky's mind goes blank. He panics, cuts straight to it.

'So er, you want to do something? Perhaps in a week or so?'

'Like what?'

'Well you know, I wasn't thinking that far ahead. Anything.'

'Oh.'

'Maybe I could take you to dinner?'

'How very gentlemanly.'

'Hey, some of us have got it and some ain't.'

'Yeah, I remember Saturday night.'

Four days later, as Whitney Houston begins an interminable domination of the airwaves with I Will Always Love You, Micky is back on a plane heading to Palma. The process of travel lifts him, as it always did and he is happy that things are becoming clearer. Well, perhaps not clearer but there is now a certain order to things. He is earning money again through the genuinely good cocaine he scores from big Chrissie, and he is excited by the prospect of hooking up with Lisa Fisher.

On the down side the prospect of buying his dad's house back remains just that, a prospect. And an expensive one. Hence the trip to Mallorca to grab more of his dwindling stash.

But wads of money isn't the only thing that he'll see on the island.

He checks into the Rey Don Jaime and calls the Chetkins' house. Sandra answers and they arrange to meet. At sundown she picks him up in an open top Astra but they are both wrapped up warmly against the November chill. She kisses him on the cheek and drives out of town.

'I know where we'll go,' she tells him.

'Oh yeah?'

'Where we first met. Not many other places open this time of year anyway.'

Micky grins and enjoys the ride over to Magalluf. It's all good and getting better. He is alive, he has friends, he has money. His dad will be happy into his old age. He'll get the house back. There is Lisa. But what about Sandra?

Magalluf is so dead they park directly outside Dicey Rileys.

'Christ,' Micky observes, 'we could park *inside* and no one would notice.'

For some reason that joke is the highlight of the evening. They chug a few beers, do the 'Hey do you remember when?' thing, talk openly about the Ecstasy and sex days.

But it isn't the same.

Micky orders a couple of Kamikazes with the next round, tries to get the party going, but Sandra gives him the 'Take it easy, I'm driving' routine.

He tries for the millionth and, he promises himself, the last time to remember just how he saved Sandra's life on the first night they met, right here in Magalluf. But there is nothing.

They head back to Santa Ponsa and decide on The Pepperpot for dinner. This is interesting for two reasons. One, it gives Micky a chance to do his pilgrimage to Bugsy's, and two, he hasn't seen the owners, Stewart and Doreen since the bad old days, the restaurant being directly next to where Bugsy's used to be.

They walk across the carpark and Micky glances left. Absorbed by Paco's, the Spanish eaterie on the other side, Bugsy's no longer exists but Micky can feel it. He can feel the drama, the love, the pain. The triumph.

They walk into The Pepperpot where Sandra hugs Doreen. Micky stands grinning at her shoulder. She looks at him, waiting to be introduced.

'Don't you recognise me, Dor'?'

No tan, short hair and eight intervening years of human chaos have made a difference to the way Micky Targett looks, but not that much.

'Oh my good god, you're not getting another bar are you?' She isn't joking.

'Good to see you too, me dear.'

119

She grabs Sandra by the shoulders. 'Tell me. Tell me he's not.'

Sandra is laughing too. 'Christ it wasn't that bad was it?'

'You have no bloody idea.'

Once Doreen calms down the meal goes well. Knowing she only has a short drive and there will be no cops, none that her father can't handle anyway, Sandra relaxes and drinks. And once she is assured that Micky is only visiting, Doreen relaxes too and joins them for brandies.

No sparks fly but Micky knows that sometimes you can't turn back the clock. Which is why, when she drops him off at his hotel, he is more than a little surprised to see Sandra get out of the car as well. She bleeps shut the locking system and holds his hand as they stride into reception.

'Don't mind do you?' Is all she says.

For the rest of his short visit Micky wears a permanent grin. It's a shame Connie isn't there but he hangs with Sandra, Barbara and the kid. It's luxury all the way, not least because he can afford to provide some of it himself.

Barbara gives him a rucksack that contains forty thousand pounds in cash. Oh what fun we have.

On his third and final evening Micky is expecting another roll in the hay. They're strolling on the beach, wrapped up warm. Nice sunsets at that time of year. Then she stops and looks at him. Considers him.

'It's been a great little trip. Thanks to you,' he tells her, and means it.

She smiles, steps into his arms and turns her face to look out across the bay. They hold each other for long moments, moments of true happiness.

'What shall we do, Mick?'

'About what?'

They unglue.

Wow, she thinks, *is he thick or what?*

'About us. What are you thinking?'

Jesus Christ on a fucking bike! Where did that come from? His default thought process is, quite naturally, one of panic.

'Erm, I think I'm so lucky. Lucky to have you in my life. Lucky I know your family.' He knows how crap that sounds before he has finished speaking.

She looks up at him and knows already. The gentle blue-grey of her eyes glosses over but she looks back towards the pale sun so he won't see.

Micky thinks about his dad, thinks about his brother. He thinks about going to court, thinks about how weird both he and his life are. Thinks about waking up in Ben Yardley's bed. Then he thinks about Lisa Fisher and her fat, juicy lips, her gorgeous, dinky feet. Thinks about her miraculous eyes, further illuminated by the scorched gleam he noticed when they were kissing in Ben's kitchen. Thinks that he has far too much to do before he can settle down, even if it's with the daughter of one of Europe's top gangsters.

'Sandra I'm walking a ton of cash through customs tomorrow, then I might go to court to fight to get my home back. I have to look after my old man. I have to figure out what my life is *for*.'

'I see.'

'I want you in my life, Sandra. We're good together. When I can get through some of . . .'

She flats her palm into his chest.

'It's okay.' She sniffs and takes his hand and they walk back to the car.

The journey back home is bittersweet. Achingly sentimental. Sandra is so lovely, he thinks. All those boxes ticked except . . . What? Just what the fuck does he *want?*

Part of him wants her and the stability. And when he thinks what being related to Connie Chetkins would do for his cred, what it would do for his bank balance it all but fries his brain.

But what if it doesn't work out?

Shit, why is it all so complicated?

But if Micky thinks all that is complicated, things get a whole lot worse when he is dragged over at Luton airport customs and they lift forty thousand pounds in cash off him.

*

The phone in the busy office rings and the powerfully built man in the smart suit picks it up.

'Ray Pitts.'

121

'Hi mate.'

'Who's that?'

'It's Bill you plonker, your man on the inside.'

'Hello, mate. How goes it?'

'Good, better than I expected.'

'Tell me. I could do with some good news.'

'Caught a live one.'

'Oh yeah?'

'You're going to love this – Micky Targett.'

'Is that his real name?'

'Apparently, but this gets interesting. Cupla years ago a girl OD'd in custody. East End somewhere.'

'I remember that.'

'She'd been caught dealing. I don't know her name but it wouldn't take you long to find out. I think my man Micky supplied the gear that killed her.'

'So who's this bloke?'

'Found him in a pub in Upminster. He told me he was behind the Midnights and Stingers that were all the rage back then.'

'He told you that?'

'Yeah and guess what? Yesterday he sells me four grams of chop. Pretty good stuff too. Got them all here for you.'

'*Now* I'm interested. Can he get more?'

'As much as I want.'

'Pukka, but for the minute don't do anything.'

'He's primed and ready to go.'

'I don't care. One, I don't want to spook him and two, it might pay us to see if we can chase it up the ladder. The fact that he may or may not have been involved in the death of that girl changes things.'

'Okay so you want me to hold back?'

'Yeah. Maybe one more and then we'll tee him up for the big one. I'll get back to you.'

'You got it.'

CHAPTER NINE

ESSEX - APRIL 1993

If your mind's neglected, stumble you might fall
Stumble you might fall

The Spring of ninety-three is a testing time for Micky Targett. Things haven't turned out like he planned.

After his return from Mallorca a year previously he was rolling in money, ideas and dreams. Now, as he tries to get his dad into the Scirocco so that he can get him off to hospital for his operation, he realizes that he has been tripped up by all three.

'Where are we going?'

'You're getting a new hip. Don't you remember?'

Micky recognises the glazed befuddlement. As per usual his dad has forgotten something and, as per sodding usual, he chooses to lie about it.

'You never told me about this.'

Micky has packed a small kitbag for the four night stay. He is looking forward to the respite. As they drive over there they hear a girl singing on the radio. Apparently all that she wants is another baby – Aheyey.

At The Nuffield hospital in Brentwood, Micky suffers the accustomed embarrassments of the old boy being a bit of a 'character' out in public. Every nurse is called 'Babes'. Every doctor is called 'Boss'. On their way to the ward a massive porter ambles past. Eddie stops him.

'You're not going to give me any trouble are you?'

The stunned man looks at Micky for guidance.

'Just kidding, son. Hope I see you around.' He pumps his hand energetically.

Four days, Micky thinks. *Four whole days.*

The arthritis in Eddie's hip has been worsening since forever, to the stage where he is in constant pain, so the hip op. has to be done. What also has to be done, in light of the ridiculous NHS waiting list, is paying for a private procedure. Hence the Nuffield. It is another ten large or so that he won't see again but Micky knows that if the old granite-hard bastard is complaining then it must be bad.

What also turns out to be bad, badder than he ever thought possible, is the period of rehabilitation.

Whilst Eddie is as tough as they come, his forgetfulness means that Micky is constantly on the go. When Eddie shuffles through on his crutches to the lounge and, with a blast of relief, lowers down into his chair, it is Micky who needs to go back to the bedroom to fetch whatever it is that has been forgotten. Likewise when Eddie makes it to his bedroom he yells for Micky to bring through whatever he's left in the lounge. And there is *always* something.

And there are months of it.

What helps Micky through it is an unexpected, windfallen by-product of the whole thing.

'Make sure he gets up and moving every day, see that he does his exercises and give him enough of these as and when he needs them,' the chief nurse tells him as she hands over a large white envelope containing several boxes. 'Maximum eight a day.'

Okaaaay, thinks Micky, what have we here? And what he has there is Tramadol, which he remembers with some affection from the accident that mangled his own knee a few years before.

Of course he doesn't deny his dad what he needs, and he finds that when he encourages the old guy to wash the green and yellow caps down with a few glasses of Merlot, he actually doesn't need too many at all. Which leaves enough for Micky. This is a good thing because Micky has pain of his own, namely the colossal one located in his arse on account of the shit with the house still going on.

His weekly calls to Ben Yardley became monthly, because his

brother is fighting the case.

'This is fucking ridiculous,' Ben declares over drinks in The Beedle And Bastard one evening.

'You don't have to tell me, Ben.'

'First the full defence, now he's stalling at every turn. What's wrong with this man?'

Micky has a few ideas about that.

'Every time they need to reply they deliberately leave it to the last possible moment. Why does he hate you so much?'

Because he knows, Micky thinks. Him and his shitbag ex. They know where the violence came from.

Not only do the delays mean the ownership of the house is still in limbo but the longer the case drags on the more Micky is obliged to shell out. The initial five grand back when they met a year ago was supposed to bring the whole fiasco to its satisfactory conclusion. He doesn't want to think how much has been piled on top of that.

'How's your dad doing?'

'Yeah he's making progress but it's slow. Poor old sod.'

Ben sees that Micky is struggling. He knows the bloke has always had a quip, always had a smile. Lately, though.

'How's Lisa?'

'Fine thanks. We're getting on well. One of the few good things at the moment.'

He's not joking.

One of the other good things is the Tramadol.

Of course it is nothing like the heroin he had so enthusiastically embraced just a few years previously, but when he's on enough of it Micky doesn't think too much about anything. Which is the point. He just goes to that place. That place, the blue-walled grotto of comfort, where no one and nothing can get to him. Where he is safe and unmolested by the madness of the world. He'll be going there quite often in the coming months. And years.

Ben talks on, something about another party, but Micky zones out and doesn't hear him. Micky is thinking and what he thinks is – Why does weird shit keep on happening?

His current fugue state started months back. Getting his forty K

125

swagged off him at customs on the way back in from Mallorca the previous November.

'I'd just like to check your bag, Sir.'

The bloke was away to one side of the walk-through area so Micky kept going, pretended he hadn't heard.

'Sir!'

Fuck!

The shortness of the trip had meant he'd only taken a rucksack so wasn't long before the bloke pulls three cherries.

'Lot of money to be carrying with you, Sir.'

It had been so easy the previous time, he'd paid the possibility of a stop scant attention.

'I won it at the casino in Mallorca.'

'Oh, congratulations. Would you be able to prove that?'

Bollocks, thought Micky.

'I can but I don't have that on me. It's at home.'

'At home? So you live in Mallorca?'

Oops. 'No I live in Essex. You see I actually won quite a bit more than this a while ago, earlier this year. I brought some of the money, along with proof of the win, back with me then.'

'I see. How much did you win in total?'

'I won a hundred and fifty thousand pounds. I brought back a hundred last time. There is exactly forty thousand there.'

'Did you declare the money last time?'

'No.'

'Why not?'

'I didn't know I had to.'

'I'm going to need to deal with this in private, Sir. Please re-pack your bag and follow me.'

The upshot was Micky had to find that letter from the casino. The last time he saw it was in the case in the loft with what was left of the wonga. Or was it? Shit, getting as bad as the old man.

The bloke had counted the money in front of him and gave him a receipt. He also gave him a form C9011, told him to fill it in and call the number on the paperwork when he'd got the casino note. Then they could talk about him having his money back.

He didn't have the cash for a cab from the airport so had to slog it into Paddington on the train, across town on the tube to Fenchurch

Street and then all the way out to Essex. His nerves were so minced there was no way he was going to fall asleep and go to Shoebury.

He piled into the house, hauled the steps down from the loft hatch and scrambled up. Then it all went into slow motion. With a concussive slam of dread, he understood instantly that he wasn't going to find the proof of winnings letter in the suitcase. That was because the suitcase wasn't there anymore.

He trembled precariously on two ceiling joists, gulping long and hard on the musty air. The old man. Could only be him.

He calmed himself as well as he was able, and completed a slow three-sixty of the entire loft area. Then he got down again, as low as he could, to peer into the gloomy corners, at one point grinding his screaming knee into one of the joists. No, definitely no case.

Clambering back down, he heard the radio from the kitchen. Heard that twat warbling on about his achey breaky heart.

Eddie was there slathering butter on thick white slices.

'Alright, boy. Want a sandwich?'

Micky pointed his quivering left index finger skywards. 'Dad, think carefully. My suitcase up in the loft . . .'

'Yeah?'

'Do you know where it is?'

'Yeah. Why, you don't need it do you?'

Micky sagged so much with the relief he could have been carried around in a bucket.

'Whoa. Thank Christ for that.'

'What's the matter with you?'

'There's something important in it. Where is it?'

Rock Steady Eddie jabs his chin towards the kitchen wall. 'I gave it to them.'

'What? Who? Who did you give it to?'

'Them. Next door. The oldsters.'

'Mr. and Mrs. Rogers?'

'That's them. For their holiday.'

'Did you take the money out first?'

'What money?'

Jeezus.

'When are they going away?'

Eddie's expression of benign detachment only added substance, crushing substance, to what he said. 'They've already gone.'

As he powered out through the house and across the driveway, Micky's legs felt like they were made of reconstituted chicken. The Rogers' ancient Nissan Micra was nowhere to be seen. A solitary hall light indicated that, yes indeed, the occupants were away on holiday. Micky's desperate, fruitless ringing of the bell and hammering on the door confirmed his misery.

He tottered back into the bungalow, out once more into the kitchen.

'Told ya. Want a tea?'

'Please.'

He leant against the counter top, supported himself by his elbows, and considered the damage. Loveliest old couple you'd ever meet but why didn't they bring the money in when they found it? Never see that again.

Truth is Micky wasn't too sure how much was in there. A hundred he parked with Ben, then there was the money for the car, the hip operation, fixing the house up. Three large to Chrissie for the chop. Plus, of course, the ongoing and seemingly endless legal bills. Maybe there was fifteen. Plus the proof of the win at the casino. That meant if he had a prayer of seeing the forty K being held by customs again he'd need to call Connie to get his contact at the casino to write another one. How would that look and what would it cost?

Micky heard the mug of tea land next to him.

'Cheers.'

Then he heard his dad opening and closing a cupboard, heard the wrinkling of a plastic bag which Eddie also put on the counter top.

'Found that in the case.'

Micky looked up, saw the bag. The bag in which he kept the money and the proof of win at the casino. The bag that he thought it best to bundle up everything in less than week ago but had completely forgotten about.

Despite eventually retrieving his forty thousand, Micky's torment continued with the uncompromising stance taken by his brother. Full denial and defence, which was ludicrous because he had the evidence. So the title of the house would be staying where it was for the foreseeable.

But two beacons of fun and inspiration were shining through the gloom towards the end of nineteen ninety-two. The first was his burgeoning cocaine business.

He'd bought three ounces of quite pokey gear for three thousand flat, and knew that he could gram that out at current rates and gross well over five. The question being, how long it would take?

That noisy cabbie, PC, had promised much, as a lot of them do, but he'd heard nothing more from him since that first drop. That wasn't a problem because Micky was re-learning a solid fact he came by years before, namely if you have the right product at the right price you will end up knowing a pleasing amount of people who regularly phone you up wanting to give you money.

That most of them were friends of Ben and Lisa or friends of theirs was an added treat. Nice, professional people who knew what they wanted and always had the cash to pay for it. Micky established an ordered, discreet round and with it a rewarding solvency.

Of the forty grand he brought back from Mallorca he gave thirty to Ben Yardley as added payment to the bank for the title of the house. The other ten went upstairs with the rest. In a new and, Micky hoped, impossible to find location, tucked under the layer of insulation behind a ceiling joist.

The income from his coke round, together with his dad's two meagre pensions, would support their modest lifestyle until they got the house back. Get over to Connie in Mallorca and start living again.

The other thing making Micky smile at that time was Lisa Fisher who was as exotic, luscious, sexy, intelligent and fun as he'd thought when he'd first met her at Ben's party.

He ended up getting round to see her again just after his trip to Mallorca, when he'd collected that second block of his cash. Her two-bedroomed terraced house in Ilford was, if a tad chaotic, cosy, welcoming, and tastefully decorated. She greeted him in simple jeans and T-shirt and Micky couldn't believe she was a teacher. He copped an immediate stiffy as soon as he saw her barefoot.

He followed her along the hall and through into the kitchen, checked the rear end that he should already know all about but doesn't. Note to self – go easy on the shots in future.

A wall had been knocked down to enable a large kitchen-diner arrangement.

'Want a glass of wine?' Lisa asked.

'Sounds good, cheers.'

On the radio Michael Jackson was taking it upon himself to Heal The World. She turned down the volume. She splashed Frascati from an already opened bottle. She steered them towards comfy seats, slung a leg over the arm of her chair. Smiled. White teeth and dancing eyes.

'So . . .'

Micky knew she had the upper hand. She's been up for it and he crashed out on her. Quite funny when you think about it.

'Yes indeed.'

'Did you have a good time at Ben's?'

Those dimples. Jeezus.

'Well I had a fabulous time, thank you. Yourself?'

'Yeah.' She tittered delightfully, touched her upper lip with the tip of her tongue. Christ, look at that tongue? 'It was interesting.'

'Interesting. Yeah, I suppose.'

'Did you get home alright?'

'Yeah, cabbed it back soon after you left. I don't live too far from there. Shame I didn't get to see you.'

'I was there,' she shrugged playfully.

They stared at each other.

'You're really hot.' It's all he wanted to say.

'Yeah, never mind that. Tell me about what you do.'

The good thing about taking drugs with people, Micky knows, is that they're effectively criminals, just like he is. You have that over them. Especially the respectable types. Like teachers. Lots to lose. So he doesn't mind relaxing. It's good to talk.

'I'm not doing anything at the moment.'

'How was your trip to Spain?'

He thought back. Sandra. Lots of sex, her fumbling offer on the beach and his fumbling avoidance of it.

'It was alright thanks.'

'Only a couple of days? Why did you do that?'

He looked her in the eye. 'As I think I told you, my dad has been defrauded out of ownership of his own house. Ben is helping me get it back which is expensive. I have some money I keep in Mallorca. I went to bring some of it back.'

'That's terrible.'

'It is.'

She sipped her wine.

'You mean in cash?'

'Yeah.'

'Blimey.'

'Yeah well, I won't be doing that again. A nice man at customs took it off me.'

'Oh my God! How much?'

Micky took a large gulp. 'Forty thousand. It *should* be alright. Bit of paperwork. It *is* my money.'

She exhaled extravagantly. 'Whoa, that's some heavy shit. Why have you got lots of money in Mallorca?'

That really was a good question, and Micky had no doubt he could keep her entertained for hours once he started answering it.

'Look we know, from the other night, that I used to be at it.'

'Sorry?'

'Criminality. I remember telling you that much. I made a lot of money and, for reasons I won't go into now, that money in cash, ended up in Mallorca. I can prove I came by it legally, but I'd rather not run it through the banking system.'

'Much better to stick it in your case and get caught, right?'

'Suitcases full of cash is something else I could tell you a lot about.'

She tossed her head back and laughed, her corkscrew hair doing its mad dance. 'Damn, you *are* good fun.'

'You have no idea.'

'So is that all over? You a good boy now?'

'Trying to be but hey, I'm easily led.'

She spotted the tease behind his eyes. 'Yeah, butter wouldn't melt.'

He reached into the pocket of his jeans and pulled out the plastic bag which he placed on the coffee table between them. It was at least five grams.

'Ooh, look at that.'

'I like drugs. Part of life.'

'So why did you bring that here?'

'I thought it might be nice. Just the two of us. I am aware things got a little out of hand last time.'

She carried on looking at the bag. 'I see.'

He was momentarily distracted by her eyelashes, like two brand new wallpaper pasting brushes.

'It's no biggie. I'm not suggesting now . . .'

She stared him down as he talked and for a second he began to think he'd misjudged it.

'I just wanted to let you know I deal but I'm not a bad man, okay?'

She placed her glass on the coffee table and stood.

So then he figured he'd misread the entire scenario, figured he's going to get bashed.

'It's er, there if you want it.'

Hands on her hips now. She going the can of mace and fingernail route? Get ready to run, Micky boy.

'Haven't you ever heard of a certain phrase?'

'Which one is that?'

'Never on a school night, dickhead.'

'What?'

'It's alright for you international playboys. It's Thursday evening. I'm taking a bunch of seventeen-year-olds through Animal Farm at nine in the morning.'

'Holy crap.' Micky folded into himself with the relief.

She stepped over his legs, swiveled and sat on his lap. She took his face in her hands. Christ those eyes.

'I'm afraid we'll have to do this the old fashioned way. When was the last time you got laid straight?'

Now *there* was a question.

She presseded her lips onto his.

Back of the net, Micky thought.

And the sex was beyond description. Beyond being just sex. It was everything he'd been looking for and, unfogged by any chemical imbalance, he was a full and vigorous contributor to the evening. More than once. Which he was able to remember.

And once more before school in the morning.

And in the car on the way back out along the A12 he knew what he wanted to hear. There was a time, a bygone and less thoughtful time, when he would have gone for Brown Sugar. But this was a different Micky. He rammed the CD in, turning the Blaupunkt all the way up. The slide guitar took him away.

Hey babe, what's in your eyes?
I see them flashing like airplane lights
You fill my cup, babe that's for sure
I must come back for a little more

So it was all as good as it could be. In fact things looked up even more towards the end of the year when that gobby dickwad PC got back in touch saying he was after more gear. Ker chiiing!

'Gonna be a whiiiiiiiiiiiite Christmas, Geez!'

He took another five grams straight away with the promise of mega biz over the holidays. Any chance he could lay on an ounce? He still had more than that in the garage but he called Chrissie Jarvis to re-up anyway. Nice.

As if to confirm the spirit of goodwill to all men was in the air, Micky got a call from HMRC telling him he could, upon production of appropriate identification, go to Luton airport to collect his forty thousand pounds. Thank fuck for that.

Since his mother had faded away throughout the winter of eighty-six into eighty-seven Micky had never done the Christmas thing. It was only ever a crass excuse to get on the razz anyway. That said he was looking forward to a little festive celebration round at Lisa's. Sadly that was not to be.

'Family.'

'Oh yeah? What, Nigeria?'

'Nothing quite so exotic. Kidderminster.'

'Right. Who's there?'

'My daughter.'

'Daughter?'

'Yeah. You see, we can find out stuff about each other without that funny game.'

'Right.'

'Her father lives there too.'

It was the most bizarre thing but Micky felt the jealousy tearing through him like a fever. The fuck was that all about?

So he hunkered down with Eddie, slipped up the Yeoman to see the lads and made sure he was available to all his customers as and when the need arose. It was Micky Mouse business compared to the old days but he knew it was a different world now.

On Christmas eve he got the call from PC.

'How we fixed for the oz, Geez? My pals are gagging.'

'Ready when you are.'

'Suhweeeeet. Carpark of the Huntsmen? Seven?'

'Shall be done. I'll be sitting in the car. The Scirocco, yeah?'

'Good man. See ya.'

PC hung up the phone, looked at the muscular man sitting at the desk next to him and smiled.

'We on?' Detective Sargeant Pitts asked William Hubbard.

'We on, boss man.'

Before Ray Pitts arranged for his arrest back-up, he made another call, tried to find out what he could about this bloke. This Micky Targett.

UPMINSTER, ESSEX - DECEMBER 24TH 1992

Micky sits behind the wheel of his car as the Huntsmen and Hounds fills up for the Christmas Eve yahoo. It's six forty-seven pm. He has got there early because that's what he does. Matter of habit.

He's also in no rush. His dad needs a lift up the golf club but that's later on and, that aside, Micky has sod all to do.

He pulls the plastic bag from the front of his underwear and slips it into the door pocket. He goes over the phone call. Goes over the history of his association with this bloke. Dealt with him twice before. If it was going to happen it would have already . . . As this thought runs across his brain he is poleaxed by another one; why, if PC needed a bunch to move on at Christmas, has he waited until seven o'clock on Christmas Eve to score?

Fuck!

Micky looks at his watch. Okay, keep it calm. He's a mate of The Stomach's, that's good. He's very high profile, that's good. He's already a buyer.

Micky looks through the windscreen, scans the carpark. Away to his left the pub doors open and, to the sound of festive merriment, a couple dive into the throng. A car pulls into view, drives past Micky. He watches it slow and stop. But no one gets out. The reverse lights illuminate and the car drifts all the way back across Micky's line of sight. Like a shark. It stops ten yards away with the engine running.

Micky reaches for the keys but right then a minibus full of howling females enters the carpark, stops right there and completely blocks any getaway. Micky tries to swallow but it feels like he has dirty golf ball in his throat.

He watches as the driver's door of the car opens, watches as the elegantly shod feet hit the ground. Then there is a man, a very big man and the man is walking towards Micky. Thump thump thump goes his heart. Twang twang twang go his nerves.

The man walks closer, his hands in his Crombie pockets. Micky has never seen him before but he can see that he's big and he's tough and, one way or the other, he is going to destroy Micky's life. He stops walking only when he is standing next to the Scirocco. They are close enough to touch.

'Open the fucking window.'

The minibus driver is looking for a parking spot, there just isn't one. He's not moving. Micky's shaking hand is on the keys. He has no weapon which is undoubtedly a good thing. He hits the button.

The man looks down at him, exacerbating the dynamic. Micky is nothing and this man could crush him like the bug he is. They stare and Micky can't look away.

'He's not coming.'

'I'm waiting for me girlfriend, mate.'

A smile tells Micky what he found out first time around, earlier in the year on Connie Chetkins' terrace in Mallorca. There is so much knowledge in the world and Micky Targett is in possession of so little of it.

'Well she ain't coming either. Your lucky night, boy.'

Micky says nothing. He doesn't understand. He's not clever enough, he's not strong enough. He has to take care of his dad. All he wants to do is go. He looks up and sees the minibus pull past him to the pub entrance where the women pile noisily out.

'I'll head off then.'

'Best you do, son. Not every time you'll get a free pass. Nice looking boy like you, wouldn't last long in there.'

Micky starts the car, finds gear, handbrake off.

'Merry Christmas,' he hears as he drives off.

As Micky passes the car he looks in at the passenger. He knows that he knows the man, but he can't remember from where.

ESSEX – APRIL 1993

'Mick? Yo, Earth to Mick.'

Micky stirs from is recollections, looks around. He's in the Beedle And Bastard with Ben Yardley who finishes off his Pepsi.

'Yeah.' Micky straightens, gets himself together. A hundred and fifty emgees of Tramadol can slow a chap down, especially with a couple of beers. 'What you saying?'

'I said maybe we should have another evening at mine. You up for it?'

'Hmm. That could be good.'

He thinks back to the last one. It was a total hoot but maybe all the good questions have already been asked. Then again, Micky reasons, if he can remember fuck all about that it would be like starting again.

Fact is Micky isn't feeling his dynamic, electric best these days. He tells Ben he'll think about it, says they'll talk about the case again on Monday and they go their ways. April ninety-three. The country is still talking about the Warrington bomb. Two kids dead.

It was only a couple of months before that he'd learned what happened to PC. He'd caught up with The Stomach during a rare visit to the Yeoman.

'Bloke got busted. Turns out he was a cocaine dealer.'

Micky's pint of Stella all but gets blasted over the pub wall. *'What?'*

'Yeah. Who'd a thunk it? My money was on you.'

So that was why the bloke had just disappeared. Being warned off the meet with him on Christmas Eve was freaky enough but knowing PC had gone down for the same thing was just too weird. Too close.

He'd carried on gramming out to the others because he knew he was safe with them. But then he thought he was safe with PC.

And then summer is on its way but he is stuck at home looking after his dad.

Thinking about surgery Micky hadn't failed to notice that renowned Premier League onion-bag botherer Alan Shearer had undergone surgery on knee ligaments that he'd wrecked on Boxing day the previous year. Word was coming back that he would indeed play again. Micky figured that if that Geordie fucker could do it then so could he.

As Eddie ditches one crutch and then the other and regains a little mobility, Micky made enquiries at the Nuffield about a rebuild for himself. He winds up in front of his dad's surgeon, Miguel Ferrer.

'Yes, knee ligament rebuilds are becoming effective. Yours is a posterior though.'

'That a problem?'

'No. That can be done. As to its effectiveness . . .'

'So what do you actually do?'

'Firstly I won't be doing it. I just do hips, but I know someone who can help you. He will take apart your knee, cut a slice from your patella tendon, thread that through and secure it by way of screws to the bottom of your thigh bone and the top of your shin bone. That will become your new ligament to replace the one you have damaged.'

'Okay. Recovery time?'

'Two months in plaster and then you can get down the gym. Maybe another two months and you'll be good to go.'

'As in running and playing sport?'

'I wouldn't recommend contact sports but running yes.'

Micky gives it thought.

'I couldn't get this on the NHS could I?'

'No.'

'Do you know how much?'

'I'll need to check that along with my colleague's availability. Perhaps twelve thousand.'

Ten days later Micky is getting slammed full of Propofol which, he is informed when he comes out of surgery, is a substance he made urgent purchase enquiries about in the euphoric seconds before he went fully under.

His chopped about knee, along with the ankle to thigh plaster, makes life difficult at home but Rock Steady Eddie rises to the challenge doing whatever he can for Micky.

Business ticks over as Micky invites his customers to collect and they all, Ben and Lisa included, are more than happy to do so.

Two things colour the summer of nineteen ninety-three; one, absolutely nothing happens in his case with his brother other than the same, interminable lurch towards an eventual confrontation in court where the winner would, in every single imagination, take all. If Micky won he would get the house back free of any charges. The bank would lose everything and Micky would be entitled to claim all his legal costs from his brother. If Micky lost he would never get the house back, would get stuffed for Ben's fees *and* would be liable for all of his brother's costs as well.

As Bill Clinton hammers Iraq, just to send the uppity raghead motherfuckers a 'message', the second feature of that summer has Micky taking full advantage of his practically unlimited access to Tramadol. His *own.*

'Do you have any kind of opiate taking history, Mr. Targett?' This is the head nurse upon hearing Micky specifically request the magic painkiller.

He thinks back, chasing the dragon as he tried to see off his own demons, only a few eventful years before.

'Certainly not.'

One day the devil in him leads him to unload one of those caps onto his bedside cabinet. He racks the fifty milligrams into two 'Tramlines'. He liked the joke more than the effects and doesn't bother doing that again.

Mostly though, he passes his days drifting in and out of that place, that place where he likes to go more and more.

His lay-up doesn't unduly affect his relationship with Lisa. From the new year up until the operation in May they'd had a great time. Bundles of sex, quite a lot of cocaine (and weed), some great conversations; books, films, dreams et al, and many, many laughs.

Micky wonders if he is in love. He figures he deserves it, and if he is he's not afraid.

You got my heart, you got my soul
You got the silver, you got the gold
You got the diamonds from the mine
Well that's alright, it'll buy some time

After the operation, even though she comes by the Upminster bungalow occasionally, everything necessarily changes. There are one or two rushed blow jobs in his bedroom when Eddie is zipping around the block for his daily rehabilitative walk, but that's it. He wants it to last but at the same time he's thinking of getting the house back. Getting fit. Getting to Mallorca. He knows there is conflict waiting for him round the corner.

Two months later the cast comes off and, for the second time in his life, Micky looks down and wonders where his right leg has gone. Muscle wastage, some weird shit.

Two months after that, having religiously hammered the quad and hamstring machines down the local gym, his leg is looking more like the real thing, but his knee still hurts. In his mind the original X Rays shows why. The tip of the upper screw looks like it had been advanced half a rotation too far and is digging into the bone of his knee. He raises the issue with the physio and eventually the surgeon himself. He is told everything is fine and he should keep at it down the gym.

And it keeps hurting.

And he keeps taking the Tramadol.

And he knows it's not right. Six months on from the operation it's worse than it was when he went in. So he goes back to the surgeon and sees what he's dealing with. Across the desk, as this man shuffles papers and squints at X Rays, he sees a car mechanic who's screwed up a service but won't rectify it because it'll eat his profit. Sees a shop owner who won't change a sub-standard shirt because it's been worn once. Is everyone a shyster?

'Something's wrong. That screw is in the wrong place. Do you think I would be saying this if it wasn't serious.' Micky stares him down.

So this bloke, this so-called orthopaedic surgeon, Mr. El-Zebdeh agrees. Has no choice.

'Alright. If it is in the wrong place it will be safe now for me to remove it,' he says with a combination of boredom, disquiet and virulent dislike.

Micky is pleased for two reasons. One, he'll get his knee back. Two, he'll get another blast of that Propofol shit.

He wakes up with the screw in a jar next to the bed.

So he goes to see Ben Yardley and they sue the bastard.

'Very difficult thing to do. You will need to get testimony from at least one other surgeon saying this guy messed up, and doctors are notorious for closing ranks.'

At the beginning of December of ninety-three Micky, along with the rest of the world, hears some news that many thought was long overdue and therefore caused little fuss. Following a sustained operation involving elite Colombian forces working in tandem with American DEA agents, Pablo Escobar is gunned down fleeing across a rooftop in his home town of Medellin. El Don Pablo. El Padron. The man who more than any other, gave cocaine to the world.

The horror of his legacy is as well known as his incredible rise to wealth and power. The richest criminal the world has ever seen. Not for the first time Micky pondered the misery the cocaine trade had and was causing. He shooed the thoughts from his mind and carried on knocking out his wares.

Over the winter of ninety-three into ninety-four Micky and Ben find not one but two sympathetic consultants to verify Micky's grievances. Using their opinions they put the case together and threaten El Zebdeh with eternal damnation. Or at the least some very adverse publicity. They settle on seven large. Micky feels the thrill of vindication more than the buzz of the cash, three grand of which goes straight to Ben as his fee anyway.

'Anyone else you want to sue?' he asks Micky cheerfully.

Then, in the new year of nineteen ninety-four, Ben tells him it looks like the whole case with the house is going to mediation. Micky isn't too sure what that will mean practically, but it sounds like a lifeline.

'Avoids court,' explains Ben. 'Somewhere neutral. Perhaps the offices of the bank's solicitors in town. No independent mediators. Just thrash it out around the table between the three of us.'

'Three of us?'

'Us, your brother and his wife and the bank. Plus everyone's legal representatives of course.'

'Ben, tell me again what you think of our chances in court.'

He hears the unmistakable sound of air getting sucked through teeth.

'Look, it doesn't matter now but for arguments sake I would say sixty-forty to you. Maybe even more but nothing is ever certain. We don't know what lies they might come out with.'

'But the evidence.'

'And some of that evidence is solid and some of it isn't. And what should be our ace in the pack, your dad, may well turn out to be a liability. He's just too fragile. I would hate to put him on the stand.'

Micky knows he's right.

'Trust me. This is the best way. We'll try to get the best deal for you we can, but one way or another you'll get the house back. Eyes on the prize.'

Damn, thinks Micky Targett, *nearly there.*

Bouyed by this development, and by the fact that he is largely pain free in the knee department, although that of course doesn't stop him bleating for more Tramadol from his GP, Micky embarks on a spree of getting seriously shitfaced.

There are a few riotous nights out with the lads down the Yeoman but he finds that these days the drink does it for him less and less. Some of the hangovers are just crucifying. What he wants to do is score some Ecstasy and go out with Lisa. Also what he wants to do is score some Ecstasy and stay *in* with Lisa but that can wait for another day. The problem is he can't land any of the stuff. Oh how the mighty are coming up short. Then he has a thought.

'Ben, fancy a beer.'

Such is Micky Targett's world in the early months of nineteen ninety-four. He can buy class A drugs from his lawyer in one minute and take his teacher/girlfriend out to enjoy them the next.

By that time they are up to seeing each other a couple of times after work during the week and all day Sunday. Micky is stunned to realize how good sex can be without drugs. That's not to say they don't get on the gear some of the time as *well*, but mostly it is Lisa's preference to keep it clean.

And Micky feels the power of his blossoming love taking him over. He knows it's for real when he considers the basic facts; she's crowding forty and she's black. Well not black, beautifully brown. At any time in his prior life he knew the whole deal would have been inconceivable. Now not a solitary fuck could be given.

Sometimes they read together. The fact of it freaks him out but he loves it. Cuddled up with a book each, enjoying the silence which is only disturbed when one of them needs to quote to the other something that has moved or impressed.

One Sunday in late-February they are at her place and it is *all* about the sex, and whilst it interests neither of them to get into anything seriously off-piste, Micky is gratified to discover he shares Lisa's appreciation of tasteful underwear. Inspired by her preferences he even takes it upon himself to do a bit of shopping for her. For both of them. Lace, silk. Stay-up stockings. And pastel colours. Blues and greens look best against the caramel of her immaculate skin. And with her eyes.

So they have a few drinks and maybe a smoke of nothing too heavy, put something rhythmic on the stereo and off they go. For hours.

And it is perfect.

Slow and tender when they want it to be and some proper headboard slamming stuff when they feel like that. They've both been around the block enough times to know when they're onto something good.

Micky encourages her to hold her legs back so her feet are up beside her head. Then he supports a muscle-filled buttock in each palm, drifts his tongue lightly across her anus, into her vagina, takes a few laps around her clitoris and goes back again. Over and over. He knows enough about her to tease her right to the edge, gives her about fifteen minutes, then feels a seismic orgasm rip through her. She calls time and they settle back for a break.

'Well,' she coos as her calmness returns, 'this is all turning out rather well.'

'Hey, stick with me, kid, you'll be farting through silk.'

'Thank you for that, Oscar Wilde. Y'know, I knew you'd be a decent shag when you walked into Ben's that first time.'

Micky gags on his wine.

''Scuse me, did you say *decent?*'

'Well, we're getting you there.'

'I believe there are certain rules about that sort of thing.'

'Such as?'

'Any man who can dance and ride a motorcycle fast, that's the dude you need to be getting in the sack with.'

'What about dudes who fall *off* motorcycles. How is the knee by the way?'

Coming on thanks for asking. Did the scar help?'

'Didn't do your chances any harm.'

'God bless you, Cut-throat Jimmy.'

'*What?*'

'That was the bloke who did it. Cut-throat Jimmy Mulroney.'

'Jesus Christ. Are you for real? You crims are actually called things like that? What was your nom de guerre?'

'Micky 'Sex-god' Targett.'

She hoots with glorious laughter.

With a hard-on that has no idea why it isn't getting any action, Micky slings his leg across her thighs, lays a palm on her stomach and kisses her cheek.

'About that . . .'

'About what?'

'You getting hurt. Couldn't you go to the police?'

'No.'

'Weren't you out for revenge?'

Micky doesn't really want to go there.

'He was too far down the ladder for that but he was warned off.'

'Who by? A big, scary man?'

'By a big, scary employee of a big, scary man.'

'You're friends with people who hurt other people?'

'Lisa . . .'

'It's okay. No biggie.'

'Look, you know I'm not a bad man.'

'Yeah.'

'I've met some bad men in my time, Jimmy Mulroney was one, but I don't know them anymore. I *do* know some very powerful people who I've worked with in the past. They seem to like me. I've been in a corner once or twice in recent years and they've helped me out.'

'Why do they like you?'

'Well, half a lifetime ago, I pulled a girl out of a fight. She was getting beat up by her boyfriend. I did the Bruce Willis thing. She was pregnant too.'

'Oh my god.'

'As it was she nearly lost the kid. She turned out to be the daughter of a very heavy duty individual. He and I are close. Well, close*ish*. He's the man in Mallorca.'

'Ah the Mallorca connection.'

'Yup, all roads lead there.'

'And you think you might go back?'

Now that is the kind of question that gets Micky on the back foot. If he was honest he should just give a straight 'yes'. But then part of him is starting to fall so completely for her, he's wondering if Mallorca is really the move for him.

Blue Lines by Massive Attack slips around on Lisa's multi CD player.

'I got no plans to go anywhere until my dad's house is sorted.'

'Any word from Ben on that?'

'Not recently.'

She shuffles onto her side, turns to face him.

'I still can't believe your brother did that.'

He wonders if this is the moment to tell her more. He gave her the lite version, but everything? How would that go down? The violence. The addiction. The counseling. The madness. He has this stunning woman on-side, why jeopardise that? Not now anyway, not at a moment of such delicacy. He actually wishes she'd just shut up. He's losing his perk-on for Christ's sake.

'This isn't helping the mood.'

'Sorry.'

In response she reaches out and takes his dick in one hand and his scrotum in the other. Gentle, stroking motions. She knows what works. He sighs in gratitude, closes his eyes and gives himself over to her care.

'You like kids, Mick?'

He sees images of young James, Sandra's boy.

'Yeah. I know a couple. They're cool.'

'You never considered having any of your own?'

He's thought about it. Often. Knows he'd do a much better job than half the bozos around. But where do you get the time? Even when he has sod all to do he knows there is no *way* he'd have any time for a sprog. And how are you supposed to know what to do? He's into his mid-thirties and he's still trying to work out how to take care of himself.

'I'm the kind of person who doesn't handle stress very easily. Even if things went smooth all the way I don't know if I'd have enough of myself left to give.'

He opens his legs to give her more room, which she takes. The opening percussion and the bass line behind it signal the start of Safe From Harm. He breathes deep.

'You're such a thoughtful person. You'd be great.'

'That's nice of you to say so. But the dark side of me thinks that the last thing the world needs right now is another target to aim at.'

She shakes her head at the pun.

'Christ, you should've been a poet. You've got the words and the angst.'

'One day I'll find out what I've been put on this planet for.'

She keeps up the teasing, knows she is making him burn. She leans forward to touch her tongue against his lips. He tries to respond with a kiss but she pulls away.

'You've been hurt a lot, haven't you?'

'More than a few but not as much as some.'

'Would you like to meet my daughter?'

He opens his eyes. This is a development as Lisa doesn't talk much about her girl, the girl's father and how things work. He understands things aren't easy but he can't help but feel the sting when she spends most of her holidays away.

'That'd be cool.'

'Couple of weekends time.'

'How old is she?'

'Six.'

'Hannah, right?'

She smiles. 'That's right.'

'Yeah, that would nice. She look like you?'

Lisa grins. 'Yeah, in some ways.'

'She got your eyes?'

She stares at him from inches away and Micky is once more lost in the beauty.

'Only I've got my eyes.'

There is nothing else for him but to admit he is falling in love.

'Jeezus fucking Christ.'

She grins and says, 'You're turn.'

She pushes him onto his back and kneels between his legs, forces his thighs apart and gets to work with her tongue and those big, fat juicy lips. Micky lies back and gasps, marvels at how they both know exactly what to do to the other to push the buttons. Looks forward to a future filled with pleasure and with love.

But before he gets to try on his family man hat there's a party to be had. He and Lisa are going out, hard.

Ben calls him and he picks up ten pills for fifty, the ones with the $ stamp on. Happy days.

They meet at Lisa's mid-evening, Saturday night. Micky is so psyched for the whole deal he is literally shaking. She takes her time getting in and out of the shower then dresses in tight jeans, girlie motorcycle boots and a black T-shirt that says 'Fallen Angel' and features a naked, black woman nailed to a cross. He is speechless with both admiration and desire.

In the kitchen the radio belts out Rocks by Primal Scream. Micky can taste the froth of want and excitement bubbling up his throat.

'Do we have to get there really late? Is it one of those?'

'No no. In fact I'm all for getting over there. I doubt I'm into the staying up all night thing these days. Test driving me knee too.'

'So what is it?'

'I just saw a flyer the other day. Two blokes from a couple of years ago. Americans. Jeff Mills and Richie Hawtin.'

'And they are . . ?'

'Techno DJs.'

'Hmm. Is that good?'

'Hey don't go all mumsy on me.'

She grins. 'Let's just hope you can keep up with this old mum, white boy.'

Fuck yeah.

'Where is it?'

'Dungeons under London Bridge.'

'Sounds delightful. Wanna drink?'

'Yeah. Let's have a drink, a line and drop the first one, that way we'll hit the ground running. It's all in the planing.'

She grabs the wine, he racks out a couple of six-inchers.

'Precision, darling. *Military* precision. This is no ordinary mission.'

He places a couple of $s on the kitchen counter.

'How long since you done a pill?' he asks.

'I've never done a pill.'

Micky waits for the punchline. And waits.

''Scuse me?'

She shrugs. 'That's alright isn't it?'

To help with his befuddlement he hits his line with some violence. Is it alright? If not why not?

'If I get weird you'll look after me won't you?'

He gulps Chardonnay. 'I was hoping if I got weird you'd look after *me.'*

She grabs his rolled up twenty. 'There you go then, soldier, we're in it together.'

So they drop a pill each and jump a fast black to that place under London Bridge. The road in all the gangster films that literally looks like a tunnel. Lisa isn't fully out of the cab when she heaves up all over the kerb. Micky guides her to a crappy tobacconist, buys a bottle of water.

'Stay with it, take your time,' he counsels. He's well on the way himself but can't enjoy it. Not if she doesn't.

She breathes deep, a patina of fear and doubt covering her lovely features.

'Give me a minute. I get it. I get it.' She holds an index finger skywards, a look of intense concentration filtering into her eyes.

'I felt how good that was. It was just a bit too much all at once.'

Micky's natural downer has taken priority, he thinks. What he doesn't know is that, while he may feel totally flat, his own chemically febrile demeanour is there for the whole street to see. He's bobbing up and down and chewing his cheeks with the best of them.

But the best thing about all that? She brought it around. They sat on a shitty Bermondsey pavement with their backs against some piss-stained wall and he talked her through. She drank her water, did some deep breathing and then pronounced herself ready. And he could tell she wasn't kidding. All concern gone, replaced by the bliss. She got it alright.

So by the time they queue up with the scuzzy ravers and get in there the place is *jumping.* And by then Micky is able to relax and go with his buzz too. Which is considerable.

They queue up again to dump their coats and *again* to buy some more water and then he takes her by the hand and leads her through that ludicrous warren of alleys and rooms and passages and suddenly she's howling her head off.

'This is fucking *insane*!'

'Et voila,' Micky declares.

'Why didn't anyone tell me about this before?'

'I've been telling you for months, you muppet.'

And suddenly Micky is laughing too, that uncontrollable, almost unbearable, gut-heaving laughter. They have to hold each other up. He takes her face in his hands.

'Please don't tell me you've got an Animal Farm class in the morning.'

Panic overtakes her as she worries that she really *does* have an Animal Farm class in the morning. Then she sees his cheeky grin, realizes he's joking. She ponders the wild and irresistibly lovable man before her. He's a bit dangerous too, but he's so fucking funny. She collapses into his arms and laughs so hard it hurts.

They find a little space against the far wall of the main room. Mills might be on in there but Micky doesn't know when and he doesn't really care. It's all good. He catches Lisa's spaced out eyes, like two massive dinner plates with some alien kind of vol au vent in the middle. She grins.

'Can you dance to this?'

'I think so.'

'Do you want another one?'

'Another what?'

'Another pill.'

If possible her eyes widen even further. 'Noooooooo!'

He laughs, starts to shuffle, feels for the groove. She tugs his sleeve.

'Are you having one?'

He thinks about it. He's Micky Targett.

'Yeah fuck it. Why not?'

She holds her face, shocked and awed at their decadence.

'You're a teacher who's pushing forty,' he tells her as she drinks down the pill. She laughs and coughs, showers him. They both giggle like idiots.

'And I've got a child.'

And so it goes. And it goes wonderfully. They bounce from room to room like a pair of drunk teenagers. At one point she has him up against a wall that is literally running with condensation. They don't notice that, but what Micky does notice is that as they start to kiss and he feels her cheeks and touches her breasts, and as he reaches around to her arse, her buttocks fill his palms so perfectly he thinks he will explode with the joy. His senses, pulped to perfection by the pills, acquiesce still further under the relentless hammer of the music. In the strobe lacerated darkness their hands are everywhere and dreams are made to come true.

It's everything he has ever wanted. Sure he'd done it before. The first time he ever took Ecstasy. Little Jen over at that rave in Catford somewhere. But this is with her, with Lisa. This is with the one.

The perfection of that moment, of those hours affect him deeply, even if he doesn't know it at the time. He would find other highs in other worlds but nothing would come close to what he feels in a grimy London dungeon with a schoolteacher mum.

But even though he gives himself to it fully he has some kind of trip mechanism, a safety valve in his head. All the things that have happened to him. He's seen how good things look from up there, from the mountain top. He knows that moments like this one, moments of oneness and of love, can never be trusted.

And he's right.

They are both chronically horny and having such a good time they don't want to leave, but they manage to drag each other out around four. They need to be naked together and soon.

They fall into the first in a line of iffy looking minicabs ranked up outside. Micky gives the driver the address. Lisa leans into him and four hands go everywhere. A few seconds. Through wildly oscillating eyeballs he looks around him. He can't focus at all but he realizes they haven't moved. He smiles at the back of the driver's head, gives it a couple of beats.

'You,' someone says.

He looks into the rear view, their eyes meet. He doesn't know who it is but he knows something is wrong. He can tell by those eyes.

''Sup, mate?'

'You.'

Lisa, looking forward to a warm ride home stirs in Micky's

embrace.

'What's going on?'

He's changed. Been a year. Lost weight. That stupid moustache has gone.

'I got nicked 'coz of you.'

Then Micky understands.

'Holy shit.'

'Been alright has it, Mick? Had a few pills? Nice looking bird. Few quid in your pocket'

'What's happening, Mick?'

'PC. Jesus!'

'I just done a year, mate. Cheers.'

'The fuck you talking about?'

'Had to be you.'

'Why did it? I was waiting for you at the Huntsmen. Christmas Eve. Then I . . .' Micky sits forward causing Lisa to flop over and behind him.

'Then you what?'

Micky remembers the man at his window, the face in the car.

'You didn't show.'

'Because I'd just been dragged over and fitted up. I had nothing on me.'

'Are we going anywhere?' This is Lisa. She sits up straight and, through the fog of the drug, she senses something wrong.

'Why is that anything to do with me?' Micky wants to know. 'If I'm selling to you what would I have to gain? What are you fucking saying?'

'I'm saying I've done a year, lost my license, lost my house. I've had to borrow money to buy this pile of junk just to go minifuckingcabbing. I nearly lost my family.'

'You've lost that soppy accent too, PC. You speak quite nicely. What's that all about?'

PC swivels in his seat and hangs over into the back of the car. They face each other from inches away.

'I'll tell you something, Mick. You think you've got back up. We'll see. However long it takes. Wherever you go I'll find you and I'm gonna fucking *melt* you, bruv.'

The words hang in the confines of the car like fanged animals, like stinging insects.

'Now get out the fucking car.'

'Let's go,' Micky says to Lisa.

They pile out and jump in the cab behind and get the fuck gone. Lisa is panicking but Mick calms her. He's through the roof with confusion, panic and a little anger but he sure as shit doesn't want to lose the monumental buzz he's on. At his insistence the driver floors it through the empty streets.

But it's no good. Back at Lisa's they put music on and have a drink and share a spliff but Micky can't get it out of his head. Just what *was* that?

And Lisa isn't smiling either.

They shower together, wash away the cigarettes and the sweat and it's still horny, but as the new day begins to make its presence known, Lisa tires quickly and drifts in and out of sleep. Worse, Micky can't keep his hard-on. PC, he thinks. The Pro Cock. What the actual fuck? He remembers hearing he got nicked but that same night? Christmas Eve of ninety-two. Fuck my old boots, he thinks.

He smells the sex through Lisa's freshly cleaned pores, feels her impeccable skin as he spoons her from behind. He reaches down and tries, half-heartedly, to tug himself back into life. Not *now*, he tells himself, I got the buzz, I got the woman . . .

But the last thing he thinks of as he starts to drift is PC. The hatred in his eyes.

'Had to be you.'

Neither of them really sleep but around mid-morning Micky feels he's ready to party to the extent that he considers suggesting they drop another pill and *seriously* get after it. But Lisa is in a very different place. She gets out of bed without speaking, goes to the bathroom and then straight downstairs. Micky hangs in thinking, hoping, she'll be back with the coffees and the condoms. But, no.

On his feet he winces in pain, and it's not just the knee. More and more of late he feels discomfort in his left hip. The initial injury and the surgery mean he's done a lot of limping on the same side.

Lisa is sitting in one of her chairs looking out through the windows into the garden. She has her own coffee.

'Morning,' he greets.

'Hey. Kettle's just boiled.'

'Cheers. Want another one?'

She shakes her head, shakes the curls.

Micky fixes himself a strong one, figures he might need it.

'So what was that with that driver last night?'

'Haven't got a bloody clue.'

'But you do know him?'

'Yeah, I know him.'

He sits in the chair opposite, quaffs the instant. She's staring at him.

'So what was he saying?'

'Lisa can we talk about the rest of it? The good parts?'

'I was very disturbed by that, Mick. Tell me.'

'Look he's some bloke I met a couple of years ago. Bit of nuisance really. I ended up selling him a few grams. That's it.'

'He said he'd done a year. Is that prison?'

'Yeah.'

'What happened on Christmas Eve?'

'I really wish I knew. I was waiting for him and . . .' He thinks again about that night. The man telling him to get lost, the familiar face in the car as he pulled away. And he knows he's not going to mention that.

'And what?'

'He didn't show.'

'Is that it?'

Micky shrugs. 'That's it. I heard he got nicked and I never saw him again until last night.'

'What did he get nicked for?'

Micky looks into his cup of Java, then back into her mesmerizing eyes.

'Selling cocaine apparently.'

She sighs, looks away. Mick is suddenly scared. Has to bring this around.

'Look I met the bloke two or three times.'

'Something happened you're not telling me.'

'Something happened that I don't know. I got no secrets from you.'

'It's too close.'

'What is?'

'Your life. Your past. You.'

'What's that supposed to mean?'

Her silence tells him all he needs to know.

'Ah I get it. You're okay with your white-collar chums sitting round a nice table in a nice house playing games but . . .'

She looks at the garden, into the coffee, anywhere but at him. He feels a nudge of nausea, breathes. Then she turns to him, decides.

'You say you're going to Mallorca again anyway, right?'

And there it is, Micky boy and no mistake. And it kills him.

CHAPTER TEN

But maybe you ain't never gonna feel this way
You ain't never gonna know me, but I know you
Things can only get better
Can only get better if we see it through

Three weeks after getting dumped Micky exits Chancery Lane tube and meets Ben in a coffee shop close by. With him is their barrister, Miles Crenshaw and his assistant, a young woman whose name Micky doesn't catch. *Christ, I'm paying for all this*, he thinks.

They walk around the corner and enter a shiny new high-rise, home to the lawyers representing ABN Amro in the case Micky hopes will return title of his parent's lovely bungalow to his father, free of the ludicrous bank charge with which his brother had grotesquely saddled it.

Micky's heart is like a techno beat as he enters the boardroom where the meeting will be held. His brother and his ex sister-in-law are both expected to attend. He is not sure how he might react to seeing them.

He scans the room and looks into the faces of the six people, five men and one woman, already seated. Relief cools him as he sees that the woman is most certainly not the starched, unattractive, middle-class twat who married his elder brother a dozen years before. Another sweep of the room relaxes him further as he can't see his brother there either.

Breathe.

Micky and his team settle into chairs and he wonders why the fat, derelict old guy in the corner, clearly there to empty the bins or take the coffee order, is actually sitting at the polished mahogany and not doing his job. Why would . . . Noooooooooooooooo!

It's only been three years, or perhaps four since Micky last clapped eyes on his vile sociopathic, narcissistic, deceitful sibling. How the fuck could he let himself go like that? Then again, thinks Micky, if a bunch of professionals entered my house, put out one of my eyes and snipped off the toes of my wife it might age me too.

Micky tries to catch his brother's eye, the one that isn't made of glass, but he's not having it. In lieu of that confrontation Micky scopes the entire office looking for some objet d'art, item of decoration or small furniture to lump over the fat, ugly bastard's head, should the need arise.

A heavy ashtray on a far shelf is noted.

But Ben Yardley has told Micky that, whatever happens, he must keep calm. They have to settle today. They *can't* go to court.

Weirdly enough, Micky knows his brother's lawyer. He represented Micky in a motorcycle accident claim half a lifetime ago. Rob Renner. Nice guy, decent brief. But they're not budging. Yeah, they'll sign over the house but Micky pays their costs, currently running at a scrotum busting twenty-one thousand pounds.

Micky is very tempted to leap from his seat, lean across the table and holler those fateful words, 'See you in court, motherfuckers.'

But he doesn't.

Miles Crenshaw, smoothly eloquent and massively persuasive talks for many minutes on how put upon Eddie Targett has been, how much this has already cost the family and, basically, look, do us all a favour and split the costs so we can all get out of here.

Rob Renner tells him to get fucked. Not in so many words obviously, but that is the gist of his contribution.

'My client denies all of the accusations put to him. Mr. Targett senior knew precisely what he was doing when he signed over title of the house to his son and ex sister-in-law. We will consider signing over title to the property once assurances are received that all costs incurred are covered and that these accusations will be put to bed once and for all.'

Cunt.

Micky has been to Rob Renner's office. It's a room above a Chinese in Sidcup. No way have his costs hit ten grand much less twenty-one. Ben Yardley asks for a break and he, Crenshaw, Micky and the young woman leave the room, go to an office next door to talk it through.

'No way,' says Micky.

'Mick, think calmly.'

'I am. No way. For one thing those costs are so over the top it's ridiculous.'

'We can ask for proof of all of that. If any claim for costs is found to be inflated we can counter.'

Micky strides around the smaller room, hands on hips. One of the things bugging him is this whole mediation process. If this is happening today, why could it not have happened a year and many thousands of pounds ago?

He's close but he can't quite bring himself to take it up the arse from that scumbag. Best part of two years *and* twenty-one grand. That's without all his own costs that have mounted because of the delaying tactics. And that's all it is, Micky knows – tactics. Nigel's done this deliberately just to stick it to him. Still, he thinks, if I had to look in the mirror every day and see what he sees, I wouldn't take it lying down either.

'One thing though, Mick. When we get the house back it should go into your name. Might save a lot of trouble further down the line.'

Micky thinks about that. Inheritance tax, all that crap. Hmm, good point but then his principles, not for the first time in his life get in the way of a logical decision.

'No, mate. It's not my house. It will be but not yet. It needs to go to the old man.'

Having started to think the day would never come Micky finds himself a tad unprepared for both the moment and its implications. It begins when his mobile trills in his pocket. It's in the evening which makes it more unexpected.

'Hello?'

'Micky? Ben. How are you today?'

'Hey, Ben. Yeah not so bad thanks. You?'

'Yeah fine. Sorry it's so late. I was out and my phone ran down. You sitting down?'

'Do I need to?'

'You can't dance if you're sitting down. All done.'

'Well well.'

'The Land Registry confirms your father's name is back on as the sole owner of the property which is completely free of any charge, covenant or caveat. Mick I know how difficult this must have been for you and your dad and I am sorry it has taken so long. Well done.'

Mick doesn't really hear much after that. Something about attending to the final bill or something.

He gets off the phone and thinks about the first cup final he ever saw. He was never into the football, preferred rugby, but on that day he knew he was seeing something different.

Nineteen sixty-seven. The winners, the imperious champions, all in white. But it wasn't the football or how they looked that was important. It was about how they *were*. It was about that man climbing all those steps and lifting the cup high into the air. Everyone cheered but Micky wept. Wept at the achievement and the total glory of it. Vowed there and then that one day that would be him. In honour of that occasion he walks into his old room. Looks at the poster and pays homage to the mighty Scot.

Of course he never matched anything like that, but he didn't forget that sight and with it the curiosity of how that must feel. To do something, to finally accomplish *something* you've worked towards for so long.

Then comes this day, this moment and with it he is able to appreciate that very feeling as it sweeps over him and breaks him down in tears. The achievement and the glory. This is his cup final, the best and the most important thing he has ever done.

He walks, sniffling from the bedroom into the long, extended lounge. It is a beautiful house. Worth saving. As he walks towards his father, sitting in his usual chair watching television, he stops at the framed photograph on the cabinet. The black and white. The darling couple in their East End finery. Him in the sharp suit, the thick mop of black ringlets. The woman, dazzlingly pretty.

'I did it, mum,' Micky whispers, tears rippling the image. 'I did it.'

He stands beside his father who is watching two preposterously dressed grown men fighting with what look like giant cotton buds. They are perched on a platform high above a padded landing mat. Thousands of people howl like imbeciles. One of the men knocks the other off the platform. The victor rips off his protective helmet, leers into the close up, holds his hands like claws. Growls for the audience. He has *very* bad hair.

'Look at this two-bob nonce,' comments Eddie Targett.

Micky composes himself but he doesn't know why. It is, after all a momentous occasion. What's wrong with a little emotion?

But him and his dad aren't like that. Never have been. So he sniffs, wipes his eyes and takes a second. He sits on the coffee table, leans his elbows down onto his knees and grins.

'That was the solicitor, Mr. Yardley.'

'Oh yeah? What he have to say?'

They knew it was coming but after all the setbacks and the delays it seemed like it would never happen.

'We got it.' Micky bobs his head, grins some more and worries he'll start blubbing again.

'Got what? A job? Is he going to give you a job?'

Micky blinks in confusion. 'What? No.'

He raises his hands, looks around him. He wants to hug the walls.

'The house. He just confirmed it. It's back in your name.'

Micky's dad isn't known as Rock Steady Eddie for nothing. Micky should aspire to such monolithic stoicism. Such infinite unflappability.

'Blinding,' says the old guy, a flicker of a smile at the corner of his lips. 'Put the kettle on.'

Micky busies himself in the kitchen, (where's them Garibaldis?) his head buzzing with ideas. This was supposed to have taken a few months, but two years of his life passed serving his need to achieve his goal. Two sodding years and a ton of cash. All because that thieving arsehole . . .

But now he's home free and cruising. His prosaic, black and white world has suddenly switched to glorious technicolour and he is already thinking about Mallorca. Thinking about Sandra. Thinking about the good life with Connie Chetkins. Better get over there quick. But he knows he can't leave the old man on his own. The old guy, bless him, has clearly been losing it for a while, and Micky knows there's only one way around it.

'Fancy coming up the golf club for a couple tonight?' he asks appearing at Micky's elbow.

Micky doesn't much care for the golf club. There's a couple of good people who helped Eddie through the nightmare of his grieving. Eight years on, some of them still do. In fact he's even seen one of the barmaids drop Eddie off home when he's had a few. What's that all about?

But some of them are the crass, bigoted embodiment of everything Micky hates about privileged Essex life. Daily Mail reading wankers. And in nineteen ninety-four, women still weren't allowed in the back bar. What was the point, Micky wanted to know, of going to a boozer where there were no girls and only witless, chinless, gutless Nigels and Archies to talk to? It was bad enough down the Yeoman with the lads and he loved it down there.

'Aah no thanks, pop. I've got to talk to someone about going to Spain tonight.'

'Are you still going on about that?'

'Now that all this shit with the house is sorted I'm going over there as soon as I can.'

Eddie looks momentarily stunned and Micky feels like dissolving when he sees the little boy lost in his father's rheumy, slate eyes. How can someone so tough be so vulnerable?

'You need to come with me.'

'Where?'

Deep breath. 'Spain, you plonker. What have we been talking about all this time?'

'I'm not sure, boy. They got any beer over there?'

'Fucking tankers of it. Are you mad? Look, I've got this mate, I've told you about him. He's got the concession . . he's got this bar and a restaurant that he can set me up in. The house is safe now and going up in value but I need to get working and I have a good chance over there.'

'So what do you need me for?'

'I don't nee'. . Look, the summer is starting. Howzabout we go over there for six months? I'll get meself set up and you can take it easy.'

'What about this place?'

That is a good question, Micky concedes but he also has a good answer.

'We'll rent it out.'

'Who to?'

'We'll find someone. It'll rent for top dollar.'

Rock Steady Eddie sups on his tea, dunks a biscuit. He doesn't look happy. Then again he hasn't for eight years.

'If you're working what will I do?'

'I won't be working all the time. Probably only in the evenings.'

'Hmm. I dunno, boy.'

'When we get there I'll buy you a new set of clubs and you can . .'

'New set of what?'

'Clubs.'

'What, they got golf over there?'

Micky can't help but smile. 'Dad one of the best golf courses in Europe is a twenty minute drive.'

'Well why didn't you say so? Prat. Now let's get up the golf club for a beer.'

That night, when they come home, Micky retreats into his room with his phone. He is still in bits about Lisa but knows there's no way back. He yearns for the relationship and mourns it as well. He makes two calls.

One is to Sandra Chetkins and he puts it on the line, tells her he's ready. Tells her he is on his way to Mallorca and wants to meet her there. There is a chance him and her dad are going to put something together. It's all going to work out. Everything will be okay.

The words – 'I need time to think' – aren't exactly what he is hoping to hear.

He clicks off the phone. He thinks, *fuck! Am I trying too hard? Did I lay that on too much?*

He knows he's reaching. Knows he's running out of options. He is thirty-four years old.

The second call is to the big man himself.

Micky's faith in Connie Chetkins is as unshakeable as it was on the day he realized he wasn't about to be murdered by him. He puts the call through to let it be known they'll be over sometime soon and he's buzzing on the prospects. Disturbingly there was no sign of the enthusiasm from the man that he was hoping for.

*

Sandra Chetkins stares into her phone, completely unable to believe what has just come out of it. If only. If only.

As she does a *lot*, she reaches for the large glass of white wine which lately lives charged and ready on the coffee table in front of the luxury sofa upon which she spends just about every evening. The sofa is in the roomy lounge in the spacious two-bedroomed Chelmsford flat her parents have provided for her. She is privileged to the point of being spoilt rotten but she tries not to hold a grudge against herself. She knows how lucky she is.

A bottle of Sauvignon Blanc in the fridge, her young son playing happily in his room and East Enders on the TV. Can life get any better?

Well actually, she reckons, *yes it can.*

She's lonely, and as she cruises through the early years of her fourth decade she believes, along with just about everyone she knows, it's high time she settled down.

Sure, now she has baggage, but she never realized how much it might weigh.

She thinks back to the men she has known in her life. To the ones she can remember anyway. The spotty, fumbling berks at school. Then the occasional wannabe tough guy who saw her as nothing more than a cute stepping stone into the orbit of her legendary father. Then Spain. Mallorca. James's father. That ridiculously good-looking, charming, seductive boy who took bed-talent to a completely different level.

Then came the night he saw her talking and laughing with another man and gave vent to his jealous rage by all but beating and strangling her to death. Along with the unborn son she had no idea she was carrying.

She's pinned against a wall behind a bar in Magalluf. He has her by the throat. He punches her. She can't move, can't breathe. Then, as the edges of the world start to blur, she hears the flat smack of a fist crash into the side of her attacker's face. She leans against the wall to stop from collapsing, gulps air. Stays conscious enough to pull the flailing man off her boyfriend before he kills him. They run to her car and get the fuck gone.

161

Then she thinks, as she always does, about the man she'd just been talking to, the man who saved her. Micky Targett. Mad name, mad man, mad times.

She'd left Mallorca soon after that night and only saw her hero again years later when he sought her out back home. And they'd loved and laughed and done everything young lovers should do, and quite a lot they shouldn't. It had been brilliant and she'd adored every wild moment of it.

She is transported back to the passenger seat of the black Ferrari as it howls soulfully through the lanes of Essex. They're both flying on Ecstasy. She shuffles around in the seat, all the easier to lean across to stick her tongue in his ear, grab his crotch.

The good times they shared.

Then the change in him, the wreck he became. Gone from being strong and handsome to looking like a street druggie. The nightmare of their last evening together when he couldn't even talk properly.

He was flawed and had problems he could only solve by diving deeper and deeper into the bag of drugs that never left his side, by delving deeper and deeper into his own toxic psyche. Maybe he could have been the one she thinks as, not for the first time, she wonders how the fuck Ricky Butcher puts up with that wailing slapper Bianca Jackson.

But he came back, with her dad's help. Made it through and proved his worth to his own family, or what was left of it. She thinks back to that time a year and a bit ago when they'd had a few days together in Mallorca. She'd instigated their lovemaking and was glad to do it. Then she'd asked him what he wanted to do. Do together. The three of them. Like most blokes he'd danced around responsibility like it was an unexploded mine. He made his excuses - he called them reasons.

And now she gets that call.

If only, if only.

I could have loved you, Micky, she says to herself as she empties another glass.

Barefoot she pads through the luxurious pile, so deep she feels it on her ankles. She goes to the fridge for a refill and thinks about this new bloke. Ian. Lovely daughter. Great job with Credit Suisse. Reliable. Dull as ditch-water but hey, when a girl is staring down the barrel of her thirties . . .

So she returns to the sofa, mutes the television and does what comes naturally. She's her daddy's girl and she does what daddy's girls do. She picks up the phone and dials.

Connie Chetkins has a busy evening ahead of him. He prepares for this in the manner of a successful, legitimate businessman, by escorting his post dinner brandy onto the terrace of his magnificent house overlooking the Mediterranean Sea, from where he will watch the sunset.

He also takes three phones with him. He will both make and receive calls and, whilst he never writes anything down he knows pretty much who he'll be talking to and about what.

He parks his behind on the terrace wall, looks down the cliff to admire his magnificent Sunseeker launch. His eyes roam the exterior of the seven-bedroomed mansion he designed and had built three years previously. He has every reason to feel pleased with himself and his accomplishments. He is in his late-fifties, has amassed a fortune rumoured to be in the hundreds of millions of pounds, has a beautiful family and multiple income streams that mutate and expand continuously. He is at the top of his game but feels the need to keep pushing himself, and hopes that he always will.

His peace is interrupted by the soft warbling of a phone. He is expecting calls, but not this one.

'Hello?'

'Con? It's Micky.'

'Micky? Ah, bang on Targett. How are you, boy?' *Could really do without this,* he thinks.

'Very well, mate. Yourself?'

'Yes, Micky, I'm fine thanks. Are you calling to tell me you're finally over the line?'

'Yeah, man.'

Both of them hear Micky's voice crack with emotion. *Bless him,* thinks Connie. *He's a good kid. Flakier than a snowman but I did the right thing with him.*

Micky takes a gulp of Essex air, tries to hold it together.

'Got the call from my lawyer today. It's all done, the house is back in Pop's name, all charges lifted.'

'That is great news, son. It took a while and it took a lot but that was the proper thing to do, am I right?'

'When aren't you right, Con? I am in your debt.'

'Are you bollocks.'

'Ha! Anyway, least I can do is buy you a cold one.'

'Anytime but I'm not due back for a while.'

'No no, I'm coming there.'

'You are?'

'Like we agreed two sodding years ago, can you believe that? Me and the old fella are heading over.'

'Ah, right.'

'Just got to rent the house and we'll be over for the season.'

'Brilliant.' *Sod it,* thinks Connie.

'I know there's not too much dosh left but I'm hoping I can get working with that.'

Good luck with that, boy, thinks Connie. 'I'll do what I can to help.'

'Nice one. Alright, I know you're busy so I'll get out your way.'

'Let me know your dates. We'll get two rooms ready.'

'You're a gentleman, Con.'

'Yeah well, don't spread that around. No good for business.'

'My love to Barbara if you would please.'

'Of course. Be lucky.'

Connie flicks the phone off.

He doesn't need the visit but a promise is a promise. And the kid still might be useful, and there's always Sandra.

Connie knows he isn't psychic, doesn't believe in any of that old shite, but sometimes when he's got something on his mind . . .

The phone rings. Sandra.

'Well well, young one. Was just thinking about you.'

'Oh yeah? All good I hope.'

''Course, my dear. How goes it?'

'Yeah very well. How are you and mum?'

'Missing our daughter and our grandson. Well, not so much the daughter but the boy we'd love to see.'

'Oi! Easy there, old fella.'

'Ha ha. How is he?'

164

'Very well. Loving school. Would you believe he's good at art?'

'Art? What are they teaching him about art for?'

'Free expression innit? They're very big on that at this place.'

'Jeezus. How's his football?'

'Well he's getting big but he doesn't seem to have an aggressive bone in his body.'

'So he's going to be a thinker?'

'About time we had one in the family.'

'Good point. So when you coming out? Ooh, hold on.'

'What?'

'A heads up. Just got off the phone to an old friend of yours.'

'Who's that?'

'Micky Targett.'

'Oh my God! He just called *me*. What did he say?'

'That's he's coming over here. What did he say to you?'

'That and he wanted to try to make it work with me and James.'

'I see. How do you feel about that?'

'I'm not sure.' Then silence

'If you're not sure, that probably means no.'

'I know he's nuts but he's such a sweet bloke. So well-intentioned.'

'But?'

'Well, I kind of asked him to give it a go a couple of years ago. It was over there. You weren't around.'

'And what happened?'

'Well he could think of every reason not to do it and none to go ahead.'

'That kind of sounds like your answer then. Something else, I asked him to behave and keep his head down but he's been dealing again.'

'Oh, has he?'

'Yeah always had a wild streak and you got other considerations now.'

'I know. James is growing up and I can't have someone so . . unpredictable around him. He said he'd be doing something with you.'

'Well time was maybe, but he's almost out of cash and I don't know if he'd like being just offered a job. He's bringing his dad too.

'You see? He's so sweet.'

'Can you see yourself with him in five years? Ten?'

Connie listens to his daughter breathe. Knows the answer and is happy about it.

'No. He wants me to meet him there but . . .'

'Well just stay away darling. I'll talk to him if you want.'

'No, it's been a while since I was there anyway. Easter's coming. Best he hears it from me.'

'That's good of you. Now listen, sorry and all that but I'll be needing this phone tonight and your mum wants to talk to you anyway. Can you call her on her mobile?'

'Okay, will do. See you soon.'

'Kiss the little man for me.'

Connie clicks off again. *Now, this* is *a development,* he thinks. Potentially. Question is, can he use it? Because there's this situation developing in Essex.

Connie's not psychic, doesn't believe in that shite. Then another phone rings.

'Hello?'

'Hey, Con.'

'Evening, Georgie.'

'What's the scam?'

'Well funny you should say that. Just had two calls; one from Micky Targett the other from Sandra.'

'Oh yeah?'

'Yeah. You remember two years ago we had him over here and straightened everything out? I kind of invited him back.'

'Uh huh.'

'Well he's gone and done it. Got his old fella's house back and now the pair of them are coming.'

'What, to live?'

'For the summer at least.'

'Bit in yer face isn't it?'

'It is. I could do without it but here's the thing. My only concern about using the kid has always been Sandra.'

'They got history, right?'

'Correct. As you know he dug her out of trouble in Magalluf all those years ago and they got it on when they were both back in Essex.

She's always been sweet on him but . . .'

'But he's not exactly settling down kind of material.'

'Exactly. But Sandra doesn't want to be the single mum all her life. She's seeing this bloke. Futures trader. Bit of a dick but he's what she needs. Earns well. Civilian.'

'So Micky boy is out of the picture.'

'Well I do have a grandson that might not have been here if not for him, but he's dined out enough on that. Unless . . .'

'You thinking of this problem?'

'That I am.'

'Happened again. We lost another parcel today. Why I was phoning.'

'Saucy fuckers.'

'Thing is they don't know it's us.'

'I'd prefer to keep it that way.'

'Sure sure. But if we're hiding behind freelancers this could continue. There are three of these nutters, and they *are* nutters. They're on everything they nick, plus steroids plus whatever else. Imagine Mike Tyson completely off his face times three.'

'Oh great.'

'They may well get busted, but if we don't take them on or if we don't officially warn them, this could get worse.'

'Maybe our boy could get us in there?'

'We need to do something. They're not stupid. You never get the three of them together. Not in public anyway. He's done undercover work before hasn't he?'

'Yeah, he's a good liar. Used to front a stolen car ring for Terry Farmer.'

'He'd feel flattered being back in with us.'

'Indeed. Tell you what. Let's wait for him to get over here, then you pop over too. We'll tell him he's got no future here, and at the same time let him know we flicked that grass away from him. He'll be on his knees, then we offer him the gig.'

'There's a plan.'

'Okay, my man. Catch you later.'

Connie clicks off the phone. What a funny old life we lead, he muses.

Another phone rings.

'Hello?'

'Hello, Con. Francois here.'

'Francois, I was just thinking about you.'

'Well that's nice. How's sunny Spain?'

'Sunny and Spanish.' He effects his best South African accent to match that of the caller. 'And life on the veldt?'

'All good here, boss. Thank you. Just briefly as I know you're busy. We heard back from that fella. You know, the one that works on the safaris?'

'Oh yes?'

'Yes and it came back as a positive.'

'Oh well that's good news.'

'Yes indeed. This could be the start of what we were talking about. Says he can get us the access we were discussing.'

'Great stuff, Faf.'

'But like we said, the markets we have are limited. You want to make real money doing this. It's Asia. It's China.'

'Yes, my friend. I'm working on the way in over there. This is looking good. I'll call you in a few days and we can go through this properly.'

'Okay, Connie. I'll wait to hear from you.'

'Thanks, Faf.'

Connie clicks off the phone. Sits. Takes a sip of the brandy he'd forgotten about. Then says one word. 'Thailand.'

PART TWO. DO THE RIGHT THING

CHAPTER ELEVEN

SANTA PONSA, MALLORCA - MAY 1994

Inside you're pretending, crimes have been swept aside
Somewhere where they can forget

The Yellow Pages throws up several local rental agents and Micky gives a couple of them a shot at the business.

The first to get there and check the place out is a brassy looking sort with a provocative pout, wearing jeans that are waaaaay too tight for her. Micky has to admit he takes an instant liking. When she tells him the place will easily pull in around a grand a month he likes her even more.

A week later she shows up again with, what looks like, an ideal family. There's an old guy who must go about seventy, his daughter, late-twenties, her boyfriend (no visible tats or piercings) and their toddler. Micky loves it. No wild parties, early to bed and the place will be immaculate when they get back.

Subject to references and various checks they sign on for six months with a view to rolling that over should both parties agree. Sweet. He gets two sets of keys cut, him and Eddie say their goodbyes to the Rogers next door and Micky leaves Connie's Mallorcan number with them in case of unpredictables.

In the run-up to departure day Micky goes through his stuff. What he's going to take, what he can throw in the loft and what he can just throw? In a draw in his bedroom he finds a box of Citalopram and this pulls him up very short very sharply.

Wow, he thinks, *did that really happen?* That basket case on anti-depressants, going to a 'unit' for therapy? The paradigm shifts evermore, and if you can't shift with it then you're done. The box goes in the black plastic bag he lugs around his room. Onwards and, finally, upwards.

His biking gear, boots, helmets go in the loft as do all his winter clothes. Not that there's much. He's in his mid-thirties now and doesn't own a lot. Of anything. But what does he need? Stuff? Furniture? Things? A tremble of longing seizes him. Why isn't he like his friends? House, wife, kids. Why does he now admire the people he once derided, the norms of this world?

He wants to be ordinary, but then where is he off to? Chasing the sun. Chasing dreams again. And wasn't it sunny Mallorcan dreams that got him in trouble in the first place?

By the time the big day comes around Micky gets that awful feeling he is making a dreadful mistake. The worry is that in doing the right thing in taking his dad with him, he is at the same time shooting himself in the foot. But Micky needs to go, and the last two years have told him that there's no way the old guy can be left on his own.

Apart from his national service (Iraq and Palestine) and before that his evacuation from London during the Blitz (Devon) the furthest Eddie Targett had been from his native Wapping was hop picking down in Kent and a day out to the beach at Southend. It might possibly have stayed that way if he hadn't met Micky's mum. She picked him out, sorted him out and made a life for him.

Then, just after they bought the Upminster bungalow with retirement around the next corner, she went and got it. Started in her pancreas and from then it was just a couple of months. On top of that, shortly thereafter, his eldest son stole everything he'd ever worked for. And it was Micky's job to pick up the pieces of that. Which he'd managed to do, in a roundabout, blundering kind of way.

But it was only on the flight to Mallorca that Micky fully understood that his *real* task was only beginning.

170

His dad sat beside him sobbing so loudly and so painfully that the entire neighbouring section of the plane cast their glances down in shocked, mortified embarrassment. The stewardesses whispered among themselves, shot concerned looks down the aisle.

Micky did the only thing he could. He ordered bundles of gin and tonics, most of which he necked himself. He used the napkins to dry his dad's eyes.

'I want your mum.'

But when they step out into the Mallorcan sunshine of early summer ninety-four it's like nothing had happened. Connie is there to greet them and Eddie, all warm smiles and positivity, immediately recognises a fellow old-school tough guy. He makes an effort to crunch Connie's hand when they shake and Connie lets him do it. Not only that but Connie is in the white, open-top Rolls and Rock Steady Eddie loves it.

Micky knows that Connie didn't have to do this and is touched by the gesture. He's thrilled to look around to see his dad in the back seat with a massive grin on his face. Maybe it will be okay.

For their first few nights on the island, until they get their own place, the pair of them are guests of Barbara and Connie, and if Eddie was impressed by the Roller he is totally blown away by the house. They are unpacking when, for about the one hundred and twelfth time, Eddie asks Micky how he knows Connie.

Micky sighs and goes over the well-practised lines.

'I told you, I know him through his daughter who I met out here first time around. Connie has a restaurant in Essex and I used to sell him booze and tobacco when I was going to France.'

'Didn't he care where it came from?'

'Do me a favour. He's one of us. Except he's rich.'

'I see.'

'So then I came over to see him and his daughter Sandra a couple of years ago. That's when I had that massive win at the casino. That's how we got the house back.'

'What house?'

Micky's not sure what to say to things like this. One minute he seems fine and the next he's a stranger.

'Our house. In Upminster.'

'Right.'

'And that thing with his daughter Sandra. She was getting beat up one night and I pulled her out of it. Connie's never forgotten that and he's a real good friend to me. He kind of owes me. And now that we have got the house back I'm over here to see if me and him can do something together.'

Eddie nods.

'I like it here. Mallorca's great. I was just a kid last time so I want to give it a proper go. Maybe you'll like it too.'

'What can I do?'

'What do you mean?'

'A job.'

For one awful moment Micky thinks his dad is serious. Then he realizes that he is.

'Dad you don't have to work. You're here to relax, remember?'

'Well what am I going to do then? I don't know anyone.'

'Tomorrow me and you go out looking for a flat. Then we're going to buy you some golf clubs. Then you . . . Then we're going to start having some fun. Golf, food, drink. Fun! It's gonna be great.'

Rock Steady Eddie Targett ponders what he is being told. He looks at his son and wonders why he has become so difficult to understand lately. He's a good kid but can he be trusted? Of course he can. Doesn't seem like he's ever going to properly fill out, but he is the total spit of his mother.

That heavy bloke at the airport though, who was he and what was that all about? Why was he there to meet them? What's he up to?

And where are they? On the coast for sure. Brighton? Margate?

Golf, food, drink and fun.

He thinks hard and remembers what two of those are.

But he keeps quiet, doesn't let on. He knows there's some kind of problem, but until he can figure out what it is he's just going to play along.

The thing about Eddie Targett is that everyone, at least within the confines of his limited orbit, falls in love with him. Once he relaxes, gets his feelers out and is comfortable in the present company, he can undeniably be a real hoot. As so it proves chez Chetkins junto al mar.

Barbara, for one, thinks he's magic. She's been around Essex and East End 'characters' all her life and would invariably choose a quiet night in rather than go somewhere they're likely to be, but she can't get enough of his offers to wash up, peel onions, uncork a bottle of wine etc. He even volunteers to walk the dog. It's almost a shame she doesn't have one.

And because Barbara likes him then Connie does too. Not only that but Connie loves to hear about the old man's tales of dock life and how things were back in the good old days. Connie admits to being born in London Fields and is amused to hear Eddie describe that as 'out in the bleedin' country'.

Inside a week Micky and his dad are installed in their new flat. It's back in towards town in a modern block in the Carrer Gran Via Menorca. It's not too far from Captain Francis but Micky is under no illusion about touching base with him under present circumstances. No temptations, no falling off any wagons is the order of the day.

But boy could he ever do with a line. Or a gram. Get bent for a few days because things are not well, or at least haven't gone as planned. He thinks back two years when Connie handed him both his past, his present and even offered him a glimpse of the future. A glorious, sun-splashed future in which all things seemed possible.

But it took too long and too much money to get the bungalow back and now he's only got about twenty odd grand left, plus a chunk of change he brought over, and a shrinking list of options. That kind of wedge in nineteen ninety-four will score you zip.

In those two years Connie bought into the newly constructed Hotel y Apartementos Casablanca, close to the beach. Micky couldn't get involved though. Because he wasn't there and he wasn't sure if he had enough cash. The chance went.

Connie talks about the possibility of another project. He's got his eye on some land on the far side of town, right out past where Bugsy's used to be. But it's not now, and Micky needs now. Then Connie says he can have a job any time he likes. The Casablanca has a lively bar, and he knows he can make the place jump. But it's not Bugsy's and it never will be, and most of all it's not his. He didn't go through everything he went through to get a job as a barman working for someone else.

And then there is the Sandra situation. He was asking after her and out of nowhere she just arrived. With young James. It had been a little awkward. Eddie was at his 'nudge nudge – wink wink' best. So they'd taken themselves away for an afternoon. And she'd laid it on him. Cleared the air, which was for the best.

'You not seeing anyone?' she asked casually as they strolled the beach at Paguera.

Lisa's dazzling eyes pulse into his mind. He misses her but if she can't handle him then it's over.

'Er no, nope. Been too busy. You?'

'Erm. Yeah kind of.'

The pile-driving thump to his chest is so much more than disappointment he might just as well call it despair. Lisa broke his heart, now Sandra is grinding the pieces into the Mallorcan sand.

'Kind of?'

'Well there's this bloke. He has a daughter at James' school.'

Micky doesn't know what to say. Doesn't even know what to think. She is one of the reasons he is here.

He feels a familiar and a very worrying uncertainty overtake him. Feels the earth move beneath his feet. Now, after a few weeks of 'settling in' and 'looking at opportunities' Micky is no nearer to knowing how he is going to make the move work. The flat for him and his dad costs money, the hire car costs money. Eating and drinking and being alive costs money, and of course with the Chetkins living just around the corner there's no way Micky can get at it.

Knowing what he knows now about the drug trade he could score a fortune in the season. The Captain has the Charlie connection with, presumably, weed and pills too.

But Connie warned him off all that which is another thing that's starting to piss Micky off. He's blazed through his dosh and not only isn't he going to marry into the family fortune, the only gig Connie can offer him is a crappy job pulling pints. Micky has an extra mouth to feed and is starting to resent Connie's insistence as to how he should go about it.

Maybe it's time to tell Connie Chetkins where to get off because it seems that's what Connie is trying to do to him.

Fact is he is starting to think there's not a lot of point to them being there. This is compounded by his dad's ongoing and increasingly iffy behavior.

'When we going home, son? Who are all these people? Why can't I understand what they say? Where is Match Of The Day?'

174

As promised he hooks his dad up with a set of clubs and membership of the exclusive Son Vida course outside Palma. When he's there the old guy is in his element. Loves the course, always meets some old ex-pat to have a round with, loves the nineteenth hole. Depressingly expensive, but that's Micky's worry not his.

But as the summer takes hold it is invariably too hot for Rock Steady Eddie to thrash that little white ball around. Which means he is on Micky's hands full time. Usually moaning. Always asking questions. Never understanding. Never understanding anything.

One afternoon Micky, Eddie and Connie are out on the terrace having a chat and a couple of beers. Micky is anxious to talk business to Connie but he can't with his dad around. Someone brings up the Kray twins.

For some reason Micky has no knowledge of, this subject is catnip to Eddie Targett. If catnip turned human beings into inflamed, homicidal maniacs.

'Don't talk to me about that pair of fucking queers!'

Connie gags on his San Miguel. Micky freezes. He knows Connie's second in command is Georgie Harper, a man who has pulled Micky out of deep shit on at least one occasion in the past. *And* helped put a chunk of cash in his hand. And Georgie used to be with the twins. Made his name and his fortune at their knee.

'Fucking despicable people.'

'Dad . . .'

'Keep quiet if you don't know what you're talking about, boy.'

Micky holds his head in his hands.

'Never hurt their own, they say. Only fought with other villains. Fuck off!'

'You ever meet them, Ed?' Connie asks calmly.

'No I didn't. Could have done. I knew where they went, knew where they drank. People fawned over them. People I thought were my friends. Wankers.'

The silence-laden hiatus threatens Micky's sanity. He looks at Connie who patiently regards Rock Steady Eddie Targett with a quizzical yet uncommitted stare.

'They picked on anyone. Pub guv'nors, tobacconists, car salesmen. They'd hurt anyone if there was a shilling in it. Bullies. And a pair of pansies, both of them. That's why his wife killed herself. Yeah they could handle themselves, good boxers, but they weren't the toughest. You might know him . . .' Eddie points at Connie who doesn't quite know what to do or so.

'Sorry, Eddie, who's that?'

Micky starts to cringe as he has done so many times over the last couple of years. His dad is trying to remember something. A place, a name, a thing. Something. And he knows from excruciating and very embarrassing experience this will drag on all day because there is absolutely no way . . .

'Buller Ward.' Eddie shouts, suddenly with a memory like a steel trap.

Connie slams his bottle down onto the table. 'What!'

'Ward. Buller was his nickname.'

'You are the first man I've ever met outside of . . . business that has ever heard of Buller Ward.'

'From your way, yeah? Hoxton?'

'Hackney,' corrects Connie, sporting a grin the size of a melon slice.

'Toughest man I ever knew.'

'What? You *knew* him?'

'Yeah, me and a nephew of his used to work in my dad's gang in the Royals. End of the fifties. Lovely man.'

'Oh my God. He is a legend where I'm from.'

'Thief, which I don't like. But *hard*.'

Eddie now has his audience in the palm of his hand. Micky can't quite believe what he is seeing. Connie looks like a little kid who has met his favourite pop star. Any minute now he's going to get his autograph book out.

'Real good boxer too. Big man. Could have made it but preferred the villainy.'

A gentle breeze ruffles the fringe of the canvas awning above them.

'They bashed him up, cut him, shot him and he just laughed at them. But he was a gentleman, this is my point. He never hurt anyone who didn't need it. Them brothers . . . Horrible. Bullies. Let's have no more talk of them.'

The resounding silence is, once again, overwhelming. Then, as if none of the outburst had happened, Eddie suddenly jumps nimbly from his seat and heads towards the house.

'I'll just see if that nice lady needs any help with anything.'

Micky wonders if he'll get away with that. Keeps schtum.

'Wow,' says Connie shaking his head.

Schtum.

'Small world it certainly is.'

'He's seen a few things.' Micky finally says.

'That he has, son. Damn. The great Buller.'

'Who's that?'

'A face from the past. Legend.'

'Ah.'

'Mick your dad is a fine, fine man. You are so lucky.'

Micky feels himself choking. There is so much he doesn't know about the teak-tough little guy he's mostly never got on with.

'Yeah. Yeah, Con. I am and I know.'

'You also know,' Connie asks, turning towards him in his seat. 'You also know that he is very unwell don't you?'

'I know he's not the same as he was.'

'Don't kid yourself. I've seen it before. Barbara's mother.'

'He's not a young man, Con but you've just seen him. Sometimes he's as sharp as a gangster's razor.'

'And sometimes he doesn't know what country he's in. I'm not wrong, am I?'

Micky breathes deep, looks at his shoes, feels the sick dread that he always tries to shoo away.

'Listen, me and you need to have a proper sit down. He's twenty-four carat and you have to do right by him. Georgie's coming over again as well.'

'Jesus.'

'Don't worry,' he grins, drains his beer. 'He never liked those two much either.'

There is another reason why Connie Chetkins is smiling. Micky is surplus to his requirements in Mallorca. But bizarrely he could use his help back in Essex. Connie thought he might have to lean on Micky a little, let him know he wasn't welcome. Since he's seen how Eddie is though, well, there's his way out. He and Georgie Harper, they'll get Micky on his lonesome. Read him his fortune.

Two days later Micky and his dad are having lunch on the terrace

177

of the restaurant at Caesars apartment block. The sun is blazing but they are under the shade of the low slung awning. Neither man speaks.

Micky ruminates on the way things have gone. All the work, all the hassle and the expense of the last two years getting the bungalow back. Was it worth it?

He thinks of his mother. Thinks of the way, at the weekends and after work, she practically lived in the greenhouse and the garden. Thinks how she never went anywhere after they'd moved in, she loved the place that much. Only a few years from her retirement. Her house. Yeah, 'course it was the right thing. Not for him so much, and not necessarily for the old man. For her.

He looks at his dad, shoveling food into his mouth, some making its way onto the table, some onto the floor. Why are they here? What was this for? Hadn't Connie done enough for him? Did Micky really think he'd be taken into the firm? What could he possibly bring to *that* table.

Eddie Targett suddenly stops chewing. Looks straight ahead and concentrates like he's a fox that's scented a chicken. Then he stands, walks across to a group of three men at an adjacent table. He is calm but his hands are fists.

'You reckon do you?' Micky hears him say.

Micky had never seen his dad throw a punch until that day. He'd seen his old boxing trophies, heard the family talk about him, but this was a first.

Women scream, men shout and two of the blokes at the table are unconscious even before they know what's going on. Micky flies over there and rugby tackles his dad to the ground before the third one gets his share.

'What the fuck are you doing?' Micky wails.

'Get off me you moron.'

Micky drags the old boy to his feet. Two waiters run from inside. The third man, in his attempt to get away from the flailing geriatric lunatic, pushes himself away from the table and lands heavily on his back. As he is going down he grabs at the tablecloth and drags the whole Mallorcan, lunchtime experience over with him.

'Jesus fucking Christ, dad. What the fuck?'

'He called me a cunt.'

'No he didn't.'

'Don't you go against me. You're the same as all of them.'

Micky has him by the shirt front, watches as the waiters attend to the two stiffs. He hears the word 'Policia', sees a waitress inside reach for the phone.

'We got to get out of here.'

Micky grabs a bunch of notes from his pocket, more, much more than their bill will ever amount to. He thrusts it at one of the waiters.

'*Siento. Lo siento. Este muy infermo. Siento.*'

He hustles his dad through the packed interior and out the other side. Up the stairs to street level and to the car.

Rock Steady Eddie Targett is back in the knocking people out business. He is seventy-one years old.

On top of that, two things happen in the coming weeks that tell Micky Targett Mallorca is no longer the Shangri-La he once thought it. As if he could possibly think anything else.

Firstly, and two days after the Caesar's incident, he and his dad are invited to dinner at the Chetkins'. Georgie Harper is there. Micky hasn't mentioned anything about the scene at Caesar's but knows that Connie has ears everywhere.

Eddie is in high spirits but he is drinking. He was out on the beach during the day and his face is sorely sunburnt. Barbara fusses around him and he likes the attention, purrs as she smooths in the aftersun.

Over dinner he is loud and mostly incoherent. He thinks he is endearingly charming but everyone squirms with embarrassment. Fortunately Barbara redeems the situation by suggesting Eddie and Micky crash over for the night.

'It's getting late, Eddie. I'll show you to your room.'

'Yeah, good idea. I'm turning in too.' says Micky, latching on.

Miraculously Eddie falls for it and complies, the three of them head into the house. It is eight-thirty.

Micky puts his dad to bed, his emotions awash with worry and forboding.

He turns off the light, rolls his dad onto his side and leaves him to it. He makes his way back downstairs, joins the others at the table.

'Listen everyone . . .'

'You don't have to apologise for anything, Mick.' Barbara tells him.

Teary-eyed he flops exhaustedly back into his chair.

'I don't know what to do.'

'He needs care. Proper care.' Connie says.

Micky nods but doesn't speak.

'There are things they can do. Drugs. Slows it down.' This is Georgie.

'I thought my future was here. Thought I was doing the right thing.'

Barbara leans across and places her hand over Micky's. 'No one could have done more than you, my love. You're a good son and a good man, but you need professional help. You won't get it here.'

Micky knows it's over. Knows going back is unavoidable.

Then he notices that Georgie, Connie and Barbara have flinched, are looking past Micky back towards the house. All three wear stunned expressions. Micky turns, sees his dad standing there. Not moving. He doesn't speak, just stares out towards the sea. He is naked.

Micky has two thoughts. The first is that the life he has known up until this point is officially over. The second is that his father is indeed possessed of a fair old chap.

Later that night, after Micky has got his dad back into bed *again,* he and Georgie and Connie surround a bottle of Macallan's. Micky is emotionally spent and getting a reasonable drunk on. He is confident enough to say what he wants to say.

'I need to get back at it.'

Georgie and Connie swap glances.

'In this precise spot two years ago you made a deal to leave that alone.'

'So what? What do you want from me? I need help and I'm going broke.'

'You're no good at it.'

'Yes I am.'

Then Connie and Georgie do that thing. They look at each other and swap thoughts.

'Let me tell you how good you are at it,' Connie tells him as he considers the whisky in the heavy crystal. 'You were buying a few ounces from a car dealer in Seven Kings. You were probably bashing about ten to twenty percent filler in that. Then knocking it out at point eights, maybe nines. Few hundred quid a week. Nothing wrong with that.'

Micky feels himself weaken, feels the oxygen draw away from him. No. No. This is not possible.

'All's going well then you meet a bloke. Starts off smallish. Pays on the nose. Then he slips in a bigger order. You can handle it but you sense there's something not right.'

'Connie how . . .?'

'But you're greedy so you look for reasons to kid yourself it's all okay. You go along with it. Nice little tickle for Christmas.'

Micky's world tilts. It's not just the booze. It's not *even* the booze. It's just everything else. Life, he's just not good enough at it.

'So you're sitting there in your poxy Scirocco, thinking you're the kiddie. Right out in the open where you can be photographed, watched, jumped. Then along comes a man. Yeah, along comes a man who saves your life.'

Micky holds his face, hopes the others won't see the hot tears of panic and confusion.

ESSEX/EAST LONDON - NOVEMBER 1992

Ray Pitts has been making enquiries. He wants to know more about this bloke, this Micky Targett. Those Midnights and Stingers from a few years ago and that girl who died.

Word comes back. Jennifer Baddows was her name and it happened in Stratford nick. Pitts doesn't know anyone over there so he just calls up and gets into the desk Sargeant who, well well well, was actually on duty the night it happened.

'Yeah I remember, she was working the clubs, had a pharmacy's worth of gear on her. Half of which she must've done herself because she started going into one. Foaming at the mouth, the whole number. We called the doc but she checked out that night.'

'Did she say anything before she left us?' Pitts wants to know.

'Nope. We did hear that she called someone that night but nothing came of it. He was looked at but nothing could be proved. Funny name but I can't remember.'

'Maybe I can help with that. Targett?'

'That's it. He got a visit but he was clean. Well obviously not *that* clean because he was wrapped up with Denny Masters and Pete Chalmers.'

'Jesus, really?'

'Apparently so.'

'Hey what happened to them? Anyone know?'

'I think Pete lives abroad. Denny's around though. Very low key. He's buying up property around here. Mad bastard seems to think the price of bricks will go through the roof because he's heard a rumour the Olympics are coming to Stratford.'

'Wow, that's nuts. So this Targett character, nothing else on him?'

'Not around here. Why the interest?'

'He's cropped up out this way. Lives in Upminster and he's dealing coke. We're setting him up for a nick. I was going to hold off but if he's all mine . . .'

'I'll have a word but if you don't hear back then it's an open goal for you.'

'Alright, mate. Appreciate all that.'

Sergeant Richard Jaynes of Stratford police puts down the phone. As he does so one of the station's detectives walks past the desk on his way out to lunch. Small world.

'Oi, Guv'.'

'Yeah, Rich.'

'That's a weird thing. You were on that case a few years ago when that girl died in here. Jennifer Baddows. Remember that?'

'Yeah, what about it?'

'Just had a call from Romford. The bloke that may or may not have supplied her. Micky Targett. He's on their radar.'

The detective stops, thinks back. He remembers it well.

'Really, what's he up to?'

'Selling coke. The DS there says if you have anything on him he'd like to know. He's going to lift him soon.'

'What's his name?'

Sergeant Jaynes looks down at the notes he has just made. 'Pitts. DS Pitts.'

'Right,' says Detective Inspector Steven Black. 'Interesting. Leave that with me. I might need to get involved.'

Blackie thinks it's probably not worth bothering about, but remembers that Connie Chetkins pays him what he pays him because things like this are *always* worth bothering about. So he gets on the phone.

'So don't tell me how good you are at crime, Mick,' says Connie Chetkins as he gives the three glasses a major splash. 'The only reason you are sitting here enjoying the environment is because you know me and Georgie and we know Blackie of the Yard. You were selling to a police informant, you dozy twat.'

Micky is too weak, too bashed-to-fuck to find words. Breathing is tiring. Just sitting still is exhausting. The man in the car. As he pulled away from the carpark of the Huntsmen pub that Christmas eve. Blackie.

'He got nicked selling coke himself.'

'And how do you think that was made to happen?'

'Bit strong wasn't it? He lost his cab license. He's got family.'

'Have you been at the bong water again? Bloke was a fucking grass! What are you, the fairness police now? You'd rather it was you?'

A terrible silence descends. Micky is at a loss what to say or do. It feels like it's all over. Okay he's got the house back but after the doomed dalliance in Mallorca he's down on the cheeks of his arse again. He's got no job and a mad dad who is dependent upon him for everything. It's all gone wrong. *Again.*

He looks around. This place, the terrace. This is where truth lives, in this fine-aired, opulent chancellery of criminal reckoning.

Then Micky hears the words he wants to hear the least and wants to hear the most. Georgie Harper begins to speak at the point of Micky's lowest ebb. And there's obviously a reason for that.

'Thing is, Mick,' he says leaning forward to lay a brand new phone on the table in front of them. 'There might be something you could do for us.'

The second installment of conclusive proof telling Micky he needs to head home comes the next morning. He is roused by the sound of a coffee mug being landed on the bedside cabinet. A presence in the room.

The hangover is brutal. He doesn't even like Scotch.

'Your dad's up.'

Their eyes meet and Barbara Chetkins' kindly expression tells him that the horrors of the previous evening were much more real and unpleasant than the traditional nightmare he was hoping for.

'Ah right. Cheers, Barb. How is he?'

'He's fine. I doubt he remembers. That's how this thing is. A lot of the time they've no idea what's going on and it's better for them that way. It's those closest to them that get hurt.'

Micky hears that.

Downstairs the old guy, sunburnt to look like a trodden-on pomegranate, is in good form.

'There he is,' he calls to his doddering boy. 'Can't handle his drink, this one. Never been able to.'

Micky sits and Barbara plops some toast in front of him. At that moment the house phone rings and Barbara picks up right there on the kitchen extension.

'Hello? Yes, that's right. Mister who? Rogers?'

Micky's blood stops moving. Surely not. The last time he got a call from his elderly next door neighbours was when they imparted the news the property had been seized by bailiffs. He knows that whatever this is about is going to be bad. Emergencies only, they agreed.

'Yes', Barbara says, 'they're actually here right now. Hold the line please.'

On trembling legs Micky stands and walks to take the phone

'Mister Rogers?'

'Hello, young Micky.'

'You alright?'

'Yes. I'm fine. Dorothy is too.'

'Good. That's good.'

'How is your father?'

'Yeah he's cool thanks. We had a few drinks last night and stayed over at my friend's place. You're lucky to catch us.'

'Oh lovely. That's really good.'

'Yeah.'

184

'And how's life in the sun. Warm enough for you?'

'Well,' Micky answers, starting to calm down. Just a chat to catch up it seems. 'I like it but Eddie boy is giving it his lobster impression today.'

'Ah ha. Buy him a hat. A big white one.'

'Yeah. Yes will do.'

'Anyway, son . . .'

'Yes, Mr. Rogers. Good to talk to you again . . .'

'Bit of a situation here.'

'Oh?'

'Yes. Fifteen policemen kicking your front door in at six o'clock this morning.'

The words rattle around Micky's brain like actual seeds of a plant so aggressively poisonous that when it matures and flowers it will kill any living thing that touches it. What? What did that man say?

'Yes, there was this strange smell but none of us in the street knew what it was. Then we had a change of postman. Young chap. He knew what it was and he called the police.'

Micky reaches for his chair with a shaking hand. 'No,' is all he can say.

'I'm afraid so, son. It seems there was a marijuana plantation in your lounge.'

Micky knows he has to move fast. He gets his dad out onto the golf course then hammers back to their flat in Santa Ponsa where he hits the phone. Firstly he gets Len Rogers back on and gets him to run through it all once more.

Firstly, the only one out of the 'ideal family' who was ever there was the old guy, and he would come and go at random hours of the day and night. Secondly, he closed the curtains. Permanently. Thirdly, how the hell did they think they were going to get away with it anyway? In a quiet street, cheek by jowl with dozens of people who, being retirees, never went to work?

But perhaps that was the master stroke because, as Len Rogers had told him when he first called, even though everyone within range could smell something pungently unusual wafting down the close, none of the geriatric fuckers had a clue what it was.

Anyway, eventually Plod was called and they certainly knew what it was. Soon enough a van full of uniformed goons was deployed and the lads lined up and the knock was made. No answer. So out came the big red key and in went the nice, old original door. And sure enough, the lovely old fifties-build that Micky spent a fortune and two years fighting for was a bona fide ganja factory.

So he gets the name and number of the investigating cop and, after a lot of getting pissed around, has him in his ear.

The initial problem is that this bloke, DS Pitts, sounds like a bit of an idiot.

'Targett?'

'Yes, that's my name. Our name.'

'What's your Christian name, Mr. Targett?'

'Micky. Michael. I live in the house with my father Edward.'

Heavy static down the line from Essex.

'You're Michael Targett?'

'Yes.'

Jeezus! Another one who has had his brain removed at Hendon, thinks Micky. But he gets it. This cozzer reckons Micky is in on the scam, which is understandable.

'You're in Spain you say?'

'I am.'

'Ok, well I can't discuss anything with you until I am sure you are who you say you are.'

'Len Rogers, the guy next door called me about it this morning.'

'Okay but would you be able to fax me some ID? Passport plus something with your address on?'

'Yeah I can do that.'

'Good. Are you planning on staying there for long?'

Micky thinks about his dad and knows it's all over anyway.

'Not anymore, no. I'll finish up here and get home as soon as I can.'

'Ok good, difficult to talk over the phone.'

'How is the house?'

'I can't really talk about it until I see some ID. You could be one of the growers fishing for information.'

Micky sighs. Being a victim of crime totally sucks.

'Fair enough, but is it secure? I understand from my neighbor your boys didn't mess about getting in the place.'

'They were as careful as they could be and by law we have to secure properties. It is padlocked and I have the only keys right here on my desk.'

'Okay, cheers. What's the fax number? I'll do that today and then look for a flight.'

After he finishes the call DS Pitts sits and thinks deeply. Of course he already knew, from talking to the neighbours, the name of the family that lived at this address. And he knows there ain't too many people in Essex, in the bloody *world*, with a funny name like that. A name that keeps cropping up.

After Micky finishes the call he dials up the estate agency in Hornchurch that found those wankers. In fairly non-uncertain terms he lets them have it. He is changing the plans of his entire summer to fly home to deal with the situation that their tenants have created. How was this allowed to happen? He will need to see the work, character and previous landlord references for all three adults that were originally promised.

Then he digs out the insurance policies he has fortuitously brought with him. Calls up the Prudential, lets them know what's what and that he'll be in touch in a couple of days when he's back on the ground.

On the topic of insurance, Micky figures there could be a result here. Davey Watkins and his property repair/maintenance business. Get some inflated bills, claim for some work that doesn't even need doing. Bish bash bosh, nice little earner.

He grabs a San Miguel to help with his hangover, smiles and tries to look on the bright side. Then he heads to the travel agents to score the tickets home.

*

Eddie Targett hears a loud, whirring sound and feels a tugging at his armpits. He can't figure out if they are related but he knows this is no time to panic.

The noise is a new thing for him. The feeling under his arms, the rope holding the entire weight of his own body, is not. That has been with him for a while. Being lowered down into the pit. Into the dark confusion. He's thought of talking about it but he doesn't know who he can trust. Who's left anyway? His son? He's a good kid, but sooner or later, they'll all let you down. It's just a matter of when.

Slowly slowly. He can't remember how long it's been going on, but he knows as sure as he can sometimes hear his wife calling to him, that someone has a rope around him and they are lowering him down. Not all the time. Not every day. Now and then he can think clearly and he can feel the sun on his face and he knows there is love in his heart for his boy, his Micky. That and a sense of loss for his darling Florence, his 'Florrie', that is crushing him alive. But more and more the bad days get the better of him, and down he goes, into the pit. When he looks up he sees the square of daylight get smaller. The darkness closing in.

Now he is sitting in this place and he's got this dreadful whirring, this droning sound going on. His head hurts.

He holds his hands up to his ears, presses tight.

Then he hears a voice, distant and frail but even before it becomes clear, even before he can make out the words, he knows who it is. He calms and the droning sound fades and he knows everything is going to be alright. He knows all the pain will go away once he sees her and they are together again.

He gets up from his chair, limps a couple of steps to get the blood moving through his old legs, and goes to the door to let her inside.

*

The aborted relocation to Mallorca is in tatters, and that's how Micky feels himself. Connie and Georgie, for the second time in two years, have told Micky what has been going on in his life when he had no clue whatsoever himself. They'd read him his fortune and then offered him a lifeline.

He is so tired that even the worry dogging his every moment can't stop him sinking into the refuge of much needed zeds. But even then he's not free. Even in sleep there is no escape.

Squabbling, cawing sounds. High pitched bickering. Then angrier noises. Men noises. Shouting. What the fuck is it now?

He surfaces back to the inconvenience of the real world. Except this time it's more than mere inconvenience. He awakens to pandemonium. People are running, shouting, screaming.

'Oh my God! What is he doing? Stop him!'

Then he remembers where he is. He stands and over the heads of the people in front of him sees three rows further down the aircraft. Two stewardesses and what looks like a concerned passenger, are literally hanging off of the back of a fourth person. In the midst of the melee the fourth person is hidden from view but Micky can tell he must be very strong because the three others are unable to control him in any effective way. It's only when one of the stewardesses is literally bucked away from the thrashing ruckus, to land with an audible thump on her back, that Micky can see what is happening.

He sees his dad. He sees his dad trying to open the aircraft door. They are somewhere over the Pyranees.

Wrestling his baying, weeping father to the ground in the plane and then sitting on him, along with two other male passengers for the remaining hour of the flight wasn't the only drama, as terrible as it was.

Spending several more hours with the police and the airport authority reps, when they finally touched down back at Luton, explaining, pleading, cajoling until they were both allowed to continue their journey wasn't the finish of it either.

Unable to bear the thought of a journey by train, Micky decided he had no choice but to spring for a cab all the way around the M25. Things actually picked up a little on the ride home because Eddie took a liking to the driver and, relaxed once again, didn't shut up all the way back. Okay so you can't physically open plane doors like that from the inside but that wasn't the point. Eddie didn't know that. So it was like being that close to killing a hundred and twenty odd people earlier that day simply hadn't happened. Which, in Eddie Targett's mind, it hadn't.

And the fun just carried on when they got to Eddie's sister, Frannie's place out in Laindon.

The thing Eddie doesn't like about staying at Frannie's house is that he doesn't really like Frannie.

'Why do I have to do that?'

Micky has explained to him a couple of times what's happened but still isn't sure he has properly understood.

'It will just be a lot easier. I'll get the house sorted out and then you come back. Won't take long.'

'How long?'

'I'm not sure.'

'What's wrong with the house?'

Jeezus. 'I told you, dad, the people renting it weren't very clean.'

'I can sort that out.'

'Just go and stay with Fran, yeah. She says she ain't seen you in ages.'

'There's a reason for that.'

'Look just *go* will you.'

The cab rolls past the A10. Micky is *unbelievably* stressed. He rubs his temples with his fingers.

'Where?'

'Frannie's.'

'Who?'

'Aunt Fran.'

'What about her?'

Jeezus.

Micky resorts to staring out of the window and Eddie seems to calm. Until the cab pulls up outside Frannie's house and she comes toddling down the path to meet them.

'What the fuck is she doing here?' Eddie wants to know.

Micky closes his eyes, breathes. He gets out of the car and gives his aunt a hug, whispers in her ear.

'Fran, I'm sorry but I need help. He's much worse. Can you keep him here for a few days.'

'I'll do me best, boy.'

'I need to see what state the house is in. I'll call you tomorrow.'

She takes his face in her hands, sees what he is carrying. 'I always knew he'd be the first to go.'

Eddie doesn't bother to hide his displeasure, *not that he ever fucking did,* Micky thinks.

'Alright, girl?' He practically snaps at his sister.

'Mr. Happy, very nice to see you too. How was your holiday?'

'What am I doing here?'

'How long ago was it you gave up being pleasant? Your son and me are doing you a favour. He's got a lot of worry.'

Micky hauls his dad's case from the boot of the cab and drags it past them to the front door.

'He's up to something.' Eddie bawls. 'What the fuck are you

playing at?'

Micky stands there totally shattered. He even bends down to rest with his hands on his knees, like a knackered, Sunday morning, pub footballer. His breath comes in rasping wheezes. He sounds like a fucked accordion.

Right there in his aunt's front garden he tries so desperately hard not to cry. He wants to cry because this day has, finally, brought him an understanding of how serious it all is. He tries to kid himself that this understanding is progress and he'll be able to handle whatever happens next. But what he doesn't know is that this is pretty much as good as it gets and that, barring occasional glimpses of happiness and drug oblivion, each day of the coming years will bring fresh and increasing heartache.

As the driver pulls his cab away he says, 'Tough day, mate?'

He drops Micky off at the Upminster bungalow and lifts half the national debt from him in the form of a fare. Micky goes to the front door and inspects the damage. It actually doesn't look too bad. A chunky but basic hasp and staple held by a padlock secures the door to the frame. He can't see in because the curtains are closed. Maybe, he thinks optimistically, it's just a bit of tidying.

He chucks his suitcase into the boot of the Scirocco and belts over to Romford nick. Presently he is sitting down opposite Detective Sargeant Raymond Pitts.

Micky is not sure how to feel about this bloke. He's good-looking, in a tough, vibrant kind of way. Looks like he can handle himself. Obviously gets down the gym. He certainly crushes Micky's hand when they shake.

And he looks at Micky, talks to him like he's met him before. Like he knows him. Maybe this is how he goes about his business. After all, Micky rationalises, he's only got that daft 'Receiving' charge against him from the way back, so how the hell would a low ranking cop from the suburbs know anything about him? Or indeed *want* to know anything?

Not only that but this cop may still be thinking that he was in on grow. Which is fair enough, but then Micky reminds himself there's nothing to be worried about here because he is the sodding victim.

When Micky walked across the room to meet and shake hands, it was all Ray Pitts could do to hold himself back from slamming a head butt into the bloke's nose. *Piece of shit scumbag pusher,* the cop was thinking. Strolling into a nick like he owned the place. Least he can do to try to break his hand.

'Firstly, Detective, you said on the phone that no one has been arrested for this.'

'That's right. No one was home.'

'Would it not have been possible to just plot up in a car across the street and wait for someone to arrive?'

The bloke smiles and that pisses Micky off.

'No. We just don't have the resources for that.'

'I see. Well, they shouldn't be too difficult to find.'

'What was the name of the lettings agency again?'

'Bromley Estates in Hornchurch. I have the tenancy agreement and copies of ID back at the house. I've already let them know what's happened and I'll get all the paperwork to you tomorrow.'

The cop nods, doesn't seem too bothered.

'How is the house?'

Ray Pitts looks back at Micky and thinks, *who the fuck are you coming in here telling me how to do my job?* More front than Southend. And there's that thing wth PC. His living gone, his life turned upside down. And then there's Jennifer Baddows.

'It's a bit of a mess.' He has trouble not smiling. 'We counted a hundred and fifty-five plant pots full of soil in your lounge, each one containing an adult. Seedlings and cuttings up in the loft.'

'Jeeeezus. Not hydroponics?'

Yeah, thinks Ray Pitts, *what do you know how to grow, fucking tomatoes?*

'Nope, that part of it was old-school. The rest was pretty up-market. They used a foil-lined, steel-framed grow tent which filled the room. The plants were in that and the lights were suspended from it. Keeps the heat in and doesn't show up through the roof to helicopter heat sensors.' *Like you don't know this already.*

'So the Met can afford a helicopter but not a car for a day or two to make an obvious nick?'

Pitts chews down another impulse to bash the vile shithead into next week. 'They also punched a hole out through the lounge wall. Ventilation I suppose. Might be some wildlife in there.'

Micky surprises himself by how much hurt he is feeling. Quickly followed by anger. He thinks about his mother. Thinks about her lovely house.

'They also bypassed the electricity. Real fire risk that. The whole place could have gone up.'

It's almost as if the bloke is enjoying all this.

'I can't believe they thought they were going to get away with it.'

'How long was the let for?'

'Six months for starters then maybe more.'

'From a seed to harvest takes four months. Hundred and fifty-five plants gets at least two hundred ounces and skunk is going for at least a hundred and fifty quid.'

'Thirty grand,' says Micky.

'Minimum. They would have got that first crop away then got in touch with you to see what your plans were. They would have got away with it had it not been for that new postman. First day on the job and he smelt it walking up the drive.'

Micky has to smile at that. He looks out of the window, sees it's dark already.

'Well I better get to it. Not looking forward to this.'

Detective Sargeant Pitts opens a draw in his desk and pulls out a padlock key which he hands to Micky.

'Cheers. I've got the bloke's previous address. And his daughter's. Wouldn't surprise me if they've got their heads in the sand, kidding themselves they're clean away. I'll bell you tomorrow.'

Pitts thanks Micky for his cooperation. Doesn't tell him that it's Met police policy *not* to chase down marijuana growers if they aren't present at the time of the raid. He also doesn't tell him that he will do his bare minimum to help a parasitic villain like him. Doesn't tell him that one day he's going to nail his sorry arse to the wall.

Pulling into the drive Micky gets the same sick feeling the night he came over when his dad had been evicted. This house, what is it, cursed or something?

His heart thumps as he undoes the padlock, as he enters. He flicks the hall light switch. Right, no lecky.

He feels his way through to the kitchen and finds his torch in the cupboard under the sink.

Scoping the light around he sees the kitchen looks unscathed as does the hallway he has just walked through. Checks out the bathroom which is okay too. Back out into the hall he turns right into his own bedroom. His bookshelves have been stripped of their cherished cargo, replaced with empty cider tins. The duvet and sheets are nowhere to be seen, the bare mattress looks to be stained. Unwashed plates on the carpet.

He checks his dad's room and is relieved to see it pretty much as it was when they left. Obviously the old bastard was running the thing on his own.

Back out into the hall and then a right into the lounge.

He feels and hears plastic underfoot. He takes a couple of shuffling baby steps, stub his toe against something heavy. He flashes the beam down. A plant pot, about the size that would support the average domestic Christmas tree. Full of dirt. There's also one next to it. And one next to that. Micky shines the torch towards the far end of the room. Wow!

As his eyes adjust to the dark he takes in the scale of the operation. They may have been stupid but what they lacked in brains they more than made up for in ambition.

He hears the whisper of a breeze, feels the movement of air on his skin. He shuffles between the pots towards the source and flashes his light on the plate sized hole in the far wall.

Flooded by boiling blood, his mind is considering everything he will do or have done to those fuckers when he catches up with them, when he thinks he hears something. That copper said there might be wildlife in the house. A fox? Rats? He flashes the beam to all corners of the room.

He hears something again, but not from in the lounge this time. It's out in the hall.

All I need, thinks Micky. *Things ain't bad enough I'm getting me arse fanged by rodents.* When was his last tetanus shot? He's scouring the room for some kind of weapon to lump the bastard with when everything slips into slow motion. Which, he will later think, is just as well, because surreal scenes such as the one which follows really need to be fully savoured and appreciated.

He is staring at the door when he sees it start to move. Even thinks he hears a whisper. Or possibly a chirrup, or whatever fucking sound a wild Essex animal makes. Then. . .

The door explodes inwards and something comes piling into the room. And it's big. And it's very noisy. And the noise it makes is; 'Police! Stay where you are!'

Micky is okay with that as he isn't able to make any kind of move whatsoever. He is totally frozen and mesmerized by what is happening. His torch light picks out at least four policemen filling the space between him and the door. Then they all trip over the plant pots and land in a thrashing, bellowing, serge heap of constabularial incompetence right there on the floor in front of him. If he hadn't been shatting himself he would have roared at the sight. Keystone Cops R Us.

But there are more. Overtime must have been cancelled because bodies just keep pressing into the lounge. And falling over. Eventually one of the first ones in scrambles to his feet, grabs Micky, spins him around, shoves his arm up his back and slams him into the far wall. Whatever humour there was in the situation instantly vanishes.

'Jesus Christ,' wails Micky. 'Fuck you doing? This is my house.'

He hears calls from outside in the hall. It's a large, three-bedroomed bungalow but it doesn't take the A-team long to scope it out.

'Room secure. Okay here. Bathroom clear.' And so on.

As the jokers in the lounge pick themselves up and turn on their torches the room is illuminated sufficiently to reveal the only potential threat is already neutralized. This doesn't stop Micky getting his face smeared into the wallpaper and his arm heaved further up his back.

'Easy easy. Fucking hell, mate. I just got the keys over at Romford. What is all this?'

'We just got a call from one of your neighbours. Said they saw one of the bad guys coming back.'

'Oh great. I've had villains renting the house for months and that's fine, but as soon as I come back I got the Sweeney all over me. Can you let me go?'

'Who are you?'

'Michael Targett. I live here. I've got ID.'

The policeman releases Micky and turns him around but gets right in his face. Two other cops flank Micky on either side. *Very* closely.

'You know I think you Met. lads are the best.'

'You want some medical advice? Fucking show me something, smartarse.'

Micky reaches into his rear pocket for his wallet. Flashes his driver's license.

'You blokes don't talk to each other? I was literally at Romford station getting the keys from Ray Pitts twenty minutes ago.'

The tension leaves the room faster than air leaving a pricked balloon. As the policemen exit both the lounge and the house, the sense of disappointment among their ranks is palpable.

The one giving Micky a hard time hands back his license.

'Sorry about that, Mr. Targett. Umm . . .'

'Can't be too careful these days, right?'

'Exactly. I'm sure you understand.'

'Yeah yeah.'

Micky follows them all out, hears the crackle of radios and sees, as he gets to the front door, the unearthly scene of his small suburban side street bathed completely in flashing blue lights. In a daze he stands totally captivated.

The Met's finest pile into one Transit van and three squad cars. Curtains twitch in most of the houses across the road.

Having hardly slept, Micky is up early. He needs to be as daylight reveals the extent of the carnage. Not only is the lounge wrecked but his bedroom is covered in cans, bottles, sweet wrappers and food packaging. Micky can't understand this. Just because you're a villain do you have to be uncouth? Jeezus.

He checks the electricity meter and sees the wrangle of wires and croc clips, bypassing the legal system. He climbs up into the lofts and sees the ranks of seedling propagators, bags of soil. What he also notices is he doesn't have to stand on the ceiling rafters. Someone has laid boards. And while he is annoyed to see crap everywhere, he is equally delighted to find his collection of Chateauneuf Du Pape, accumulated from his channel hopping days, completely intact.

Next thing he does is to call Davey Watkins, explains the situation, tells him he needs a decent spark, a van and preferably the man himself. There's proper cash in it. All of that, plus coffee, will arrive in around an hour. Then he gets at it.

When they crashed the place the police severed every plant in order to remove it as evidence or for destruction. This left an approximate foot long stem protruding from each bucket of dirt. Micky opens the French doors into the garden and removes one hundred and fifty-five pots of dirt which he shakes onto the garden's extensive flower beds. The stems he shoves into black plastic bags. The pots he hoses out and stacks.

He removes the plastic sheeting from over the carpet and bundles that up. The carpet doesn't look too bad but the thought of a new one on the insurance claim cheers him.

Davey walks straight in, calls his name.

'Jesus, mate. You need to be a bit tidier around the house. What the actual fuck?'

Micky laughs, shakes his hand.

'Rented it out while I was away. They was growing dope. The Feds crashed the place last week. I've had to come back to deal with it.'

'Ah, mate I'm gutted for you.'

'As it goes I think I might get away with it. Worse thing is the hole in the wall over there and they bypassed the lecky meter. I've parked me dad up at his sister's so he don't have to see this but I'm up against it.'

Micky is talking to the right man. Davey calls out a spark to sort the electricity. Then they fill, plaster and paint the hole in the wall and rip through the place like a whirlwind. Everything that needs to be dumped is taken out and everything that needs to be cleaned or left damaged, or indeed damaged *further*, for insurance purposes is attended to appropriately.

At the end of the day Davey asks for just two hundred quid and a oner for the electrician. Micky hands him four. They discuss masses of work they could claim for and the prospect of the necessary receipts. Fifty-fifty is agreed. Good to have mates.

Also good to have a decent home insurance policy, which, sadly, Micky most certainly does not.

'I'm very sorry to tell you this, Mr. Targett,' says the friendly, sweet-voiced girl he had first called from Mallorca. 'But it would appear you are not covered.'

Micky's wold tilts again. ''Scuse me?'

'As ever it's in the small print. Do you have your policy document to hand?'

'Not right now I'm afraid.'

'Well I can read it to you. Page thirteen halfway down. 'No claim shall be paid whereby the property is damaged either willfully or deliberately.' It goes on and on but that is the essence of it.'

Micky sighs both willfully and deliberately.

The next day, with the electricity restored and the place looking roughly like it did when they went away Micky heads out to Laindon to collect his dad. He expects the usual bollocking. He finds the old guy and his auntie Frannie drinking tea in the neat, little back garden.

''Allo, boy,' calls Eddie from his chair, his shirt at his feet as he enjoys the sunshine, an empty teacup on the grass.

Warily Micky approaches, but far from the clip around the ear he fears, his dad grabs his hand and pumps it enthusiastically.

'Where you been, son?'

'At the house.'

'Ah, right.'

Micky flicks a glance at his aunt and she catches the confusion it carries. She smiles and shrugs.

'All good here, Micky boy. Everything ok with you?'

'Yeah. Yeah, turned out okay, Fran. How's he been?'

Curious how they both already assume it is fine to talk about Eddie even though he is sitting right there.

'Like the pussycat he always was,' says Fran, stroking her brother's silver curls.

'The only one who ever got the better of me in a fight when we were kids.' Eddie informs Micky matter of factly.

Eddie is in the passenger seat of the Scirocco as Micky hugs his aunt.

'Cheers for that, me dear. I owe you.'

'You owe me nothing, boy.' She looks at him with genuine affection. And genuine concern.

'You're a good kid, Micky. Tough, but a different tough to him. And you're gonna need to be.'

 Back at the house, while Eddie, completely unaware of what had happened, pads around with a massive grin on his face, Micky has a moment to take stock, and on the face of it, knows things aren't too clever.

As usual it's about money. For someone who, only two years

previously, was handed a suitcase containing two hundred and twenty thousand pounds in cash with no tax to pay he has to admit things could be better. But then there are mitigating circumstances.

After fighting for two years to regain title of the family home for his father, the sums do not make comfortable contemplation. One hundred and thirty bought off the bank. On top of that he was obliged to spend almost forty thousand on legal fees, the tragedy being more than half of that was to pay the fees deliberately incurred by his own brother.

In the last two years he had made himself a couple of grand selling cocaine but had blazed through most of the rest of the two-twenty simply by living, and living not particularly well at that. Okay so he had shelled out for an essential surgical procedure for both himself and his dad and he had ventured abroad to Santa Ponsa for a doomed and very costly trip. So now he's down to about his last ten thousand.

But there are two plus points; firstly the bungalow. He had achieved his goal. Redressed the obscenity. Made good, and that was all money in the bank.

And the fuckwits that rented the place had at least seen fit to board out the loft.

Secondly he is cozy once again with Connie and Georgie. He isn't on any wages as such but the game is the game and, albeit quite tenuously, it seems Micky is back in it.

*

'Thing is, Mick, there might be something you can do for us.' This is Georgie Harper.

Micky hears the words like a Labrador hearing a high pitched whistle from two feet away.

'We've got a situation.'

It isn't enough Micky knows his Mallorcan dream is over. He's had to sit on this terrace and once again get his own arse handed to him. He's drunk, it's all turned to shit, his dad is on the way out. Where does weirdness come from? he asks himself, and why does so much of it head his way?

And now there's a situation.

'But we don't want you to fall over and roll around in your own shit again.'

Micky feels the best way to deal with that comment is to ignore it. He waits for George to speak again.

'Out your way. Pills.'

Now Micky is very interested.

'Coming in the usual route. Through Harwich and Felix.'

Micky's concentration is total. He knows this is a very important conversation that would not have been instigated unless there was some serious news incoming.

'Problem being there's a bunch of jokers out there. Injun country.'

'You losing product?'

Connie and Georgie do their swapping looks thing again. Georgie says, 'You sure?'

'Tell him,' Connie replies as he reaches for the bottle.

'We've got everything lined up. Shipping company, customs. It's all good. Problem isn't getting the things into the country, it's keeping hold of them once they get in.'

'I see.'

'Now this is a big market. Essex and East Anglia. All those field raves. But it's being hamstrung by these three maniacs. They want a slice of everything the easy way.'

'Always been the problem with Essex,' Connie observes dryly. 'Everyone wants to get rich quick.'

'Rather than work alongside the importer and make a fortune they keep ripping everyone off, including us. We've tried fronting them a few packages. They have the market but come pay day they're happy to tell our middle men to go fuck themselves. Mental.'

Micky starts to wonder where this might be going. What's he supposed to do against a gang of chancers?

'Word is they're bang on everything themselves, totally out of control. Everyone is afraid of them. Massive gym bunnies on steroids.'

Now Micky really doesn't understand. Connie and Georgie managed to see off Terry Farmer, Denny Masters and Pete Chalmers, why are they worried about some Essex wannabes? As if to read his mind Connie contributes.

'We can't go in there all guns blazing and we can't show our faces in any way. We have no police help outside of the Met. If these berks find out we are involved then it could all turn a bit lively.'

They both stare at Micky. He finally gets it.

'So you want me to go there and find out what I can.'

'Told you he was a natural,' Connie says.

'A minute ago you told me I was a dozy twat.'

'And I am yet to revise that assessment. Shut up and keep listening.'

Micky shuts up and keeps listening.

'You've worked plastic and kites before,' Georgie goes on. 'Fronted car scams. You might have the right gearing for this. If we can sort this mess out, there'll be a nice few quid in it for you.'

So upon his return, and having straightened out the house, Micky has two things upon which to concentrate his energies. Connie and Georgie's mission out in the wilds of Essex would wait for the time being. Immediately he needed to get down to the estate agents and do a bit of straightening there.

One look at Carly Bromley told Micky everything he needed to know. She had fake tits, a fake tan, fake eyebrows, and fake lips. In short she didn't mind dressing things up to look different from reality.

They know he is coming and he hopes they'll have all the information ready for him, although he isn't sure what he is going to do with it, the information. It was obvious from his meeting with DS Pitts at Romford nick that Five-Oh wasn't interested in looking for these jokers. So Micky thinks he'll find them, do his civic duty, and just hand them over. Something like that.

First he needs to have sight of all the references. Then he'll track them down. Then he'll see.

An orange teenager called Dottie greets him upon his arrival and parks him in front of her desk. She turns to address the woman seated at the desk behind.

'Carly this is Mr. Targett. The house with the marijuana people?'

The bottle blonde hair was that rigid Micky thought it might have been held in place by scaffolding. She looks through him and reluctantly heaves herself off her seat and totters over on eight inch fuck-me heels. Respect for *that* thinks Micky.

'Dot, 'ow we getting on wiv them dippy shits at the insurers?'

Micky regards the woman closely and soon sees that her expressionlessness is not manifested through lack of interest or concern for his predicament. When she speaks none of her face moves. Not even her mouth.

'Still nothing, Carl'.'

Then she is addressing him. 'See it's all with the insurers. Nuffing we can do.'

'What's all with the insurers?'

'The references. But they're rubbish. We're changing them soon.'

The oft bandied phrase – Never bullshit a bullshitter is in Micky's mind in that instant and he knows already she's scum.

'Do you not have copies of any of those references here?'

'No. We don't need them.'

'Well,' says Micky calmly, not wishing to show how wound up he is rapidly getting, 'sadly I do. But they *were* taken?'

'Yeah. 'Course. What are the police saying?'

'Not too much at all. Looks like it's down to me. And with your help I'm sure I'll find out what's what.'

'Right. Dottie'll do what she can.' Then she turns her back on Micky (implants or just a fat arse?) and makes a meandering return to her desk. Dottie doesn't quite know what to say or do. Micky does.

'Dottie what I need you to do is write down the name and number of your insurers, and the name of the person you've been dealing with there.'

The call he later makes reveals everything he suspected. A helpful agent at the insurance company tells him the reason why Bromley Estates will shortly be changing their insurers. It's because the insurers will be dumping Bromley Estates from their client list.

'They are impossible to deal with. There is something wrong with them, particularly *her*.'

'Have they been talking to you about me?'

'Yes, we know who you are and what happened.'

'Do you have the references that were taken from my tenants?'

'No. That is because we never received any.'

'Do you know they're blaming you for not sending them back?'

'That doesn't surprise me. It's that kind of agency that gives the rental market a bad name. They charge both you and the tenant and don't do any checks.'

The next call Micky makes is to Ben Yardley. They get the dream team back together and sue the skanky, fake bitch. Ben is so sure of this one, along with being aware of Micky's circumstances, he hands him a no win-no fee deal.

CHAPTER TWELVE

Lose myself inside your schemes
Now open up, make room for me

That Saturday Micky edges the Scirocco through the outskirts of Basildon. He doesn't want to be there, for many reasons, but suitably chastised by Connie and Georgie for his almighty cock-up in dealing to PC, he knows he has no choice. He's also broke.

He finds a parking space, locks the car, genuinely not knowing if it will be there when he gets back, and walks towards the town centre. He is going to Raquels.

Even when he was getting on it every weekend Micky simply didn't bother looking out to Essex for a good time. Why would you? The furthest east he ever went was Beckton for the legendary Raindance. Now he finds himself in with the bumpkins, in with the Ford workers and the window cleaners. Not that he was a snob about such things but, you know.

then he's in some kind of hellish concrete precinct and the place looms over him like a disused abattoir. He follows a few scraggly kids and joins a short queue. He gets eyeballed and patted down by some ugly goon on the door and through he goes. Ten quid before ten, up the stairs and he's in.

It's a reasonable kind of place, he thinks as he heads towards the bar, if you're happy hanging around in a school disco. Perhaps that's harsh but he senses that kind of atmosphere. It's cleanish, modernish, the music is middle of the roadish. It's provincial and boring. The men all look like they want to have a fight and the women all look like they've already had one. He scores an orange juice and ponders the two ways he can play this.

He still has half a dozen of the pills stamped with the $ sign on that he copped from Ben Yardley at the start of the year. They're in a plastic bag in the Y-fronts. Push comes to shove he can hang around and knock those out and see what kinds of conversations he can strike up. But then he thinks that if he did that then push might very easily come to shove because, after all, Basildon is a shithole and he doesn't need to be stepping on anyone's toes. Certainly not out here in bandit country.

No, by far and away the best play is to hang around, scope the place and try to score. Keep it together and find out what he can. And failing that well, he's got six decent Jacks in his bin so if it comes down to it he can always get shitfaced and pass the time that way.

The place is licensed only until two am, so there is no lounging around taking his time. He's tempted to drop one of his $s just to relieve the tedium but across by the back wall near the toilets he sees what he wants to see. Two blonde girls are talking to a bloke and he's not doing much talking back. Micky edges closer and sees it's not a conversation. It's a deal. The guy nods then spends an inordinate amount of time quite obviously fishing in his jeans pocket. Eventually he comes up with the pills and plops them into the palm of moose number one. Moose two slides the cash into his other hand. Strictly amateur night.

Over the next half an hour Micky clocks a constant stream of customers and is ready to move, but then panics because the bloke disappears though an unmarked door over by the bar. Five minutes later he's back in his normal spot. Drop off the cash and re-up, reckons Micky. Yup, he's the resident go-to pill dispenser clearly sanctioned by the venue. Interesting.

So over he goes, leans in.

'Can I get two, mate?'

The bloke stands back, looks Micky over. 'Two what?'

Well, Micky thinks, if we're going to play silly buggers. 'Er . . two *please*?'

Something only occurs to Micky at this precise moment of potential difficulty; he is without doubt, at thirty-four, the oldest person in the place. The man he's looking at, for example, is early-twenties tops. The cream of Essex youth beginning to whirl and bounce all around him; mid-twenties on average. How much more like undercover Plod could he look? He holds the bloke's stare.

'Who the fuck are you?'

'Micky.'

The bloke clearly doesn't know what to make of it. Micky wonders that perhaps this is a routine he feels the need to work through whenever he is approached by someone he doesn't know.

'I think you're in the wrong place, Micky.'

What is he doing here with these Neanderthals? He's on the verge of walking away, but through sheer bloody-minded refusal to be beaten he digs in. Takes a chance. He pulls his little bag of pills out and shows them to the kid.

'Look, I've got me own, but I need these for tomorrow. Thought we could do some business. I heard there's good stuff in here. Don't matter.'

He replaces the bag in his pocket, moves away then gratifyingly feels the hand on his shoulder.

'Oi, you don't want to be bringing gear into *this* place.'

Micky starts to think he has to draw this dickbrain a picture. 'This is what I'm saying. Do me five, bruv, c'mon. '

The kid gives him some eyeball but Micky knows he's over himself and his own ego. He fishes in his pocket.

'How much?'

'Tens.'

'What are they?'

'Question marks.'

Micky reaches for the folding and to close the deal he says, 'Sorry to spring it on you like that but I'm new down here.'

Money and drugs do their dance. The kid nods, wants to come across as the tough guy.

'Appreciate it,' says Micky.

He moves away. He's heard of Question Marks but has never tried them. Just in case they're not up to scratch he double drops. Precisely forty-seven minutes later, when it's gone eleven already, he is sufficiently bolloxed to know he's going to need something to do when the place kicks out at sodding two o'clock in the sodding morning.

Either way he feels a certain aptitude for this undercover business and sets about making new friends. He decides it will be quicker to talk to some fat, unattractive people, and bearing in mind he's in a club in Essex, he has no shortage of options.

Soon enough he's bouncing along with a couple of hairdressers and a trainee plasterer from Billericay. He's not too sure where it's all meant to go, but it's kind of fun and they're nice kids and it takes him away from where his life is and back to a time and a place where he'd prefer it to be.

At one point he's got his head together over a couple of pints of piss-weak Carling with the plasterer. Invariably, as Micky remembers it being the way of things, the subject comes round to the gear and they slip into the lingua franca.

'What you had?' Craig shouts over the music, his breath a rancid gust of burnt Rothmans.

Micky isn't enjoying the beer, pushes his glass to one side. 'Couple of Question Marks. You?'

'One of them. Good eh?'

'Yeah, nice buzz. Where'd you get yours?'

'In here.'

'Oh yeah? You a regular?'

'Yeah. It's alright. Local and you know what you're going to get. Used to get a bit heavy a while ago but it's alright now.'

'Is there anywhere to go after?'

The kid laughs. 'Probably home. Coming down already.'

'Wow. That's not a real Saturday night.'

'Bit skint and I don't get paid for another week.'

Micky dips into his pocket, slips it across. Jason looks at it like it's a lump of enriched uranium.

'I told you I'm skint.'

'On me. Can't a bloke help a brother out?'

So then the four of them are dancing and Micky even forgets he's 'working' for a while. He's ten actual years and a million light ones away from this lot but the drugs make it okay. The drugs always make it okay. Then Craig slings an arm round Micky's neck, presses his sweaty face close to his ear.

'I don't suppose you could do me a solid could you, man?'

'Yeah wassat?'

'The girls want to call it a night but I'm flying. They're on shit wages too. Don't suppose you got anymore?'

Micky grins. Ingratiate oneself with the natives. He delves deep once again, hands over the last two Question Marks. The guy can't believe his luck. Micky looks across at the two girls who have seen what's going on. Smiling, one whispers to the other. Micky starts to panic, scared he might have to shag one of them. Craig hands out the sweets and they both step over to embrace and thank their new found benefactor.

So it's all good. Micky is *convinced* he isn't going anywhere near either of the girls but then one slides over and kisses his cheek and she's dancing next to him. Then the DJ sticks on Short Dick Man by 20 Fingers and that's a laugh and they're all singing along. Then one of them says they know a friend who's having a back-to-his-place-afterwards thing. All in all, Micky thinks, this has been a proper success. Good info for Connie and Georgie and some new confederates he can work with. Then he goes for a leak and the evening takes a radical lurch.

He is *nicely* toasted as he makes his way off the dance floor. Relaxed. Too relaxed. He leans into the door of the toilets aware of, but not troubled by, the man walking in behind him. It's a standard club khazi; communal urinal to the left, couple of traps beyond that and three sinks below a mirror along the wall to the right. He's unzipping when he feels the shove between his shoulder blades that sends him flying ten feet into the far wall. Oh fuck.

He is instantly straight, adrenaline kicking in, senses on the razor's edge. Nowhere to go so he scopes out the opposition. Three. One is the dealer he bought from, young, fit, hard-looking. Next to him is an older man, maybe early-forties, tall, lean, greying hair combed back. But behind them is the problem, should there be one. This fucker is massive and not in a good mood. Long hair. *Bad* hair. Micky's furiously working mind goes back to Connie's terrace. Three nutters. Gym bunnies.

'So what's the story then, soldier?' This is the older one to Micky's left. The light is behind them which doesn't help.

Micky is holding onto it. He's been in worse situations. Christ he's been laid out cold by the best in London, what can these yokels do?

He thinks about dropping names – Do you know who I'm with? No, front it.

'Well there I was having a nice time in this nice club.'

'Yeah well, now you ain't.'

At that precise moment a toilet is flushed and a twenty year old space cadet with eyes like golf balls comes out of the trap directly to Micky's right.

'Alright, lads. Are we 'aving it or what?!'

The looks and the silence calm him waaaay down in about point two of a second.

'Ah. Excuse me.' He picks his way through the showdown and gets gone.

Micky eases himself off the wall, makes himself as tall as he can. Not that that's going to do him any good. He's got about a hundred quid plus the $s on him. Plus the keys to the Scirocco. They'll never find the car because it's about half a mile away. Worth fighting for? He thinks back to some advice Rock Steady Eddie gave him when he first started going in pubs.

'If someone is lining up to hit you, forget hitting them back. Doesn't it make sense to hit them *first*?'

He is genuinely pondering the veracity of that question when the bloke carries on talking.

'Word is you've been dealing in my club.'

Micky hears him but can't help but look over his shoulder, to the big man. Scary, big, weird-looking dude.

'You're mistaken.'

'Oh am I? This him, Jace?'

'Too fucking right it is. I told ya.'

'Look, I bought a few from this bloke . . . and?'

'You've been seen dealing.'

'I gave a couple out to some friends. It's all about sharing the love isn't it?'

'You got some bounce, boy.' This was the first time the big man had spoken.

At that moment two sweaty kids enter the toilet. The big man turns and calmly speaks.

'Toilets are closed, lads.'

Micky sees their reaction, one of complete and utter, awe-struck supplication. They can't even speak. Then they're gone and Micky's knows he's in with the A-Team.

'This isn't the way I thought my night would go, fellas. I've paid to get in, I've paid good money for a few pills, I've shared, not sold, a couple of those. I've bought a few drinks, I've enjoyed the music . . . and here I am in the khazi talking to people who don't seem pleased to see me.'

He can't be sure, because of the light, but was that a tremor of a smile on the face of the big man?

'He brought his own in. The cunt showed me.' Jason the dealer.

'Empty your pockets.' The older bloke.

No way out so Micky does what he is told. Car keys from the front right, bag of six $s from the front left and his wallet from the back right. He holds them out in front of him in his upturned palms.

The elder man, the club owner, snatches the bag, holds it towards Micky.

'So what's this?'

'Back up,' Micky says. 'First time here. Brought those along in case I couldn't score. Jesus, what are we talking about here? Can't a bloke get shitfaced these days without a fucking interview?'

'Look in his wallet.'

Jace the dealer grabs Micky's wallet, thumbs past the cash. Pulls out a bank card, a driver's license and Micky's membership card for Havering libraries.

'Michael David Targett. Upminster.'

'Is that a fucking library card?'

'Hey, reading's good,' Micky tells the bloke, feeling his confidence grow. 'If we don't read, how might we learn?'

'Christ I've heard it all now,' says the massive bloke from behind. With that he simply turns and leaves. Danger over, Micky thinks, trying not to let his relief show.

'Where'd you get these?'

'From a friend last week.'

The guy holds them up to the light. 'Dollars, right?'

'Yeah.'

'Any good?'

'Fine. On a par with your Question Marks.'

'Jace give this man back his wallet. I'll take it from here.'

Micky can't believe it. Not only is he not getting rolled but this is looking like it's heading to exactly where he wanted it to be. Jason gives him another dirty look before walking out and now Micky and the owner of the place are alone.

'Weird name you got. Do I know you from somewhere?'

Micky walks to a sink, runs a tap and ducks low to drink, breathes. He stands again, wipes his mouth and looks at the bloke. He thinks about talking to him about the old days. Midnights and Stingers. No, he doesn't know him. But he wants to.

'I don't think so. Spend most of my time in London. Sometimes Mallorca. Listen, maybe we can do something here.'

'Like what?'

'I know a lot or people.'

'So do I. So what?'

'You got good pills. That's starting to become a rarity these days. I can move some.'

'You know what, mate, you got Plod written all over you.'

'Do me a favour. I can just about stand up. Look at my eyes. I bought those pills from your boy two hours ago. If I was Old Bill you'd be answering questions down at the station already.'

The man considers Micky's words.

'You might want to rethink how that works as well, he's right out in the open doing what he's doing.'

'Give me your wallet again.'

Micky hands it over once more, watches the bloke fish out his driver's license, hands him back the wallet.

'How many?'

'Dunno. Will they always be those ones?'

'Who fucking cares? Answer the question.'

Micky has to get some sense from his broiling brain and quickly. He's had this plop right into his lap but he could easily fuck it up. He can't buy tons because he needs an outlet and he's starting from scratch, but if he pitches too low and looks like a wannabe . .

'Say five hundred.'

'A week?'

'Probably. Me and my friends have never seen those ones before. Need a bit of time to get going.'

'Your friends not trust your word?'

'They will. What's your name?'

'John.'

'How much, John?'

So now the bloke knows *he's* on the spot. Go in too high and Micky might walk away, pitch too low and he's stiffed himself.

'Cash up front,' Micky tells him. 'Always been my way.'

'Sixes,' the bloke tells him. 'You buy three lots of five hundred in three weeks it goes down to fives.'

That's actually not bad, Micky tells himself.

'You're on. Where?'

'Here. Tomorrow night.'

'Done.' Micky reaches for his driver's license but John pulls it out of his reach.

'I'll hang onto this. Until I know you better.'

Micky heaves up the volume in the Scirocco as he heads home along the A127. Fuck. My. Old. Boots.

Late as it is he feels the need to give Connie a shout with the news. Not only is he in with the bad guys but he's sure the big fella lurking at the back was one of the gruesome threesome. Could he have really fluked it on his first attempt?

He sneaks in through the front door. He's accustomed to treading like a cat when he enters this house. All that practice when he was a lairy pisshead.

But as he enters the hallway, his head ringing both with the drugs and the success of the evening, he is surprised to notice the illuminated crack around the ajar living room door. He enters.

His dad is in his usual chair watching the television. Micky checks the clock on the wall. It's just gone two. The television is not turned on. His father leers at the screen in manic concentration. He has the remote control in is hand.

'Dad?'

Without looking at him Eddie says, 'This is fucking ridiculous.'

Micky sighs. The old guy had been okay since they had returned from Mallorca, no mad episodes. But it's not going to go away and he knows it.

'It's getting late, pop. Why don't you go to bed?'

'Fuck bed. Look at this shit. TV license. And another thing, don't you ever bring that nigger bird into this house again.'

As lit up as he is Micky is floored by what he is hearing.

'Are you talking about Lisa?'

'You know who I mean. Don't you ever do that again.'

Micky rubs his eyes, holds his head in his hands. He can't think how long it has been since Lisa was there. 'You want a drink?'

Eddie neither speaks nor moves. He looks truly possessed.

'I'm going to get a drink. You want one?'

'When are you going to get a job? Put the kettle on.'

Micky gets up, feels both his hip and his knee. He grabs a bottle of gin from the drinks cabinet on the way to the kitchen. Going to be a long night.

The following evening, having grabbed three thousand from his pathetic stash, Micky heads back to Basildon. He gets pointed towards the cramped office next to the bar. He knocks on the door which is opened by the unsmiling John. Behind the desk is someone else, and he isn't smiling either.

Christ, Micky says to himself, if crime and money don't make you happy then why get involved?

John shuts the door. There's nowhere to sit down so Micky guesses, correctly, that his place is to stand in front of the desk while he's being dealt with. The man he's looking at is in his mid-twenties with short dark hair. Heavily muscled and good looking, in a blunt, council- estate kind of way. His nurtured fringe is smeared forward by some foul unguent or condiment. He gives Micky the eyeball, says nothing. Now Micky could understand this if he was asking for the goods up front on credit. That might necessitate a warning, a bit of a show. But he has already assured them he's paying cash.

The man sitting down opens a draw in the desk and pulls out Micky's driving license. He looks it over and smirks.

'Michael Targett. That really your name?'

'Sure is.'

'Upminster boy.'

'Yup.'

He's not sure what he's supposed to do. If they want him to tell them he's scared then he could do that. He'd much rather everyone got along. Clearly they've all seen *Scarface* too many times and all this old bollocks is thought necessary.

'So you walk in here out of nowhere, no introductions, and you

213

want to start buying from us?'

'You got good product at the right price but if it's a problem then I can do without.' The words travel with the confidence of someone who means what he says and the bloke gets that.

'You got some money on you?'

'You got some stuff for me?'

'Put it on the table or fuck off, smart arse.'

Now Micky has to admit he is scared. Just a bit. For his money mostly but for himself as well. He can't just let them take it without a fight. Can he? He sees the man's biceps and pectorals straining under his shirt. He reaches into his jacket pocket, pulls out the wad and places it carefully and quite respectfully in front of the man. Like it's a tribute.

Eyebrows are raised and the man is now smiling. 'What's there?'

'Three as agreed.'

'Bang on target, Mr. Targett.'

Above all else Micky is bored and he really hopes that Connie and Georgie don't end up getting in bed with this firm. With no haste whatsoever the man reaches into the drawer, pulls out a plastic bag full of white pills. He leans forward and drops them on the desk. Micky can see some Question Marks, and they all look the same. But he can't be sure.

'And what's there?' Micky asks.

'Five hundred. As agreed. 'Samatter? Don't you trust me?'

'Well I was just thinking, it would be really good if neither of us needed to waste our time counting.'

He purses his fat lips and bobs his head. 'I hear that, Micky boy. Can't argue there. The good thing being you are totally outgunned and we know where you live.'

Micky doesn't want to push it, he just wants out. He's got *some* pills and he has information. He takes the bag and pockets it. Holds out his hand.

'My license.'

The man looks Micky in the eye and places it back in the desk drawer.

'All in good time, me old mate.'

He hasn't been able to catch up with Connie to give him the good news but that will happen soon.

As it turns out he has bought four hundred and ninety-five Question Marks and a lot of dust. So someone had a dip, and a cheap, insignificant one at that, but again Micky doesn't care. He knows that Connie will take the pills from him at cost, but if he can't find him or someone on the firm to make that happen soon then he's going to get stuck with the things. More than that he will need to keep fronting the cash to maintain the supply coming. This he sees not as a problem but as a challenge. He used to be a top Ecstasy dealer and wonders if he can be again.

He also goes to see his doctor to talk about his dad who tells him Eddie needs to get into the surgery. How is Micky supposed to propose that? 'Dad you need to go to see the doctor because you're going mad'. Yeah great. He makes the appointment anyway.

He also gives DS Pitts a shout to see if they have made any progress with finding the dope growers. They haven't. So Micky checks the crude photocopy of the old bastard's driver's license that Bromley Estates did manage to take. He drives round to the Chadwell Heah address and parks up opposite.

While he's there he takes out his old little black book.

His first call is to Ben Yardley to let him know that from now on his Ecstasy comes at favourable rates and gets delivered. Then he calls Chrissie Jarvis and lets him know he'll be over tomorrow for a five minute sit-down.

As he flicks through the dirty, dog-eared pages he is staggered to see the names of so many people he doesn't know. Or can't remember.

A few he recalls but the world, he understands, has moved on. People who were once single and in their twenties when he ran with them as both friends and customers are now married in their thirties. Careers, mortgages, children. He works the numbers. Interestingly some can't remember *him*. This makes him smile because it means, presumably, that he did his job and did it well.

He flicks all the way through to the back, to the Zeds. There he sees a magic name even though it doesn't begin with a Zed. He sees the word 'Ishy'. Ishmael Zamaan. It was partly thanks to Ishy that Micky made the big time. The best double-run there was. Coke down to Brighton for sale and raw Mdma from Ishy back to London. Into the caps. Midnights and Stingers. Ishy, the man.

Micky thinks back to two calls from Ishy's girlfriend, Kerry Pattison, herself a throwback even further to his time in Mallorca in eighty-five. The first told him that Ishy had been busted and it was Micky, a regular visitor to the pair of them, who had lead the enemy, Masters and Chalmers and through them the police, to their door. Then later a peace offering of a sort. Ishy had done his time, had learned a new trade inside and was heading north to be with family. Going straight. Starting over.

Micky smiles and thinks back, but that was as far as he got. He looks across the street to see a young woman pushing a kiddie chair. It's the girl in the family that rented the house. And their escape plan? Move back into the family home. Except they hadn't even bothered to move out. Hardly major league, innovative crime, he thinks as he starts the car and drives away.

Back at his house he makes three calls. The first is to DS Pitts. No answer but he leaves a message to say he has found the bad guys. The second is to Connie Chetkins. He's not there either but he leaves a message with Barbara. She asks about Eddie and they shoot the shit for a few minutes.

He breathes deep before he calls Ishy. Must be three years. Phone's bound to be dead. But then it rings. And then he answers.

Next morning Micky drops five Question Marks off at Chrissie's car lot.

'Samples, mate. Don't do them all yourself, let's get something going.'

Then he parks up at Seven Kings station and jumps the train into Liverpool Street. Forty minutes later he's drinking coffee across from Ishmael Zamaan. And they're both doing the same thing, sitting there with big, stupid grins on their faces, shaking their heads in disbelief.

'Not having this shit.'

'You're telling me.'

'I was thinking, he ain't gonna have the same phone number.'

'You know what? I saw your number come up and recognised it.'

'Really?'

'Yeah and my nose starting running. Pavlov's coke dog or what?'

They both break up.

'So how you been?' Ishy asks. 'What you doing?'

Where to start? 'Jesus, how long you say you got?'

Ishy eyes his chunky Omega. 'Half an hour.'

'You really doing a nine to five thing then?'

Ishy manoeuvres his immaculate tie into place. 'Yeah, man. Welcome to the machine.'

'Mate if I had a month I wouldn't be able to describe what's been happening. Fact is I lost my way a bit. My family fell apart. My head fell apart. Got bashed about a bit. Actually I got bashed a *lot*. Then I managed to pull off a couple of scams and ended up on my feet. But then I had to lay most of that down to buy back my dad's house because my own fucking brother had stolen it.'

Ishy's eyes all but leave their sockets. 'What da fuck?'

'Yeah, mate. But I'm back rolling again. More or less.'

'Christ,' returns Ishy, 'all I did was go to prison and get myself a career.'

The word lands on the table between them like a grenade. Micky casts his eyes down then back up to the face of his old friend.

'Mate . . .'

Straight away Ishy is waving his hands around in front of him.

'Dude, don't. Really, don't worry about it.'

'It was down to me, Ish'.'

'No it wasn't. Kerry told me. It was down to some scumbags you know.'

'That's good of you, son.'

'Hey, it's all turned out well. I got my head down in prison, learnt computing. Then I got a job working with my brother up north. I have a knack for this shit. But I was missing London so I applied for this job and, in spite of my record, I landed it. 'Sall good, man.'

'So what is it you do?'

'I.T..'

'Don't talk like an alien.'

'Computer technology. You not up on all this?'

'I know somebody that's *got* one but that's about it.'

'You're a class act, Class, always said it. We're talking about the future here, and it's not just a simple machine to write stuff or store information on. Computers are already talking to each other. And soon everybody all over the world will be able to talk to everybody else. Instantly. The technology exists. It's called the Web. Or the internet.'

'I got news, mate, you can already do that. It's called the telephone.'

'Not like that. You'll learn. Everyone will. And soon enough all the information that there is in the world will be available for free. Libraries will cease to exist. Soon enough there will be cyber-crime. Villains will operate in the digital world. People will be able to dip into someone else's bank account on the other side of the planet.'

Micky sees his eyes gloss over with a film of passion and infatuation.

'It's coming, mate. Invest in tech stocks. It will take over the world.'

'Next time I'm in a meeting with my broker I'll mention it.' Micky smiles to let Ishy know he's kidding. 'But in the meantime . . .'

Ishy raises his eyebrows.

'Mate I'm double chuffed it's all worked out for you. You're one of the only people I cared about back then. You and Kerry.'

'She sends her regards by the way.'

'I was just about to ask. And her kiddie?'

'They're both good. In fact Kerry's pregnant.'

'Oh get the fuck *out*.'

'Yeah, man. Some wild shit, eh?'

'Hmm, the whole family thing, don't come cheap, does it?'

'I do alright and I'm going to do better. I knew what I was getting into.'

Micky stares at him. His old friend did time over drugs because of him so he knows there is no easy way to say it.

'What?' Ishy says.

'Fancy getting back into it?'

'Is this why you wanted to see me?'

'Ishy I wanted to see you for a million reasons, but I've been scared to pick up the phone these past years.'

'And now you're not scared.'

'Mate whatever happens I'm thrilled to see you and I hope we stay in touch. I thought I'd mention it and now I have.'

Ishy stares at him then out the window to the insane throng that is weekday Bishopsgate. Micky watches him chew his lip. Checks him out. The boy looks good in a suit and tie.

"Sfucking 'orrible inside. You wouldn't believe the scum in there.'

Somehow, having broken the law pretty much every day for several years, Micky has only ever seen the inside of a jail on visiting days. Okay so he'd racked up a few arrests and one conviction, but none of that was for anything worth shouting about. He keeps quiet.

'It's so tiring because you don't really sleep. I didn't anyway. I only made it through because of Kerry. And what I was learning.'

Micky suddenly feels desperately uncomfortable to the point of wanting to get out of there. Did he get hurt? He's a good-looking bloke but no tough guy. Did he get raped? He wants to know but he doesn't.

'I'm so sorry it happened, mate. Look, forget it. Forget what I said. We're in touch again and that's the thing.'

Ishmael Zamaan looks down at his coffee, swills it around his cup. Then he replaces the cup in its saucer, looks across at Micky.

'There is so much of everything flying around up here. The City. People. Information. Money. Gear.'

'Oh yeah?'

Ishy purses his lips again. Nods. 'Yeah. But it's all shit. Talk to me.'

Ducks, thinks Micky Targett. Tremendous things, especially when you get them all in that neat little row. Which he appears to be doing. He finally gets to talk to Connie who is delighted with the progress made in Essex. He tells Micky to keep at it and, as Micky knew he would, he agrees to underwrite any purchases Micky makes that he can't sell himself.

'I'd prefer if you could keep that to a minimum because I'm buying back my own pills which I've already paid for a lot cheaper, but keep in with these fuckwits, son.'

Brilliant.

On top of that Ishy is back on the firm and starts to move some of Chrissie Jarvis's coke and quite a few of the Essex pills to his money-no-object City chums. And on top of *that* Chrissie likes the pills and he starts to take plenty too. Double run time again.

Ben Yardley and his friends continue to buy both.

So Micky puts the Mallorca disappointment behind him and starts to enjoy the way things are working out. But such is the manner of his life that it doesn't last for long.

It was a huge surprise to Micky how easy it was to get Eddie round to see their doctor.

'He just wants to have a chat to see how you are.'

Eddie glares up at his younger son and Micky gets that claw of dread scraping at his insides. Then a simple shrug and Eddie finds his pullover and off they go.

The doctor is a cool, mid-forties Korean bloke. Smiles, handshakes. Just three mates sitting down for a chat. Eddie looks more than happy to be there.

'Okay, Mr. Targett. Michael is a little worried about you so I just want to ask you a few questions. Won't take long.'

'He worries too much. Like his mother.'

The doctor smiles, checks a pile of notes on his desk.

'Okay, Mr. Targett, what is your middle name?'

Eddie concentrates, flicks his eyes around the cramped surgery, takes his time.

'I haven't got one. Private Edward Targett. Royal Fusiliers, City of London Regiment. 46097231.'

Micky is astonished, confused and proud all at the same time. He has never heard that before in his life. The doctor carries on.

'Okay, Edward you live in Clayton Avenue, yes?'

'Of course.'

'What number do you live at?'

Eddie thinks hard once again. Then he grins as if he's been caught out in a childish game. 'I don't know.'

The doctor points at Micky. 'What's Michael's middle name?'

Eddie feels the walls inch a little closer to him. Feels himself lowered a little further down into the pit. This one is a trick question, he can feel it.

'I dunno. He'll tell you.'

Micky feels his strength begin to drain from him. He looks at his shoes.

'This area where we live, Edward. What's it called?'

'England. London!'

'Yes, sir, but where in London?'

Eddie thinks hard again but doesn't even reply. The doctor scribbles a note.

'What size shoes do you take, Edward?'

And that's all it takes. A couple of simple questions. Not only do the doctor and Micky know what has just happened means but, as he feels himself lowered just that little bit lower, Eddie Targett does too.

Then the doctor does that thing, that thoughtless, dismissive thing. He talks to Micky as if Eddie isn't there.

'Touch of Dementia then. There's a clinic where you'll need to take your father from here on in. I'll make an appointment for you and they'll contact you. Good luck. In the meantime I'm writing a prescription for Aricept. It may help to slow it down, but that's all it will do.'

Another unpleasant development comes his way when he returns from his weekly shopping run. He'd left Eddie in the garden and was gone less than an hour. Upon his return he struggles to pull into the drive on account of the massive, badly parked Mercedes outside the bungalow.

He lets himself in and hears voices coming from the lounge. Not unusual. Eddie sometimes has golfing mates or neighbours popping around. Micky hears a male laugh, a big, luxurious laugh. He doesn't recognise it but smiles. His dad is on form.

'Here he is,' Eddie declares.

Micky looks to the sofa across from his dad's usual chair. He meets eyes with the man but doesn't know him. Maybe forty. Big fella.

'Your mate's here,' Eddie tells him as he raises himself from his seat.

Micky sees the four cans of Stella and two glasses on the coffee table.

'I'm just off for a leak. Back in a sec'.'

Eddie walks past Micky and Micky approaches the man, stands before him and he can see, even though he remains seated, he is colossal. Muscled, tanned, good-looking. He smiles the smile of someone who is used to being assessed in precisely that way. With admiration and with fear. Silence dominates the moment until Micky speaks.

'I don't think we've met.'

221

Then the man stands up and, again it's something he's done before in the way that he does it now. He knows the effect it has because he just *keeps standing up*. Slowly and deliberately he draws himself up to his natural six-five. Towers over Micky.

'Micky, right?'

'Yeah.' He's not sure whether to shake hands, hand over his wallet or run.

'Been hearing a lot about you.'

Micky's been in a few spots before, been under the cosh but never in his dad's house and that infuriates him. But what can he do?

'Thought I'd come over and say hello in person.' He reaches into his inside jacket pocket and pulls out the plastic covered square of pink paper. 'Give you this back.'

And Micky gets it. He's being checked out by the third man. Or rather they're gathering information on him. Make sure the license is real. See what the address is like. See if there is anyone at that address they could hurt, should the need arise.

'You're the five hundred a week man who pays cash up front.'

Micky accepts his license as it is passed over.

'That's very impressive.'

'What's your name?'

'The man shakes his head. 'That doesn't matter. What matters is we know *your* name, who you are and where you are. Nice old guy, your pop.'

Micky wants to be sick, thinks *yeah, you prick, and a few years ago he'd deck you before you saw it coming.* But he's in now. He feels a finger prod into his shoulder, a finger that looks like a forearm.

'Keep it up, Mr. T. Good work like this deserves its reward. You're on your way to being part of the family.'

A wave of revulsion sweeps over him. He feels like calling Connie right now. Feels like getting in touch with Georgie. Get these scumbags out of his life before they get too far into it.

'It's just business.' Micky shrugs.

'Yeah it is but we all got to get along. I understand John's given you a target. Ooh, *target.* See what I did there?'

Wow, Micky thinks, *you made a pun out of my name. How clever are you?* He sees the smug grin. The gleaming veneers against the fake tan. Is that make-up?

'Let's get you through that and then we'll hang out. Get a buzz on maybe. See what makes Micky Targett tick.'

They both hear the toilet flush.

'Better be going. See you soon.'

Micky follows him out to the hall, sees his back flex as he walks, sees his deltoids and lats congest and then sweep out. Bloke looks like he's got wings, Looks like a sodding Manta Ray. They meet Eddie in the hall.

'Eddie, my friend I am way behind schedule. Got to run. It was lovely meeting you.'

They pump hands and Eddie loves it. Loves the sheer physicality of the man. This is someone he could swap the old-school, on the cobbles type stories with.

'See you, son. Call round anytime.'

'You're a gent. And you've got a good boy here too. Look after him.'

'He's ugly enough to look after himself.'

The man throws his head back and laughs. Laughs all the way across the front drive to the big fat Mercedes. Micky and Eddie watch him go.

'Nice man,' observes Eddie. 'Can't you get a job with him?'

'He's a lump, ain't he?' Micky observes.

'Never forget, boy, the bigger they are . . .'

'The more it hurts when they hit you.'

As the summer of ninety-four becomes the autumn and the Great British public gets so pissed off with Wet Wet Wet assuring them that love is all around, they finally feel compelled to swap that soppy horseshit for slightly different horseshit called Saturday Night by Whigfield, Micky Targett begins to feel the press of a number of irritations.

Firstly, even though he discovered where the dope growers live and has passed this information on to the boys in blue, nothing has been done. This is because the only one of them the police are interested in nicking is the old guy. His name is Barry Pye. And they can't find him.

'He's the only one you want? Why?'

'We wouldn't get a conviction against the others. The CPS wouldn't even look at it.' DS Pitts tells him over the phone when he finally deigns to pick it up.

'So have you looked for him?'

'Yes.'

Micky thinks he might have lost the line.

'Hello?'

'Yeah?'

'Is that it? So he's hiding behind the sofa when your boys go round there and that's it?'

'Mr. Targett you must understand this is not a priority for us. I know that's not what you want to hear but we are understaffed and overworked.'

'My father's house got wrecked because of these scumbags and . . .'

'Look, I know you're angry but there's really not a lot we can do. This man is on our list. He'll show up.'

Micky puts the phone down, looks at it and says, 'Fuck you twat.'

DS Pitts puts the phone down, looks at it and says, 'Fuck you twat.'

Another thing twisting a knife in Micky's guts is this ugly, fat witch called Carly Bromley. She actually answers her summons and turns up for the day in court, that convinced is she that she's done nothing wrong.

'She's going to flop the company down, mate,' Micky tells Ben as they walk up the steps to Romford magistrates court. 'She's like my brother, she's never wrong. Proper sociopath.'

'Costs a lot of money and agro to do that. We'll win today, she'll be ordered to pay my costs for the day and then we'll have a deal. We'll smack her arse for her.'

'That's a scenario I don't wish to visualise.'

In court Micky is gratified to see Ben Yardley recognise and greet the magistrate who is to deal with their case. Not that they need any help. Ben lays out what has happened and then the skank of the year is asked to repost.

'I don't even know why I'm 'ere. Can someone tell me why I'm 'ere?'

'Your company may have been negligent in this matter, Ms. Bromley,' the magistrate,   mid-forties and smoother than silk informs her. 'I believe Mr. Targett is expecting to see the references you took for his tenants. I wouldn't mind that either.'

'I told 'im. They're wiv those insurers.'

She screeches like some horridly put upon harridan for as long as the bloke is prepared to let her, which isn't very long. He addresses Ben.

'Day costs?'

Ben looks at his Breitling, shrugs. 'Time away from the office, four hours. Travel. Say eight-eighty. Call it eight hundred if that helps.'

The guy looks across at Carly Bromley. 'Okay, Ms. Bromley?'

'Wot?'

'I am finding in favour of the plaintiff. His solicitor's costs are eighty hundred pounds.'

'What's that got to do with me?'

Micky grins massively as the guy rolls his eyes, sighs weightily. 'Because I'm ordering you to pay them.'

Momentarily stunned she scatter guns the room with panicked looks. The magistrate addresses Ben with technical jargon and they begin to converse professionally. Realising her day has significantly and irreversibly darkened, Carly Bromley grabs her bag, walks and slams the heavy oak on the way out. Outside Micky is chuffed. Either way he's not too fussed about money as Ben is on a no-win no-fee and straightening out the house really did cost very little. He just wants to squeeze this old slapper.

'I'll tell her what we want. Can you get some bills together for say, three grand if we need them?'

'Sure.'

'Okay let's go for that. If she doesn't pay we'll send the Sheriffs round.'

'Jesus. Does that really happen?'

'Sure does. Anyway, don't worry about that. You won.'

But they didn't celebrate. This was because Carly Bromley did what Micky knew she was going to do, she folded Bromley Estates Management Ltd and on the same day began trading as Bromley Estates Property Managers Ltd. Nor did she pay Micky's costs or Ben

Yardley's fees. The Sheriffs went to her office, embarrassed the crap out of all the staff for an hour but came away empty handed because what she was doing was perfectly legal and she had all the relevant paperwork lined up to prove it.

*

Micky bought the three lots of five hundred Question Marks in three weeks and, as promised, gets his discount. Down to five quid a pop. This, apparently, warrants a celebration. His invitation to 'let his hair down' feels more like a summons. The VIP room of Dukes nightclub in Chelmsford. Money is good by this time so he doesn't mind cabbing it up there.

He doesn't drink or take any drugs beforehand and doesn't take anything with him.

From the get-go the night is a mess. He approaches the huge black bouncer and tells him his name and he's on the VIP list. The bouncer tells him there isn't a VIP list. The conversation doesn't last long and Micky is standing around in the street feeling like a total plum. Then it starts raining. He calls the only number he has, John the sullen manager of Raquels but gets no answer. He spots a pub over the road, gets out of the rain with a beer.

While he's in there Jason the dealer together with the younger of the three amigos walk in. They are both wrecked on something yet they both recognise Micky straight away. He isn't sure this is a good thing.

'The fuck you doing in here?' This is the massive man, Cory.

Micky sighs. How the fuck has this happened to him? 'They won't let me in.'

The two swap glances and both crack up. Exaggerated, false laughs. Micky has no option but to listen to it.

'Who won't let you in, Mary? Those big, bad men in monkey suits?'

Micky shrugs gormlessly. 'Bloke says there's no VIP list.'

'Of course there's no list. We *are* the VIPs,' Cory tells him, holding his massive arms out wide. 'Jesus. Go back and tell the twats you're with me, Tommy and Pete. But keep your voice down. The three of us don't get in the same place at the same time. Not with anyone knowing. Fuck sake, boy, you need to sharpen up.'

Micky doesn't even finish his drink. Outside he thinks of just jumping a cab and getting out of the place, but knows he can't. He goes back, gets in and gets shown upstairs, through a door, down a corridor and then through another door. It's empty but quite cool. Space for maybe twenty people, waitress service and you're looking down on all the plebs on the dance floor. He orders a Becks. It's just gone ten and he wishes he was in bed.

He thinks about his dad. The day before he came out of the bathroom and walked into the kitchen. Three of the gas rings on the hob were blazing at full tilt. His dad was in the lounge eating a carrot.

They'd gone over to the NHS mental health centre in Harold Hill near Romford, but there was nothing there for them. Just advice and not much of that. Micky was told that perhaps it was time one or two carers would be useful in looking after Eddie, but just when he was thinking the old sod was beyond understanding anything he was on that like a shot.

'There's nobody coming in *my* fucking house. There's nothing wrong with me!'

The man smiled sympathetically at Micky. 'One other thing, your father, now diagnosed, is no longer legally qualified to drive. Best of luck.'

So Micky decides he has no choice but to fly solo and do the looking after himself. To this end *he* registers as Eddie's carer. For this he is rewarded with the princely sum of thirty-one pounds per week. He also takes the step of applying for power of attorney over Eddie's affairs. By October ninety-four things are still just about manageable but he knows it will get worse. He knows Eddie will be helpless soon, will live forever and it will all be on Micky.

A switch goes in his head and he decides he needs to get totalled. He orders another Becks and a large gin and tonic and curses himself for not loading up with gear on the way out. He tries to think of his life's positives but when he does the only thing he can come up with is the drug sales which, he has to admit, are going well.

When he first started taking the parcels of five hundred Georgie Harper arranged for one of his boys to meet up with Micky to collect what he hadn't sold and to weigh him out for the difference. The bloke gave his name as Wrenny. Late-thirties and totally solid looking. Very quiet, clearly not a party boy and with an air of toughness and complete reliability. A pleasure to meet and to deal with. A younger, better-looking version of Georgie.

The rest Micky had sold to Chrissie Jarvis, Ishy and Ben, Ben's friends plus a couple of others. In total he was shifting maybe a hundred a week plus less than half an ounce of coke. Total cleared was around two-fifty to three hundred quid. Soon though, things gathered speed. Chrissie was always shouting for pills but the main man was . . . Would there ever be any doubt?

Ishy was a natural drug dealer. Man was born for it. Sure he was working in the City in nineteen ninety-four, (heavy snow in London) but that shit still needed to be sold. Soon enough Micky was shifting two ounces of coke and the whole five hundred pills. His end was always well over a grand a week.

So everyone is smiling. Chrissie Jarvis is Micky's new best friend.

'Here's one for you; cocaine dealers eh? Always sticking their business in other people's noses. Hahahahaha.'

But the best part was not needing to bother Connie to subsidise him. That was as important as anything.

The door to the VIP room flies open and Cory, Jason and three girls stagger in. They are horribly loud.

'Oi, there's Mary. Get in alright this time, you nonce?' This is Jason the club dealer. Micky's never been a fighter. Why bother? But if this twat didn't have that gorilla standing behind him they'd soon be finding out who's a nonce.

They order a raft of drinks from the already harassed-looking waitress and settle in the seats against the wall behind Micky. Immediately after, the door swings open again and Tommy and Pete squeeze in.

'Here we go.' Cory calls out. 'You two benders been out in the carpark together?'

Jason forces out more laughter than he clearly isn't feeling. Big Pete smiles, holds up a massive finger and points to the door which opens a few seconds after it has closed. A gaggle of short-skirted females, tripping and giggling pour into the room, along with two or three hefty-looking men.

The room is suddenly full, but of the two dozen people in there Micky only knows four. All of whom he thoroughly detests, and, on first sight, he's not fussed about meeting the others.

'If there are any benders in this place then I'm looking at him.' Pete counters. More laughs from Jason. Everyone's favourite pet audience.

Pete walks centre stage and is so big the room shrinks accordingly. When he moves the walls move around him. He spots Micky. Approaches.

''Ello, son. Glad you could come.' He offers his hand into which Micky's disappears completely. It comes as no surprise that Pete makes an extra special effort to break as many bones as he can. Micky squeezes back, tries not to let it show.

'You got a drink?'

'On the way.'

'Good. In the meantime you're on line duty.'

From his inside jacket pocket he produces a bag of white powder that must go five ounces, hands it to Micky. He points to the table.

'Here'll do.' Then he moves away.

Micky gets at it and makes sure he's his first customer. Something not quite right about the Charlie though. Very rough on the schnozz. Typical of these arseholes that they bring sub-standard gear to their own party.

For the first half an hour he's kept pretty busy but then as the girls start to get a bit wayward there's less of a queue at his table and he can get up, move around and have a look-see.

The music is standard crap club stuff. The kind of diluted rubbish to be found in the charts. There was even a bit of Kylie, bit of Madonna. Then it turns a little harder and Micky gets up and gives it some mild shuffles.

Swamp Thing by The Grid, that one with the mad banjo. Then it was Eighteen Strings by Tinman, with the Nirvana riff. Yeah, not bad actually, Micky thinks as he stretches out and gets his groove on.

Then he's dancing with one of the girls and even though she doesn't say a word, despite him trying to get a conversation going, and even though she has her eyes closed all the time, Micky starts to feel *unfeasibly* good. It's a weird buzz but he puts that down to his somewhat foreign environment. He checks her out and it's the usual Essex thing; high, silver sling-backs, tight, black, stretchy mini-dress which is way low at the top and equally high at the bottom. Grazes on both her knees. She is fit in an emaciated kind of way. Drugs and dancing, Micky reckons, better than any Jane Fonda workout.

Figuring the girl is going nowhere Micky is feeling well enough to kick-start a conversation with the bosses. The younger one and the one with the mad hair he first met in the khazi at Raquels, are knee deep in girls themselves. This only leaves big Pete. His massive frame occupies a significant portion of the long bench seats and he is in sporadic conversation with one of the other men. Micky heads over and flops down on the other side of the man mountain. Catches part of the conversation.

The other guy is struggling to find the words. 'Gotta pay yer d . . . d, d. He's . . . Y'know. Jeezus. Yer debts, Pete. Fuck . . . Err, what we supposed . . . Y'know? To do!'

Big Pete considers this. Micky can't fathom what kind of response might be coming but feels high enough to give it time.

'You telling . . . You telling me what . . . Me, what to do? Innit!'

Well, ponders Micky, it's not exactly the kind of cerebral exchange of views likely to be reported in the Sunday Times cultural section but hey, these are quite extreme circumstances. He himself feels the warm glow of camaraderie and is quite looking forward to a conversation but he has to admit he's not too sure what kind of sense he might make.

'How's it going, Pete?'

It takes a while, many seconds before the big man responds. Then he turns slowly and his moist eyes fall upon Micky. Then for several more seconds a look of bored confusion infests his walloping great features. Micky fears he has no idea who he is. Which, for a short while, is actually true.

'Bang on target!' He eventually shouts.

Micky thinks it's genuinely hilarious. He creases with laughter, claps his hands together, the whole number. An arm the size of an adult Anaconda makes its way across the wall and around Micky's shoulders. He gets an appropriately constricting squeeze.

'There's my man. Oi Andy!' He calls to the bloke he was just talking to.

Andy squints through the gloom and the smoke and the noise and the drugs.

'You met Micky?'

They're waiting for Andy to respond. Even Andy is waiting for Andy to respond. He doesn't seem to understand it's is turn to speak.

'Well you're not going to. Fuck off.'

Andy stays where he is because now he doesn't understand it's his turn to fuck off. So Micky has Pete's undivided attention, such as it is or ever likely to be.

'Having a good time, son?'

'Yeah. Yeah all good, Pete. Cheers for the invite. One thing . . .'

Micky feels the crush as Pete leans into him.

'That coke is blinding. Maybe I could move some of that.'

Micky feels the rocking, the mighty undulations of Pete's body as he laughs deeply and, quite weirdly, without sound.

'See this is one of the reasons I know me and you are going to get on. Deep down you're an innocent and there ain't enough innocence left in this world, son. That's what I say.'

Micky bobs his head but hasn't a clue what's just been said.

'That's not coke. Well, it's *some* coke but there's mdma and ketamine in there as well. My own special mix. Good innit?'

After a few seconds Micky can begin to appreciate why Andy was having such trouble trying to say or do anything, because now it's Micky's turn to not be able to say or do anything. He can't believe what he's just heard yet it's the most believable thing he's heard in a while. There's only one thing he can do under such circumstances. He slaps Pete on the thigh, hauls himself into a vaguely upright position and heads back over to dance with the fucked up, skinny, girl.

And he has a great time because now he understands what she's feeling and he can get into it with her. Up until that night he'd never done ketamine before but becomes an instant convert. He has his hands on her waist and she's moving to the beat and it's hot and sexy and she is soooooooo fit. Through the fabric of her dress he can feel each individual muscle and sinew twitch and turn. But then her waist, hips, torso all begin to move fluidly. He can feel it. He can feel her turning into liquid in his grasp. But how? How is all this possible?

He's trying to work it all out at the same time as wondering if this is the best night of his life. He can hear colours. He can see music. He can speak braille.

Still the girl is in his arms, and still she hasn't said a word, still hasn't even looked at him. He's facing into the room with the bannister to his right. If he looked further across, an effort he is certainly not about to make, he could peer over the edge, down onto the dance floor.

Away to his left, on the bench seats he notices Pete haul his massive frame off the seat. The room shrinks. Then Micky thinks he sees something, dismisses it as too weird because he is now seriously off his face. But then no, there it is, Pete has just picked up the bloke he was sitting next to. Andy? Anyway, it's someone, and Pete has this grown adult male in his arms like he's a fucking baby. Micky watches this and is in no way alarmed. Because he knows it can't be happening. Except. . .

Then in three massive strides Pete and his wriggling armful are at the edge of the room, up against the bannister. And Micky watches with intrigued detachment as Pete empties his arms of his burden. The man is gone.

Micky looks around to see if anyone else has noticed what just happened. No one seems to be upset, shocked or disturbed in any way. So Micky lets it go, knows he's messed up. In fact maybe another line of that shit . . .

Then he sees the one with the mad hair get real close to Pete. Like, he's in his face. Micky thinks, Jesus, if those two bastards start going at it! Then he notices one of the girls over by the door with her hand across her mouth. He sees her eyes, staring, frozen.

Micky decides to play a hunch. It's all bollocks he knows, but just to dispel this moment of confusion he's going to check it out down below. He empties his arms of the dancing girl, not that she notices, and leans slightly out over the bannister. There he sees a circle of shapes. Squinting through the smoke and the dry ice, he makes out that those shapes are people and they are all gathered around and facing in towards a central point. And that point is Andy.

Micky struggles to remember how he got home. He must have bundled out of the room, out of the club and found a cab. He can't remember anything, apart from Pete dumping a human being from his grasp like it was a refuse sack. That and the crowd encircling the stricken man, like the petals of a flower.

*

232

Deeply affected by both what he saw and by that in which he is inextricably embroiled, Micky adopts a robotic kind of existence. Through the winter and into the next year he takes care of his dad and he takes care of business and that is it. His doctor still prescribes Tramadol but, Micky figures, the bloke must know it's no longer for the pain in his knee.

Desperate to bring some levity into his life, he chops in the Scirocco for a cream Jag XJS. Chrissie Jarvis was smiling even more than usual. Micky didn't even check the prices.

The papers, national as well as local, are regularly featuring stories of gangland violence in Essex. Micky knows who is involved in most of this because he works for them. Big Pete was never investigated for what he did to Andy that night at Dukes. If he'd died then maybe he would have been. As it was he got away with a broken leg, pelvis and concussion. It was called an accident. Essex man in 'Pissed idiot falls off balcony' shocker.

In the summer of ninety-five as Blur and Oasis pretend they are like The Beatles and The Stones vying for the nation's affections, Connie Chetkins gets in touch.

'Need to step this up, son. Thousand a week.'

'Wow. Er, okay.'

'Same as before. Anything you can't move I'll have off you.'

The deal is duly done but Micky is refused the price cut he asks for. Cheapskate, maniac bastards.

Then, at the beginning of November, as Coolio's Gansgta's Paradise takes the charts, things escalate.

'Tell them you want ten thousand in one go. You'll have a mate with you. Wrenny. If that goes well you'll need more. A lot more.'

'Connie how long is this going on for?'

'Stay with it, son. You're playing a blinder.'

That's it, Micky thinks as he puts the phone down. It's all playing. It's all a fucking game.

And the deal goes down, except now Micky is the golden boy and he has all three of those lunatics all over him. Which, he figures is kind of the plan. And then it's fifty thousand. Fifty thousand fucking pills.

'Tell them that Wrenny doesn't want to go to the club anymore. Out in the open. Somewhere quiet where everyone can take their time

233

counting.'

Micky officially shits himself. He is terrified they'll smell the rat that he is. Astonishingly they go for it.

'It's a good idea, son,' big Pete tells him, as all four of them cram into the office at Raquels. 'We don't want that kind of quantity coming anywhere near where we're known. We know a place. Out near a farm not far from here. Just you and your pal again, yeah?'

'Yeah, and can it be just you blokes? Not John, no one else. We're making a fortune here but I only trust you three.'

'Aw ain't he sweet?'

So Micky finds himself in a car down a remote track on an Essex farm in the last week of November nineteen ninety-five. It is a gin clear night and punishingly cold. He is with Wrenny who is so rock solid and calm Micky wonders if he feels anything. He doesn't even look like he's breathing. Bang on time a dark-coloured Range Rover inches down the track towards them. Three men get out, two of them are carrying bags. The two with the bags get into Wrenny's BMW so that Wrenny can go through the pills. Micky gets into the Range Rover so that Big Pete can count the money that Micky is holding.

It all goes down without a hitch. Then. . .

'Two hundred thousand pills,' Connie tells Micky.

Micky is dizzied. 'Fuck's sake, Con.'

'It's the last one. Offer them a quid a pop but take whatever they come back with.'

'This needs to be the end of it.'

'It already is, boy. Just set it up. You don't need to be there. Wipe that phone and then break it into a hundred pieces and then lose those. And get yourself a solid alibi for Friday night.'

CHAPTER THIRTEEN

Is it worth the aggravation to find yourself a job when there's nothing worth working for?

DS Ray Pitts is reading the fax that has just landed on his desk. It is from someone he knows well. He did his detective training with Roland Carter, now a DS himself at Chelmsford nick. He knows Roland is going through it out in Essex. The ongoing scene of drugs and violence was one thing but the recent murder of three underworld figures and the savagery of those killings have shocked the entire country.

Everyone wants answers and Roland is right in the middle of it, out there in bandit country. Havering is London's most easterly borough and is therefore Met., but it's all hands on deck for this. Operation Century is underway and results are expected. The fucking Home Secretary has been on the phone.

'Ray, looking for all the help I can get. It's gone nuts out here. I've got some good obbo shots of a couple of clubs and other places. Been a lot of comings and goings and I need to put some names to a few faces. I'm biking a bunch of photos over. I know you never forget a face. Cheers. Ro.'

Later that day Ray Pitts is thumbing through those images taken of the entrance to various pubs and clubs in Chelmsford, Basildon, Colchester and Tilbury, along with a couple of targeted private addresses. Of the faces captured by the lenses he knows a couple by reputation, the rest mean nothing to him. Except one. He spots Micky

Targett going into Raquels. Never forget a face.

ESSEX - MARCH 1996

One day, three months after what become known as the Rettendon murders, Micky Targett is sitting in the Essex Yeoman looking into his beer. On top of everything else he finds himself depressed by the recent massacre of sixteen kids in a school in Scotland.

There is no one else in the pub. This is because it is eleven in the morning and the place has just opened. He's into the habit lately. Gets him out of the house.

He enjoys the peace and quiet at that time of day. Then the barmaid turns the radio on. Walkway by Cast. 'Walkaway – Walkawaaaay' the bloke sings.

Yeah, that would be nice, Micky thinks. Just walk away from it all. What could be easier? He's still got some cash, sell the Jag. But he can't. He has responsibilities.

He sits in his usual seat. He always sits these days. The old lot don't go in there much, not during the day anyway, and everyone else knows to give him a wide berth because he's starting to look like one of those nutters in a pub it's wise not to talk to.

He's halfway through his first pint when his phone rings. He checks the screen and is more than a little alarmed to see the word PLOD stare menacingly back. He hesitates to answer, what with everything that's happened since last December, but he knows that unless he does something mad like skip the country, there is no getting away from it.

'Hello.'

'Mr. Targett? Detective Sargeant Pitts. Are you able to talk?'

'Yeah, why not? But nothing's changed. I still can't help you with any of that.'

'That's okay. It's not 'that' I'm calling about.'

Oh yeah? What else might the police want to talk to him about other than three Essex gangsters with their heads shot off in a Range Rover parked down a lonely track in the middle of Essex?

'Barry Pye.'

Micky knows the name. Or does he?

'You might have to help me with that?'

'Last year. Someone was growing dope in your house.'

'Jesus Christ. Yeah, sure. What's up?'

'We have him.'

'No way.'

'We found him just as we'll find the Rettendon killers. Sometimes these things take time.'

'Right. So, what's the move?'

'Sadly there is no move. I believe it was him alright. He went 'no comment' to every question. He was subsequently released on police bail pending a couple of things. Then we contacted the evidence facility to check the sample plants we retrieved from your house.'

Micky gets a horrible swell of nausea in his guts.

'Unfortunately they were not stored correctly.'

''Scuse me?'

'Whoever received them was obviously supposed to use an air tight container, but the plants were simply stored in a cardboard box. They have degraded to the point where they are no longer viable as cannabis plants, evidentially speaking.'

'Please tell me you're joking.'

'When I'm dealing with crime, Mr. Targett, I never joke. Without proper evidence Mr. Pye will not be charged. I apologise on behalf of the Metropolitn Police Force.'

Fuck. My. Old. Boots.

Micky can't help but sense the glee in the bloke's voice, but that's not the thing. What really winds him up is that old scumball getting away with it. He thinks about what was done to his parent's lovely house. His mother's house. Can't let that go.

Micky has no doubts that Pye's been busted for something else, traffic offence maybe, and that his name has been flagged up and he got nicked that way. He also has no doubts that the bloke, dumb, useless and in the wrong business, may will be back living at his original address. Which Micky still remembers.

As he seethes and rails against the injustice of that bullshit, he becomes aware of a figure standing next to his table. He looks up to see a big man staring down at him. The man is strong and still, shows no emotion.

'Come outside, son.'

They walk around the corner to the car park where Wrenny points to a black Alfa Romeo. Micky gets in the back next to Georgie Harper.

'Hello, boy. How you holding up?'

'Well, George I've been better you know?'

'You'll be fine. Had to be done. You know that don't you?'

'No, George I don't know that. I don't know anything about it, as per fucking usual.'

'Listen . . .'

'Why didn't anyone tell me?'

'Because we didn't know. Not until near the end when it was too late.'

'What does that mean?'

'We gave them the chance. It was all going okay. We're fronting them the pills, the Question Marks. Everyone's happy, everyone's making a few quid. But they get greedy. Not paying their bills. Not paying their debts.'

Micky is jolted into memory. Something he heard once - Pay yer debts.

'They were given warning. You weren't the only one. The bloke that animal fucked up? Andy? The one who took a flyer at the club?'

That was it! Micky thinks. 'What about him?'

'He was one of us.' He stares across at Micky. 'Look at me.'

Micky looks.

'He was doing what you were doing but he was looking out for you. Look where it got him. He's an old mate of Wrenny's. That could've been you.'

'Ah Jeeezus,' Micky says.

'And at the end there, when we stepped it up . . . they were going to kill us. That could've been you too. Had we not seen it coming that was you and Wrenny dead and not them.'

'You don't know that.'

'Yes I do. There are two main armourers in Essex and I know both of them. One of them was approached by those morons. They were gearing up to come against us and *that*, Micky boy, is a bell that you can't unring.'

Micky sits in stunned silence. Once again he thought he knew everything but now understands the opposite was true.

'And we were right. No pills in their bags that night. Just guns. We tried but that lot were too wild. I guess when the only tool you have is a hammer then you look at every situation as if it's a nail.'

Micky sighs, looks out of the window at real people living in the real world. How did he get so far away from normality? Again.

'But it's done now. Now things will run smoothly and you're in a chair down the front.'

'You what?'

'You got a clear run at this, son.'

'Are you kidding? I've got Plod all over me as it is. I was the idiot out in the open.'

'And?'

'And? Jesus, Georgie the whole fucking country is talking about this. Okay so they were scum, but three murders in one night! The Old Bill won't stop until this is wrapped up.'

'It'll be fine. At some point in the future two men will be nicked for this. Steps are already being taken.'

'Yeah and I'm taking steps as well, away from you lot.'

'Don't be silly, son. Connie is grateful. We hold Essex. This is going to be big and you are on the inside.'

Micky thinks he's going to be sick. He opens the door. Breathes.

'No George. I'm not on the inside. I'm out and I'm done. Leave me alone.'

Micky gets out of the car and walks back into the pub where he finishes his beer and six others after that. Then he walks down the hill back to the house to look after his dad. As he walks he asks himself if he is any better than the dross he's been dealing with.

Back at the bungalow Micky goes into the lounge to check on Eddie who is dozing peacefully in his chair. He looks at the photo nearby. The two of them young and full of hope. He knows his move.

So for the next four nights he finds himself parked up outside Barry Pye's house, his guts twisting into knots as he asks himself precisely what it is he thinks he's going to do.

On the fourth night he finds out. Because there he is, on his own and it's dark.

He thinks back to what his dad always told him. Don't wait to get hit, retaliate first.

So he leans into the back seat, grabs the crash helmet he thought it prudent to bring along, and walks quietly across the road. He's ten yards behind when he pulls the helmet on, five yards behind when the bloke hears him and turns, and three yards away when he launches himself into the air to heave his head downwards, smashing the helmet into the old fucker's face. Micky sees his eyes roll back into his head and knows the bloke is sparko before he hits the pavement. He gets himself gone.

He knows it is inevitable he will get a call and he knows who will make that call. This copper, this Pitts, has it in for Micky, it's obvious. The reason why is equally clear. In fact the *multiple* reasons why Pitts fancies Micky for something, *anything*, he can pin on him are clear. PC was Pitts's man, Micky can see that now and PC got busted selling coke on the *same evening* Micky himself was due to be nicked. Pitts may not understand exactly how that happened but Micky knows it's not something he's going to let go.

Then there was the dope farm. Sure, Barry Pye was a safe nick until the cock up with the evidence, but Pitts can't help thinking Micky was in on the grow somehow.

And now, just a few nights after telling Micky that, having found the bloke, he won't be prosecuted, he winds up lights out in the street with his face rearranged.

But all that is just fluff compared to Micky's involvement with the murder of three men. At least he wasn't arrested. At least his dad didn't know. It was just a phone call. Pitts belled Micky and invited him to Romford nick for a chat. Back in the previous December of ninety-five just before Christmas. How could he refuse?

So Micky is there at the same desk in the same office talking to the same man. He thinks of saying 'people are gonna talk' but decides not to.

In front of him are two photographs. One clearly shows Micky entering Raquels. It's a summer evening and the telephoto has done its job. The second is not of similar quality.

'This one was taken from the CCTV footage filmed in the foyer of Duke's nightclub a few months ago,' Pitts explains. 'You don't look happy, Micky. You look like you're in a hurry to get out of there.'

'You ever been?'

'No.'

'Well if you do go, you won't want to hang around either.'

'Who were you there with?'

'I went there on my own.'

'You went there on your own?'

'Yeah.'

'And Raquels?'

'Same.'

'You always go out on your own?'

'Usually.'

'You cut out of there at exactly eleven forty-seven that night.'

'Bed time for me.'

'There was an incident around about that time.'

'I remember it.'

'Oh yeah?'

'Yeah. Some berk fell off the balcony.'

'The *VIP* room balcony.'

Shit, thinks Micky. *Getting close.*

'Whatevs.'

'Where did you spend your time that evening?'

Fuck! 'Dancing.'

'Downstairs?'

Micky answers without hesitation because he knows he has no choice. 'Yeah.'

'You weren't upstairs at all that night?'

No names. No lists. Safe. 'VIP room? Me?'

'How many times have you been to Dukes?'

'Just that once.'

Pitts clocks him. *Christ I need to nail you you piece of shit*, he thinks.

'And Raquels?'

'I go there a lot. Well, I used to go there a lot.'

'But you don't go there now?'

'Not for a while.'

'Why not?'

They both know the answer to this one, how best to say it?

'We all know what's going on around here. In Essex.'

'What's going on?'

He says it because he knows he has to. 'Those three blokes.'

'What about them?'

'You seen that film Tombstone? It's a bit like that around here isn't it? Besides I'm getting a little past it.'

'Did you know any of those men, Micky?'

'No.'

'Because they were known to operate out of Raquels.'

'I never met them.'

'And that bloke who came over the balcony, word is he had a bit of help.'

Micky says nothing.

'In fact the word is the bloke who helped him on his way was one of the blokes dead in a Range Rover in an Essex field.'

'Detective I'd really like to help you but . . .'

'You didn't see anything.'

'I'm afraid not.'

'Where were you on the night of Friday December 6th into the early hours of the following Saturday? Couple of weeks ago.'

Micky's got it all down. Connie made sure of that.

'The last few Fridays I've been going to Upminster golf club with my dad. Two weeks ago on a Friday I was definitely there.'

'You sure about that?'

'Yes.'

'Plenty of people saw you there I guess.'

Micky gets the inference, doesn't like it. 'I guess.'

'What time were you there until?'

'About eleven. My dad is not too well. I'm his carer.'

'And after that?'

'Back to the house.'

'You and your father?'

'Yeah.'

'And you stayed there all night?'

'Early to bed these days.'

Pitts makes a few more scribbled notes then lays down the yellow Bik. He stares at Micky and takes his time doing it.

'Thing is, mate, there is a lot and I mean a *lot* that seems to happen around you. But you're never involved.'

'There's not much I can tell you about that either. I should get going if that's it. I don't like to be away from my dad for too long.'

242

You dirtbag, piece of shit, thinks Ray Pitts.

Close but no cigar, thinks Micky Targett.

He wasn't joking about the early to bed thing. Not only does he take to his bed early but he stays in it as long as he can. That's usually until his dad, now having forgotten that his own son actually lives in the house with him, walks into his bedroom every day. Neither of them is sure why he does this but even though Micky asks him not to do it, Eddie always forgets by the time the next morning comes around.

Micky wakes feeling warm and safe. The night before was fantastic. Out for drinks with friends, then they all dropped a pill and went to a club. Lisa was there, how about that? All forgiven in an instant and then they were all over each other to the point where they couldn't stand it any longer. They cut out early and cabbed it back to Micky's loft place in Metropolitan Wharf where they had *crazy* sex until the sun was coming up. Christ knows what time it is now. He edges over to her and lays his arm around her waist.

'Mmmmmmm.' He hears her purr.

Most mornings he is somewhere like that. Sometimes it's back in Mallorca, sometimes with Julie or Sandra, sometimes out on the razz with Romanov.

The moment as he is surfacing from sleep plus the one or two hazy seconds after he actually wakes are always luscious, meaningful and happy. Then the shit descends.

The day after Micky lays out Barry Pye it happens again. Eddie walks in, edges his way around the bed to open the curtains. Micky says hello, Eddie is delighted to see him, shakes his hands. And around we go.

And that day Micky makes an executive decision. He doesn't regret the assault of the previous evening but he knows that he is now an even larger blip on Ray Pitts's radar than ever. He decides he needs to get away from law breaking completely.

In the kitchen, as Eddie splatters the walls with fat in his attempt to make bacon and eggs, he realizes he should have done it a while ago. He feels safer and better already. No. More. Drug. Dealing. None.

The previous December, when it happened and when he finally saw he'd been used to commit multiple murders, Micky couldn't see how he might continue. With any of it. Okay he kept buying the coke from Chrissie and moving that on because he needed the money, but he rejected every attempt Connie made to get in touch. Sandra even called him but he remained unmoved. Ishy was gutted.

'Ace it's rolling. We be making the big bucks now. We can't stop.'

'Sorry, mate. You'll be reading about it in the papers.'

And now, with the murder investigation grinding into ever higher gears, and with Barry Pye spectacularly laid out in the street, Micky knows he can take no more chances. He calls Chrissie Jarvis and Ishy (again) and all his Charlie customers, severing his one remaining connection to the game.

He thinks about the money he is giving up, knows how tough things will be without all that tax-free, but he sees he has no choice. It's not a moral issue, simply one of self-preservation. Micky Targett is finally, once and forever, out of the drugs business. He is thirty-six years old.

CHAPTER FOURTEEN

I'm the bitch you hated, filth infatuated, yeah
I'm the pain you tasted, well intoxicated

Lampang is a mountainous province in northern Thailand, east of Chiang Mai. It's an important centre for ceramics and is known for Buddhist temples dating back to the 13th century Lanna era. The province's capital, also called Lampang, features horse-drawn carriages available for use by fascinated tourists.

Thus the guide books describe the province and its capital. It is where Paithoon makes his home.

The weather is agreeable and the location perfect. Simple enough for him to travel to Chiang Rai and into Burma where he organizes the production of his drugs and the border crossings. Not only that but the city itself is an important transport hub, enjoying both train and road links to Bangkok and the south. It even has a small airport with daily flights to the capital.

In Lampang he built a magnificent home with wide lawns that roll down to the banks of the meandering river Wang.

Paithoon runs two versions of two different types of drugs, all of which come from Burma. Firstly there is methamphetamine and it's cheap derivative Yaba. Secondly there is the drug that made the Golden Triangle famous in the first place; opium. Along with that comes its refined finished product, heroin.

Paithoon can buy a kilo of dried opium gum from the farmers for the equivalent of one hundred and fifty pounds per kilo. He owns two labs in Burma that refine the opium into heroin, both near the border in Shan province. If one gets busted, production is maintained.

The logistics are straightforward. His main man on the Burmese side, Wunna, brings whatever is needed to the border rendezvous points. There he is met by any number of young Thai men or boys anxious to earn a few Baht. He currently uses a tough, local boy called Thanawat who has proved reliable for the last few months to the point where, should extra help be needed to carry larger loads, he organizes contacts of his own.

Once in Chiang Rai the goods are taken either directly to Bangkok or to Lampang. The couriers all use the Phahonyothin Road or to give its more user friendly name, Thailand Route 1. This is the longest road in Thailand running for over six hundred miles from the Burmese border all the way down to the Victory monument in Bangkok.

Those parcels staged in Lampang are then moved south either by individual couriers on the train, if the package is small enough, or most usually in cars and trucks to their final destinations, once again on Thailand Route 1. Paithoon is a silent partner in a fruit distribution company and it is occasionally expedient for him to move larger shipments in with the sugar cane, rice and pineapples the company normally transports.

Half of the Meth and Yaba goes to Bangkok and the other half goes to the rapidly expanding markets in Pattaya and Phuket. Most of the heroin and opium goes to Bangkok for export, usually by sea but occasionally by air.

In March of nineteen ninety-six Paithoon receives an order for twenty kilos of pure heroin. Thanawat collects it from Wunna and carries it across the border in a rucksack into Chiang Rai town. For this he is paid four thousand Baht, about seventy pounds.

Thanawat gives it to a man called Channarong. Channarong is a twenty-eight year old cab driver who makes a reasonable living driving tourists around but is always ready to supplement his income. He chucks the rucksack into the passenger footwell of his Nissan, gets onto Route 1 and drives the one hundred and forty miles to Lampang town. For this service he is paid fifteen thousand Baht, about three hundred pounds.

Channarong drives to the Sop Tui area of Lampang town where he parks in his usual spot outside the post office. He waits twenty minutes before he sees the squat, inelegant figure of Boon-Mee ambling towards him.

Boon-Mee gets in the passenger seat. He wants to talk because he has a while before his train, but Channarong is anxious to get going. If he's lucky he might be able to grab a fare back to Chiang Rai.

Boon-Mee buys a Krating Daeng at a 7/11 and shuffles to the station. He takes the slow train because that is his most economical option. It takes over twelve hours and will arrive in Bangkok early the next morning.

The old train lumbers noisily through the night and Boon-Mee doesn't get much sleep.

He walks out of Hua Lamphong station just before two in the morning. He buys another Krating Daeng from a chuck wagon in the street, downs it in one and walks to the nearby rank of motorcycle taxis. He'd prefer a real taxi but they cost more.

There are five guys on bike duty. Three of them are asleep, one is talking on his phone and the fifth is drinking directly from a bottle of Sangsom Thai rum. He puts down the bottle and stands when he sees Boon-Mee approach. Boon-Mee can see from his eyes that he is lit up on Yaba but he doesn't care. He'll get there a little quicker.

'*Bai yoo tee nai, mai?*' He asks.

'*Nana.*'

Notwithstanding the state of the guy's wrecked Suzuki, the engine rips into life on the first kick and Boon-Mee clambers on. There's nothing to hang onto and he knows the rider will go for it like a lunatic. He knows this because *all* Bangkok bike taxi riders go for it like lunatics. Especially when they're drunk and out of it on Yaba.

At the top of Ratchadamri the kid pauses at the massive junction with Sukhumvit Road. Not even he can jump those lights. On green he dumps the clutch and leans way over to aim the bike right, heading East past the Erawan Shrine. Even at two in the morning Sukhumvit Road is carnage and Boon-Mee feels no shame in hanging onto the nutter in front, but he knows it's not too far now. A few more junctions into the Khlong Toie district then the kid is over to the middle of the road to turn right into soi 4.

It's a walk from the junction but Boon-Mee has had enough. He pats the kid on the shoulder and points for him to pull over. As he's

Thai he is charged fifty Baht, about eighty pence. If he was foreign it would have been double.

As he walks down soi 4, soi Nana, he looks to his left to see the legendary three story 'Nana Entertainment Plaza' begin to empty out. Along with Patpong Road and Soi Cowboy, Nana is one of three major red-light district in the city. He sees two large *kathoeys* or ladyboys escorting a drunk *farang*. Does the guy know? Boon-Mee smiles. He loves the life. Better than working. He figures once he gets enough behind him he'll move to Bangkok. Move further up the chain.

Three hundred yards into soi 4 he takes a left into an unnamed and unlit soi. Fifty yards into that on the right is a gate. He reaches through the grill and unhooks the clasp, enters and closes it behind him. Across the small yard a dilapidated and unlit, two-storey house looms out of the dark. Boon-Mee approaches the door and knocks three times, then once more. He hears the bolts go. The door opens and there stands a short, wiry man in his mid-forties. His greasy hair is prematurely grey. He wears a frayed Manchester United football shirt, shorts and nothing else. This is Gan.

Gan is the case man and the first person, quiet possibly the only person in the chain, apart from the cooks back in Shan in Burma, who possesses any skills to speak of.

Without words Boon-Mee slides the rucksack off his shoulders and passes it across, walks away. He will be paid six thousand Baht, about one hundred pounds.

Gan goes upstairs to his work room, unbothered in any way by the fact that it is the middle of the night. He works when he needs to and rests when he can. He empties the rucksack of the twenty plastic bags of brown powder onto his work counter. Behind him are two new suitcases ready to go. Same design but different colours. The ones with wheels and a retractable handle. Substantial. Not cheap.

 He begins by laying a sheet of thick cellophane down onto the work surface. He doesn't measure it because he doesn't need to, knows he will end with twelve bags measuring fifteen centimetres by fifteen. He slits open one of the bags and pours out some of the contents onto the sheet. Again he doesn't measure, his guides being the keenness of his eye and the depth of his experience.

He smooths the powder out to all four corners with the edge of a piece of plywood. Once he has the powder in the approximate shape he needs he lays another sheet of cellophane over the top. He trims the edges with scissors, has his approximate shape and size. He plugs in his heat-sealing machine and locks the powder in.

He does this twenty-three more times. This will provide him with the twelve bags he requires to fill the sides, bottom and top edges of each suitcase.

Then he starts work on the cases. He eases his way deep into the seams that hold the lining to the walls. Once in there he can slice away the glued lining with a scalpel, exposing the space he needs into which he will pack his bags. He fills both sides with four bags and the bottom and top with two each. The bags are glued in place to stop any movement in transit and over the bags he glues thin card. He adds a pinch of ground coffee before he carefully re-glues the lining.

He takes his disc grinder and slices across the telescopic handles. To fill these he rolls more heroin-laden cellophane into long, pencil like shapes which he drops into thin plastic tubes. These tubes he then glues into place inside the two lengths of the handle. He fills the grip in the same way. This is finessing on a scale that isn't strictly needed. The amount extra he can fit into the handles is insignificant compared to what he could pack into the front and back panels of a case. But being greedy gets people caught. Gan is an artist which is why he is the most sought after case man in Bangkok.

He solders the grip back onto the handle rods. Then he grinds off the excess solder, takes an hour smoothing it down. He has matching paint to hand. By the time he has packed and prepared the cases they both weigh five kilograms more than they did when he started but visibly and to the touch there is no difference whatsoever.

It is past seven in the morning when he makes the call. Twenty minutes later he hears three knocks and then one more. He drags the cases down the stairs and opens the door to the blinding sunlight. In front of him stands the grinning figure of Benjy who has two identical suitcases.

Gan doesn't particularly like Benjy. He's too rich and good-looking for a start. He's half Thai - half American and is fluent in the languages of both countries. He speaks some French and Italian too. All the girls love him because he's friendly and looks like a rock star and that is precisely why he is so good at his job.

They swap cases and Gan drags the new ones back upstairs. He has a few days to prepare them with the remainder of the heroin but for now he can sleep. He re-enters his cramped factory and approaches the counter. He looks at the small pile of brown powder he has requisitioned for his trouble. Maybe two grams which he has diligently replaced with filler. Perks of the job. He takes a banknote from his filthy shorts and rolls it. He hits the edge of the pile.

For his services he will be paid ten thousand Baht, about a hundred and sixty pounds. Per case.

He feels the drug taking him away almost instantly. Taking him away to that place. He clambers onto his bed and drifts.

Benjy rolls the cases out into the small soi and places one on the back seat of his Lexus and the other in the boot. He reverses down to soi 4 and heads up towards Sukhumvit road. Turns right and heads west, through the Pathum Wan district and out to Ban Bat.

Benjy likes Ban Bat because it's relatively up-market, discreet and is close enough to his hunting ground. Close to Khao San road.

Benjy has had money all his life. He grew up and went to school and college in San Diego. He's into computers, cooks like a pro, can play decent guitar and is genuinely bi-lingual. He really could be anything he wants. But what he wants is the action. He *needs* to be in the game. He likes taking drugs, except the smack obviously, and he likes fucking western women. In truth Benjy likes fucking *any* women but it's the Europeans and Americans that stoke his ego and that's where it's at for him.

He drops the Lexus into the underground carpark of the block in which he currently lives, parks up and takes out the cases. Then he grabs a cab and goes over to Khao San road to meet the girls.

He ran into them three nights ago. He's seen it so many times he can spot them a mile off. Travellers. On the hippy side, coloured hair or dreads. Flowery clothes. Tattoos. But miserable. Going home miserable. Broke and back to the grind miserable. So Benjy breezed over, said hi and bought a few drinks. Then he suggested a club, dished out a few free pills. Everyone was happy and he even got to do one of them. The night made their comedown that much worse, which was the point.

'There's a way. A way to get some money. Then you can come back.'

Of course most of them tell him what he can do with his way to come back. But some don't. Some are up for it. Benjy knows it's a numbers game. You ask ten, they'll probably all say no. You ask twenty, one of them could bite. Either way he's bound to get laid.

He tells them no one ever gets caught, especially flying into Rome, London, Paris, Madrid, Boston or wherever the dozy bitches are going to. 'Security is poor at that airport. How many times you been stopped?'

So he meets them as arranged at a café on soi Rambutri. Mango shakes all round. Then they go back to their ratty little hotel.

He urges them to find anything wrong with the cases. Gan's expertise means they can't. No one can.

'It's in here already?' asks Eloise.

'Yup,' grins Benjy.

'Okay how does it all work again?' This is Francoise.

'I go to the airport with you. You check-in and I give you sixty-five thousand Baht. When you come out at the other end a man will be waiting for you. He will be holding a sign that says Nina DuPont. You go with him. He will check the cases. Then he will give you two hundred and fifty thousand Baht each or whatever that is in Francs. I'll work it out and tell him. That's it.'

'What if we get caught?'

'Don't talk or even think like that. These are your cases and there is nothing in them but your stuff. Okay?'

Eloise, the one he got it on with, thinks it's the coolest thing ever. Francoise isn't so sure. But Benjy, as he usually does when things have got this far, wins her around.

When he leaves Eloise notices that her flip-flop is worn to the point where it occasionally comes loose and falls from her foot. She tells herself she'll buy a new pair in the morning.

The next day they both get on the plane to Charles De Gaulle without incident.

Having paid them, Benjy drives away from Don Meung, his job done. One top of what he has fronted the mules, he will be paid eighty thousand Baht, about one thousand three hundred pounds, for his trouble.

For both girls the flight is a nightmare. Even Eloise has lost her confidence. They drink too much and try to sleep but the twelve hour hop from Bangkok to their home city is full of doubt, fear and recrimination.

'It'll be fine. Think of the money.' That's all Eloise can tell her oldest friend.

At the luggage carousel Francoise feels that everyone can see her heart thumping and ready to burst from her chest.

'Okay, there's mine as well. Let's go.'

They head towards customs. It's busy and they see no officials. Aiming for the green channel Francoise steps in front of Eloise. Nearly there. No customs officers at all. They're going to make it. Francoise raises her pace.

'Slow down,' Eloise calls to her.

Then Francoise hears a yelp from behind her, then the sound of someone falling. She stops and turns. Eloise is lying on the tiled floor. The worn flip-flop lies a yard behind her, the toe strap hanging loose.

'Fuck, my ankle.'

'I'm going through.'

'Wait. Let me get up. Ow!'

Francoise panics. If she goes now she's okay – if she stays . . .

'I'll see you outside.' She turns and heads for the exit.

Eloise clambers to her feet but can't put any weight on her ankle. The pain is incredible. She hops to her flip-flop, bends to pick it up.

Francoise bursts out into the bedlam of Charles De Gaulle's arrivals hall, sweating and gasping for breath. Is she home free? She scans the milling throng for the sign. She's forgotten the name. Shit. There! Nina Du Pont. She pushes her way through.

'Yeah, it's me,' she says.

The thick-set Arab glares at her. 'Where's the other one?'

'She's coming. I need to get out of here.'

'I need both of you.'

'Where can I meet you. I want to go.'

'Go with him. Wait by the car.'

She hasn't even noticed there are two of them. The tall, greasy north African flicks his head to the side. She follows him out into the air. The French air. She's going to be alright.

Out of the bedlam of the airport, into the cool and the quiet of the multi-storey. Even if she just ran now, left everything, she would be okay.

The lanky youngster takes her to a Renault Espace. He picks up the case and dumps it in the rear. Francoise climbs into the back seat, sees the man get in behind the wheel.

Then they wait.

Eloise tries not to cry. The pain from her ankle is so bad she can't put any weight on it. She hops to her case, tries to bend down to grab the handle. The incident has caused a stir right in the middle of the green channel.

'Miss? Oh, Miss! One moment please.'

Eloise, tears burning at the back of her eyes, stops and turns. Two customs officials move towards her.

In the Renault, Francoise estimates they have been waiting for an hour. In reality only twenty minutes have passed, the worst of her life. She knows she should have stayed, should have helped.

The front passenger door opens.

'Let's go,' orders the man even before the door is closed, Eloise isn't with him.

The second man starts the car, pulls away from the bay.

'Wait. Where is she? My friend!'

'She's not coming.'

'What?'

'Listen to me. If she was with you and she is not through after twenty minutes then she has been stopped. If she has been stopped she is probably telling them about us right now. We can't wait around here.'

'Oh, my God! No!'

'Get used to it. You got through, be thankful.'

Out of the airport and away. *Be thankful*, she tells herself.

They drive for less than an hour but Eloise has no idea where they are. In a daze she follows the men into an apartment block. Up some stairs, into a small, grubby flat.

The shorter man, Hmed, hands Francoise a black plastic bin liner.

'Put your stuff into this.'

He dumps the case onto a table. Francoise opens it and transfers all her clothes and possessions into the bag. When the case is empty Hmed sets about it with a small, sharp knife. The second man, Adid, produces a hacksaw from the kitchen and gently saws at the handle. It's not long before Gan's twelve flat packs and long, thin tubes from the handles are lined up.

Adid says, 'I'll weigh it.'

Hmed turns to Francoise who is sitting patiently on a sofa with her head in her hands.

'Try not to worry. What's done is done.' He hands her a piece of paper.

'If she gets through call me. If she has been stopped and she tries to involve you then you say you know nothing. And say *nothing* about us. And lose that number.'

'What will happen to her?'

'That's not my problem.'

'Five exactly.' Adid says.

Hmed reaches into his jeans pocket and pulls out a roll of notes, hands it to Francoise.

'You did good. You going to do it again?'

Eloise will be sentenced to five years and three months for importing five kilograms of pure heroin into France. Francoise doesn't go back to Thailand.

Hmed and Adid get busy. They are unusual in that they handle a lot of jobs themselves. Picking up the couriers at the airport for example. They could get someone to do that but it would mean someone else they'd need to pay. And someone else they'd need to trust. Likewise the labourious process of cutting, weighing and bagging. It's not so much the money they resent paying out, it's more people knowing who and where they are.

Whilst they were looking forward to working with the full ten kilos, developing new markets, the five they receive still takes some shifting. This is because they're not into moving big amounts. They and their contacts mainly supply the users of St. Denis, Barbes-Rochechouart, most of the ninth and the nineteenth arrondisements and the island itself. Sure they move the equivalent of ounces on to favoured friends and contacts, but they're good at working the streets. They like the street numbers.

The five kilos has cost them two hundred thousand pounds, so forty thousand a kilo. The first thing they will do is fill it by one hundred percent. They use a pre-prepared, pre-dyed mix of flour, pain-killers and whatever else is to hand. So out of that forty thousand pound kilo they now have two kilos. They weigh that out into small plastic bags. A *lot* of small plastic bags. They have plenty of customers who take grams which they can sell for the equivalent of fifty pounds a pop. So if they simply grammed it all out that would gross a straight one hundred thousand pounds.

But they go further by selling point eight of a gram as a gram. It's accepted. So if they simply did that they would gross one hundred and twenty-five thousand pounds.

But they go further by selling point four of a gram bags at thirty quid each which would squeeze out a gross of one hundred and fifty thousand pounds.

And of course they can go even further than that by selling ten pound bags to the low-lifes. So the bottom line is from a forty grand kee, which takes them about three weeks to move, they'll usually be *clearing* a hundred grand. And they have five kilos.

Sure they have a team of kids working the stuff who need to be paid, plus all kinds of rent on apartments to operate from along with general exes blah blah but hey, it's a living.

So Hmed and Adid are happy doing what they do the way they do it. They have a great source in Benjy and his people in Bangkok and they don't step on the gear *that* much. Everyone's a winner.

Of course they only pay for what comes out at their end, so when daft hippy girls get caught at the airport why should they care? Always more where that comes from and Benjy keeps them well fed. Since they started using him three years ago they've never run out.

It's for that reason, when they are still only halfway through the five kilo load, that they take seriously an offer to buy a whole kee. Sensibly they kept back two untampered-with kilos.

Olivier is someone they've known since they were kids. He's from the neighbourhood, from L'ile St. Denis itself, but he moved to London with his parents a few years back. He fancies himself as a Techno DJ and he's pretty good. There's little money in it at the moment but that doesn't bother him for two reasons: one, he's really in it for the girls and the fun and two, he's in position A selling drugs. Some of which he gets from his old running mates Hmed and Adid.

He picks up the smack when he visits and occasionally they post it over to safe addresses he has access to. Now though he figures he can make his move. Now he wants a kilo.

There's this bloke he knows. A Londoner he met on the club

scene. Older, fortyish, and heavy. Olivier has never seen him fight but sometimes you just know. Anyway this bloke is involved in the promotion of a couple of the nights he's been playing at so therefore he's involved in the door security and the pill distribution. They get talking. Turns out the heavy guy can move some smack, but he can't find a reliable source.

The guy's name is Paul. He has a nickname but it begins with an R and Olivier still has trouble with the English R, so he just calls him Paul.

So he called the boys and asked them if they had a kilo he could take. But there's a problem, Olivier doesn't have the funds. Hmed and Adid talked about it and decided, for old time's sake, they'd take a chance and front him the gear. He's one of them.

'How you going to get it across?'

'In a van. I'm going to rent it, drive to you. Stay one night at my cousin's house, drive back to Calais, chuck some beer and wine in the back and go home on the ferry. If I get pulled over I'll say I'm helping to throw a party.'

And that's precisely what happens. Hmed wants to charge him the equivalent of fifty thousand pounds but Adid talks him down to forty-five. To compensate for Adid's generosity, Hmed skims ten percent and fluffs it out with the filler. Everyone's a winner.

Olivier does get pulled over at Dover customs, but a cursory look in the back sees him on his way. They would never have found it anyway, his cousin is a mechanic.

So now he's in the big league.

He bombs back to his flat in Newham. It's a scruffy kind of place but he can afford it and it gives him the privacy he needs. Enjoying that privacy he gets to work on the powder. He pulls out ten percent of it, intending to cut that still further and small-bag it out to some people he knows. He fluffs out the bulk back to exactly one thousand grams with a mixture he learned from Hmed and Adid.

He calls his man.

'Hi Paul. Everything okay?'

'Hey Oli. Yeah. You good?'

'Perfect. I have a present for you.'

'You're a good boy, Oli. Come over.'

Olivier has been to Paul's house before. An after party. Nice house in a nice street with an ace car out front. Olivier knows that'll be him soon enough.

The door is opened by some dude Olivier has never seen before. This freaks him a little but the guy calls him by his first name and invites him in. Olivier notices, as he follows the man along the hallway, that he walks with a limp. They go all the way through to the kitchen where Paul shakes hands and embraces him, which makes him feel special. He pulls the kilo from his rucksack.

'Over to you, mate,' Paul says to the guy with the limp.

The other man has everything ready on the counter top. He lifts a small amount from the bag with a knife and deftly lays it on a square of double-folded silver paper. He has a three inch length of drinking straw already cut which he holds between his lips. He picks up a cheap, plastic lighter and holds the flame under the silver paper. In seconds wisps of spectral pleasure turn their way into the air, the man chases, inhales. The other two watch intently.

He hasn't been into heroin long. Dabbled a bit when he was a kid but since he got hurt he finds it helps with the pain, both physical and mental. He doesn't inject, though. Tells himself he'll never do that.

He draws in deep on the smoke, holds it. He drops the straw, the lighter and the paper. He looks down at the black slicks left on the foil. The runs. Not too much debris he thinks. Could be good gear.

He exhales slowly, hears some static from somewhere. He is aware the other two are looking at him like he's levitating or something but he doesn't care about that. Then, in less than five seconds, he doesn't care about anything because he really *is* levitating.

He limps to a chair at the kitchen table and sits. Oh yae.

'All good, mate?'

Andy doesn't really want to talk. He wants to concentrate. He wants to concentrate on the joy and to fully appreciate that, when he smacks up, all that shit goes away.

He thinks back to the end of the previous year. The way that maniac simply picked him up and tossed him over the balcony, like he was throwing away a dirty nappy. Sure, the wrong has been righted in that all three of those arseholes are now in the ground. But the hate never goes. He'll always have the hate. Except when he's on the brown.

'Yo. Andy boy. You with us?'

Andy stirs, back in the room. He nods.

'Pay the man.'

Paul leaves the room and goes upstairs. Three minutes later he is back with a plastic bag. Olivier grins.

On his way back into the room Paul grabs a set of scales from a kitchen cabinet. He knows that if the kid didn't stitch him on the quality then he wouldn't on the amount but he weighs it anyway. Then he pulls out five purple bricks, lays them on the sparkly granite.

'Fifty.'

Olivier thinks he'll die of happiness. He's just made five grand and he'll make another ten easily over the coming weeks. The big time is now. He looks up at this amazing Englishman he barely knows and determines to work on his accent. He wants to be able to say his name like everyone else. He's in with Paul Wren. He's in with Wrenny.

Wrenny shuts the door on the French kid and goes back to the kitchen. He needs to get busy. First thing is to drag his old mate Andy to his feet and lay him out on the lounge sofa.

'You okay, mate?'

Andy's head lolls slowly back and Wrenny catches the squalid vacancy of his numbed eyes, knows he is already gone.

Wrenny hits the phone. He's new to moving this amount of heroin. Georgie doesn't like it but fuck Georgie, he thinks. If it wasn't for Georgie playing his stupid undercover games then Andy would still be able to walk properly. Okay so those idiots *had* brought two hundred thousand pills to the meet that night, but seeing as it was only Georgie and Wrenny there pulling the triggers then Connie didn't need to know that. And they split the pills fifty-fifty.

Their firm was essentially the three of them and with all three of them gone there would be no comebacks. To be sure to minimize any adverse ripples in the business the pills went up north to contacts of Wrenny's in Manchester, Liverpool and Brum. Out of the way.

Split into smaller parcels the two hundred thousand Es went for at least three each and half of that was Wrenny's. Plus the thirty large Connie paid him for offing the fuckers anyway. On top of that, as Georgie had said, they now held Essex. Good times. Except Andy would always carry the limp. Always bear the pain.

Now Wrenny, having padded out his kilo, finds the smack busness not as easy as he thought, especially as he needs to keep it quiet from Georgie and anyone Georgie might know. He was hoping to have it gone in a month and clear at least twenty but on his first round of calls he comes up way short. He goes to his B list, calling people who didn't put in any advance orders, people who may even be users themselves. Small time, but it's an untried market and he's starting from the bottom. To facilitate this process he even digs out a couple of old little back books crammed with numbers and contacts.

As he is flicking his way through one of these books he hits the Ds and is brought up sharp. *Oh my fucking god,* he thinks. A known smackie herself and everyone's favourite bike from the old days. Wrenny thinks back to the two or three occasions he even had a dabble himself.

He can't believe the phone is going to ring, but it does. Not only that but Juliette Dixon picks up. After the brief conversation he sits shaking his head. Unreal.

He drives from Theydon Bois to Walthamstow. It's only five miles but it's light years away in every other conceivable notion. As he draws closer to the address Dixie has given him he starts to itch, but still considers the possibility of a quickie when he gets there. She was quite the athlete in the old days.

As soon as she opens the door he tells himself no. She's a few years older than him but, seriously?

He can tell she's been in and out of the shower and done the hair, make up and clothes thing but she still looks like someone's aunt dressing up as someone's niece. She clearly wants to talk, wants him to take his shoes off and have a drink and part of him is tempted. He heard about some shit that went down a few years ago. She was with Denny Masters and got tangled up with . . . something. And Pete Chalmers moved abroad and no one knows why. Word was Connie was involved but then when *isn't* Connie involved?

So no, thanks for the invite and all that but he's out of there. He leaves her half an ounce and tells her to phone him when she has seven hundred quid and don't take too long.

Dixie closes the door, both enthused and saddened by what has just happened. Wrenny has always been a nice bloke and, while she sometimes struggles to remember such things, there may be the outside possibility they got it on once or twice. She's heard he's going great guns lately. Has his own club nights, runs a team of doormen, fingers in loads of pies. Then out of the blue he calls and lays some smack on her. On tick.

When she got the call she thought it was a social visit. Had something she might be interested in, he said. Then he takes one look at the flat and one look at her and he's offski faster than Michael Johnson.

So Dixie sits on her grotty sofa looking at what is on her grotty coffee table. No time like the present, she tells herself and racks out a line.

But if that wasn't weird enough, two days later she gets a call from someone else from the way back when.

*

Micky Targett can see no way out. He kicks himself for getting back into the game, for getting back into crime. Why would he do that when he knew all along he's no fucking good at it?

And now, in the spring of nineteen ninety-six, he's starting to project those feelings of darkness and defeat onto life itself. Yeah, he tells himself, as he sits on the edge of his bed, deliberately hiding from his dad. Life! No fucking good at that either.

He took the bold step to walk away from Connie and Georgie and a shed load of money. He had no choice. He's in the frame for a multiple murder (investigation ongoing) and knows that soon enough he'll get another call from the police wanting to know where he was the night someone jumped the old git that grew dope in his house and cleaned his clock for him..

His knee isn't too bad following the second operation, if he doesn't spend too much time on it, but his hip bothers him sometimes. Moderate arthritis at thirty-six.

He has a nice car that is starting to lose money, but he has saved about thirty odd grand from the last year's drug sales.

He thinks about getting a job but wonders what that might be. He can't remember the last one he had. Was it riding dispatch? He thinks he used to work in the City, but he can't remember that either.

There's something else he is thinking of doing, and if he knows that if he does this thing he can't get a job. So he thinks, fuck it, don't be a wuss, get a job. Buy a van, go parcel delivering.

He gets up, leaves his room.

It has got to the stage his dad is so unpredictable Micky doesn't know what is going to happen next. He's living on his nerves.

The house is beginning to smell.

Micky can hear the TV on in the lounge. It's loud because Eddie's hearing has started to go as well. He won't entertain the idea of going for a test, he prefers to just turn up the TV. Prefers to make his son shout.

Micky goes into the bathroom, takes a leak. Yeah, he reckons, I'll buy something like an Escort van. Nippy. A turbo diesel with a proper stereo. Get out of London on some long runs. The thought starts to cheer him.

He zips up, turns on the cold tap at the sink and something catches his eye. He looks at it for several seconds. He works out what it is but carries on looking. He knows what it is but can't *believe* what it is. He's seen loads of them before, most days in fact, but never on the edge of a sink.

It's a human turd.

He's embarrassed for his dad more than anything. What's he supposed to do? Rub the bloke's nose in it?

He knows there is nothing to do or say because ten seconds after he does or says anything, Rock Steady Eddie Targett forgets what he's just heard. He knows that from this point on, his life will be mostly about looking after a baby. A baby in its seventies. He breaks some toilet paper from the roll, picks up the turd and flushes it.

It is for that reason that Micky Targett knows that he isn't going to get a job. He knows this because he appreciates he won't be able to drive a van at the same time as doing the 'something else' he was thinking of doing; running a substantial heroin habit.

So he goes back into his room and feels the drag of grim inevitability. He feels it like it's a court summons. He has no choice but to call Juliette Dixon.

'I do not fucking believe this,' she squawks as he sits in the chair across the coffee table from her. On the way over he was thinking about the possibility of a dabble with the old bird. Rekindle that flame. But even though he can't remember the last time he got laid he knows he's not up for it. She's put on a lot of weight and in those tight, faux leather trousers her arse looks a bit like the cheap sofa she's sitting on.

'Ditto,' he tells her.

There is so much history he doesn't know where to start. But so much of that history he knows she has never been privy to. The secreted devices in his house and hers. Are they still there? The phone calls that were recorded and listened to that incriminated her so completely.

From her angle it is so weird to see him again but mostly in a good way. She can still remember their first meeting. Terry Farmer had brought them together. An unmarried couple out shopping with stolen credit cards and chequebooks. And it worked so well that when Micky stepped up to work for Masters and Chalmers he took her with him. And then they took their act international. Made a bundle.

And they got it together. Nice bloke, if a bit out of his depth.

But she wonders how much he might know about how she stitched him up. Got him fucked up on crack and heroin and betrayed him to Demon Denny Masters.

So it's a stand-off and a very awkward one, but they both decide to let it go. Not the time for questions, just business. Micky wants something that Dixie has. It's very good stuff so she doubles the weight and puts point eights into gram bags and charges Micky fifty a pop. He doesn't quibble, smackheads never do. He hands over the oner from a small wad.

'You doing okay, Micky? Business alright?'

Yeah, like you fucking care, thinks Micky. *Four years ago you were asking me that question and feeding the answer to the bloke who tortured me in a cellar in Spain.*

'Yeah. I'm okay, Dix'. You?'

She doesn't answer straight away because she knows that all Micky needs for a reply is to look around him. At where she is living. *How* she is living.

'Getting on.'

He gets up to go. 'Still down the market?'

How the fuck do you know that, she wants to know. Then she looks in the corner at the boxes of fake Nikes and Sergio Tacchini's. Pretty obvious really.

'It's a living.'

'You got a good source of this?' he asks.

'Yeah.'

Then he leaves.

Back at the house he is almost delirious with excitement but, ever the pragmatist, he's not sure how it might work. He thinks the best way to do it is to wait until he goes to bed, snort a line and get his drift on. His dad won't know and it'll all be fine. So he hangs with Eddie, they watch a bit of telly, Eddie cooks something horrible to eat. Micky looks at the clock.

'I think I'll have an early night, dad.' It is five past six.

'Okay, boy. Sleep well. I'll probably get off myself soon enough. 'Ere . . .'

'Yeah?'

'I was thinking . . .'

'Steady.'

'Maybe we should get a dog.'

Knowing full well Eddie will forget all about this conversation sooner than Micky leaves the room he says, 'Let's talk about that tomorrow.'

In his room Micky decides a two-incher will suffice. He wonders what it would be like for his dad if Micky died in the house and it was explained to him how it happened. Then he hits the line. A dog, he says to himself. Maybe that could work.

And then he's there. Five years, and the warmth and the safety and the joy are all exactly as he remembered. He's finally home and nothing will bother him. All the shit from the first time around. His brother doing what he did. All the beatings. Losing everything, including his mind. Watching that bloke Andy go over the balcony. The Rettendon killings. Knowing that could have been him. His dad going downhill, and knowing it will become inexorably worse. None of that bothers him. He doesn't forget about it, that's not an option, it's just not a problem anymore. Nothing's a problem anymore.

Then he has a brilliant idea. He doesn't need to get a job because he still has a few quid behind him. No, he just needs to *pretend* he's got one. This has two benefits. Firstly it gets him away from the house and secondly it gives him the reason to arrange for some professional carers to come in to look after his dad while he's out busy not working.

'Why are you getting a job? What do you need a bloody job for?'

Great, thinks Micky, *bawls me out for not having one all these years . . .*

'I need to get something going dad.' Emboldened in the glow of the previous evening's hit.

'And while I'm at work there'll be one or two women come round. Say hello. Maybe cook you something.'

If there was a tin hat handy Micky would have put it on sharpish. He cringes as he awaits the verbal retribution coming his way. But he doesn't get it.

'Women?'

'Yeah.'

'What women?'

'Couple of people I know. They'll just look in on you.'

Micky knows Eddie likes the fairer sex. Never been a ladies man but he can flirt up a storm, the old boy. So he gets onto the council and arranges for a carer to come in morning and afternoon and for Meals On Wheels to drop something round at lunchtimes. So in the space of no time at all Micky has relieved a ton of pressure off himself and cheered the old boy up no end, all at no cost whatsoever.

This enterprising initiative frees Micky up to drive the Jag to a variety of local spots where he can bung heroin up his nose and not be pestered by anyone or anything. He usually takes a book with him. Stephen King, Neil Gaiman and Chuck Palahnuik all publish decent reads in ninety-six, although, he has to admit, he rarely gets too much reading done.

Music on the radio is generally garbage. There's a novelty song about three lions or something, heralding the start of the football that summer. There's a gorgeous Roberta Flack soul song corrupted into tuneless shite by a bunch of talentless wannabes called The Fugees. But then just when you think all hope is lost for the music scene, along comes Born Slippy by Underworld.

The radio gives him snippets of news. Charlie and Di get divorced. Boris Yeltsin scores another term as Russian President. A massive IRA bomb (are those fuckers still doing this shit?) injures two hundred and slaughters whole areas of Manchester city centre. And a Saudi national, writing about his own country pens a cheery ditty called 'The Declaration of Jihad on the Americans Occupying the Country of the Two Sacred Places.' His name is Osama bin Laden.

During this period Micky's day starts with him struggling out of bed around eight. He readies a breakfast for him and Eddie, waits for the morning carer to show and heads off. Then he spins around the corner, parks up and gets his mangled. He may occasionally go somewhere else to get something to eat but that's never a priority. Before he knows what's happening the day is almost over and he heads back, timing his return to coincide with the departure of the afternoon carer. Towards the end of the day Micky, or usually Eddie, still believing himself to be a master in the kitchen, will get some food on the plates and then, shortly thereafter, Micky will declare himself exhausted by his energetic toil and hit the hay. He's normally in bed before seven where he smacks up for the night time session.

In essence his only goal of each and every day is to make it through to that blessed time when he doesn't have to be awake anymore. Far from simple, but achievable.

A week in, his new regime was indeed interrupted by DS Ray fucking Pitts asking him to pop into the office once again. And once again, Micky is relieved to appreciate, Pitts has nothing that is going to unduly inconvenience him. Yes, it was about Barry Pye getting laid out and no, he had nothing with which to charge Micky. On account of the crash helmet, they had no meaningful description. It was an appalling waste of police resources and Micky's time. Nothing to see here, folks.

One day, you appalling spunk bucket, thinks Pitts.

I'm sure I've been in this place before, thinks Micky. On his way out he mistakenly walks into a storage cupboard. Then, when he gets out of there, instead of heading down, he walks up the stairs and into someone else's office. He is lost for several minutes before realizing he is totally shitfaced on heroin in a police station. This he finds hilarious.

But all the while Eddie slides away.

'I had to clean him up today,' says the afternoon carer, an Irishwoman possessed of a charmingly affable brio.

Micky is flying, nods contemplatively

'Sooner or later it all comes down to shoite,' she counsels wisely.

'Ah.'

'I've been doing this job for five years and it always happens. They just lose all sense of what's going on. Most of the time your father, instinctively, still manages to get to the toilet. There will be times when he won't.'

Micky starts to straighten.

'He was in there today but he basically missed.'

Micky hopes that is about as detailed a description as he gets.

'I took care of it but you need to be ready. Buy a lot of bleach, rubber gloves. A mop. Does your machine have a boil wash?'

'Er . . .'

'It's going to be tough. Sorry. Another thing, the bathroom.'

'Yeah?'

'That's pretty grim in there. Can you afford something new?'

Micky knows this has to be done. He only did a partial job when he got back from Spain with the stash and now it's four years further down the dirty road.

'What's your name?'

'Carol.'

'Do you have any free time?'

'Sometimes. I work and get paid by the hour. Six pounds fifty and I have to use my own car and pay my own petrol.'

'He really likes you. If I pay you a tenner an hour can you come by more often? Weekends?'

Eddie Targett runs all the possibilities through his head once again and it always comes back to the same thing. Trust. You can't trust anyone, least of all, he is gutted to admit, that lanky twat of a son of his.

Something is going on.

Suddenly there are these women around. Not just now and then but every sodding day.

Couple of them are okay. One of them is really very nice, helped him in the shower the other day. One of them he doesn't like. Foreign. They're always up to something. She calls him Edward. *No one* calls him Edward.

They keep making him take pills as well. They give him pills every day and stand next to him to make sure he swallows and that tells him everything he needs to know. Why would he need pills if there's nothing wrong with him? Something is going on and his own son is behind it. It cuts him to realize it but he knows it's inevitable. If this shit carries on, if the deceit continues then he's going to have to start taking people out. Starting with the boy.

One day, as a new band of old slappers assault the airwaves with something about Zigazig aaah! Micky is in the kitchen looking for something. He doesn't find it but what he does find is a plastic bag with over half an ounce of cocaine in it.

Christ! How did . . .?

Then he remembers. Back at the turn of the year he'd finished dealing Connie's pills but he'd carried on buying the Charlie from Chrissie and selling that. Then, when he'd boshed the old dope grower bloke, he'd even knocked that on the head. He'd kept the one remaining leftover bag in his bedroom, but then moved it because, for some reason, his dad was always prowling around in there. Stashed it safe in the kitchen.

He grins massively at the unexpected windfall but then wonders just what the hell he's going to do with it. He could maybe move it on and make a few quid but who does he know anymore? Resurrect things with Ishy? Not for a one-off like this. Ben? They haven't spoken for a while.

He figures he could do it himself but the idea revolts him. Back in the day he would obviously have jumped on it. Back in the day he had no comprehension of how or why people took downers. Now he can't understand why anyone would take anything else. He considers the cocaine in his hand. All that socializing, dancing and drinking. *Talking* to people. What was he thinking?

So he shoves it back where he found it knowing that he'll certainly remember this little stash.

Then he forgets all about it.

What he doesn't forget is the bathroom. A new one will cheer the place up. He has a rudimentary measure up and drives to his local B&Q in Romford where he orders a new suite in white along with

267

modern flooring. In anticipation he gets on a pair of gloves he finds in the garage and rips up the carpet he had laid in the bathroom four years ago, wondering just why the fuck he had replaced the old carpet with a new one instead of something washable.

He finds a plumber in the Yellow Pages.

All the while he is doing this he keeps Eddie calm while giving him updates.

'What happened to the floor?'

'It was dirty. We're getting a new one.'

'It was alright. Why do you have to change things?'

'It was really dirty, dad.'

'How much will that cost?'

'Not much. I'm paying.'

'About time.'

'We're also getting a new bath, sink and toilet.'

'What? Why?'

'Because we need a chisel to clean it all.'

'When?'

'The bloke's coming on Wednesday.'

'What? Why?'

Micky can tell how disgruntled Eddie is. With everything. The little of life he can still understand makes him horribly suspicious. Nothing brings him happiness and Micky senses the black clouds gathering above them both.

By the summer of ninety-six, Micky is getting through his money. He pays Carol the carer to come round to look after his dad when she can, over and above the official slots allocated to her by the council. Evenings and the weekend. She's good for him.

Micky also has bills of his own, namely the Jag, which he doesn't really need, and with Dixie. He knows that the money will run out one day. That obviously worries him but he has the answer, the antidote to that concern. To *any* concern. He keeps it in a little bag in his bedside cabinet.

Wednesday arrives and the bell rings at just after nine in the morning. Micky hasn't slept well.

The plumber, Rick, in his mid-twenties and as cheery as you like, grabs a cup of tea from Eddie and gets stuck in. The plan is he is to remove the sink and the bath, leave the toilet and then return the next day to fit the new units. Micky explains everything several times and Eddie is content.

Come lunchtime Eddie insists Rick eats lunch at the table with them, even though he has brought sandwiches of his own. Passable fried eggs on toast are produced without the kitchen getting burned down.

Micky feels so much warmth for his mad old dad. He really does have a good soul. Later that day and into the next his affection will be tested to its limit.

Things are still good when Rick leaves.

'Thanks a lot, son.' Big handshakes all round.

'See you tomorrow, Eddie.'

Then the B&Q delivery truck arrives with the new bathroom suite and, once again, Eddie is in his element as he joshes and jokes with the driver, helping him lug the boxes into the lounge.

But with the dusk a change comes over Eddie Targett.

He looks out from the kitchen window into the garden. Looks at his bench and thinks about his darling Florrie. He turns and walks towards the hallway. As he moves he feels himself lowered a little further into the pit, down further into the darkness. Something is *very* wrong.

He turns right, pulls the draw string to illuminate the bathroom against the falling night and freezes in horror. Someone has stolen the bathroom. And he knows who. That little git was always a thief, always nicking a copper or two from the change he left on his dresser when he came home from the pub in the old days. Born bad, the kid.

He turns and strides to the lounge, finally ready to lay the fucker out. As he makes it into the lounge he can't believe his eyes. How much torment can there be in the world? What the fuck is in those boxes?

Maybe he should just smash a hammer over the back of the boy's head and have done with it.

Micky, who has only snaffled a couple of half-lines all day, help with his nerves, is idly watching an episode of London's Burning before he hits the hay. And another line. He feels eyes on him. Looks, and there is Eddie wearing a genuinely murderous glare.

'You,' he says, his gnarled index finger a foot from Micky's nose.

Micky's heart hits his stomach.

'What's up, pop?'

'You. Come with me.'

Micky tries to hide his sigh, gets up and, knowing full well what will happen, follows his dad.

They enter the stripped bathroom where Eddie holds out an accusatory hand.

'What the fuck have you done?'

Micky thinks about his mum, she's just about the only thing he can turn to these days that helps. Apart from the smack obviously.

'Dad, we're getting a new bathroom. The plumber was here today. Remember?'

'Don't you fucking lie to me, boy!'

Right there right then, standing on the rough concrete Micky knows he can't do it much longer. His life shouldn't be like this. In spite of his crimes he knows he doesn't deserve this, was meant for something better. Once again he thinks of all his friends with their homes and their wives and their children and their careers. He looks at his dad, this grizzled, mangled little ball of resentment and madness. He looks into his eyes and is chilled by the paranoia and the hate.

'Dad we're getting a new bathroom tomorrow. The man will be here in the morning. He did this work today.'

Eddie here's the words, tries to work them through, tries to process. He doesn't say anything but Micky knows he doesn't understand.

'I'm putting the kettle on,' Micky tells him and walks away.

In the kitchen Micky fills the kettle and sees he has been followed. Eddie is glaring at him, his leathery, jowly face fractured into a grimace of suspicious loathing.

'Go and sit down, dad. I'll bring it in.'

He watches Eddie back away from him, disappear into the lounge. Five seconds later . . . .

'What the fuck have you done *now*?'

Micky rushes to his dad's side. Finds him clutching his head as he stares down at the large boxes on the carpet.

Micky wants to cry.

'Dad, please. Try to understand, this is the new bathroom.'

Eddie holds his head tighter and tighter, seemingly in an effort to pull it free of his shoulders and so end his torment.

'Why the fuck are you doing this to me?'

The scream and the pain within it are enough to finish Micky for good. But this night he will find out how strong he is. Because it goes on. And it goes on. And on.

After the second cycle Micky decides, no, Micky *knows* that, short of simply walking out, there is only one answer to this. He considers his own complete and utter *depletion* of energy and initiative and knows he has no choice.

By this stage of the game he has stepped things up to the point where he is buying ten gram bags from Dixie so he dives into his bedroom and, not even bothering to rack out a line, he simply holds the bag and pushes his face into it, inhaling both greedily and dangerously. For an instant he thinks about offering some to his dad.

Back out in the lounge he can't find the old fella. This is because he is back in the bathroom.

'Michael! Michael! Come here quick.' There is genuine horror in his voice, and Micky knows from memory that if he's getting called 'Michael' then things must be bad.

He sniffs hurriedly, no time to lose. He rushes to the bathroom and in the few seconds it takes for him to get there he begins to slow down, begins to process the good news. He finds Eddie in his default position. His eyes are on stalks, arms outstretched beholding the ruination of the landscape.

Micky's head lolls back and he goes with it. *There we go. Not so bad now is it?*

And so the evening goes on. Eddie is caught in his terrible loop and Micky loses count after seven circuits of it. He explains what is happening as well as he can until he feels the drug along with a natural exhaustion overtake him. He loses patience and feels awful about that. He seeks his bed.

But he doesn't sleep. He goes somewhere and visits his favourite place of solace and comfort along the way, but he spends the dark hours on some strange, worrisome journey, a welter of doubts and recriminations shadowing him along darkened passages. He feels himself chased once again. The black, shifting shape hounding his every turn and move. It doesn't get to him but he can't shake it. He can't get away.

Then, in his darkest moment, he does what he thought he would never do. He actually says the words out loud.

'Dear God. Please help me. I don't know what to do anymore. I know I've fucked up, I know I've done wrong, but please help me. If you help me then I promise, I will sin no more.'

He knows it's bullshit and he knows that the smack is more of a god to him than the other one that doesn't exist anyway. But that's how desperate he is.

The light wakes him. He doesn't know what time it is but knows it's before eight as he has set his alarm. Rick the plumber is due at nine. Through the fog of the smack hangover he lies inert, the drama and sadness of the previous evening still on him like a sheen of day old sweat. He doesn't want to move until the last possible moment. No chance.

The door flies open and Eddie piles in, strides powerfully to the curtains. Micky reckons he'll rip them wide open, chase him out of bed and call him a lazy bastard. If only it were that easy.

Micky feels his heartbeat surge as he watches Eddie part the curtains by two inches and peer out. His eyeballs flick manically.

'They're out there.'

Micky feels himself slip. Slip from his already tenuous hold on the world, on reality. He's falling and even the safety net, even his heroin sanctuary can't help him.

'Dad. . .'

'It's happening. They're on the roof.'

'Jesus fucking Christ.'

'Get up. Get your boots on.'

'There's no one there.'

'Are you going to let me down all of your fucking life?'

And that does it for Micky. He can't pretend any longer. He can't pretend to himself or the world that this is any way tolerable. Is this what his life is now?

So he starts to cry. Lying in his bed, unable to move, he lets go and allows himself to break down. Huge, great wracking sobs. He cries and cries and cries because it is the only thing left for him to do. And he doesn't care how it looks and he doesn't care what his old man thinks.

Disturbed by the noise, Eddie's attention is drawn from the threats outside. He looks down at the prone figure of his youngest son. He doesn't look right. His face is screwed up, he's making a strange sound, his eyes are wet and Eddie, momentarily wrong-footed, doesn't know what to make of it. Then he remembers this same boy, years and years ago riding his bicycle. First time off the stabilisers. Plucky as you like he'd pedaled furiously, made ground, but then lost balance and went over. Scraped his knee. He did the same thing then, cried because of the pain. Eddie Targett remembers that.

Then he understands that's all it is, the boy is in pain. He says nothing but shuffles across to the bed. He sits down on the edge, leans forward and embraces him. Holds him close, protects him as he always did.

Micky clings on, like the child he has been reduced to. It takes a while but eventually the sobbing ebbs and he feels for a hold on what could laughingly be called normality. He wipes his eyes with the back of his hand. Sniffles. Takes deep breaths.

'Right,' says Eddie forcefully, 'Get you boots on. This is happening.'

Micky finds the strength, gets up, gets dressed. He makes himself a mega-strong coffee, slaps his own face until it reddens. But now he's on his feet he wonders what Eddie is actually going to show him. Exactly who or what is on the roof?

Eddie's agitation is now focused on the boxes. He paces around them like a cat circling a defiant mouse. Pushing his luck Micky goes out to stand in front of the house to look up on the roof. From inside Eddie watches him.

'Anything?' he shouts.

Micky takes a chance. 'Nah. They've gone.'

He checks Eddie out, sees him sigh expansively with relief.

But he knows it's not over, knows it's *never* going to be over.

Rick's knackered Transit rocks up bang on nine and Micky lets him in thus avoiding the door-bell.

'Listen, mate. The old boy is having a bit of a rough morning. Sorry and all that but well, he's harmless.'

'I've seen it all, mate. No worries.'

Eddie hears the talking and confronts the pair of them.

'You two going to clear up this fucking mess?'

Rick laughs nervously but Micky knows it's not a joke.

'This is Rick from yesterday, dad. We'll get on it right away.'

The two edge past Eddie and his withering looks and into the bathroom. Ten minutes later Eddie is all smiles and it's cups of tea and bacon sandwiches all round, and the rest of the day goes off without a hitch. Likewise the following morning when a different tradesman rocks up to fit the flooring.

The bad news at this time is that smack, once again, has it's hands firmly around the throat of Micky Targett to the tune of over a gram a day. The good news is he can still afford to buy larger amounts to keep the per unit cost down. Dixie lets him have an ounce at a time for eleven hundred. Sadly for Micky he will never know that just one link in the chain separates him from the one person in the business, Wrenny, that he still likes and respects.

And the grind grinds on.

Sometimes he thinks the situation is bringing him closer to his dad. While they no longer go to the golf club together they hang at the house drinking beer, watching TV and talking. And it was a great summer of sport. Okay, despite the wizardry of Paul Gascoigne, England lost to Germany in the semis of the Euros but there were other treats they savoured together.

A stunning end to the U.S. Masters saw Greg Norman blow a six shot lead on the final day to lose to Nick Faldo. Later in the year a Thai-American kid will turn pro. His name is Tiger Woods

Manchester United dominate national football once again.

But Eddie really comes alive when there is boxing to watch and discuss. The most talked about figure in the sport is a human hamburger called Mike Tyson. He dumps the hapless Bruno onto his arse in March only to be similarly dispatched by Evander Holyfield later in the year.

On such occasions Micky and his dad are content in each other's company.

But mostly there is disharmony. Micky, for all his rough edges, can be fastidious. Has a thing about noisy eaters. Eddie with his soup slurping and his caprine mastications, his belches like a Doberman's bark, is a constant source of irritation.

Then there are all the things that Eddie no longer notices about himself. He no longer notices his collars and shoulders are covered with dandruff. He has to be taken to the barbers. He doesn't see the rambling, grey, wire wool twists of his eyebrows. He is no longer able to reach down to his yellow, twisted toe nails. Micky hates attending to these things, but he does.

Eddie has also forgotten where, or indeed how, to buy anything. He is no longer able to deal with any piece of mail that arrives for him. So Micky does all that too and, while he dutifully goes about it, he knows he is sacrificing a lot of himself to these tasks, and when he watches his dad shuffle away from him, he sees the shadow of his own happiness, ephemeral enough to begin with, drifting away too.

One evening, as the summer of that year fades into the autumn, he returns from picking up another bag from Dixie to find his father devilishly busy in the kitchen. He prowls expectantly next to the oven. The heat is overwhelming.

He's tried to talk him down from this in the past but got nowhere. The thought of him anywhere near a naked flame, let alone the prospect of actually eating anything he might put on a plate in front of him, scares Micky shitless. But there's no stopping the bloke. The old sod really enjoys it and it's good for his self-esteem so, Micky wonders, what's the worst that can happen?

As he walks through the hall towards the kitchen he guesses, quite correctly, that Eddie is working on a cake, because it looks like it's been snowing in there.

'Alright, boy? I'm all over this. You better be hungry.'

'Yeah. What we got?'

'Er, not too sure. Some dried fruit. Currents, dates. That sort of thing. Be about ten minutes.'

'Okay. No main course?'

Eddie ponders and thinks. 'I suppose we could have something later. Go in there and put the telly on.'

Micky does so, shifting the bag of heroin from the front of his underwear to his pocket. He grabs the remote, gets the early news. Ford are introducing some mad little thing called a Ka.

Not for the first time he wonders if, perhaps, things will stabilize for his dad. Perhaps this is as bad as it will get? With the help he gets from the two official carers and Carol coming over whenever she can, he figures things are as covered as they can be. But he shudders when he thinks about the bathroom and the trouble it caused. Deep down he knows that despite unaccounted for pleasantries such as today, he's strapped in for the long haul. And Eddie is made out of proper Wapping granite. He'll outlive everyone.

Then in he walks with his game face on. Cooking, to him, has always been a discipline of the utmost seriousness and he is known to get the hump when Micky isn't hungry or says things like, 'Can I just have some cheese?'

So it's a dried fruit cake and, no expense nor trouble being too much on this day, custard. He dumps a tray load on the coffee table and sets about cutting into the cake, decants a lump into a dessert bowl and hands it over. Micky splashes custard all over it. It smells and looks great. Eddie gets stuck in too.

After a couple of mouthfuls Micky is struck by two things firstly the cake doesn't actually taste of anything. The custard is fine, the cake – nothing. Secondly, as he chews and searches for the merest tincture of flavour upon which he might focus, comment and compliment, he notices something really weird. He takes another spoonful, chews carefully and slowly. Yes, his mouth is going numb.

He looks across at his dad. 'That alright?'

Eddie is powering through the bowlful like he hasn't eaten since last Wednesday. 'T'rific. You?'

'Not sure. Did you put any coconut in it?'

'Coconut? Don't think so.'

Micky sniffs it, nibbles a little more. The inside of his mouth and now his lips are definitely . . .

Fuck!

Keen not to alarm the old boy he sets his bowl aside and stands with no apparent haste. 'I think a coffee with this, don't you?'

'Please yourself.'

Micky breaks into a gallop. Out in the kitchen he scrabbles frantically through the cupboards. *No, no, please don't let this be . . .*

Sad, but yes indeed, true. Eddie has chucked at least fifteen grams of decent cocaine into the cake mix.

Fuck. My. Old. Boots.

Back in the lounge Eddie has cleaned his bowl and is eyeing the rest of the cake.

'Alright, that isn't it?'

'Do you want a curry?'

'What?'

'I fancy a curry. Takeaway. Shall I go to the shops and pick one up?'

'Dunno. I was going to have some more of that.'

'We'll have it for afters. I'll stick this in the fridge and nip down the road.'

Micky gathers the bowls, spoons and custard and gets it all out to the kitchen. By the time he gets back from the Indian he's buzzing his tits off.

He finds Eddie with Matt Munro blaring, his shirt off and three cans of Stella lined up in front of him.

'You alright, pop? Turn that shit down a bit will you.'

Eddie complies, a big grin splitting his face.

'Not sure I want any of that, boy. Anymore of that cake?'

The devil on Micky's shoulder tells him to go with it but he knows he can't so he plays a hunch instead.

'What cake?'

Eddie thinks and the strand of memory snaps. Yeah, what cake?

'I got a hell of a thirst on. Fancy coming up the club?'

*

The uncertainty of living with and caring for a dementia sufferer continues for Micky into the winter of ninety-six. Some of the time he looks upon this duty not as some onerous burden but as a privilege. He sees it as an opportunity to give, to give something back. Not just to his dad but to the world. He is *contributing* and he likes that.

Other times he feels like it is going to break him.

Towards the end of November he is driving home from wherever he's been. It is bitterly cold. He's taken to hanging around in shopping centres and, on occasions, pubs. Sometimes he'll have a beer, sometimes just a line of smack. He always takes a book. Neverwhere by Neil Gaiman gives him a view of London and The Beach by Alex Garland makes him think of a place he's always wanted to visit. And, as the weather worsens, he wonders more and more what that place might be like. Thailand.

He listens to the news on the radio. Chaos in the channel tunnel. A fire has brought the whole thing to a standstill. Micky says a prayer for everyone making a beer run that day.

He turns off the main road and heads up Tawney Avenue in the direction of the bungalow. A raw sleet begins to fall and through its mean slant he thinks he sees something heading in the opposite direction on the other side of the road. A shambolic, shuffling figure. For a nano-second the light from the Jag's dipped beam glints off a pair of heavy spectacles. Micky checks his wing mirror, slows to a stop.

He slams it in reverse, pelts back towards the hunched old man dressed only in light slacks, shirt, pullover and slippers. He jumps out.

'Dad!'

The old man ploughs on, huddled against the wind.

'Dad. Stop.'

Micky grabs his arm and he turns to look. His face is blue, his eyes are streaming.

'Where you been?' Eddie demands.

'I've been working. Get in the car.'

Eddie stops for a second, looks down at his son. A vicious gust of wind slices down the street like the edge of a broken bottle and suddenly the shivers overtake him. He knows he has something important to do.

But it's not the weather that chills Micky Targett, it's the look of both confusion and fear in his father's eyes.

'Get in the car, dad.'

Eddie does what he is told, shivering like a skinny old dog left out in the snow.

'Don't do this again, alright? Where were you going?'

Eddie thinks. Thinks as if his life depends on it but he just can't remember. He says nothing and Micky gets them home and into the warm.

Shocked by what he's seen Micky makes the decision to stay in the whole of the next day.

That night sleep is impossible.

The following morning, his squeamishness means he is reluctant to venture into his dad's bedroom when he wakes. Eddie has always been an early riser and Micky worries when he doesn't hear him shuffling around. He fears the worst. But would it be the worst?

Of course, since Eddie started to deteriorate, Micky has considered the possibility and the ramifications of his demise. How would he feel? What would it mean?

He hates himself for the answers his brain suggests to these questions because his unshakeable instinct is to feel that it would be for the best. Eddie has a shit life and that is making Micky's life shit and that is the beginning and the end of it. Micky knows the old boy is going to die but there is no way of knowing when. So he remains permanently on edge.

He heads into the bathroom and is stunned by the smell. It is not a large room so it doesn't take him too long to find the source. Carol was right. The bath is splattered with excrement. Lots of it.

He goes to the kitchen and grabs rubber gloves and bleach from under the sink. He is calm enough to flick the kettle on while he is there.

Back in the bathroom he turns on the bath taps but leaning over the bath the stench is overwhelming. He dashes back into his room, soaks a T-shirt in aftershave and ties it over his face. Back in the bathroom he opens the window, arms himself with the loo brush and gets to work.

Ten minutes see the room clear. Apart from the smell. To counter this Micky picks up the air freshener spray and empties half of it over the bath. He resumes his morning ritual by taking the leak he went into the khazi for in the first place. He has a pounding headache.

In the kitchen he makes himself a coffee and turns on the radio. He hears the fucking Fugees massacring another classic, this time No Woman No Cry. He rolls the tuning wheel, catches a blast of Breathe by The Prodigy and decides that's a bit too much under the circumstances. He stands in silence. Then he sees his father's bedroom door open and Eddie emerges, his slippers dragging on the carpet.

Micky doesn't know what to say. Should he mention the bath? Is there any point?

'What you doing here?'

Micky thinks he would be able to spend more time more easily around his father if he wasn't such a blunt, curmudgeonly fucker. But then again if Eddie knows and fully appreciates what a state he is in then he has more than enough reason to be the way he is.

'Day off.'

'What is it you do?'

'Drive a van.'

Eddie refills the kettle. 'Want some breakfast?'

Micky thinks of the coke cake fiasco. 'I'll do it.'

He slots some bread in the toaster and they stand next to each other waiting. Micky finds himself smelling his father and wonders how far away the day is when he has to put his hands on him. See him naked. Wipe away the shit from his buttocks and legs.

Eddie takes his tea into the lounge leaving Micky alone to marmalade up the toast and think about where his life is. Where it will go.

The day passes without incident. A carer shows up mid-morning. Micky doesn't know her and Eddie doesn't either. She makes more tea, ensures Eddie takes whatever is in his dosette box. They hang around in the lounge listening to the radio. She tries to engage him in conversation but he really has no idea who she is or what she might want with him.

At noon a ring at the door announces the arrival of the Meals On Wheels service. In a Pavlovian reaction Eddie launches himself forward and powers into the hallway. Micky follows him, keen to see how the thing works. He is standing behind Eddie as he opens the door and thus gets an immediate understanding of why the old boy is so eager to get there. Probably not much to do with the food.

'There's my favorite boy.'

''Ello, Sweetheart. How are you today?'

Micky has to admit, the old bastard always did have an eye for pretty face.

'Steak pie, mash, peas and gravy today, Eddie.' This is the smoking hot blonde, mid-twenties, who hands over a box wrapped in metallic foil. She notices Micky hovering in the hallway.

'Hello.'

'Hi.' Micky says.

'This is my son.' Eddie tells her.

She nods at Micky.

'Why don't you come in for a cup of tea?' Eddie asks.

'Love to, Ed but I've got me route. Got to keep moving.'

'I might have to chase you down the road one of these days.'

She laughs a lovely, kind laugh. She must have heard every single word of every single line of lonely bullshit going, Micky reckons, but she's still smiling.

'Well don't do it today, it's bloody freezing out here. See ya tomorrow.'

She bounces down the drive to the little van and pulls away. Both Micky and Eddie check out her arse as she goes.

Micky is lifted by this brief encounter. Sure she's getting paid, but the goodness of her heart was clear and obvious.

It's a day that drags with blood-thickening boredom, but there is a glimmer of interest that comes the way of both of them during the late afternoon of every weekday. It is then that Micky and his dad both find they have developed an unfeasibly committed appreciation of human calculator and all round cougar-like TV personality, Carol Vorderman. So it is, when Micky can get himself back to the house at the appropriate hour, often still cosseted in the arms of Morpheus, they congregate in front of the television for their usual hit of Countdown.

'Where is she, where is she?' Eddie wants to know as he sinks into his chair.

Micky has to laugh but he knows full well the old boy has a point. It doesn't matter how long into the past he commands his memory to go he really can't recall a subject upon which the pair of them so wholeheartedly agreed. Yeah, the woman has got the goods, but the main reason he always tries to be there is for the warmth generated between him and Eddie by this rather unlikely patch of libidinous common ground.

'She adds up a storm, the bird.'

'I wonder what she's wearing today,' Micky says.

And there she is, clad snugly in a contour enhancing velvet number that does everything in all the right places.

Eddie's grin is wider than his face.

'So she does all this in her head? She hasn't got one of those machines to do the sums with?'

'Nope.'

'She's unbelievable.'

'You'd think they might give her a chair.'

'Then we wouldn't be able to see her arse.'

That, Micky knows, is a fair point.

It's a fun and unifying diversion, albeit a temporary one, at the end of which, Micky always tells himself he will have an evening off the gear. But as the music plays the show out it's his turn to be Pavlovian and, once again, he shamefully but inevitably creeps into his room and hits a line.

This is just as well because soon after he hears his father shouting for him, and he's angry. Always so angry.

'What the fuck have you done now? Why are you here to fuck my life up?'

If Micky wasn't so depressed he'd laugh and if he wasn't just about to come up on the brown he'd weep once more. His father is trying to pull on a pair of trousers over his emaciated legs. He can't manage it. The reason for that is the trousers aren't trousers. He's trying to wear a pullover on his bottom half.

'Why the fuck do you keep doing this to me? You've been a useless arsehole all your life.'

Soon enough the afternoon carer shows up. Pleasingly it's Carol and all three of them hang in the kitchen while Micky makes tea. It's almost fun but Micky knows it's just a moment, a moment that he isn't really able to enjoy.

If only I knew how long this will go on for, he thinks. *Then I could plan.*

Two things happen that let Micky know he can do all the planning he likes but he's still in a prison. Firstly, Eddie goes to the toilet and Carol puts down her teacup.

'You been in his room lately?'

He knows he's been a wanker about this. He hasn't been in there for months.

'Erm . . .'

Someone who's seen it all before, she helps him out.

'I know it's tough but it's getting very unhealthy. This place smells like someone took a shoite in a haddock factory. It's literally ground into the carpet. His sheets haven't been changed since forever. I can help from time to time but all of that really isn't my job. You need to step up.'

Micky starts to panic. His mountain, already too big for him to climb, gets bigger by the day. He doesn't know it then but inside a fortnight, in a manner too awful to even contemplate, there will be an answer to his dilemma.

The second jolt that rips into Micky happens after Carol has left. He's watching the early news. He has, of course, heard of Tony Blair but never really took much notice of him. Apparently though, despite a recent pull back from the Conservatives, Labour are still way ahead in the polls for the election no less than six months in the future.

Eddie is in his room. In spite of what Carol said Micky feels reluctant to even check up on him so afraid is he of what he might find. Then Eddie is standing right next to him. And he's crying. Crying and shaking.

'She's gone, boy.'

'Jesus! What? Who's gone?'

Eddie's eyes are terrified whirlpools. 'Your mum.'

Micky is speechless.

'Please, son. We have to go. We have to look for her now.'

Micky watches him shuffle from one foot to the other.

'Dad.'

'Please, boy. She'll freeze. We have to find her.'

Micky sees this as something of a watershed because he knows it won't get any worse than this. How can it?

Someone has to give Eddie the good news that his beloved wife is not in fact missing. Then that person has to tell him the reason she isn't missing is because she's been dead for ten years. How's that for job of the day?

And of course that person is Micky. He does the only thing he can, he gives it to him straight. And he watches as he sees another part of his dad's soul simply cease to be. He sees the devastation in his eyes turn to realization, and then be seized, yet again, by more devastation. Eddie finally understands. He stops crying but the agony goes on.

But the next night, something happens that passes to Micky a glowing, warming light he will carry inside of him for all of his days.

Early evening and Eddie asks Micky what he wants for his tea.

'It's alright, dad. I'll get us something. Fish and chips?'

'Fish and chips nothing! Shut up and sit down.'

With that he is gone and Micky knows there is no point in arguing. So all he can do is sit in the lounge watching the telly and try not to be too disturbed by the sounds coming through the wall. The crashes of the pots and pans as they are dropped to the floor, the accompanying curses. *Best off not to know what's going on out there,*

Micky thinks.

Eventually Eddie bundles into the lounge carrying a tray which he dumps on Micky's lap. His face is tortured with concentration. He shuffles off to retrieve his own dinner.

Micky looks down at the plate and sees what his dad intended to do. Boiled potatoes, fried sausages and onions. Ordinarily a meal Micky could have devoured with great pleasure. Ordinarily. But upon closer inspection and initial sampling Micky soon discovers this was no ordinary culinary endeavour. For a start the potatoes, crispy on the tooth, seem not to have been boiled at all. Conversely the onions are clearly not fried but boiled. The sausages are black on the outside and a shocking pink inside.

He can't be bothered to mention any of this, knows it will be much more trouble than it's worth. He threw away what was left of the coke cake because he knew it was out of sight and there was no way Eddie would have remembered, but this is right here and right now.

Eddie rejoins him.

Micky finds part of a sausage that doesn't look like it will kill him and eats that. Four chews in his mouth feels like it is melting, a horrible sensation that consumes his entire head in seconds. He throws the tray from his knees, gets to his feet and runs out of the room.

'What's wrong?' calls Eddie.

Mouth full, Micky can't answer, he just carries on across the hall and into the bathroom. He spits whatever was in his mouth into the toilet, gagging luridly in the process, runs the tap in the sink and holds his mouth under the stream. He reaches onto the shelf, grabs his toothbrush and gets to work with that. *What the actual fuck?* Micky wants to know.

A moment later Eddie rushes in to join him.

'Boy,' he informs his son helpfully, 'don't eat the sausages. There's something wrong with them.'

Enraged Micky glares back.

'You're fucking telling me!'

He barges past and out into the kitchen, searching the debris strewn counter tops for a clue. Eventually he sees what must have happened. What *has* happened. A certain manufacturer of washing up liquid was, in nineteen ninety-six at least, making its product in a variety of colours other than the traditional dark green. One of those bore a great similarity to the normal colour of cooking oil. Both bottles of the washing up liquid and the cooking oil were standing next to each other on the counter top next to the hob. Micky snatches them both and holds them up for closer examination as his dad joins him in the kitchen.

'Look!' Micky squeals. 'Look what you did. You fried the sausages in Fairy liquid.'

Eddie clearly reverts to the found-out schoolboy inside. 'No I didn't.'

'Yes you did. Look, there's fucking bubbles in the frying pan!'

Eddie looks. *Shit,* he thinks, *totally busted.*

Micky glares at him expectantly. Then something happens which gives Micky hope. Hope in adversity, and if you have hope . . .

Micky will later swear he saw a lightbulb illuminate above Eddie's head. There is certainly no mistaking the impish grin.

'Maybe so, son. Maybe so. But I'll tell you what, they may not be the best sausages in the world, but they're certainly the *cleanest* aren't they?'

Long seconds pass. Long seconds in which Micky tries to process and understand what is taking place in front of him. And at the end of that brief period he is left with just one word; genius. You just cannot write that shit.

So he starts laughing and, realizing that he's not actually going to die from food poisoning, he carries on laughing. The two of them, once Micky returns from the chip shop, laugh about it all evening.

Yeah, thinks Micky Targett, maybe there's something in this praying to God bollocks.

Three days later, while Micky is out picking up more heroin from Dixie, Rock Steady Eddie suffers a massive stroke. Carol, by this time holding a key of her own, finds him on the lounge floor.

*

Micky arrives home from his dash to Oldchurch hospital to a house that is perfectly quiet and still. His mind whirls with thoughts and concerns, drowns in an ocean of self-recrimination. He should have been here. He should have been here.

He closes the door and walks through the hall and out into the kitchen. His first thought isn't to hit a line from the bag in his pocket. He doesn't want tea nor can he stomach anything to eat. He only piles more guilt onto himself by doing what he does next but he doesn't care. What he does next is nothing. He stands in the kitchen and he listens to the silence.

He walks through to the lounge, sits on the faded green Draylon. He looks at his father's chair. That chair is as old as Micky and it followed them from Stepney to Rainham to the first house in Upminster and then to this place. He is as familiar with that chair as he is with the man who spent the last four decades or so relaxing in it. Now it's empty and so is Micky.

Should have been here.

He listens to the silence and feels the peace, and he can't help but enjoy it, the silence and the peace. He knows that now nothing weird, nothing unpleasant, nothing insane will happen, and that knowledge and the serenity that comes with it is most definitely his due, he reckons.

'Your father has suffered a haemorrhagic stroke,' the neurosurgeon at the hospital told him. 'It is of the intracerebral kind. He is quite frail and you say demented as well?'

'Yeah,' Micky mumbled, suddenly very scared.

The guy sighed and did the looking-straight-into-the-next-of-kin's-eyes thing. 'Well, I can tell you that surgery is not appropriate. Your father is in emergency care and we are doing everything for him that we can. I should, however, tell you that I think it unlikely he will survive. But we can never be sure about these things.'

Micky sees a tea cup on the window sill next to Eddie's chair. He goes to it and picks it up. It's not one of those crappy 'World's Greatest Dad' ones. It's just a simple white cup. But it's *his* cup and as he holds it Micky is overwhelmed by sadness.

He takes the cup to the kitchen, washes it and places it on the rack on the counter. He looks out into the garden and sees Eddie's favourite place in the world, his wooden bench. Where he used to sit and talk to his beloved Florrie.

Then he notices the kettle has a fingermark on it. He looks at the kettle and smiles. It is the third Micky needed to buy in recent months on account of Eddie filling the previous ones with milk and wrecking them all. He wipes it clean.

Having done that he fills a bowl with warm soapy water, narrowly avoiding using the cooking oil, and wipes down all the surfaces in the kitchen. He doesn't dare look in the oven but he sets about the hob and gas rings. Then he hits the bathroom.

He tidies and cleans his bedroom. Then he goes into his dad's bedroom. The smell is terrible. It is the smell of decay, and the guilt of his previous inaction is there to punish him once more. If he can do this now then why not when his dad needed it? He opens all the windows.

He looks at the nasty little bed. He bought a new mattress the previous year but the bed and the sheets and the headboard all look cheap and old. He strips the bed, taking the sheets and pillows, at arm's length, out through the kitchen, into the garden and in through the side door of the garage. The soiled mattress goes the same way.

Back in the bedroom he notices brown hand prints on the side of the bed. He gets rubber gloves from the kitchen then removes the supporting slats and stands the bed frame on its side. He leans on it and it cracks and folds immediately. It's probably as old as he is, Micky guesses. He carts all that out too. In the garage he finds a Stanley knife.

Back inside he considers the floor and is pleased he is wearing shoes. He does the after shave soaked T-shirt routine again. He rips up the carpet and cuts it into manageable slices, drags it all through and out to the garage. Then the pulverised, powdered underlay. He removes the curtains. He leans his nose against the wallpaper and knows that the smell has even permeated that.

Then he cleans and tidies the lounge.

Then he goes into the third bedroom, his own when he was younger. Nothing to do in there except look up at his three heroes.

'Might be moving on soon, boys.'

That evening Micky Targett does something weird. He doesn't take any heroin. Simply doesn't feel the need. He has abstained before because he likes to test himself. He keeps it in his room and it calls to him every night. Most nights he answers that call and it helps him get through, but sometimes he tells it to fuck off. To let both it and him know he's not some scuzzy, addicted smack head. That's what he thinks anyway. But this night there is no craving, no desire.

Yeah, moving on. Lucky they didn't get that dog.

CHAPTER FIFTEEN

Paithoon drives Priow's little sister to his house in Lampang. She cries most of the way in spite of his shouts and threats. In the end he just punches her and turns the radio up.

He occasionally picks up a kid. Sometimes to settle a debt, sometimes if the parents are just strapped for cash and the price is right. Most of the time it's those Rohingas from Burma. Generally he doesn't get too involved because the money in it is next to nothing compared to the drugs he moves, but points have to be made and examples seen to be set. It's all business.

He locks her in the cellar where he can't hear her and calls A-Wut and his partner Nong who pay reasonable money for good-looking kids. An hour later they show up. A-Wut, a tattooed ex-meth head, has a rucksack containing fizzy drinks, sweets and crisps. It also contains rope, gagging material, duct tape and a bag with a draw string for the kid's head. Diazapam too.

Paithoon unlocks the cellar and the couple goes in. Girls this age don't normally take too long and they go with the nice routine first. The 'you're coming with us to have a lovely time by the seaside' number. This is accompanied by the drinks and the sugary snacks.

They know that there will be objections. They'll get plenty of 'I want my mum', but the crushed pills in the drink will wear her down or at least keep them docile for the journey. There will be tears and shouts and tantrums but it's often surprising how quickly the spirit of a young human can be extinguished.

Occasionally, usually with boys, the resistance necessitates the other approach in which the pair of them participate also. Beatings, the bag over the head, disorientation. Sensory and sleep deprivation. More beatings. It's all the same to A-Wut and Nong.

Just twenty minutes behind a locked door with Mayuree tells them they are in business. She's a pretty kid who will do as she is told. They emerge from the cellar smiling, Nong holding a stunned looking Mayuree by the hand. A-Wut peels one hundred thousand Baht, about sixteen hundred pounds, from a chunky roll which he gives to Paithoon. They leave.

Their cheap Hyundai isn't suited to the motorway but they aim south on Highway 1, making a start on the four hundred and sixty mile journey, pretty much all of which will be on high speed concrete. They want to complete the run with toilet breaks only. Firstly the quicker they get there the quicker they will start earning. Secondly they don't want anything incriminating happening en route. Overnight stops might have the kid say something, do something to raise alarm. CCTV cameras may pick up an image.

Keep her quiet, drugged and out of sight.

A-Wut takes the wheel first, Mayuree is asleep in the back. Nong heaves her bulk in beside her and is soon asleep herself.

It is a boring, uneventful shift for A-Wut. No radio. He smokes constantly, thinks about dropping a Yaba pill but decides against it. Keep it straight until he gets there, he tells himself. Then maybe have first crack at the kid for a treat.

Five hours in he needs a piss and the car needs fuel. He pulls over at the next pit stop, wakes Nong and tells her it's her turn. He goes straight to the urinals around the back, then fills the car and, in the 7/11, buys more cigarettes, a couple of Krating Daeng and a few bags of nuts and crisps. He leans against the car as Nong waddles to the ladies. He sparks up another Marlboro as he looks in at the slumbering infant he has just bought. Pretty, which is unusual for most kids from that area. Slender nose, a lot of the farang seem to like that. Slim without being skinny. *Yeah,* he thinks, *if we break her well enough she'll be a good earner for years.*

Nong squeezes in behind the wheel and A-Wut gets in the back next to the kid who stirs and trembles. They both look at her as she grizzles and mewls feebly. Then she finds flatter ground, calmer waters and settles back into a darkly troubled sleep.

Nong starts the car and they pull back onto Highway 1, heading further south towards Bangkok.

An hour later they hit the outskirts of the original city of angels, but rather than plough on into the bedlam, Nong gets onto Highway 9 to skirt west. As she heads through Saphan Sung she takes the off road and picks up Highway 7 to move away from the sprawling conurbation and south towards Chon Buri.

The sky is beginning to change as they near their destination. The velvet of the darkness can only conceal a clear blue tint for so long. Then the world lightens as the car eats through the last of the miles. Soon they can rest. Well, A-Wut and Nong can rest. For Mayuree rest is a privilege she will soon have to learn to live without.

Nong slows for the exit road off of Highway 7, heads towards the sea. The upper reaches of the Gulf Of Thailand.

Heads in towards Pattaya.

Onto the South Pattaya road and into the diseased heart of the city. They finally pull over some five hundred yards back from the beach. Five hundred yards from the luxury chain hotels and the expensive restaurants. Five hundred yards from the sand where normal people with ordinary children play and swim every day. Five hundred yards from freedom. But in this world, in Mayuree's new world, making it those five hundred yards will be like travelling to the moon.

Just in time she wakes up. Wakes up so that A-Wut doesn't have to carry her over the threshold into the cheap apartment block that is her new home. The home where she will either be beaten and starved or have sex with men for money that she will never see.

Mayuree is now working as a full-time prostitute. She is still only ten years old.

ESSEX - DECEMBER 1996

Micky visits Eddie every day. Not that Eddie knows because, as he clings gamely to life, he is completely comatose. Micky sits at the side of his bed, holds his hand.

The hospital staff envisage very little chance of him making it, but hint at the fact he has survived a week since the stroke as being a positive sign. Micky has no idea what that might mean.

He cleans the house over and over for the whole of that week. He hires a steam powered wallpaper remover and strips Eddie's bedroom and finds the walls themselves are in pretty good shape. He buys paint, a roller and brushes. He buys new curtains, replaces lamp shades and light fittings. He calls in a carpet company. While the rep is there Micky looks around, thinks that if he's doing it he might as well do all of it. Once carpeted the place looks and smells like the fantastic home he remembered when his parents first bought it an eon ago. He hires a van to empty the garage, not just of what he pulled out of Eddie's room but of a ton of crap that had been accumulating over the years.

He asks an estate agent to call round to value the place.

He has also heard that the library has a computer that is connected to this thing that Ishy mentioned all that time before. The world wide web thing. He's keen to investigate it and wants to find out what he can about a place he'd like to visit.

He dresses for the conditions. He likes hearing his footsteps creak in the thick snow, so opts to hoof it through the streets into town, noticing the place is unusually quiet. He gets to Upminster library to find it closed. There is a notice taped to the inside of the front door. 'Closed on 25th and 26th'.

Jesus, he thinks, *it's Christmas sodding day.* He wonders where all his friends are. Not literally, he just thinks it's odd no one contacted him. Does nobody really care?

He calls the hospital and is told there is no change in his father's condition, so he decides there is no point in going to see him. He celebrates the birthday of our Lord the Saviour by drinking neat gin with ice, all he could find in the drinks cabinet that he likes, and by hitting a few lines of Dixie's smack. He has a little left in the current bag and decides he'll stop when he gets to the end of that.

He settles in for the evening enjoying every second of his solitude and tranquility. Joy to all men.

Two days later he goes to Upminster library where a bloke there tells him about this new mechanism that helps you find stuff on the web. He calls it Ask Jeeves and shows Micky how to use it.

'Type what you want to look for in there and hit Enter.'

So Micky types in the word 'Thailand'. He reads a lot and checks out the photographs and loves all of it. He is even able to print out what was on the screen and bring it home with him.

Later that day, the hospital calls, something they haven't done before. His heart thumps violently. They tell him that, miraculously, Eddie has made tremendous progress over the last forty-eight hours. He looks like he is going to survive. They ask him to go in to discuss the next move.

Over the coming weeks and into the new year, as Rock Steady Eddie lives up to his long held nickname, Micky's overwhelming feeling is, once again, one of guilt. Of course he doesn't wish his dad dead. Does he?

After talking to the staff at the hospital he feels, or rather he knows, that it would be a lot better for everyone if he did succomb because, despite his 'recovery' his life, from this point on, will be one of complete dependency.

In his innocence Micky asks the doctor, 'How will it all work then? What's the word? Palliative? You give him palliative care?'

The doctor, used to giving people much worse news than this, doesn't blink when he lets Micky have it.

'Oh no, Mr. Targett. We don't care for him. He has made amazing progress. *You* care for him. He's coming home.'

On numb legs Micky wobbles out and to the car, gets home without knowing how. Inside he slumps on the sofa. If life was unbearable when Eddie was mobile and semi-capable and only had dementia, what's it going to be like now? He feels like phoning his brother and telling him it's his turn. He has another idea.

He calls Carol the carer and invites her over. He suggests dinner or whatever but she is happy to simply come to the house.

'Wow, good job. The place looks grand.'

'Thanks. Didn't take long. Maybe I missed my calling.'

It's mid-evening and Carol is dressed in her civvies. As they take tea through into the lounge Micky can't help noticing that she is indeed an attractive woman. Early forties, five foot two of eye-catching bounce very artfully preserved. He loves the tinkling scales of her Waterford lilt. Okay she's married but maybe if . . .

'So how's Eddie?'

'Well the old boy is confounding medical science. The grim reaper had one hand on his shoulder but Eddie boy turned round and nutted him square between the eyes. Not only is he going to make it but he's coming home.'

'Oh my God that is amazing.' But she knows, both from Micky's expression and from the past nine or ten months of helping to handle Eddie, that 'amazing' is a relative term. She's seen it all before and knows Micky is the one who is suffering.

Micky sighs. 'It is.'

'But . . .'

'Yeah. But. I was practically a basket case before. I feel terrible for thinking about me when it's him that's so sick . . .'

'But . . .'

He nods. 'Yeah.'

'I know. Don't feel bad. You've done well and you can be proud of yourself.'

It's good to hear although it doesn't change much.

'Do you know what kind of care he'll need?' she asks.

'Round the clock, probably wheelchair bound. He'll need everything done for him.'

'The good news is you won't be involved too much.'

'Right. Well, I don't see how I can be. This is real nursing, yeah?'

'Yes it is. If he's coming back here and he's in that state then you'll probably have to get a live-in.'

''Scuse me?'

'A live-in nurse. A nurse who lives here. There's a third bedroom, right?'

'Well yeah but . . .'

'He's too sick to go into a nursing home and he's taking up a bed where he is. He needs round the clock medical care. He'll only get that here with a qualified live-in.'

'I see.' Micky thinks this might not be too bad. A nurse, eh? He wonders if she'll be obliged to wear the outfit. Not an outfit, what's the word? Uniform. And if there is full-time care on hand that will relieve him of a lot of his duties.

'Could your company get in the frame for it? I mean could *you* . . .'

'Me? No. I'm a carer not a nurse but my lot could arrange everything. They do what you need.'

'Okay, well, you can slag the Tories as much as you like but as least we're hanging onto the NHS.'

Carol casts him a wary glance. She gets a feeling Micky is in for a shock.

'This kind of thing isn't on the NHS if your father has any money.'

'He's barely got anything. I haven't got much either.' Micky thinks of his once magnificent stash, glad what is left of it isn't public knowledge.

'Okay. What about this place though?'

'What about it?'

'Who owns it?'

Micky feels very sick very quickly. *No,* he says to himself. *Just, no.*

'He does.'

'Shit.'

'What?'

'They'll take the cost out of this place.'

'What, you mean we'll have to sell it?' Panic and fear grip Micky in a terrible embrace. *No. No. No.*

'You won't be forced to sell it because this is a perfect place for him to be. But they will take a charge over the property. As and when Eddie dies, depending on how much is owed, you'll have to pay the bill. If you have that money yourself that's how you pay. If you don't, you'll be obliged to sell the house to pay it.'

Micky struggles to hear what she's saying. After everything he has come through. This house. This fucking house! But what's a nurse going to cost? Everyone is always banging on about how poorly paid they are. Can't be more than a couple of hundred a week. Three tops.

'So what would be the cost of that, a full time, live in nurse? Any idea?'

Carol feels for him, she really does. Nice bloke, she knows that. Bit scatty but he has a lot of soul.

'About three and a half grand a month.'

When Carol has gone Micky thinks back to the conversation he had with Ben Yardley. The title of the property. Micky could have had it diverted into his name and thus avoided these costs. But he didn't. He wanted to do the right thing, get the house back for his dad and for the memory of his mother. And by the time he'd managed to do that Eddie was far enough down the road to not even fully understand what had happened anyway.

And, after everything he's done, Micky has shot himself in the foot for three and a half grand a month. For how long?

As he makes the call to Dixie to line him up another ounce he resolves *never* to do the right fucking thing again.

It's good to see Chrissie Jarvis. He's doing well, has a better standard of motor on the front. He mentions the drug business but an immediate and curt shake of Micky's head warns him off. He's there to chop in the XJS.

'What you after, mate? Got a nice Audi just come in.'

No, Micky doesn't want an Audi. He's not there to trade up. 'Give me the cheapest piece of shit in the place that runs.'

Micky needs money. The only income he has is the thirty-odd quid a for being a carer plus his dad's two pensions. That's it.

Having thought about the money he would receive for selling the house in the eventuality of Eddie's passing, something else he feels horribly guilty about, he is now informed of the costly alterations he needs to make to accommodate Eddie and his nurse.

Fortunately the third bedroom is big enough to take a small double so he doesn't need to bash any walls around. He relocates his three heroes into his own room.

But he needs new beds and mattresses and everything that goes with that. A wheelchair needs to be bought. A ramp to the front door. Widening of the interior doorways.

Micky should be glad. His old man is hanging in there.

Eddie returns to the home that he owns, in the spring of nineteen ninety-seven. Also into the equation comes a short, dumpy Malaysian nurse called Akma who moves all her stuff in too. Micky still pays Carol a tenner an hour to call around when she is free. Eddie is as well cared for as he can be. Micky not so much. He gets so depressed, so fucking *down* he's got his own private bathysphere for the journey.

An NHS physiotherapist comes round and works with Eddie on his muscle strength. Strength being a contentious word. The word muscle is a little generous too. Eddie Targett, once so powerful and robust, has shriveled to the point of no return. Mentally the stroke has robbed him of just about everything the dementia didn't. No one seems to know what, if anything, he can understand.

He can say one word they all make out; at first it sounds like Orrie. Then, when he finds a way through his debilitating restrictions and starts to form words again, they understand he is saying, 'Florrie.'

But he's a fighter and he works at his exercises to the point where

Akma can get him out of bed and into his wheelchair on her own. That's as it good as it gets, but at least it frees Micky up with the time to nurture his heroin habit and to sit around asking himself the same question over and over again; when can I have my life back?

And the clock turns and time, more sluggish than ever, rolls by. For Micky though, stupefied by the drug and by chronically unfair twists of fate, and for his dad, simply stupefied, life is a quagmire of depression and inertia.

It was always on the cards but on the first of May ninety-seven Tony Blair's 'New Labour' victory ends eighteen years of Tory control. The ethos, the 'take the money' values that kick-started Micky's quest for fortune are at an end. But of course they aren't.

He, his dad and Akma gather around the TV for the evening news. Eddie's speech is improving although certain letters at the beginning of words are still lost to him. The W, H, N and S.

'Oo ee?'

Both Akma and Micky know this translates as, 'Who's he?'

'Tony Blair,' Micky says. 'New Prime Minister.' Blair looks good as he whips his speech notes from his pocket outside number ten. Doesn't look like a lefty though because well, he's not. This is Centrism. This is 'New'. Meet the new boss - same as the old boss.

''anker,' Eddie comments acidly.

He's still got it, Micky thinks.

Ninety-seven rolls by. Hong Kong goes back to the Chinese, the IRA declare a ceasefire. On the morning of the thirty-first of August Micky slouches against the counter top in the kitchen listening to radio. Akma is with Eddie. He rolls the tuning wheel but there seems to be no music, just talking. He listens and hears talk of a car crash in Paris. The Princess and the Fayed bloke. Unconfirmed rumours at first.

And Micky's life as a depressed heroin addict goes on. On top of it all his guts are a mess because the smack is making him constipated, so he's dosing up on laxatives and that ain't fun either.

So he comes off it during the day and gets a job. As a Meals On Wheels driver. There is sod all money in it but he does it for two reasons; one, it gets him out of the house, gives him something to think about. Secondly the altruism is genuine. He likes doing things for people, especially the oldsters.

Actually three reasons. He enjoys the evening drift even more.

Another year.

On April the tenth nineteen ninety-eight the Good Friday agreement is signed by the British and Irish governments. Peace finally comes to the Province. On the fifteenth of August the Real Irish Republican Army detonates a car bomb in the small market town of Omagh, County Tyrone killing twenty-nine people and injuring over two hundred. The following month it too announces a ceasefire.

But it was barely into the new year when Micky was startled out of the fog of his day to day. Following a trial at the Old Bailey, two suspects were convicted of the murder of three men on a remote track on a farm in Essex. Neither man was called Wren or Harper.

Micky shivered at the memory. Georgie Harper wasn't joking that day two years previously in the car park of the Yeoman. *Steps were being taken,* he'd said. Stone cold killers with brains.

Was that really me? Micky thinks. Was I involved with that? Did I *know* those people?

Throughout ninety-eight Eddie's health is a constant concern. He appears to make progress but that progress is fragile and usually fades. Micky sits with him constantly. Thinks back. Ponders their differences.

Eddie always wanted his sons to learn enough at school so that they never had to bust their bollocks at work like he had to. But Eddie never seemed to like the boy and then the man that Micky became. Okay he turned into a bit of a smart arse, but wasn't that what a Grammar school education was *for?*

He was good at sports, which pleased his dad although his interest in slamming into the boxing bag Eddie had strung up in the garage in the Rainham house was short lived. It hurt his hands. On the rugby field Micky, a natural fly half, had a decent turn of speed and a serious side step. The same snake-hipped excellence would later dazzle dance floors across the UK and Europe. But one Saturday morning he came unstuck when he went in low against a six foot black kid playing for Stepney Green. Broke his nose.

He was stunned, there was blood everywhere and Micky wanted to come off. There were no substitutes in those days. Eddie was disgusted.

'Wipe yourself off and get back on there.' Even the school PE teacher was pissed off but knew not to get in Eddie's way. Micky went out again but that incident changed things.

And weirdly, Eddie couldn't get along with Micky's reading either. He always had his nose in a book. Anything, didn't matter. One summer's Sunday he was in the lounge, chuckling his way through Portnoy's Complaint. Eddie went nuts.

'What are you doing in here when the weather is this good?'

Micky was never one to waste an opportunity like that. 'Er, reading?'

Eddie grabbed the book and slammed him around the head with it.

'Get out and get some exercise. What's the matter with you? Why aren't you like your mates?'

There were several answers that rinsed through Micky's mind, foremost among them being, because they haven't got a dickhead for a father.

He was his mother's son and desired to be nothing else.

He was good at school but never quite good enough. His report card was stuffed with 2As and 2Bs.

'What's wrong with getting ones? Why are other kids cleverer than you?'

Micky was screaming inside.

'He just wants you to be the best?' Florence would tell him.

'I'm the best I can be but that's not enough is it?'

'He's very proud of you. He tells everyone about how good you are.'

'Why does he never tell me?'

Even she had no answer for that.

And now, as another year turns and Micky nears the end of his fourth decade on this god forsaken planet, he looks down at the stricken, wasted, distorted figure of the man who used to and continues to make his life so difficult. Head lolling to one side, dribbling, incontinent, useless. *Expensive.*

He thinks how cruel it all is. There he was, cock of the street. The Wapping hardman. Athlete, boxer, worker. Royal docks gang boss. Cable Streeter. Father, husband, provider. Now look.

Micky tries to find a reason to hate him but there is none, and that just makes it worse.

A few years before, Micky read a book written by a German Jew imprisoned in one of the camps. Guy was a psychiatrist so perhaps had half a chance of working out how to keep his mind in one piece. It was one of the most fascinating things he had ever read and the gist of it, from Micky's corner anyway, was this; you can take everything from a man. You can do anything to him and take everything from him except one thing. And that is the way he deals with what is happening to him. Even under circumstances as inhuman as that, it is the sufferer who decides how he is going to feel.

So Micky looks down at his old dad and knows that Eddie Targett is digging in. Surviving. And Micky is proud of him and he decides to dig in too, hoping he can be half the man his father is.

*

DS Roland Carter was perturbed by the phone call he had received earlier in the day. He'd had a few like it over the last month or so, from the same man. But things were getting a little intense. Things were *escalating.*

Ordinarily he would have put it down to stress, too much time spent on the job, but this was different. This was different because he knew the man concerned. Knew him well enough to know he wasn't that kind of bloke. Ordinarily.

So, even though the traffic was a bitch and he had other things to do, like have a life, he took the time out to drive to Romford and have a beer with his old mate from Hendon. Have a beer with Ray Pitts.

It isn't a market day so he can drive straight to that section of the town centre where, up until not that long ago, they'd been herding sheep since medieval times. Which is kind of ironic, thinks Ro Carter as he parks up outside the Bull pub. Ironic because Romford hasn't really progressed in terms of civilized living since those days back in the thirteenth century.

Ray Pitts doesn't look too good which means not only does the job have him strung out but he's been drinking to deal with it. Ro makes his way over to his old mate hoping he hasn't resurrected his cocaine habit as well.

''Ello, boy. You alright?' he asks as he holds out his hand.

Ray nods and shakes but doesn't smile. 'Be a bit better when you buy me a couple of Scotches.'

Bollocks, thinks Ro Carter as he heads to the bar.

He is aware from past experience that Ray Pitts is sometimes prone to take things personally. Shit gets to him. Not often, just sometimes. Like now.

He places the whisky and his pint on the table and sits across from him, sees he isn't happy.

He is so well acquainted with this man he actually knows what he is there for. He knows what this is all about. He could even guess the why, just not the who. But that will come. With the whisky it will all come.

'Tell me something, Ro,' Ray Pitts says by way of an opening gambit. 'Those two blokes, those two you got for the Rettendon murders . . .'

Back to that again. 'Yeah?'

'What do you reckon? Really?'

'Doesn't matter what I reckon does it?'

'All on the say-so of a grass trying to keep himself out of jail.'

'If it wasn't them who was it? Who else is in the frame?'

They sip their drinks. Ro has an outside chance of meeting up with a girl.

'What's on your mind, mate?'

But he knows what's on Ray Pitts' mind. He wants Ro to do him a favour. Maybe not even that. Maybe he just wants to be told that what he is about to suggest is okay.

Two years before, Ro Carter needed something doing. He needed a bunch of Es to plant on someone. He'd never done anything like that before.

Everyone knew this scuzzbag was at it, but he was cute and they couldn't get near him. He ran a council estate near Tilbury, bashed up his girlfriend, stabbed someone in a fight. The usual. It drove Ro nuts but he couldn't get his hands on any gear. Well obviously he could, just not safely.

So he asked Ray and the next day there they were, twenty in a bag and two days after that the bloke was in custody. It was a one-off and they didn't speak of it again.

Ray Pitts flops copies of both the Evening Standard and the Romford Recorder onto the table. Points to the headlines.

'Violence and drugs. Drugs and violence. On our patch, Ro. I am getting serious earache. I need a collar. A proper one.'

'Ray . . .'

'The thing is this is not exaggeration.' He points to the acres of lurid newsprint.

'It's actually like this now. There's little firms of these arseholes buzzing all over the East End and Essex thinking they're Tony Montana.'

'So just soldier on. It'll come.'

Ray Pitts disappears his whisky, shakes his head.

'There's this one bloke. . . .'

Ro Carter sees a twisting vein throb in Ray's forehead. Watches a single bead of sweat pop from above his eyebrow.

'I can't work it out. He's been into the nick almost as many times as me.'

'What does he do?'

'Nothing that I know about so nothing anyone can prove. He was on the fringes of the murders. He's a wrong 'un, from the way back too.'

Pitts looks aimlessly across the pub. Ro has never seen him like this, wound so tightly.

'Sounds like if you were going to give it to someone he would be your Patsy.'

'A good friend of mine did some time because of him, I'm sure of it. He's a wrong 'un. I know he is. And I've got a witness.'

'What do you mean?'

'For whatever I hit him with.'

Ro takes another pull on his pint. *Fuck this*, he thinks.

'Look, Ray, you're my man. You know that. But we said that last time we weren't going this way again. We could lose everything.'

'Feels like I've lost everything already, mate. This is bending my head. I need a nick and it needs to be this bloke.'

Ro Carter sees the pain in his friend's face, sees the pressure building behind his eyes. He looks rough. Christ, he looks fucking psychotic.

He sighs. 'What do you want me to do?'

'Do you still know that burglar? You used him as a grass a little while ago.'

'Petey Burton? Yeah.'

'I need him for a bit of work.'

*

On the first of January 1999 most of Europe gets a new currency and Micky is prompted to think about money. He's down to about ten grand but that is stable. His derisory wages and his dad's two pensions don't add up to much but then they don't need to. The little Fiesta gets him to the shops, the food bills and costs of running the house aren't high. The three thousand six hundred and forty pounds that Akma, and her occasional stand-ins, cost is only of passing concern to Micky because he doesn't see the money leaving his wallet.

But he knows what's happening and even though he knows it's a terrible, unkind, unfair thing to think, he can't help but ponder the fact that every day Rock Steady Eddie digs in and survives is costing Micky about a hundred and twenty quid. Plus at least thirty a day on the smack. A couple of years of this have slipped by already.

And Eddie is as tough as they come.

And more weeks of it.

And months and months and months.

And another year.

On December the thirty-first nineteen ninety-nine, as the rest of the country is preparing to party like well, that Prince song, the thirty-nine year old Micky Targett sits watching television with his dad and Akma. The world is waiting for aircraft to fall out of the sky and trains to plough into each other. Every computer in the world will crash and civilization will be over in a few short hours.

Staggered by the sheer joylessness of his life, Micky feels more rooted in, and shackled to, the old century than he ever has.

In London the newly erected London Eye is to be the centre of a dazzling firework display. Prime Minster Blair has promised the capital a 'river of fire'.

During the televised splendour, for which Eddie and Akma have managed to stay awake, Eddie leans towards his son and tries to speak. Micky can't make it out at first. Works through the letters he knows Eddie still has trouble with.

'Eye ull.'

'Eye full?' Micky asks. Eye full of what, dad?'
'Eye gull.'
A chill rips through Micky.
'Sorry, pop. Try again.'
''Igel. N . . n . .n . . Nigel.'

PART THREE. MICKY TARGETT'S RUN

CHAPTER SIXTEEN

UPMINSTER, ESSEX - JANUARY 1ST 2000

Born under a bad sign with a blue moon in yo' eye.

On the first day of the millennium Eddie is in bed, attended by the unflappable and indispensable Akma. Micky watches news footage of the mess the previous night's celebrations made of the streets of London.

He gazes out of the window at the damp greyness. The rhododendron sags in monochromatic fatigue. The dazzling patterns of the passion fruit plant are half a year away. The wild mint bush hangs grimly on. He looks at the sodden garden bench and thinks about his mum and realizes he is turning into Eddie.

He switches off the news and goes back to last night. The old boy wants to see Nigel. Jesus Christ, what's he supposed to do with that?

In fact what is he supposed to do about anything? He's further away from where he wants to be than ever, and he's hemorrhaging money every second. On the upside he's noticed that he doesn't suffer from too many bad dreams of late. Conversely he knows all he has to do is think of his everyday life and he'll get his fill of nightmares that way.

He doesn't want to contact Nigel. The hate is too much. He decides to do nothing, hopes Eddie will forget all about it.

He walks to the sound system and turns on the radio. John Lennon's *Imagine*, a re-released leftover from Christmas is the last thing he needs. He shuts it off

He picks up a book he has borrowed from the library. A nice bit of escapism, the bloke there had told him. The Beach by Alex Garland. Thailand seems to be calling.

In February All Saints top the UK charts with Pure Shores taken from the soundtrack of the film which Micky goes to see on his own. He wonders if it's really like that. The beaches? The girls? The weed? He leaves the cinema wrapped up against the biting cold and promises himself. One day. Yeah, one day.

He can have no idea that day really is coming, and sooner than he could rationally believe. Nor can he have any idea of the catastrophic circumstances under which it will come.

In the meantime the drudge goes on, but there's something nagging at him. Something's not right and it can't be just paranoia because he hasn't been near any coke since the night of the great cake fiasco.

He's being watched. Okay he's never actually caught anyone, never seen a car in the rear view. But something ain't right. He feels eyes on him.

One evening through into spring time he pulls the gasping Fiesta onto the drive and, as he's locking it a dark saloon cruises slowly past. Micky eyes what he can see of the passenger and is sure he knows him. He watches the car to the end of the avenue where it stops at the T-junction, waits for long seconds before pulling out of sight.

Can't be anything, he tells himself. He's long out of the game.

Then he walks inside the house, shuts the door behind him. In the lounge Akma is sitting next to Eddie who is slumped in his chair. She is holding his hand. She looks up at Micky, her soft, moon-face unusually creased with both sadness and unease.

'He tells me no more.'

Micky thinks she means he won't finish his dinner.

'Give him a while, Akma. He'll get around to it.'

She stands and beckons him forward, then points to Eddie. Micky sits and takes the gnarled, bark covered twigs of his dad's hands in his. Eddie tries gamely to turn his head to look at his son.

'What's up, pop. You alright?'

'Orrie.'

Micky's throat contracts. It destroys him when the old boy tries to talk about his mum.

'Ont . . . Want . . . to be wi' er.'

The 'er' vents from Eddie's body with a force that exhausts him and Micky starts to cry.

'Enu . . . Enuh now.'

So now it's all totally on Micky, and once again the weight of that responsibility gathers to pulverise him.

In the kitchen he makes tea and Akma shuffles out, looks up at him.

'You have to help him.'

'I know, Akma, but what can I do?'

Akma doesn't release him from her surprisingly searching gaze. 'Speak to Carol.'

He goes to his room and makes the call, explains what has happened.

'That's very illegal,' she tells him. 'Are you sure?'

'Yeah. He's done in. It ain't just the stroke and it ain't just the dementia. There was so much before that. He was a dead man walking when me mum died and that's fourteen years ago. Not even he can fight this anymore.'

Silence.

'Carol?'

'I'm coming over.'

Twenty minutes later she's there and it's like she knows what to do and Micky senses it's not the first time.

As she walks into the lounge she squeezes Akma's hand, then takes the framed photo from the top of the china cabinet. She takes the seat next to Eddie's chair.

'Hey, Eddie boy. Remember me?'

Eddie jerks and twists his head, gets a look. A twitch of a smile. ''Ello, babe.'

She shows him the photo. The young darlings together all those years ago. He sees it and starts to cry.

'Are you sure? Rock Steady Eddie, are you sure?'

He nods vigorously.

'It's important, darling. We have to know for certain so I will ask you again. You want to be with your Florrie now, is that right?'

Micky breaks apart as he watches the gutsy old bastard.

'Yes. I wan' Florrie. Pease elp.'

It's the most lucid he's been since the stroke. He cradles the photo and softly weeps.

Carol looks up at Micky and angles her head towards the door.

'I can help you,' she tells him when they are out in the hallway. 'Tell me again you are sure?'

He knows it doesn't get any more real than this.

'Yeah. There is no point to this anymore. What do I do?'

'Potassium.'

'He has supplements of that. What about it?'

'He can overdose on it.'

'How much?'

'Don't use his supplies. I'll go and bring you enough.'

'I don't know what to do.'

'Mick, I'm coming back and I'll show you, but I can't be here. You understand?'

Micky starts to recoil but gathers himself. He's Eddie Targett's son and he needs to do what he needs to do.

Inside the hour she is back and leads Micky to the kitchen where she produces an unmarked plastic bottle of large white pills.

'Okay, these are concentrated. To be sure give him a hundred.'

'Right.'

'Grind them up, sprinkle it on food, stick it in a drink. That's a lot of powder but make sure he gets through it all.'

'What will that do to him?'

'It should stop his heart.'

'Ah Jesus.'

'No easy way, boy. If we give him morphine that might raise suspicion and someone could look into it. This way it will look like natural causes. He's an old, frail chap. No post mortem.'

'Okay.'

'You might give him a few sleeping tablets too. Get him to bed and then you 'discover' him in the morning. When people die their potassium levels rise anyway so even if there is a post mortem it'll be fine. This is the best way.'

They call Akma into the kitchen where it occurs to Micky the two of them may have acted in tandem in this way before.

'Politicians, right-to-lifers, bible-bashers. They don't see what we see, people in their agony.' Carol observes Micky as he leans onto a spoon, grinding the tablets into dust.

'You do the right thing, Micky. You are good man,' Akma tells him.

Soon after, a crying Carol is hugging him in the porch.

'I know he's an old sod, Mick and I know how hard your life is because of him. But don't blame him. We're all just trying to get through. And soon enough he really will be in a better place.'

Then she calms herself, deals with the situation.

'You phoned me once tonight, we just chatted, talked about Eddie. I was never here. Wipe that bottle clean, then throw it.'

Micky nods solemnly. Then she leaves.

Two hours later, after Micky and Akma have spooned Eddie his favourite spaghetti Bolognese and insisted he drink two large glasses of Micky's finest Chauteauneuf with it, they put him to bed. Micky sits with him for a while. Soon he slips into a sleep from which, they both hope, he will never reawaken.

Micky stands and his shaking hand reaches for the lamp switch, but as he does so Eddie stirs and opens his eyes, looks up at Micky.

'Nigel no wan see me fore I die.'

He closes his eyes again and Micky's heart breaks into a thousand pieces.

*

The last of the funeral guests have left and Micky is pleased about that. He was chuffed that so many people, and he had no idea who half of them were, turned up. Now he sags with the relief they have all finally buggered off.

He was intimidated about giving the eulogy and barely made it through, but his generous, humourous recollections went down well. He thought it best not to mention the coke cake but the sausage story had them hooting in the pews.

As they played the old boy out, Micky had chosen Smile by Nat King Cole, he went across and affectionately patted the coffin, saw Rock Steady Eddie Targett on his way.

He thinks about his brother and wonders at the power of his own selfishness. He didn't try to find the piece of shit to tell him about the funeral, thus depriving both of them their reunion and final goodbye. He knows he'll carry that burden with him until his own final day.

He pours himself another huge Courvoisier, pulls off his black tie and wanders the empty house, this house of ghosts and discord, of treachery and of hope. He contemplates its peaceful, optimistic beginnings and its squally, squalid end. He makes his way, as he invariably does, to the photograph. He hopes Eddie found her. He can't consider the prospect of him still being on his own. He raises his glass in a toast to the pair of them.

He gets to bed eventually but he knows it's doubtful he'll sleep. He thinks about hitting a line but decides against it. He's nearly through another ounce and might even knock that shit on the head now. Now that it's over.

He joneses sometimes and struggles to sleep when he lays off it but he loves the fight. After what he's been through, heroin is fucking pussy.

He might be awake but isn't sure. His senses have no traction. He thinks he hears something. Something at the side of the house. Then from the garden. Foxes.

He gets up early, hits the kettle and toaster and turns on the radio. Independent candidate Ken Livingstone has been elected mayor of London.

He takes his coffee into the lounge and, inevitably, settles into his dad's old chair, uncomfortable piece of crap that it is.

He needs to talk with Ben Yardley who told him he had a conveyancing solicitor to handle the sale of the bungalow. Maybe he'll do that today, along with choosing between the two local estate agencies.

He jacked in the Meals On Wheels job after Eddie died.

He got the bill from the homecare company. Three and a half years of qualified, live-in nursing care has cost him just shy of one hundred and forty-five grand. The estate agents reckon the bungalow, in its current condition, will go for around two hundred thousand, maybe two-twenty. And he'll have bills. Commissions, fees. The funeral and the piss up for it cost over three. Ben Yardley won't be cheap.

Weird when he thinks back. Connie Chetkins handed him his life plus two hundred and twenty thousand pounds. Now he's been through, wait for it, eight freaking years of upheaval, grief and worry and he's down to about fifty. And to cash that in means he will have nowhere to live.

Not that he's counting because there's more to it than that. He did the right thing. He got his parent's house back, and he looked after the old man. Double cup final.

And he's free.

And now he can start again. He's just turned forty, his knee, hip and sometimes his back nag him spitefully, but he ain't finished yet. Still plenty of life in this old Essex boy.

He walks, slowly, into Upminster. He tells his favoured estate agents they have the gig and sets them to work. He calls into a travel agents and, although he won't be going for a while, checks the price of flights to Thailand. Thoughts of the land of smiles cheer him.

He picks up a copy of the Romford Recorder. The front page is dedicated to some black kid who got knifed in Romford. A drug deal gone wrong. He's out of danger but he'll be in hospital for the foreseeable. There's a picture of him in a hospital bed looking like a scared child. Jesus, Micky thinks, the fuck is wrong with everyone? He is so glad he is out of the game.

He picks up a few groceries and heads back home.

Couple of hundred yards from the house a blue Mondeo cruises past. Slowly. Two minutes later he thinks he sees it coming back in the opposite direction. He lets it go.

He gets into the kitchen and turns on the radio. Not only has rap music become ubiquitous ear-piss but now there's *white* rap music. There's this knobhead Eminem all over the airwaves. Micky rolls the dial and lands on Classic fm.

As the Berlin Philharmonic conducted by the legendary Claudio Abbado begins its rendition of Brahm's Violin Concerto in D Major, Micky snaps on the kettle again. Once again he can't help but think about how many of them Eddie managed to blow up. Thinks about losing half an oz of top Charlie baked in a fucking cake.

This all distracts him from what is happening five yards away in the back garden, where a number of uniformed and heavily armoured police officers have jumped artfully over the back fence and are now lining up to crash into the house.

Above the music Micky hears the front door bell ring. He goes to answer it.

As he opens the door his immediate thought is he knows the man standing there looking at him. Sunglasses confuse the issue, but the powerfully built, shaven headed figure isn't alone. Ranked behind him are five large men dressed in black and wearing blue crash helmets.

''Ello, Micky.'

At that moment the rear door opens and three men similarly dressed men advance unstoppably into the kitchen. The sweeping, orchestrated strings add a surreal edge to the procedure. Micky thinks he's tripping. Either that or he'll wake up any second. Maybe his dad will walk into his bedroom, open the curtains and life will be back to normal.

'Michael Targett, I am arresting you for the assault of Trenton Jennings. You do not have to say anything. But it may harm your defence if . . .'

The man steps into the hallway and slams a pair of handcuffs onto Micky and it's then he knows who the bloke is. It's Ray fucking Pitts, and he's arresting him.

'What? Wait. What did you say? Who?'

' . . . you do not mention when questioned something which you later rely on in court. Anything you do say may be given in evidence. Do you understand that?'

'What are you talking about?'

'Is there anyone else in the house?'

'No. What are you talking about?'

Behind him Micky hears shouts of 'Clear' as the goons from the back make their way through the rooms. There is a bizarre déjà vu to the whole scene.

But he doesn't wake up, because this is really happening. Cops are rampaging through the house *again.*

Five minutes later he is sitting in the lounge when one of the coppers brings in a bag of brown powder from Micky's bedroom. He freezes but then remembers he has no scales in the house and is down to the scrapings of that bag, so no intent to supply charge.

'Oh dear, Micky,' mocks Pitts. 'What's that? You a smackie now?'

Five minutes later Micky's world collapses when one of the other heavies, wearing protective gloves, brings in a plastic evidence bag. There's a knife in it and on the knife is blood.

'Found this in the garage, guv'.' He hands it to Pitts.

'Christ, never had you down for stupid, Mick, but thanks for handing us this case on a plate.'

At Romford nick Micky is formally charged. There's him, Pitts and the Custody Sargeant who reads out a load of stuff about the Offences Against The Persons Act of eighteen sixty-one. This is clarified instantly by the words – Grievous Bodily Harm With Intent.

'You Michael Targett on the first of May two thousand in Romford Market, Romford, Essex, did unlawfully and maliciously by any means whatsoever wound or cause grievous bodily harm to Trenton Jennings, with intent to do some grievous bodily harm to Trenton Jennings.'

Pitts then chips in. 'I believe Mr. Targett may be in some danger of a reprisal attack from the victim's associates. I also believe that due to the serious nature of this assault Mr. Targett may fail to appear in court tomorrow. I recommend he is remanded in custody.'

'You enjoy your work, Detective Sargeant?' Micky asks.

'Fucking loving it right now.'

Then it was an hour in the cell to think about things and then it was time for a nice chat.

'Well, Micky boy, I thought you was cleverer than this.' Pitts tells him across a desk in an interview room. 'All the times you been here and managed to dodge your way out.'

Micky has managed to get it together a little. Right at the start he really did think it was some kind of joke. In a minute they'd all crack up and point and laugh at the panic on his face. Then, as the car pulled away from the house and all the neighbours were out in force in their front gardens watching, then Micky started to get the horrors.

Then Pitts and another plain clothes called Carter start giving him earache.

'Don't matter you're a dope-growing, drug-dealing, murder-conspiring cunt. Don't matter you're a fucking smack-head. Don't matter you battered that poor old git outside his house that time. . .'

Christ, Micky thinks, *how did that all happen? Maybe I should write a book.*

'But what does matter is you stabbed up a boy on my patch and I've got you for this.'

Micky takes it seriously, of course he does, but there's one thing making him keep his heart rate more or less where he'd like it to be; it's all bollocks and everyone knows that.

'That knife comes back with anything on it, blood, dna, hair, anything that takes us back to Trenton Jennings then we're pushing for a lot of years and I'll make it stick. And that's assuming the little spade fucker stays alive.'

Micky doesn't even know the name so there's nothing at all for him to link to.

'So do yourself a favour and tell us all about it. We've got not just the kid with an ID on you but a passer-by saying you stabbed him.'

Micky tries to think of an answer, something smart. Something that will shut this dick up. But he knows he wouldn't be where he is if this was just some misunderstanding. And that knife in the garage. . .

So he starts to appreciate they haven't just picked him up hoping he had something to do with this thing. They're *making* it so that he's had something to do with it.

'Lawyer.' Is all he says.

Later that evening Micky is brought from his cell to finally meet in a room with Ben Yardley.

'If you didn't do it you have nothing worry about,' Ben Yardley assures him in his smoothest tones. 'This isn't Medellin this is Romford. Having said that, they're saying they have two witnesses.'

'This is insane.'

'Do you know where you were on the night of the first of May? Monday just gone.'

'I was almost certainly at the house.'

'On your own?'

'Yeah.'

'Did you phone anyone or anyone phone you on the house phone?'

'I don't think so. Not sure.'

'And this knife?'

'In the garage? Do me a favour.'

'You've never seen that knife?'

'No, but . . .' Micky jerks upright with the memory of something.

'What?'

'Last night. I thought I heard something. Someone outside, near the garage.'

Ben considers. They both know what Micky is saying. He scratches out a few notes.

'So what do you think? Should I be worried?'

'Will it do you any good?'

'Dunno, reckon I'll try it though.'

Ben stops writing and stares at Micky.

'Oi, just in case you're wondering it's all bullshit.'

'I know that.' Ben smiles. 'It's just the why I can't figure.'

'Me and that bloke have history. Pitts. There's a whole bunch of things he's wanted me for. Did I tell you he even dragged me in here to talk about the Rettendon murders?'

Ben's eyes are like dinner plates. 'No you didn't. Fuck's sake, Mick. Were you arrested?'

'No. He just asked me in for a chat. They had my picture on CCTV in a club where those blokes used to operate. That's all. But you see what I'm saying? He fancies me for whatever he can think of.'

Ben sighs, now he's getting worried. He reaches across the table and tenderly squeezes Micky's hand.

'Look you're here for the night. Court tomorrow. You will almost certainly be bailed but it will cost you. Try not to worry. I'm with you.'

Mick barely sleeps in the shitty cell but at least, on a weeknight, the place isn't rammed with drunks and Essex chavs. But he gets some serious smack shakes. Those ants under his skin, his scalp on fire.

He knows there is no way he'll be able to do any real time.

The noise of the police station starts to escalate around seven but he doesn't get taken out of his cell until after lunch. The trip in the back of a van to Romford Magistrates Court takes all of two minutes but with the pissing around it would have been quicker to walk because it is literally next door.

In court Ben Yardley is there at a desk and another suit, Micky guesses it is the CPS brief, is at another. The Magistrate bowls in and they get to it and the agreement to conditional bail is over in no time. Micky is told not to contact the victim, not to live anywhere other than the Clayton Avenue address and to surrender his passport.

Apparently, because he has lived in Spain before, he is a potential flight risk. Oh yeah, and it's going to cost him five grand.

His committal hearing is set for three weeks time.

Micky Targett sits alone in the house, the house that has, for better or for worse, but mostly worse, come to shape his life. If the walls aren't actually moving in they sure are metaphorically.

When he had smack to hand and decided not to take it he had no serious problem. Now that he doesn't have any, Mr. Jones is all over him. His skin feels like someone else's. He scratches so much he draws blood. But he's not worried. Eddie survived without his beloved Florrie and Micky knows he has the family steel inside him. Knows he can do without the brown.

On the upside he feels ecstatic that he gave up dealing all that time ago. If the police had found bundles of drugs in the house along with the scales and the bags then they would have been holding him up as a violent drug-dealer. As opposed to just violent. But that begs the question, if they planted the tainted knife, and persuaded two witnesses to falsely identify him, why not go the whole nine yards and plant drugs too?

The question is irrelevant now so he lets it go, has more pressing matters to give his time to, namely the downside. He's going to prison. DS Ray Pitts of the Metropolitan Police Force has made that his priority.

The extent of that bastard's determination came out at the committal hearing

The victim's blood was retrieved from the knife found in Micky's garage. That, combined with not one but two eyewitness statements, means Micky is a goner for GBH with intent. Load that with possession of a class A and add all that to his previous conviction for receiving stolen goods at the start of the nineties and it's no longer a question of if but how long.

He thinks about running but he has no passport to run with and no cash either. The five grand bail money all but wiped him out and Ben Yardley isn't going to work for nothing.

All he has, maybe fifty-sixty grand, is tied up in the house and his trial at Snaresbrook Crown Court is a matter of months away.

By now the extent of the fit up is clear. The knife was one thing but then they trotted out the eyewitnesses.

Trenton Jennings, the victim, aged twenty, unemployed with a record for violence and drug dealing. How had Pitts persuaded him to point the finger at Micky? But that was only the warm up act.

William Hubbard, aged thirty-eight. Walking through a deserted Romford market happened upon Micky stabbing and robbing a young black man. He looks at Micky as soon as he's called.

William Hubbard walked into court and Micky knew he was dead. Bill Hubbard. The Pro Cock. PC.

Micky is in the back of the cab with Lisa under London Bridge. The driver turns in his seat. The hate in his eyes.

'I'm gonna fucking *melt* you, bruv.

And Micky did melt.

Outside Ben takes him for a drink.

'Don't tell me, someone from your murky past come back to haunt you?'

'You could say that.'

He sees it all clearly now. Pitts has wanted him on something for years. PC has wanted him since he did time thanks to Connie and Blackie taking a hand.

'Do we know anything about this kid? Trenton?'

'He's from Bermondsey. Out this way seeing friends apparently. Says you offered him some gear in the market after the pubs kicked out, he said no and you stabbed him and nicked his money.'

'He's the fucking dealer, not me. I hear inner city gangs are coming out to the suburbs to take over the gear sales. County Lines they're calling it. I reckon he's got whacked by someone local whose toes he's stepped on. Pitts has got hold of him and told him what to say in exchange for a let-off.'

'Well I'm never one for conspiracy theories . . .'

'Well I was very much elsewhere when this happened so someone's conspiring and now we know who.'

Not that it does him any good. He sits in his dad's old chair in the lounge at home and considers his fate. Ben's advice is to simply tell the truth, but Micky knows that if the might of the Met. is prepared to lie and fabricate evidence against him then things are looking a little on the grim side. Atavistic fears and worries crowd in on him from all angles.

His other option is to plead guilty. Plead guilty to stabbing someone.

His mobile rings. Number withheld. It's happened a few times the last few days and once again he ignores it.

He goes into the kitchen, makes himself a cup of tea. He never thought he'd feel like he's feeling but he admits that he actually misses his dad. His phone beeps with a text message - 'Answer it.'

He drops the phone onto the kitchen counter like it's made of Kryptonite. Ten seconds later it's ringing. He answers.

'Yeah?'

'Hello, I understand the house is for sale.'

Jeezus. 'Yes but I think you need to go through the agent.'

'Well you know, not really. I don't like middle-men. If I like the place I'll take it. Can I come to see it?'

'Er, yeah I suppose so. When you thinking?'

'Today?'

'Erm, look I've got a lot on at the moment. Maybe . . .'

'Are you not around?'

'Not at the moment. I've . . .'

'There's a car on the drive.'

Fuck, thinks Micky Targett. 'Who is this?'

'Open the door.' The line goes dead.

So there's Micky, half expecting to get arrested for being in possession of a mobile phone with intent to send a text message, or some other bullshit, when the reality turns out to be a lot more interesting. They're in the lounge and Micky's jaw is hanging off.

'Nice place,' says the man as he ambles down the length of the lounge towards the French windows and the garden. 'Potential.'

'Jesus fucking Christ, Wrenny.'

'I called a few times, you didn't answer.'

Micky holds his head onto his shoulders. He is both shocked and pleased, although he has no idea what kind of visit this is. Good news? It's been four and a half years since the murders and four since he walked away from Connie and Georgie. And Wrenny.

'You not pleased to see me?'

'Well yeah. Just a little surprised that's all.'

Out of all of them it was only Wrenny that he really cared about and felt he could trust. Proper. Well, they were all proper, obviously, but he could relate to Wrenny whereas Connie and Georgie? They'd used him once too often.

'How's Andy?'

Wrenny smiles. 'I always liked you, Mick, and there's the reason why. You're a nice man and that's the start and the end of it. You're stand-up.'

Micky is flattered, almost bashful. Then remembers he has a hitman in his lounge.

'He's not doing bad. He'll never be right but he's getting on. Working full time for me now.'

'Good. Give him my regards will you?'

'I will.'

'Have a sit, mate.'

'No, let's do the tour first.'

''Scuse me?'

'The house. I'd like to look around.'

'Seriously?'

'Yeah. We got lots to talk about and this place is one of them.'

It makes as much sense as anything else, so Micky spins him around the premises and Wrenny asks all the pertinent questions. Seems very knowledgeable. In the loft, in the garage, down the garden, with Wrenny taking pictures as he goes.

Then they're sitting down, Micky in his dad's chair, Wrenny on the sofa.

'You had any offers yet?'

Micky shakes his head. 'Why would you want to buy this?'

'I got a building firm. I thought this might suit what we do and it does. It can be extended out the back from the kitchen and the loft is easy big enough to convert into two bedrooms and en-suite. Modernise everything else.'

'Lots of properties all over London, Wrenny. You come all this way out to the Shires?'

Wrenny smiles. 'Yeah well. I know you're in a spot, this seemed like it might be a way to help out. Sorry about your pop by the way. I hear he was quite a character.'

Suddenly there is something Micky doesn't like. Senses an agenda.

'Thanks. Yeah, it was tough at the end and he was a good old boy.'

'You stood by him.'

'You know a lot about me suddenly, Wrenny.'

'Not just suddenly. Where you at with your case?'

Micky gets that feeling again. Eyes on him.

'Come on, Mick. There's nothing we don't know.'

'We?'

'Tell me.'

'There's this DS in Romford who's fitted me up. He had a grass working for him years ago that I was selling to. Con and Georgie got him banged away. Then he figured I had something to do with the three murders so he dragged me in for that.'

'What did you tell him?'

'That I was elsewhere the night it happened and that I knew nothing.'

Wrenny stares him down and Micky gets it.

'He's been trying to nick me for years. So now he managed to plant some evidence, a knife, in the garage and there was some of the victim's blood on that. And he's got the victim IDing me along with a passer-by who just happens to be the grass that Connie and Georgie flicked away.'

'Hmm, not very subtle but if they all stand together that could stick.'

'It looks like it will.'

'You been away before?'

'No.'

'How you feeling about it?'

'How do you reckon?'

The sliding glass at the back of the house is open. It's a warm, late-spring afternoon. Birdsong makes its way in from the garden. It's idyllic. After everything Micky does love this place. But he's going to jail.

'Could have a way out,' Wrenny says. 'What's this place up for?'

'Two-twenty.'

Wrenny nods and Micky's heart begins to stir.

'We can't stop this bloke in Romford. We've tried but he's got something to prove. Got a hard-on for you. He's clearly bent but he won't listen to any advice.'

'Blackie?'

'No. Blackie can't break cover for this.'

'Why's that? Not important enough?'

'No it ain't, son, and don't give me that. This isn't New York. This isn't Soho in the sixties. And anyway, you walked away to be on your own.'

Micky holds back. Could have a way out the man said.

'It's our understanding that just offering him a bung to let you go would only wind him up. He's getting earache about all the local drug crime and he's trying to get his figures up. Sending you away at the same time is icing on the cake.'

'Nice to know I'm in everyone's thoughts still.'

'Well yeah, but . . .'

Micky tries to read him. Tries to see into his dark brown eyes. The bloke gives less away than Connie or Georgie, but Micky thinks he susses the 'but'.

'But you're also worried I might do some talking now that I'm in this position of . . . vulnerability.'

'Mick get us a couple of beers. You're a natural, Connie's always said it and he's right. That work you did getting us in with that Essex mob was top drawer.'

'Cheers.'

'In fact none of us can understand why you're such a fuck up.'

Micky takes it as the compliment he figures it's meant. He pulls two Stellas out of the fridge and brings them back into the lounge. He grabs glasses from the china cabinet. Wrenny looks and notices the photo, walks to it.

'These your parents, mate?'

'Yeah.'

'Wow, brilliant picture.'

'That was taken as closer to the eighteen hundreds then it was to this century.'

'Jesus. Good looking people.'

'Thank you.'

They sit, pour, drink and look at each other.

'Here's what. I'll buy this house. Cash. You settle your debts, that'll leave you with enough to start over.'

'What do you know about my debts?'

'I know. Then you take off.'

Micky thinks he's missed something. 'Sorry?'

'Do a runner. But not just anywhere. You'll land in the place of your dreams and there'll be a job waiting for you. That job won't be particularly well paid but it will be tax free. No one will be looking for you.'

'I can't just piss off and leave.'

'Why not? Both your parents are dead. You're estranged from your wanker of a brother, you got no kids and no woman. You're unemployed and the Old Bill are fitting you up for a long spell away. Knowing what I know you'll cop at least five.'

Micky hasn't really thought about it in those terms before.

'There isn't enough time. It could take months for the sale to go through. I haven't got that long.'

'You don't have to be here.'

'How's that going to work?'

'You got someone with half a brain you can trust?'

'Yeah, my solicitor.'

'Perfect. You appoint him as your agent, perhaps give him power of attorney over your affairs. *He* sells me the house. You trust him enough for that?'

Micky thinks. 'Yeah, but what about my money?'

'I'll weigh you out up front. What are your debts?'

'About a hundred and fifty. A care home has a charge over this place.'

'No mortgage?'

'No, that's it.'

'Okay. I'll pay you two hundred for the house. I'll give you fifty up front and I'll pay off the care home. You're out of here, off to the sun with a chunk of change and a job to go to.'

'I ain't going anywhere without a passport.'

'You haven't got a passport?'

'Plod swagged it. They think I'm going to run.'

'Don't worry about it.'

'So where am I going to run to? Wales?'

'I'll get you a passport.'

'How?'

'Don't ask. Just get me two of those little photos.'

'They'll stop me at the airport. Won't they?'

'It won't be in your name, you dick.'

By this time Micky's heart is hammering. *This could work,* he thinks. *I can get out from under this shit.*

'What's the job?'

'Bit of driving. Serving in a shop. Maybe bar work. We need an English speaker. Someone we can trust.'

'I'm done with the villainy, mate.'

'It's totally straight.'

Micky scans his brain for drawbacks. What can go wrong? Well only *everything.*

'I'll never be able to come back will I?'

'You got anything you need to come back for?'

Well, there is the million dollar question.

'Look, you're with us. We'll always look out for you.'

'So Connie's behind this? Connie and Georgie?'

'You got a problem with that?'

'That all got a bit much for me, mate. Those three blokes.'

'I know, son. I know. But you're dealing with me, now. *I'm* doing this.'

Micky knows he's selling the house anyway. Whatever happens he won't be able to keep it. So then he'll be homeless. Okay he'll have fifty large to smooth out that wrinkle but how long will that last in England in the new century? And what work can he get? After he comes out of prison with a record of violence? *Prison.* Then the wild side of him takes over. He's going on the run! He's an international fugitive. How fucking mad is that?

'They'll come after me won't they? Extradition?'

'There is a treaty but you'll have a new name anyway. You'll have a bank account also in that name. But everything is cash. And anyway, no one is going to find you out there.'

'Out where? Not Spain?'

'Spain's old news. No one goes there anymore. No, Micky boy. Nothing so mundane for you. You're going to Thailand.'

Micky was terrified throughout the whole process.

Even though he trusted Ben Yardley he didn't tell him he was going to skip the country until the last minute, not that it took a whole lot of working out.

The sale of the house was straightforward. No chain and a cash buyer so there was no need for any of that power of attorney nonsense. Ben and Wrenny's solicitor hustled through the completion in just over six weeks. Indeed even before that, upon exchange of contracts, Wrenny had given Micky ten grand in cash and assured him a further forty was on its way to an account in Thailand. The bill with Akma's home nursing company was settled.

Wrenny had also given him his new passport which was one of the weirdest things, and there'd been a few of those, in his life.

'Phillip Paul Jackson,' Micky said, thumbing through the immaculate document he had brought to the Upminster house. 'How is this possible, mate?'

'There's always a way, Micky boy. Or should I say Phil? And get used to that. You may not appreciate it now but further down the line there might come a day when you'll be grateful you told someone your name is Phil and not Mick.'

The house and the money were the main thing. But they weren't everything and his last few days were busy.

The crocked Fiesta he actually left in the drive, signed the logbook and handed it to Wrenny, told him to give it to one of his builders if they could make use of it.

He visited his doctor, who was very sympathetic, gave his condolences about Eddie. Under those circumstances, and with Micky going a little heavy on the limp, he had no trouble hobbling out with another prescription for Tramadol.

He visited his aunt Fran out in Laindon. Good old bird but she'd clearly lost something of herself over the last few years. She was in bits at the funeral. Pushing eighty by then she'd dumped a lot of weight and moved with more aches and pains than Micky could ever imagine. He looked at her, thought about his dad and snatched a glimpse of his own future.

As the days ticked down to his flight Micky couldn't think about who else he should see. He decided he would call Ben on the morning of his departure to give him the news. Then he thought, the paranoia throttling him again, he would actually call him from the airport.

Then something weird happened. Dixie called him. Okay he hadn't made any pick ups of late and she presumably knew when he would re-up as a matter of habit, but it was just strange. Smack dealers don't chase their customers for business.

'Hello, stranger, how you getting on?'

Micky is immediately on the defensive. One, he's trying to keep away from the brown anyway and two, he just doesn't trust Dixie. No, something not right about this.

He tells her he's lying low and dealing with the fall-out of the old man. Will need some soon and will call her then.

*

The coach pulls into Victoria. It is past nine in the evening, windy and raining. An air of transient desperation hangs over the place. An empty lager can rattles across the arrivals bays. Stale vinegar wafts on the cold gusts.

A motley crew of travellers descends, easing backs and cracking necks as they clump down the steps. Among them is a big, burly man. Tough looking with cropped grey hair and a neatly-trimmed, grey beard. Weary from the journey, he waits patiently for his turn to grab the holdall the driver dumps onto the pavement.

He scopes the place, like he is expecting someone to be there. He looks at his watch, heaves the bag up onto his shoulder and heads off.

He walks around the corner, blinks and gathers his skinny denim jacket at the neck as the weather hits him full on. He curses into the teeth of the rain and the wind. He makes it to Victoria tube.

Victoria line all the way to Blackhorse Road. At the other end he just about has enough money left to jump a ride from the minicab office opposite the station. Five minutes later he's standing at the door of his cousin Jimmy's house.

Terry 'The Harmer' Farmer is back.

Big Tel's incarceration had not gone the way he had hoped. Firstly bashing up five screws and wrecking half the room during visiting time towards the beginning of his stretch constituted a serious black mark against his already tainted name. Then, following the appeal against the length of his sentence, he was more than a little dismayed to be told that not only would his sentence not be reduced but it would actually be *extended*.

Upon returning to Durham prison after the appeal hearing, Terry was working in the kitchen when a fellow inmate asked him how his day in court had been. When Tel explained, the man had the serious lack of judgement to laugh out loud. Terry wrecked the kitchen. And the man.

Sufficed to say there was no time off for good behavior.

He ended up serving almost eight years, making it back to Walthamstow in the winter of nineteen ninety-nine. His house had long been repossessed. His wife had left him, met someone else. Moved away.

His erstwhile partner, cousin Jimmy Mulroney, had lacked the necessary drive, ambition and brains to make a go of criminality without big Tel. He'd taken work as an auto parts delivery driver. He wasn't married but his live-in girlfriend was also the mother of their two year old daughter.

Jimmy had visited as often as he could but, with the kiddie and all that, the trip up to Durham hadn't been possible for a few years. Terry understood.

Jimmy put him up at his rented flat. 'Couple of weeks, let me get on me feet, son.'

So Terry does the thing that recently released villains are supposed to do. He makes the appointments with his probation officer bang on time and he looks for work.

But what he mostly does is sit about trying not to get drunk while he wonders what the fuck could have happened. He's pieced it all together and it still doesn't make sense, but he knows it revolves around Micky Targett.

He knows where Micky lives, or at least used to, but he doesn't want to go there. Not yet. He understands the implications of his own temper and knows he can't take any risks, not until his probationary period is up anyway.

He has time. He'll find out what went down and straighten it if it's the last thing he ever does. He has missed most of the nineties.

He gets a job as a mechanic and rents a shitty one-bedroomed flat over a kebab shop in Tottenham.

He tries to get around to see a few faces but there really aren't that many to see. Pete Chalmers has moved abroad. Denny Masters is said to be around but no one knows where.

It's a new century and he's stuck in the previous one.

Eventually he calls Dixie. He'd been avoiding it because, deep down, he knows she's bad news. He's heard she's dealing again, got a good smack connection. He knows he can score on tick from her and bring in a few quid like that but if he gets caught . . . Screw that. Not only that but she'd be in her fifties. So he'd kept away.

But eventually, through curiosity as much as anything, he makes his way around there. It's a dump but he lives in worse.

They bullshit about the old days but that only serves to remind him of how shitty *these* days are. *Christ,* he thinks, *how we used to live.* Now look.

Then he mentions the smack, not that he's ever been a fan. She doesn't deny it but won't tell him where it's coming from.

'No one you know.'

Then she says the most ridiculous thing and Terry feels himself going into one. Knows his short fuse, and here it is getting sparked by the mention of one name.

'You'll never guess who's a regular.'

He shakes his head.

'That Micky. Micky Targett.'

Terry Farmer's world is crushed by an incoming comet. He can hear his pulse, white spots of blinding light bounce off the walls and flash across the room.

''Scuse me?'

'Yeah, few years now. Haven't heard from him for a while now though. Funny innit?'

Yeah, thinks Terry, *about as funny as arse cancer.* He breathes deep. What the actual *fuck*? He stands, leans over the coffee table and hands Dixie her own phone.

'Call him.'

'What? What for?'

'Ask him how he is. You were worried. Put it on speaker.'

Dixie does as she is told, knows better not to.

'Hello, stranger. How you getting on?' chirps Dixie.

Then Terry hears Micky's voice and knows that ultimately it won't matter if he does time for it or not, that little Essex scumbag needs to get what's coming.

Micky thinks about going to the Yeoman to say his goodbyes to the chaps but what is he realistically going to tell them? 'Alright lads, I'm fleeing the country and kissing everything goodbye. It's that or prison.'

So he doesn't go. Likewise he swerves the golf club.

He empties his bank account of the pittance that is left in it, adds that to the ten large Wrenny laid on him. He barely sleeps the night before his flight. When he gets up he smashes his phone and drops the bits into a drain.

He makes coffee but doesn't eat. Then walks from room to room. Drinks in the memories, some good but mostly bad. It breaks him up to leave but he knows he has no choice. He promises himself he'll come back one day.

He locks the front door and shoves the keys through the letter box, spares for Wrenny and his builders.

But he does pop next door to bid farewell to the Rogers. He's okay doing this because they know the house has been sold and therefore know he is moving away. He is alright with leaving them a phone number.

Lovely people, even if they have been bearers of chronically bad news over the years. He has a lump in his throat as he walks away, but he doesn't look back.

At the airport he makes three calls. The first is to Ben Yardley. He made sure to keep on top of his financial obligation to his lawyer so there was no awkwardness about money. There was just awkwardness.

'Say that again, Micky. Slowly.'

'I'm skipping the country. Today.'

Silence. Eventually Ben speaks.

'I know when you're not joking.'

'Yeah, well, I wish I was. Listen, I'm just an ordinary bloke. Alright, I see things from leftfield sometimes but . . . I'm not as mad as my life. And I'll say it once again, I didn't hurt that kid.'

'I know you didn't, Mick. Jesus, I'm so sorry.'

'Thanks, mate. It's been great knowing you.'

'Oh God. Don't say that. I can't believe I won't see you again.'

Micky feels himself choking up. Ben's work wasn't cheap but he got the job done, did everything he was asked to do and with some style.

'Where are you going?'

Yet the paranoia is still there. He wonders why Ben wants to know?

'I'll maybe send you a postcard. Do me a favour, don't call this in to the police for a bit. I'm at the er, at the station. If I don't call you in two hours that means I made it. If I do call you it's because I'm fucked and looking for some legal advice.'

'You put me in some tough positions, my friend.'

'Yeah but I'm worth it.'

Then Micky phones Lisa. Sadly it goes to voice message. He wanted to hear her voice. Wanted to know how much she cared for him, if indeed she did.

'Hey, Lease, it's Mick. Listen, I'm going away. Not sure when I'll be back. New adventures are calling. I'll miss you. Truth is I've always missed you. Even before I knew you I was missing you. Should have said something more at the time, although I suppose at the end of it that wouldn't have made much difference. Take care of yourself. I love you.'

The third call is to Carol. Carol the carer.

'Hello, Micky. How are you, my dear?'

'Hi, Carol. Yeah I'm okay thanks. Yourself?'

'You know, keeping on keeping on. This is a weird thing, I had a dream about your dad the other night.'

'Christ that must have been scary. What was he up to?'

'Smiling that big old, handsome smile. He was on good form. He was still old but with none of his problems.'

'Ha! You should've seen him when he was really like that. You would have loved him.'

'I loved him anyway, son. Thanks once again for the invite to the funeral. You did him proud.'

Micky feels himself struggling again, feels his throat seize. So much good in the world.

'You're so welcome, Carol. You made that last period bearable. I owe you everything. What you did for me . . .'

'Ah stop now. You looking after yourself?'

'Yeah I'm doing alright. The house has been sold. After your lot got paid there was a little left for me. Hey how is Akma? You seen her?'

'Yeah we bump into each other. She's a good girl, our Akma.'

Then Micky asks himself why he needs to tell her what's going on. What's the point? So he doesn't.

'That's lovely. Say hi and thanks to her from me, would you? Listen I just felt the need to call you and hear your voice. You are very important to me.'

'How the hell are you still single, you smooth-talking bastard?'

'Hahaha! That one is anybody's guess.'

'Call me anytime, Micky boy.'

'Cheers, Carol. You put the ass in care assistant, you know that, right?'

'The gob on you, boy, you must be Irish. If only I was ten years younger.'

CHAPTER SEVENTEEN

BANGKOK - MAY 2000

The neighbour digs the flavour still he's moving to another town
And I don't believe he'll come back
God damn right it's a beautiful day uhuh

Micky is so wrapped up in it all that he totally forgets he is going to *Asia!* Forgets he is travelling on a moody passport. He checks in and breezes through passport control. Nine days before he is due in court to face charges of grievous bodily harm with intent, Micky Targett leaves the UK with no idea when or indeed if he will be back.

He gets fairly drunk on the plane. Twice.

Twelve hours and ten minutes after take off his British Airways flight touches down at Don Meung airport in Bangkok.

He is exhausted, hungover but psyched to the max. He's in *Thailand* for Christ sake and the buzz of his arrival means, once again, he completely forgets that if his passport attracts any attention he'll be spending quite a bit of time in the Bangkok Hilton. Then plenty more in The Scrubs.

Wrenny told him where to walk for the cab rank and wrote down the hotel name and address where his stay is reserved. On the firm. The grinning, bowing cab driver heaves Micky's case into the boot of the green and yellow Toyota, and they head into the writhing, sweating, human anthill that is Krunthep, City of Angels, the Big Mango, Bangkok.

Windsor Suites hotel, Sukhumvit soi 20.

The walk from the cab to the hotel door is a bastard because Bangkok in May is like being in a sauna, but he's soon into the cool sanctuary of the massive atrium. He checks-in, and is stunned by the succulent beauty of the receptionist.

In his room he cranks up the air-con, rips off his sticky clothes and rolls around laughing on the king size bed. He turns on the TV and eyeballs a Thai soap for a few minutes. He hits the mini bar and tries his first ever Thai beer. Leo meets with his approval.

Whatever time it is in his head it's early evening in BKK and it will do him a bundle of good if he can stay awake until lights out, then sleep through to the next morning. But he is so happy and so excited he has no idea when he'll be able to sleep again. So he gets his trunks on, grabs a towel, gets in the lift and goes *up* to the swimming pool.

As long as he lives, Micky Targett will never be able to adequately describe just how good it felt, that gratification delay. He'd crawled the hard yards and paid his dues. Okay so he'd been a bad boy, not exactly a wrong 'un but he'd fractured the occasional law. But the amount of shit he'd had to deal with was way out of all proportion, finishing with him being set up by . . . the motherfucking Metropolitan police force.

Yet he'd come through it all, wriggled his way out from underneath a mountain of oppression and bad luck without doing a single day of jail time.

And now, as the Siam sun is slowly sinking, and as the sounds and smells of the Thai streets make their way up the twelve stories to where he stands on the pool's edge, he knows he is done with the tears and the sadness. He thinks about his mother, dead these last fourteen years. He thinks about his father, fallen foul of dementia and calamity and now safely back with his darling Florrie. Then he thinks about himself and says the words that no one else could be bothered to say.

'God bless you, Micky boy, and let the good times roll.'

He dives into the rapturous cool that feels so good he thinks he's having a full body orgasm. He surfaces, emerges from the liquid into vibrant, energizing life. He is truly born again.

He floats on his back, looks up at the dazzling array of stars studded against the black Asian night. The second half of his life begins right there. His knee, hip and back feel great. He feels himself finally start to unwind, content and very safe in the knowledge that all of the worst things that could happen in his life have already passed.

Yeah right.

*

Terry Farmer hasn't decided what he's going to do yet. In his experience it's sometimes best to just wing it. No point writing a script. Yeah, the bloke needs to get damaged, but he'll be spared permanent ill-health so he can stick to the payment plan.

He's been to the house before. Nice, suburban. Privileged. The more he thinks about it the more he hates Micky Targett.

Charlie Brown's roundabout and then out along the A12. Ilford then Romford, over the Gallows Corner flyover. Takes the Upminster turn off and drives past all those big houses he knows he'll never be able to afford.

He decides he'll ring the bell and whoever answers it gets knocked out. That's basically it. It's worked before.

Late evening. The darkness hides descriptions of the car but he's running twinned plates to be safe, and whoever is to be on the wrong end of what he dishes out will be relaxed and not expecting a visit. He pulls into the quiet little avenue and parks in the puddle of gloom between two streetlights on the other side of the road.

He knows the lounge is at the rear of the property so isn't worried he can see no lights. Up to the front door, he looks into the bedroom window to the right. Not only are there no curtains but there is nothing in the bedroom. No carpet, no light fittings. And it's the same story in the other bedroom. Got the decorators in. The bell goes unanswered.

He nips down the drive at the side of the house towards the garage. No light or sound through the obscured bathroom window. On his toes he peeks over the garden fence. No one home at all. Bollocks.

But he sees lights on in the house next door.

He rings the bell to be eventually greeted by an old fella who looks like something out of a Dicken's novel.

'Good evening, Sir. I'm visiting the Targett's next door. Do you know if Michael is around?'

'You've missed him, young man,' says the oldster, scrabbling to retain control of a wooden cane that appears to have a life of its own. 'He left this morning.'

'Oh no. Do you know when he'll be back?'

'You misunderstand. He sold the house. He's gone to live . . . abroad.'

Farmer chews down the information, tries to stay cool. Part of him thinks he'll just rush this old sod, have a tie-up. Whoever's in the house gets bound and gagged and he'll turn the place upside down. But no, he knows there are greater endeavours at play here.

'Did he leave a forwarding address? You see I'm his brother.' He guesses the old guy would know the story but will have forgotten the face. It's a real gamble.

'Are you indeed? I knew your father. Both he and Michael say you caused them harm.'

'I know, Sir. That's why I am here. I wasn't even invited to the funeral but I wanted to make it up to Micky. I have heart disease. I need a chance to put things right while I can.'

Farmer watches the bloke take it on board, think it through. *Come on, come on don't ask any questions.*

Then he bites. 'Well, under those circumstances . . . .' He looks to the old style desk cum cabinet right there in the hallway, picks up a piece of paper.

'A number is all he left. Why don't you step in and copy that out. Say hi to the young tyke from us when you see him would you?'

*

Micky has three days in Bangkok before he has to head south to go to work. On the first night he is still awake and chomping at the bit. Already five bottles of Leo deep, he leaves the manufactured cool of the hotel and plunges into the hot, fat air of Bangkok. Air pregnant with the promise of exotic delight. He takes his life in his hands and clambers onto the back of a motorcycle taxi, directing the wild-eyed kid to this place Wrenny had told him about.

'Soi Cowboy,' Micky yells above the traffic noise and off they go. Riding dispatch in London was never like this.

You'll find a god in every golden cloister
And if you're lucky then the god's a she
I can feel an angel sliding up to me

'Here's the drill,' Wrenny had instructed. 'You'll get dragged into a club, pole dancing, that kind of thing. A beer is about a quid, you buy a drink for a girl it's probably two. You want to go with her you have to pay the bar about a tenner, that's called a bar fine. To shag her is about thirty-five, maybe forty quid. That's all you need to know.'

What Micky didn't know was how gorgeous the girls were. And how many of them were working Cowboy.

At around midnight he is strolling up the middle of the pedestrianized street, maybe a hundred yards long. And there are about a million hot women wearing not much more than bikinis and boots who want to get across him. After a couple of exchanges the English capabilities of most of them run dry.

He stops here and there to buy a few drinks because he knows the girls earn a little something out of that. He's generous with tips. They clasp their hands in front of their faces in a prayer gesture and bob neatly in a dinky curtsey. A *wai*. He finds them enchanting, wants to hear their stories, and desires to marry them all. But as enamoured as he is with the girls, he is as equally revolted by the tides of fat, ugly, poorly-dressed, unpleasant-looking sex tourists. Predatory reptiles. He's been told the girls have a choice. A right of refusal.

Micky looks at the men and shudders, worries that is him now. Is he one of them?

But the night, the hours, the preceding weeks and his life are dragging on him. He jumps a bike back to the hotel and crashes.

He doesn't find the deep, rewarding sleep his level of exhaustion and discombobulation deserves. It's a shifting, dirty sleep. And the shape is back. The dark, morphing phantasm that follows him at his most exposed and unprepared. He wakes several times during the night feeling scared and disorientated.

He tries to shrug it off, thinking he has left all his cares and problems behind. What he can't know about are the problems that are already queueing up for him in the future.

He drowses and sleeps and swims and sunbathes throughout the next day.

335

*

DS Ray Pitts stares at the phone in his hand like it's a writhing python. It's almost as if he is blaming the handset itself for the ludicrous information that has just poured forth from it. Slowly he replaces it into its cradle, chews his lip thoughtfully.

The bearer of the news was erudite, gentlemanly and even charming. Lawyers often are. The news that he bore was so unpleasant to hear because, once again, *that* name was attached to it.

'My client, Michael Targett,' said the lawyer.

Ray Pitts sits up straight. Wants to cut a deal? Wants to go guilty before trial? Either way it's all gravy from here on in. Get that monkey off the back.

But no. Ben Yardley doesn't tell Ray Pitts anything he wants to hear. Quite the opposite. In fact if Ray Pitts wants to see Micky Targett in a prison cell, then not only is he going to have to start again but he's going to have to scour the country, and quite possibly the world to even get himself into a *position* where he can start again.

Jesus fucking Christ on a moped.

And he knows what his next unpleasant task is. Him and PC cooked up the whole scam together because they both wanted it so badly. Put that slippery fucker away no matter what.

Then one night there was a stabbing in Romford market. Little Trenton, knife carrying drug-dealer known to the police, got stabbed by a rival who got clean away. But Pitts was there when the call came in and was all over it, got to Trenton first and explained to him who had actually carried out the attack. Showed him a picture. It was either that or do a lot of time himself for the bags of coke Pitts was ready to place on him.

What could go wrong?

'Hello?'

'Bill, it's Ray.'

'Ray, boy. How goes it? We all good?'

'Not exactly. He's skipped bail.'

Bill Hubbard, the pro cock or PC to his mates feels his life blood, once again, slowing in his veins. Because of one man.

'How do you know?'

'I just got a call from his brief. Tells me he knows nothing more

336

than that.'

'But you got his passport.'

'Yeah but . . .'

'What?'

'I can't believe this bloke operates on his own. He must have some big boys behind him.'

'So he might even be able to get abroad?'

'Possibility. Obviously we'll get round to his house, neighbours, friends. We'll pull everyone. We'll find the bastard.'

'If it's the last thing I do, Ray.'

'I know, mate.'

'No, you don't. A year of my life. My job. My family. I don't how he did it but he did it. No matter how long this takes.'

*

On his second night in Bangkok Micky heads somewhere else Wrenny recommended.

'Might be your thing, even though you're an old git these days.'

'How you feel, mate, it's how you feel.'

'Yeah yeah. Anyway, lot of foreigners but on the young side. Backpackers, that sort of thing. Lot of dope and dancing. Very youth hostelly. But listen . . .'

Micky listens.

'Don't fuck up over there. It's fairly slack but we ain't got too much sway with the cops, with them tiddlies.'

'Tiddlies?'

'Tiddly winks – chinks. Not in Bangkok. You get nicked, you might be able to buy your way out, but it's on you.'

So Micky jumps a cab and heads to Khao San Road.

Wrenny's description was spot on. Lot of tie-dyed clothes, Screamadelica and Bob Marley T-shirts, sandals, white kids with dreads. Young Europeans and Americans walking on the wild side before they go home to their parents' loving care, their careers, their universities. To their cosseted lives. They have so much to live for, so much hope, Micky Targett thinks. But he knows that soon enough life will kick that soppy shit right out of them.

He wants to be approached by sleazy Thai blokes daring him to drink cobra blood like in that film, but it's all a bit nice and well behaved.

He breaks away from the throng and finds a chuck wagon at the side of the road. He knows from someone the night before that the word for chicken is *gai*. So he manages to order chicken and rice. There's no beer so he nips to a 7/11, scores a Leo and comes back with that, sits on a tiny plastic chair at a tiny plastic table. And he loves it. The food is delicious, the beer is cold and there's magic in the air. He feels at home.

Back on the main drag he eases onto a bar stool then gets involved in a game of pool which he loses. He tries to get some conversations going, buys a couple of drinks. But it's going nowhere and he knows why. In spite of his scar and in spite of his occasional limp he knows he looks good for his age. But good for his age means nothing here. *Age* is everything and Micky, now into his forties, is twice as old as most of these privileged pretend hippies.

He moves down the street, takes a chair at a table of a neon-splashed bar terrace.

'Beer Leo, kup.'

The waitress grins, nods and disappears back inside. Micky feels so good about everything. This country, the language, the culture. His life. It's all worked out.

Seated at a table behind him is a Thai guy hitting on a couple of girls who are both pissed. They're all speaking English so in spite of the street noise he can pick up snippets.

'Nobody gets caught. It's never happened and it never will. They don't stop girls.'

They exchange glances, one tips her drink down in one.

'It's free money. I thought you said you walked on the wild side. Here's the news, ladies, I *am* the wild side.'

Micky twists his head, senses there is something interesting happening.

'So where will it actually be?' This is the really drunk one.

'It's *inside* the cases. Stitched in. I'll bring two to your room tomorrow and you'll see. Then, if you don't want to do it that's up to you. Five thousand pounds each and you get to keep the cases.'

His little joke gets no response but he's on his way to bringing them around. They're looking at each other, smiling, goading.

338

'When are you leaving?' The guy wants to know.

'Saturday.'

'Okay, well we have time. I'll come over tomorrow, show you and we'll talk more.'

He waves inside for his bill.

'Have you got any coke, Benjy?' The not so really drunk one asks.

Micky's ears grow to twice their normal size.

'Baby I've got everything. Look if you're on the plane on Saturday you shouldn't get smashed tomorrow night. That means tonight is the big one. I've got coke, great Es and VIP passes to the Cinnamon Lounge. Ready?'

Big grins all round. The waitress hands both Micky his beer and brings the guy's bill, which he pays with a flourish. Micky takes a sip but there's something about the scene that disturbs him.

They all stand and, for a reason he doesn't comprehend, Micky stands too. The guy tries to get passed first but Micky is in his way.

'Excuse me,' he says, American accent.

Micky holds firm and checks him out. He is shorter by three inches but has confidence to burn. Good-looking bastard.

'You girls okay?' Micky asks.

They look at him blankly, then edge their way around the other side of Micky's table.

'Ginny, right?' Micky asks.

One shakes her head. 'No.'

'Sorry, my mistake. But you're okay, yeah?'

'Of course they're okay. What the fuck, man?'

He stares into Micky from two feet away and Micky holds that stare. Then he hears Wrenny's words; 'Don't fuck up over there.'

He lets it go because he knows he has no choice.

'Sorry, mate,' he tells the bloke.

He stands aside, lets Benjy pass and with it the moment itself, leaving the two girls to their fate.

CHAPTER EIGHTEEN

Never been here before, I'm intrigued I'm unsure
I'm searching for more
I've got something that's all mine

Two days later Micky checks out and grabs a cab south. Once they are clear of the city's tentacles it's all motorway. Highway 7, signs to Chon Buri. Nothing much to look at. Then he starts to see signs to his new home. Signs to Pattaya.

Off the motorway and the driver hangs a right onto South Pattaya Road. Into the dark heart. Into Sodom and Gomorrah. The driver could make this run blindfold because every day a thousand sex pests arrive at Don Meung and half of them bypass Bangkok and the rest of the country altogether. More choice in Pattaya. By the turn of the new century the conservative estimate is of twenty-five thousand sex workers plying their trade, with busloads more arriving by the hour. The skyline is webbed with cranes and cheap, easy sex is the reason why.

Halfway along South Pattaya Road the cab catches a red. Micky is buzzing again, can't sit still. The sun is going down and the adrenaline is going up.

He looks to his right at a non-descript apartment block. Something catches his eye up on third floor, a window. A face. A young girl. So young and so sad, and she is looking right at him. He stares back. She looks like she's crying. She waves, no, she *beckons* him. Then it looks like an adult pulls her from behind, away from the window. Then the cab is in gear and they move off.

340

Ten minutes later they pull into a small soi off Thappraya Road. Micky has no idea what to expect his new home will be like. He pays the driver, pulls his case out of the boot and stands before a newish five-storey block of flats.

Into the lobby and he is delighted to see, through the glass doors and behind the block, a decent-sized swimming pool.

He takes the lift to the fourth floor and finds 4C. He hits the bell, hops from one foot to the other. Wrenny has told him that, most of the time, he won't have the place to himself. But it's a big place and of a certain standard and needs to be kept that way. Micky thinks back to his recent living arrangements. He doesn't like sharing but having come from living with a demented, immobile, incontinent stroke victim he's sure he can handle what's on the other side of the door.

He listens intently and hears nothing. Then he panics. What if Wrenny has stitched him up? He's on the other side of the world on a moody passport, what if . . .?

The sound of a door opening, but not his door. He looks behind him where a chubby Thai woman has exited 4B.

'Kun Meek?' she asks him.

'Sorry?'

'You. You kun Meek? Your name Meek?'

'Ah right. Yeah. I'm Meek. *Mick*. Sa wa dee kup.'

'Sa wa dee ka.'

Keys in hand and beaming gayly, she waddles past him, opens the door and he collapses with the relief.

Inside the spacious, shiny but barely furnished apartment, the girl walks before him turning on lights.

'My name Pim.'

'Pim.'

'Ya. English Gow he give me keys, say meet you.'

'Very nice, thank you. Is Gow here?'

'He go out. Back later, maybe tomorrow. That Gow room, this your room. That room suh pare.'

She has the most endearing, squinty smile and Micky loves her instantly. He wants to tweak her gorgeously plump cheeks.

'Thank you, Pim. You are very kind.'

'You welcome. See you later.' She hands him a key and leaves.

Alone he gingerly opens the door to his room and is pleased to see a massive bed, curtains over the window and a wardrobe. That's all he needs for now. He tests the mattress and is happy to feel the firmness with just the right amount of give that his maladies require.

Wrenny had told him all about Gary Pleasant. Gow to everyone.

'Not a face to speak of but a proper bloke. Good businessman. Sure he's pulled the odd stroke here and there, who hasn't? But he keeps us all on the straight and narrer. Been in Thailand for twenty years, speaks the lingo, knows loads of Thais and, more importantly, knows loads of cops.'

'Why does he need to know loads of cops?' Micky wanted to know.

'Because of the 'never thought thats'.'

''Scuse me?'

Wrenny took a deep breath. 'Throughout recorded time there has always been a procession of people trying to make their way in this world. Some do, some don't but all of them at one time or another have been in the situation where something has gone wrong.'

Micky stared at him blankly.

'And afterwards they would always be sitting there thinking about what went wrong and they would always be moved to declare, 'I never thought that would happen'.'

Micky smiled and knew what was coming.

'Now where you're going, when things go wrong they are prone to go *very* wrong. So when you're sitting there thinking 'I never thought that would happen', you'll be glad to know that Gow Pleasant knows loads of cops. Trust me.'

Micky isn't sure what to do. He wants to go out to see how bad big, bad Pattaya really is, but he feels the needs to touch base with his new chum. He's also getting hungry and the tantalising smells of cooking wafting through the block are driving him nuts.

Then something weird happens. A ringing sound. He traces it to a wall-mounted phone in the kitchen. After thirty seconds or so it rings off but immediately starts again and this time they ain't hanging up. So Micky thinks he may as well answer it, take a message.

'Hello.'

'Hello. Is Micky there?' It's a London accent, and not only that but Micky thinks he recognises it. But it's not Wrenny. Maybe it's Gow.

'Yeah, speaking.'

Then the line goes dead.

Six thousand miles away a woman uses her Tesco loyalty card to lift a small amount of brown powder from a plastic bag. She deftly places it onto the CD case of a pirated copy of Play by Moby. She cuts it into two lines then finds a grubby five pound note which she rolls into a tube. She drops to her knees and snorts one line. She offers the note to the man sitting on her sofa.

'Everything alright, babe?' she asks.

'Yeah, Dix'.' says Terry Farmer, with a satisfied sccowl as he puts down the phone. 'Everything's fine.'

Micky unpacks slowly and hangs up his shirts. Then he takes a shower and shaves. Then he decides he is going out and thinks about what to wear. Pattaya is on the coast but is only marginally cooler than Bangkok, so he opts for his old Levi cut-downs and a well-seasoned T-shirt emblazoned with a print of Ian Gillan.

On his way out, the door opens and Gow Pleasant walks in.

'Gow?'

'Mick.'

He's tall, taller than Mick, in his fifties but in great shape. His green vest reveals taut, brown cables for arms. The logo on the vest is – 'Go Down With Gow'. An image of a floating scuba diver with his thumbs up is below. He is all but completely grey but his hair is full and healthy, swept back and tucked behind his ears. His face is tanned, lined and handsome. Grey eyes twinkle beneath a pronounced brow. Micky likes him immediately.

'Sorry I wasn't here to meet you. I guess Pim found you.'

'Yeah she did, no worries. Gow, did you just phone?'

'No.'

'Mm. There was a call and an English bloke asked for me but then rung off.'

'That's odd. Anyway, I'll get a quick shower and then we'll go out. Say hello to a few people, get some dinner. Yeah?'

'Pukka.'

'Great. Ooh, got something here for you. Hang on.'

He goes into his room, rummages through a drawer and comes back with an opened envelope and a plastic card.

'This is your bank stuff. Wrenny dropped you forty k which comes out at . . .' he looks at the account print out. '. just shy of two and a half million.'

Micky thinks he's going to die of happiness. And it's only just beginning.

Forty minutes later they are hanging on the corner of their small soi and Thappraya Road. They climb onto the back of what Gow calls a Baht bus. Open backed pick-up trucks that circle the town. Jump on - jump off for twenty Baht per person.

'Hungry?'

'I could eat a horse, mate.'

'That could well be what you get. You been to Patts before?'

'First time in Thailand.'

'Ha! This should be fun.'

Just off Walking Street they sit in a reasonable looking café. No tourists. Gow orders *Tom Yum ah haan ta lay,* seafood soup and Micky copies him.

'So, Gow. I'm hoping you know more about what's going on than me.'

Gow grins, thinks the bloke is okay. 'What did Wrenny tell you?'

'Not much. Him and you have a few businesses. Couple of shops. A bar.'

'Pretty much. I came here back in the eighties to open a scuba shop and go diving. The shop is at the other end of Walking Street and the boat is moored out on the pier not far from here. Eleven metre Stormcat, takes ten punters at a time. We do well. There's good diving around here and not everyone that comes to Pattaya is a sleaze bag.'

'Just most of them.'

'True. Which is why we got into the sex business. Me, Wrenny and one other went in on a club together, just off the main drag on soi twelve. I don't really have a lot to do with that on the day to day. I helped set it up and do all the legal shit. Got it off and running. Dealing with Thai people is not easy, but I'm the go-to man for that.'

'You're fluent in the language, right?'

'Pretty much. You know any?'

'No but I like learning. I have reasonable French and a bit of Spanish. I'm looking forward to it. So, where might I fit in?'

'Can you DJ?'

'No.'

'You ever worked behind a bar?'

'Yeah, I used to own one in Mallorca. That's where I first met . . .' He holds himself back for some reason. Keep it tight.

'Can you drive?'

'Yeah.'

'Bigger stuff? Like a van, lorry?'

'I've driven seven and a half tonners.'

'Hmm. You ever worked in a shop?'

'No.'

'You scuba?'

''Fraid not.' He chuckles. 'Feels like I'm talking my way out of something here.'

'Not at all. We'll start off with you in the shop. Nothing to it. Selling the dives, selling the kit where possible. Everyone speaks a bit of English. You can also help us load the boat when we go out. In the season it's everyday but it's quieter now.'

The Tom Yum arrives and Micky is blown away by the flavours.

'I told them to go easy on the spice in yours. Thai food will lift your head off the way they normally eat it.'

'So the club you got. Is it a proper girls-on-the-catwalk kind of thing?'

'Yeah, about forty girls grinding away. I was thinking we might be able to use you there as well but Thais are funny about some things. If you were a DJ it would be no problem because that is what they call specialized work. Bar staff really need to be locals. If we employ as many locals as we can that goes down well with the powers that be.'

'And who are the powers that be?'

'Cops and the mayor.'

'Same the world over. Are they really that bribeable here?'

'Yeah, part of the culture. They've all got their hands out.'

Micky nods, digs into the food.

'I hear you could've done with a bit of that flexibility back home.'

Micky didn't expect Wrenny not to give the man the full lowdown.

'Yeah. I've pulled a few strokes but generally got away with it. Which annoyed a certain DS who took it upon himself to fit me up. Wrenny and his contacts tried to reach out to him but couldn't make it happen. Hence I landed on your doorstep.'

'It's not a problem. He speaks very highly of you.'

'Really?'

'If he didn't rate you, you wouldn't be here.'

That makes sense and Micky is grateful, not just because he's landed on his feet, but that he's done so with such a nice man.

After dinner they stroll most of the length of the world famous Walking Street. Late May is very much off-season but the place is still bedlam. Hawkers, barkers and hookers line up on both sides of the road outside their places of business. Bar price cards and restaurant menus are waved in their faces to begin with, then, as they progress further along this most disease-clogged of arteries, they pass the gogo clubs. Outside each of these are ranked a number of the establishment's employees. Some are waitresses but some are the dancers themselves and Micky is stunned, even more so than when he was in Bangkok, by the number and the sheer brazen sexiness of some of these women.

'Please tell me there comes a time when you get bored with this,' he says.

Gow smiles broadly. 'You get used to it but never bored. I love Thai women. They are part victim – part predator. *All* of them, and I love that, what's the word . .? Paradox. But do yourself a favour, don't ever fall in love over here.'

'Advice born out of experience.'

'Correct. That's why I now live in a flat with two other men as opposed to my own villa. Which is where my ex-wife resides. With her boyfriend.'

'Sorry to hear that. Is that right foreigners can't own property here?'

'Yeah, so if you want to buy somewhere you have to do it in the name of a Thai national or a company majority owned by a Thai. My lawyer told me I should let him handle it all but I listened to my wife instead. Cost me more than I can say.'

They press bravely on. At one point Micky is literally accosted by a gorgeous woman with an impressive cleavage. She has him by the arm and isn't about to let go.

'You buy me drink, handsome maaaan,' she wails.

The bar she is dragging him towards is playing proper techno so he's already thinking they might have a beer there before moving on. But Gow shoos her away with a few curt words.

'That's Jenny's Star Bar. Don't bother going in there until later when it fills out.'

'Why's that?'

''Cos that's where the ladyboys start their evening.'

Micky pulls up sharp, checks back to the girl who has resumed her vigil of the street. She waves flirtatiously at him.

''Ang on. You mean . . .'

'Yeah, that's a bloke.'

'No way.'

'Mad innit? Most Thai women don't have much up top, so if a girl has big tits the chances are it's a geezer.'

Micky can't believe what he's seeing, or hearing.

'Upstairs there, up the escalators is the best club if you like hard house music. It's called Marine but it doesn't get going until after two.'

On they go through the chaos, past a karaoke joint, past a bar where a Thai band is annihilating Smoke On The Water, onwards past drunks, beggars, cripples, past a stall selling racks and racks of Rolex watches, past shops selling football shirts of every single leading European team.

And past girls, so many girls.

'You should see this place in the season,' Gow tells him.

Then they are off the main drag and into an alleyway that is six feet across to begin with but then opens out to about twenty. A girl wearing a gold bikini and fuck-me high heels zips between them on a scooter, a yard of ink-black hair lashing the night air as she goes. A chuck wagon is practically alive with sizzling delights. Two long-haired, tattooed Thai guys argue over a bottle of Sangsom. The sights and the sounds and the smells are intoxicating to Micky. It's a sleazy slice through the guts of the town and all the more exciting and seductive for it. Dirty and a little bit dangerous.

Micky likes Pattaya.

'You'll get used to the lay out soon enough. This is soi twelve, it runs off Walking Street to the left as you approach from the beach end.'

There is a club either side and Micky can hear the muffled thump of dance music from each. First The Witch's Coven on the left and then Diamond agogo on the right. Three beautiful women wearing silky, red kimonos and smoking cigarettes hang around outside the Coven. Outside Diamond two are dressed in knee-high, black boots, lacey, black underwear and nothing else.

Thirty yards past Diamond Micky spots a neon sign on the wall. There's a comedy red devil with a yellow pitchfork and the word - Diablos. Gow nods at a young Thai man on the door and they duck in. Out of the heat and humidity and into the cool. Into the den.

There's a bar along one wall and a raised platform along another. Bar stools attend the length of the platform and several single men, perched lecherously upon them, are looking directly into the crutches of half a dozen girls in orange bikinis who are dancing unenthusiastically to non-descript house music. In the centre of the room is a circular stage featuring more girls and around this are bench seats dotted with several more men and a few other girls.

Gow ignores the whole scene and strides to the corner of the place where he heads up a flight of steps. Upstairs it's more of the same but much smaller and no bar. Around the periphery of the twenty-five feet square room is a long bench seat and every ten feet or so is a small podium upon which a single, bikinied girl is dancing. In the middle of the room is a six feet square sofa. On the sofa are two naked girls who are pretending to get it on.

Gow is greeted by a tall man of medium build around fifty. He sports collar length hair streaked with grey and a beard to match. Even in the gloom of the UV and the low lights Micky can tell he hasn't see the sun in years.

'Mick this is Scotch, Scotch this is Micky Targett.' Gow shouts into his ear.

'Scotch?' Micky asks as he holds out his hand.

'Aye,' says the man as he takes it.

The man's warm, generous smile belies the harshness of his accent.

'Want a drink?' Gow asks.

'Yeah cheers, I'll have a Leo please, mate.'

348

'Get us a coke, dude.'

Scotch goes to get the drinks and Gow steers Micky to a small, unoccupied table by the far wall.

'He runs the place most of the time. Makes sure everyone gets paid, makes sure the deliveries have arrived. Deals with any drunks or idiots. Good bloke to have around.'

'You said foreigners shouldn't be working in bars.'

'Yeah. Officially he doesn't work here. Obviously he does and he's here because I know I can trust him. He hangs around in the shadows. Doesn't work downstairs, just runs the place from up here. He gets paid cash, as you will.'

At that moment one of the customers, a Chinese, hanging back along the wall, gets up from his seat and sits on one of the few low stools around the sofa where the two girls are half-heartedly still frolicking. He grabs one of the girls by the ankles and pulls her, on her back towards him. Then he leans forward and begins to perform cunnilingus. While not appearing delighted with this odd shift of dynamic, she seems accepting enough.

'Jesus,' Micky says. 'Is that legal.'

'Technically they're not even supposed to have their tops off.'

'So how . . .?'

'We're protected. The chief of police owns the freehold on this building. And I taught his son how to scuba dive. It's also why Scotch can work here. Costs a few quid but it's worth it. If it kicks off and Scotch can't handle it, he makes the call and in two minutes we've got ten freelance nutters in here with knives and bats to take care of anything.'

'Wow.'

'Off duty cops. Welcome to Thailand, son. Word of advice . . .'

Micky leans in close, sees Scotch and a waitress come back up the stairs with the drinks.

'Never ever go up against a Thai. Not in an argument, certainly not in a fight. Never argue with a cop, even if you've done nothing wrong. If you're sitting in a car with the engine off and someone drives into you it will be your fault. And if you take it to court they'll find you guilty. You're an outsider here and you always will be.'

Micky takes his beer and the three of them clink bottles.

'Good to know you, mate,' Gow says.

'Aye, good to have you here, Micky,' says Scotch.
'Cheers, lads. Good to be here.'
'Don't get too pissed' Gow advises. 'You start work at ten.'

So Micky's tenure in Pattaya is underway. Gow has a great little business and he is pleased to be part of it. Gow, through his years in the country, his mastery of Thai and his well-placed friends in the authorities, has made many contacts in the main hotels and apartment blocks. If you're in Pattaya and you want to go diving or snorkelling then you'll get told to head to a shop at the beach end of Walking Street and you 'Go Down With Gow'.

It's not easy work though. He helps out in the shop behind the counter and deals with customers who want to go out on the boat. He's also expected to refill the tanks with compressed air, wash down all the BCDs, masks, fins and snorkels at the end of each trip and load up Gow's pick-up with all the kit in the mornings when he's going out. He's even been out on the boat a couple of times. He considers learning to dive.

Part of him wants to get wrecked on drugs and chase pole dancers, but he knows he needs to make a good impression first. The high-life will come because Pattaya is party central every goddam night, and one lucky Essex bozo has wound up living in the middle of it.

He takes Thai lessons and makes progress. He spends time across the hallway with Pim and her ridiculously extended family, eating, trying to talk and making friends. This may not be the 'real' Thailand but he loves it just the same.

As the summer heads into the rainy season of the year two thousand, Micky struggles with the heat and humidity, but in Pattaya you're never too far away from the sea, a pool or an air conditioned interior.

In the mornings when Gow is going out, Micky rides with him along the length of Walking Street to unload the truck at the pier where the boat is moored. In the pulverizing daylight the place is revealed for the scummy, rat-ridden, roach-infested shithole it truly is. Without the neon and its cloak of night it is a truly horrible sight, this constellation of vileness and vice. Micky loves it.

One thing that does grind his gears is the cohort of morons, villains and general dickheads that occasionally show up to occupy the third room. Generally they come across as loud, boorish and privileged, expecting the Thais and, on occasion, Micky himself to pay homage to them and accommodate their every whim. He can't understand why a man with the clout and class of Wrenny would indulge these jokers.

Gow has no interest in getting involved, so it falls upon Micky to babysit while they're in town. Okay, Gow gives Micky tiime off so that he doesn't have to worry about being at work the following day but, all things considered, he'd rather not because whilst Micky himself is far from the smoothest guy in town, some of these berks make him look like Noel sodding Coward.

But karma was clearly invented in Thailand. Micky knows this because of what happened to Tony Bryant. He wasn't even on the run, he just did a bit of business with Wrenny, fancied a holiday without paying for it and somehow wangled use of the room.

Tony Bryant was a fat, scruffy, smelly, uncouth drug-dealing bully from Plaistow and the minute Micky laid eyes on him he knew it was going to be bad. Gow rolled his eyes and delegated.

Out in the clubs and the bars he left a vapour trail of upset and antagonism, and it was Micky's job to keep this knobjockey out of trouble and translate one single question.

'That one, ask her how much she wants. That one, ask her how much she wants.' That was how their time together went.

And the bloke was there for *weeks*. But by that time Micky had been in the country for five months and knows the basic ropes of how the sleazy old town works. So one night it's two in the morning and they're up in Marine and they're both a couple of pills to the good. The pills come through Scotch but, because the firm are newly into the gear in Pattaya, they come in at the equivalent of twenty quid a pop. Another reason Micky keeps large nights to a minimum.

Bryant is drunk as well, takes his shirt off, dances wildly and shouts his mouth off. Micky is flirting with a group of girls and it would be a good night but for this colossal embarrassment. The Thais are too polite to say anything.

Bryant reels around bumping into people, grabbing girl's backsides but then spots this total babe dancing coyly on the fringes of the group. He stops and stares.

'Jesus, look at her,' he says, throwing a sweaty arm around Micky's shoulders. 'That one over there in the black. Ask her. Ask her how much.'

Micky hates it but over he goes. Even in the gloom and through his juddering eyesight her beauty is apparent. Flawless complexion, dazzling white teeth, nut-brown eyes. She smiles gorgeously as Micky approaches and then he notices something else about her; her large breasts.

She and Micky converse briefly and, whilst he's still not sure, he has a pretty good idea. He looks at her throat. Yes! He slips her two thousand Baht and tells her his friend really likes her. She doesn't even look at Bryant because she doesn't need to. Work is work.

So Micky slopes back to Bryant and says, 'You're on, mate. She's up for anything. Three thou for the night.'

Bingo.

The next morning, even though he is knackered and suffering, Micky gets up especially early to see what there might be to see. Gow is in the kitchen cleaning up his breakfast things and about to leave for work. He seems in an unusually good mood, singing along to Groovejet by Spiller on the radio.

'If this ain't looooove . . .'

'Morning, mate,' Micky greets.

''Ello, son. How was last night?'

Micky can tell from his expression that he's hiding something. They're both grinning at each other but neither wants to spill what they know, or think they know, first.

'Not bad, mate. Didn't have a massive one.'

'Right. Tony okay?'

'Think so. He cut out before me. You not see him?'

'No,' Gow says, 'but . . .'

'Yeah?'

'I've seen *someone*.'

'Oh yeah?' Micky asks.

'Did you have a little friend back?'

'Not me. Came home alone like a good boy.'

Gow grins massively. 'I see. You're up early.'

'I feel okay, thought I'd come in and help out.'

'Good of you. I have something I think you'd like to know about our guest.'

'I'm all ears.'

That night they're all in the Diablos having a drink. Bryant, having slept all day, is ready for another big one. Gow, Micky and Scotch are relaxed and ready to share some news.

'So, Tone,' says Gow brightly. 'I hear you scored a bit of a babe last night.'

'Phwoar. Mate, fuckin' unreal. All over me. Best blow job I've ever had. I may have to move over here full-time.'

Scotch stifles a giggle while Micky and Gow hold it together.

'Right. Yeah, they know their trade some of these kids. Shame she was on.'

'How you know that?'

'Bumped into her as she was on her way out this morning.'

'Oh? And she told you that?'

'Didn't have to. Don't tell me, she did that thing about being shy. Lights off, lying on her side so that you could spoon her from the back and do her up the arse.'

Tony Bryant chokes on his beer. 'What the fuck? She told you all that? Cheeky bitch.'

'Didn't tell me anything. I worked it out because that's what a lot of them say.'

Scotch has to turn away, Micky edges closer on his bar stool. Bryant starts to look uncomfortable.

'That's what a lot of *who* say?'

'Don't tell me, you were wrecked last night and she left before you woke up.'

Scotch's wild, hooting laughter cuts across the music.

'The fuck you talking about?'

'I'm talking about one of the oldest tricks in town, mate. I saw him this morning without the make-up. You're in the club, Tone, and not a very exclusive one at that. You fucked a bloke in Pattaya.'

Two things, apart from much attendant mirth and merry-making, happened after this revelation. Firstly Tony Bryant ripped Pattaya apart looking for the ladyboy who had robbed him of that particularly virginity. Unsuccessfully, as it turned out. Secondly he decided it was time to move on. He swore the three of them, also unsuccessfully, to secrecy and decided that he'd like to check out this place called

Phuket he'd heard about. He was in a cab before the sun came up.

In fairness, Tony Bryant was as bad as it got. With a warning of only a day or two from Wrenny, a South African guy in his sixties called Francois rocked up in September of that year. He was polite and courteous but didn't want to mix with Gow, Mick and Scotch socially or in any way. He was in the country for three weeks but spent just a total of five nights at the apartment. No one knew where he went. Then one night he broke cover to a degree by taking the four of them out to one of the best restaurants in town. After a couple of beers he let slip that people called him by his abbreviated name. Faf. He was gone before they woke up the next day.

Then there was this time a young French bloke called Olivier showed up. Not unnaturally he didn't want to talk too much about what had happened, sufficed to say he'd been living in London and got busted selling smack. Jumped bail just like Micky had. He was actually a pretty decent DJ and Gow assured him there would be no shortage of job opportunities in Pattaya. He actually played a few nights downstairs at The Diablos and Gow even got him a slot early on at Marine. He had a bright future but told Micky that wasn't why he was there.

'It's not my kind of thing, Micky. I'm a city boy but I like the country. I'm heading north. I want to find out more about the border country. Thailand, Burma, Laos. Up there. I'm heading to Chiang Rai, then we will see.'

And that wasn't the only time Chiang Rai got mentioned. As November two thousand rolls around and the warm, dryer weather invites more tourists to swarm the town, Gow invites Micky to Diablos one Saturday night. Nothing strange in that.

So they're upstairs on their usual stools at the high tables at the back. The music is as crap as it always is. The girls, bless them, pretend they're having a good time when the punters are looking, but are clearly bored shitless when they're not.

Scotch has been reading the Pattaya News newspaper and Micky notices the headline; 'Tourist found dead on Jomtien beach'.

'Hey I heard about this today. How pissed do you have to be to go swimming and never come out?'

Gow and Scotch exchange glances.

'He wasn't pissed. That was no accident,' Scotch tells him.

'How do you mean?'

'The dangers of ambition,' Gow explains. 'That idiot was with a firm of Russians who are trying to move in here without paying their dues.'

'Into the drug game?'

'Yup. There's this weird fact that Thailand is the only Asian country that has never been invaded. Now that may be because no one has really bothered trying too hard, but the fact remains there will never be foreign criminals taking over here. That's because it would mean the cops giving up the big chair.'

'You saying the police offed Sergei boy last night?'

'Yup. He was tortured, held under and then had his body lobbed in the sea by people knowing he'd be washed up early this morning. Sends a message.'

Micky herds his thoughts. 'The *police* did that?'

'You be in Thailand now, boy,' says Scotch.

'Lucky you're on the winning side, son,' says Gow.

Micky breathes deep, takes a pull of his beer.

'So you enjoying your time here, Micky?' Scotch growls.

'Yeah, mate, all good. Can't think of anywhere else I'd rather be.'

'I'll drink to that.'

They clink their bottles.

'And yourself, Scotch. Things work out as you'd thought?'

A gentle shrug from a man who, just by looking at him, has clearly seen and done as least as much as Micky ever will.

'I got my hang ups oot the way before I came here. I had drink, drug, money, family and female problems all my life and dumped them all when I arrived. Been plain sailing ever since. Never thought I'd end up being a pimp's assistant but I've had worse jobs. Much worse. And yourself, son. You seem healthy and happy enough. You keeping it together?'

'A few things I always live by; one, never get drunk more than three times in a twenty-four hour period. Two, never take drugs on a school night. Three, always be nice to everybody, at least until they give you a reason not to.'

'Got a philosopher among us, Gow.'

'Man's going places. Right now we're going to the office.'

This is a surprise to Micky. Firstly because it's the first he's heard of it, and secondly, he didn't know there was an office.

He follows Gow behind a curtain which he thought led to the girl's changing area. It does but beyond that is a non-descript, unmarked door. Gow knocks on it and they both hear a voice calling them in.

The room is about big enough for a desk, three chairs and three adults, which is why when Micky and Gow enter it becomes crowded. Sitting behind the desk is a diminutive Thai. He is dressed smartly in a black, long sleeved shirt, his gold watch clearly visible. He wears black, plastic-rimmed glasses. His jet black hair is swept backwards away from his brow and controlled with some shiny substance or other. Micky puts him at mid-fifties. He has the look of a man who has never smiled in his life and has no intention of starting anytime soon.

He stands and leans forward to shake Gow's hand.

'Hello kun Narong. How are you?'

'Hello, Gow. Yes I am good. Is this your man?'

'Yes it is. This is Micky from London. Mick this is Narong. He's the chief of police I was telling you about. Friend of ours.'

Whoa! is all Micky thinks.

So they settle in their seats and the cop, this Narong is staring at Micky and it's *very* uncomfortable. But there's nothing he can do or say. Gow senses it.

'So you remember I asked if you could drive a truck, Mick?'

'Yes I do.'

'Narong asked me if I knew anyone.'

'Yeah, I like to help out where I can. Would my license be alright over here?'

Gow machine guns some Thai across the desk and the guy looks at Micky like he's an alien.

'Yeah, license, in Thailand. Good one. We'll have to work out some third party, fire and theft as well. Don't worry about all that. It's a big panel van.'

Micky thinks and what he thinks is there's something wrong. 'You can't get a local to do this? Driving?'

'It's not about the driving, Micky,' Narong informs him in very clear English. 'It's about the trust. Gow tells me good things about you.'

Micky nods at Gow. 'That's nice of him. Of course I'd like to help.'

In spite of the air-con Micky starts to sweat. Yeah, Gow did ask about driving and yeah, now that his senses are screaming at the max, he can even recall Wrenny telling him his job might involve getting behind the wheel. But. What's. In. The. Van?

'Good. I think this is going to be alright,' says Narong.

There are so many reasons why Micky has to do this; one, Wrenny has sent him here and he owes his freedom to that. Two, Gow is a great bloke and he owes him plenty too. Three, Narong is the chief of police and tonight seems like the perfect time for Micky to remember that for several months he has been staying in Thailand illegally.

Yeah, many reason to do it ranged against one solitary one not to. That being whatever it is that's in the fucking van.

Then Narong is opening the top drawer of his desk, reaches in and pulls out what looks like a laminated white business card which he passes to Gow. Gow looks it over, sees several lines of Thai type. Narong talks for twenty or so seconds.

'It's all cool, Mick,' he says handing over the card with a smile. 'You'll have a Thai co-driver. Proper bloke and the van is totally straight. You won't get stopped, but if you do this is your get out of jail card. This is Narong's official notice to *anyone* that you and your journey are not to be interfered with.'

Narong leans across the desk to look Micky hard in the eye. 'The boy with you is a good boy. He will look after you and you will look after him.'

Then without another word Gow is on his feet and it's handshakes all round and then they're back in the club where Mick, suddenly feeling unpleasantly sober, orders a large G&T and another beer. Gow senses his unease.

'That is one of the most important people in the second most important town in this country, Mick. You'll be fine. You're a protected species.'

Micky feels neither fine nor protected. He feels sick.

'Have Thursday off. Rest. It's a bit of a trip.'

'Where the fuck am I going?'

'Have you heard of Chiang Rai?'

Three days later Micky is up early. Coffee and some cereal. A slice of mango. Gow gets up to see him off because he feels for the bloke.

'You'll be fine.'

A cab toots from outside.

In the cab next to the driver is a well dressed Thai in his mid-twenties. Nike T-shirt, baggy Levis. He doesn't even say hello. That's okay with Micky. He doesn't want to talk to anyone either.

They head the usual way out of Pattaya but instead of taking highway 7 up to Bangkok and then north the driver stays on highway 3, hugging the coast. Half an hour later Micky is able to spot the looming hulk of a massive cruise liner over to his left. That, along with towering yellow gantries and ranks of cranes, tells him they are close to Laem Chabang docks. The driver and passenger witter and point as they find their way through side streets, access roads, past a refinery to a wire-fence dock gate. They get out and the driver pulls away without being paid.

Micky's accomplice, Kovit, walks to the gate kiosk where a shabbily uniformed Thai wearing a gun on his hip slouches in a chair. Kovit asks him something and the guy answers, pointing generally to some grey, corrugated sheds in the distance. A five minute walk across the open expanse of the dockyard brings them to an unmarked door upon which Kovit raps his knuckles. Micky fingers his wallet in his back pocket. His 'get out of jail card' was the first and last thing he checked when he came out.

A bolt is thrown on the inside and the door opens a fraction. Hushed words flash between Kovit and a man inside. Kovit juts his chin in Micky's direction. The guy leans around the door and assesses him with a sneer.

They enter a huge warehouse stacked with steel racks most of the way to the ceiling. Micky stares upwards, has never seen anything like it. They follow the man through an impossible maze of boxes, crates and cargo containers. Almost hidden among them is a white Mercedes Sprinter van. Modern and comfortable. Micky hopes it has aircon.

The guy leading them talks to someone else, mid-thirties with terrible acne and spiteful eyes, jerks his thumb over his shoulder at Micky and Kovit. The first guy walks off.

Pizza-face walks to the pair of them and stands provocatively close and stares. *Yeesh,* thinks Micky, no wonder he's in a bad mood. Doubtful he could get laid even in Pattaya.

After long seconds he pulls a key from his pocket and holds it out. Kovit takes it and they climb in. The man walks to the roller shutter door and buzzes it up. As Kovit edges the van out into the dazzling sun Pizza-face looks in through Micky's window.

'Don't lose it,' he says.

Out the gates Kovit steers them through the anonymous hinterland streets of the vast port and Micky is paranoid to the max, terrified they'll be jumped, killed or at least busted. Or all three. They pick up the 3 then head over onto the 7. No one comes near them.

On the open road Kovit floors it and in an hour they are approaching the sprawling outskirts of Bangkok. Micky, finally relaxing, reckons the sprinter takes a payload of maybe two tons and he can tell by the poor acceleration and the slight weaving on the road that they are dragging most of that, if not more.

But so far so good and he starts to relax, feels a twinge of hunger. One o'clock already.

'Kovit.'

He gets a look.

'Huw mai? Ahaan?'

'You can speak English to me.'

'Oh okay. I could do with a drink and something to eat. Can we stop?'

'Yeah. A place in ten clicks.'

They pull over at a service station, park up and stroll into the café area and Micky feels a blast of deja vu. A van hiding a load of coke that didn't exist at a service station in Kent.

They each buy a few bits. Drinks, snacks. They sit at a table and Kovit plays some kind of game on the screen of his phone. *Technology these days,* thinks Micky, an image of an exuberant Ishy flashes across his mind.

Eventually he puts the thing down and then wants to talk on the one subject Micky really can't help him with; football.

'You English. You not like football?'

'Sorry, man. Not my thing. I like rugby.'

'What about music? Beatles or The Stones?'

That's better. The kid wasn't standoffish after all. Good, because

Micky has some questions of his own. Well, one anyway.

'The Stones always. Better music and they were the original bad boys.'

'Zepellin or Sabbath?'

'Ha! Love it. I saw Sabbath around seventy-five but I prefer the Zep.'

'Techno or Drum and Bass.'

'Techno all day. Hey, you go out in Pattaya? I've never seen you.'

'Nah, I don't go out in Pattaya, it's for the farangs.'

'Fair enough, how do you know Gow?'

'Through my uncle.'

'Who is your uncle.'

'You know him. Narong.'

'Ah right. Now I got it.'

Micky gets a bit of a stare and hesitates. Then asks his question.

'So what's in the van, Kovit?'

'They didn't tell you?'

'I'm just an employee.'

'I see.'

Micky gets another stare.

'Well if you weren't told I shouldn't tell you. Your turn to drive.'

The miles drag by for a few reasons, one being Kovit likes rap music. Played loud. Micky hates rap.

He pulls over mid-afternoon for another break. Three hours after that, as night falls on the outskirts of a place called Lampang, Kovit swings into yet another truck stop. They fill the tank, take a leak and buy more drinks and food.

Micky settles behind the wheel. He takes a slug of coke.

'Got to wake up,' he says.

Kovit eyes him from across the seat. 'You're okay.' It's not a question.

Micky is a little surprised. 'Thanks. You too.'

'You want a real energy hit?'

'You mean Red Bull?'

He digs into his pocket and pulls out the ubiquitous small plastic bag. Red pills.

'Whoa,' Micky says. 'Not when I'm driving.'

'It's not Ecstasy. This is Yaba. You tried?'

Heard about it, been warned off it, never tried it.

'This'll get us to the border quick.' With that he disappears one of the pills with a swallow of orange Fanta. He offers one to Micky who feels it rude not to accept.

'You're okay.'

'Thanks.'

'Ivory.'

'What?'

'That's what we got in the back. Elephant tusks, Rhino horns. From Africa. On their way to China.'

Micky Targett fires up the engine and hits the highway north. Now he is in the illegal wildlife trade. He is forty years old.

Fifty-seven minutes later he feels like he is at the controls of an F16 jet fighter. Fuck, this thing can move! Freaking Mercedes, man. Those Germans. It's only when Kovit draws his attention to the fact that he is doing around thirty clicks an hour that he remembers he's on drugs. He's in the fast lane as well.

'I know what you need, dude.'

He rummages in the small rucksack between his feet, pulls out a cassette tape and rams it into the deck in the dash. Micky recognises the intro right away and howls with delight. The neat little scales of the guitar, the fat tom toms in after that. Then they are headbanging and Micky's boot squashes the pedal. They both time it perfectly into the first verse.

Say your prayers little one
Don't forget, my son
To include everyone

I tuck you in, warm within
Keep you free from sin
Till the Sandman he comes

Micky grins and looks out through the windscreen with a clarity of both vision and purpose he hasn't known before. His mind is clean. His mind is *pristine*. He has never been so alert and ready for whatever comes next.

He's feeling great and alive and he is the best driver in the world and if the little Thai bloke next to him tries to get the wheel off him he's going to knock him spark out. Screw it, he'll drive this thing all the way to China himself.

Exit light
Enter night
Take my hand
We're off to never never land

'You feeling okay, man? That more like it?'
'Yeah, this is good. All good.'
'It's okay. For certain things.'
'Like this. Staying awake and concentrating.'
'Right.'
'I feel really sharp. Hahahah.'

Yes, it all makes sense to Micky. Once again he's fallen madly on his feet. He's somehow got himself into the position where, with a bomber's moon lighting his way, he's driving a truck load of illegally imported African ivory through the Thai jungle up towards the Burmese border. One of the country's top policemen has virtually guaranteed him safe passage. He's getting paid. He has a cool kid with him who is into heavy metal and who has just given him some extremely powerful drugs. Of *course* it all makes sense.

They follow Highway 1 all the way into Chiang Rai town where the road is down to two lanes, slowly past temples, shops and houses and across the Kok river bridge. Then they are out the other side. Still on the 1. Still heading north. North to Burma.

Less than an hour later, as they draw near to the border, Kovit turns the music off and tells Micky to slow.

'We stop soon.'

They pass a brightly lit Shell station. Two hundred yards after that Kovit points to a crude layby with a dark car parked in it.

'There.'

Micky is wired enough to start worrying he's going to have to deal with someone other than Kovit, but at the same time there's a very convincing voice in his head telling him everything is going to be okay. This be some gooood shit.

'Wait here,' Kovit says as he drops down from the van.

362

Micky leans to his left so he can see in the nearside wing mirror what's going down. Kovit approaches the passenger side of the car, talks to the occupants. Almost immediately two men get out and the three of them advance back towards the van. Micky watches intently, sits motionless. Then Kovit opens the passenger door and pulls out his rucksack.

'Come on,' he says to Micky. 'Leave the key.'

Micky opens his door and nearly hits one of the other guys in the face with it. He gets a stare, says nothing, jumps out.

He walks around to the back, conscious of being close to the road where a huge, open-topped charabang loaded with twenty-odd field workers thunders past just a few feet away. He joins Kovit on the scrub at the side of the layby and they watch the van pull away towards the border crossing.

Micky is buzzing nicely and knows there is no way he is going to sleep. Which is why he is especially pleased to hear what Kovit says next.

'Okay, let's party.'

They pile into the empty car, Kovit gets some music going, then swings an outrageous, rubber-burning U-turn right across the road and they belt back to Chiang Rai town. They each neck another hit of Yaba and thirty minutes later they pile into an all-night brothel Kovit knows. Minutes after that Micky has the cutest little babe jabbering away as she bounces up and down on him.

Unlike when he's trying to shag on coke or Es, Micky finds Mister Floppy is nowhere in sight. They're bashing away for a good thirty minutes but, crucially, after a fifteen minute lay over he's ready to rock again. He's almost feeling sorry for her as he dishes out one of the finest pastings she's ever likely to get. Eventually he gives her four thousand and tells her to get some rest. He doesn't know if she understands, but she certainly doesn't hang around.

But he can't get to sleep and he knows he won't be able to. So he goes for a walk. The sun's up and the town is stirring itself for another scorching hot day. The main streets are concrete and tarmac but some of the smaller sois are still dirt. He ducks down one of those, looks into the shabby wooden houses and shops that are opening for business. He wonders if this is the 'real' Thailand. Away from the crowded beaches, away from the mobbed golden temples and Buddhas, away from the rows open rows of bars and clubs where young women feel they have no choice but to sell their bodies to self-serving, rapacious foreign men with too much money. Like him.

He comes across something that looks like it might be a café or 'restaurant'.

'Mee gafe mai?' he asked a woman sweeping the step with a broom.

She nods and points to a plastic chair. He sits and ponders the Yaba experience. It wasn't the best buzz he's had but, as Kovit said, it suited the moment. Crazy hot sex though. *Yeah,* he thinks, *we'll be having that again.*

The woman places a tin mug of something black in front of him. The taste of it makes his eyeballs frost over but it's what he needs. Helps get his head back on straight.

He looks up to see a Thai boy dressed in rags standing in front of him. In his hand is a plastic cup with nothing in it. Hanging around his neck on a string is a crudely made cardboard sign. On the sign are scrawled two words – Plese help.

The boy, maybe fifteen, is tall but painfully thin and when he looks up into Micky's eyes Micky feels his heart break. Maybe *this* is the real Thailand.

He reaches into his pocket, pulls out a thousand and hands it over. The kid thinks it's some kind of mistake, stands still. Micky takes back the note and pushes it into the boys pocket. Maybe he's being put out onto the streets by criminals and has to hand over the money at the end of the day. He's heard about that. Then he pulls some change from his other pocket, drops it into the cup.

'Cheu aria?' Micky asks.

The boy smiles and points to his own chest.

Micky smiles too and nods. 'Chai. Kun cheu aria mai?'

'Priow,' the boy says shyly, then moves away.

So now Micky has another income stream but, as per fucking usual in Mickyworld, there's a problem. It's quite a remote, out of sight out of mind kind of problem, but it bugs him nonetheless. He loves animals, always has.

His family came into possession of a tortoise when he was about six. Quite what a tortoise was doing in nineteen-sixties Stepney is anyone's guess but he loved that thing. Called it Simon, after Simon Templar in The Saint.

Then, when they moved out to Essex he bugged his parents for about a year before they caved and got him a dog, a gorgeous Golden Labrador. She was everything he'd ever wanted. He was twelve years old, the Lab was just one, but after just a few weeks he started worrying. Everything was fine with the dog, it was all in his head, and what was in his head was how slaughtered he was going to be when she died. All being well it was fifteen years down the road, but he couldn't stop himself.

Loves animals.

So when he actually comes around to being an active, hands-on participant in the illegal wildlife trade it really starts to eat his head. Especially when he considers the majority of it is going to be worn or eaten or used as decoration by ignorant Chinese and Vietnamese. Medicine. Ornaments. Rugs. Soup.

Tigers parts, Elephant and Rhino tusks, Pangolins. What the fuck is a Pangolin anyway? The runs become a regular thing.

The money and adventure he loves, but the whole of his existence he begins to doubt.

But there are always drugs.

As much as Micky enjoyed his first Yaba experience he found the comedown pretty grim. No proper sleep for two nights, nasty jitters and some serious jonesing. This was in part counterbalanced by Gow laying fifty thousand Baht in cash on him as his bonus for safe delivery of the load. His first thought was to get some more Yaba in.

Then he found his ideal combination by allying that shit with a decent hit of Mdma or a couple of Es. However doing that meant he often came up short when he needed a hard on that lasted more than five seconds. But a couple of hits of Cialis or pouches of Kamagra gel soon sorted that out. The chaotic hedonism of Pattaya suited him down to the ground, and there was an answer to every problem.

So, aside from feeling guilty about the animals, he was rolling. There was a time in his previous life when he had four girlfriends on the run simultaneously. In Pattaya it wasn't uncommon for him to have that many lined up in one *night.*

Not only that but it's not unknown for a man to run through an entire relationship, something that would fill up several years in the real world, in the course of a single evening. You could meet/be introduced to the girl of your dreams, fall in love over dinner, get drunk, do drugs, go out for the night, get laid, have an argument, squabble, fall out, split up and smooth things over with a sizeable divorce settlement in the course of one night.

It's kind of fun but . . .

Along with being upset about the animals, it's the girls themselves. He tries to kid on he's different. He tells himself that because he lives there, has a modicum of guide-book level Thai and is relatively young and okay to look at, the girls are really into him. It's a nailed-on fact that, assuming the same money was on the table, the bar girls and dancers would indeed chose Micky over some fat, elderly, stinking, decrepit German fucker who wanted them to shit on his chest and smear it all over him. Sure that much is true. But over time, as he learns more of the psychology of the place and of the industry, he comes to understand that it isn't about him at all. It's the money and that's *all* it is.

The girlfriend experience is on sale everywhere. But there are no girlfriends.

And they've all got the same story. They all lose their virginity to the boy next door sometime in their mid-teens. Condoms and sex education, both parental and at school, are unknown. They get pregnant and the boy legs it. Another mouth in another poor family to feed and, as they are becoming young women anyway, the societal and familial obligation to go out and earn money is upon them. But there's nothing they can do. Nothing except . . .

So even the fat, ugly ones get packed off to Bangkok. To Phuket. To Pattaya.

Micky meets some of them and talks to all of those he meets and they all tell that story and they all seem to come from up north. Isaan, Chiang Rai, Chiang Mai. Poor. Ignorant. Unchanging. Hooking in order to raise the next generation of girls who will, in less than two decades, replace themselves. The circle never breaks.

And it shreds Micky's heart and he wants to help. Many is the time he gives them money and insists on *not* sleeping with them. Slips them a few thousand and tells them to go home and have a night off. They kiss him, thank him, wai to him and he feels good.

Ten minutes later he spots them over the far side of the bar working some other sap. If there is an answer to this, Micky ponders, he has no idea what it might be.

So he thinks maybe it's time to find a girlfriend. Someone who works in a shop or a bank. He's into his forties, loves Thailand and wants to make a life here, but underneath the smiling veneer of the place he senses a meanness that shocks and worries him.

And then came the night when everything changed.

He's preparing to load up for a big one because the boat is out of the water for a service and Gow closes the shop to go to Bangkok for a couple of days. Micky's off the leash. He's an E and a Yaba to the good but, coming up to midnight an irritating, whining mosquito of a worry starts to buzz around the inside of his brain. Did he set the alarm in the dive shop when he locked up earlier? Bollocks! He can't remember and, fretting fruitcake that he is, he knows he won't be able to relax until he goes to check. He legs it down there, gets inside and what do you know? Of course he activated the alarm. He *always* activates the alarm.

Then he hears the shop door slam shut and the lock get turned. Then someone runs towards him and ducks panting behind the counter. He's in the doorway of the back room and sees what looks like a little kid, a girl. She's tiny and skinny and her entire mini-body heaves with rasping breaths. Then, through the gloom of the unlit shop, he notices she's dressed like a hooker. Short, tartan skirt, no more than six inches from waist to hem and a matching bra top, knee high boots.

Lying in the foetal position she stares up at him and all Micky has to do is look back into the desolation of her teenaged eyes to know there is something very *very* wrong.

'Hep.'

'Arai? Arai mai?' he says.

'Hep me. Please.'

'Help?' Micky kneels down next to her so he too is out of sight of whoever might be chasing her.

She nods and starts to cry, all the while terrified the sound of her own whimpering will alert her pursuers.

'It's okay, I help you.'

Outside he can see and hear a woman and a man, the man

thrashing the air with his heavily tattooed arms. They are shouting in Thai and he starts to feel as scared as the girl. He figures she's 'working' and has taken off. Maybe stolen something, maybe owes rent.

The couple outside moves off. Micky gives it about ten minutes then goes to stand. She grabs him.

'Where you go?'

'You want me to get police?'

Her eyes bulge in horror. 'No. Police no good. They hurt me.'

Micky is now really starting to panic which, along with the drugs, is a frame of mind that is totally weirding him out. Does he need to get involved in this?

'Okay, I get taxi. I have Thai friend. You talk to her.'

She thinks then nods.

'Stay here.'

Before he goes Micky grabs a kids' surfing T-shirt from the clothing racks along one wall. She puts it on. Pathetically it comes down to her knees.

Twenty minutes later they are safely in Micky's apartment. Micky crosses the hallway and hits the bell of 4C.

'Pim can you help me please?'

The ever smiling Pim is completely unruffled. She closes her front door and pads across the landing with Micky.

After a five minute conversation with the girl she is not looking so controlled. Micky hovers close by and can't help but notice the moistening of Pim's eyes.

'This is bad,' she says.

'What is?'

'She was taken from her family. Long time ago.'

'Taken? What, you mean like, trafficked?'

'Yeah.'

'Christ. When?'

'She can't remember. Maybe five years.'

Micky looks at this tiny bundle of humanity, squashed into one corner of the sofa. Her knees are tucked under her chin and the T shirt is pulled down to cover her legs. She stares dumbly ahead.

'How old is she?'

'She's not sure about that either. But sometimes Thai girls are small. I think maybe fifteen. Sixteen.'

Then the truth is on Micky like a lorry running him over. Fifteen or sixteen minus five. And dressed that way. But he has to know, has to put himself through it.

'So what has she been doing? Dancing?'

Pim asks her a simple question in Thai and the sad, silent nod that comes back is the answer neither of them want.

'Men fuck her. Sometimes farang men like children.'

That night Micky will both lose and find himself.

'Pattaya can be a bad place. Tourists not see this.'

Micky wants to be sick. His head is spinning. He would be in turmoil even without the drugs. He slurps from a plastic bottle of water.

'Pim, first thing please. Can you get the make-up off her? The nail-polish too.'

There's something unbearably revolting about that for Micky, the sexualisation of a child.

Pim stands, says something in Thai and holds a hand out to the girl, only to be greeted with a shudder of negation and a curt reply. Pim looks at Micky.

'She wants to stay with you.'

In deep, Micky boy. Getting in deep here.

'It's okay. I'll get some stuff and some clothes and come back.'

Pim leaves the room and the ensuing silence haunts Micky as much as the presence of this wretched infant.

He goes to the kitchen cupboards where he knows there is a bag of crisps. He offers it to the girl and she takes it, opens it and feeds herself robotically, looking straight ahead.

'What is your name?' he asks her.

'Tik.'

Pim returns with some clothes and a make-up case, sits next to the girl and proceeds to wipe away the obscenity of what has been done to this child. But Mick knows that's only skin deep. The internal atrocity won't be so easily dealt with.

As the last of the mascara is consigned to the bin Micky is overcome by a colossal hit of déjà vu. He looks into the face of this lovely young girl and thinks he knows her from somewhere. There's a tiny and fragile thread of recessed knowledge that he's clinging desperately onto. He *has* seen her before, but he can't think where and he feels the swirling brew of drugs and shock dragging on his senses. He lets it go.

Pim takes her into the bathroom to change and Micky sits on the sofa holding his head in his hands. He feels like crying. When they emerge back into the lounge he finds he has no choice. He looks at an innocent, broken kid and gushes tears of rage, indignation and guilt. He is ashamed to be a man, ashamed to be human.

When he comes out of it he asks Pim to translate.

'Ask her where she is from, Pim.'

The question is asked and the answer translated. 'She is not sure. She thinks Chiang Rai.'

'What are you going to do, Micky?'

'What do you think I should do?'

'You have to be careful. You said she is afraid of the police?'

'I wanted to call them but she was terrified.'

Pim speaks again and once more Micky sees the shudder of fear, the shock in the huge brown eyes.

'Tell her I know the chief of police.'

The reply that comes back from the girl seems to make Pim confused. She talks in Thai again, as if to confirm, then looks Micky square on.

'She knows the chief of police too.'

'What?'

'That's what she said.'

'Ask her what his name is.'

Micky awaits the answer with a throbbing heart and with nausea boiling in his guts.

'His name is Narong. He go to fuck her every week.'

Micky and Pim watch over Tikky as she fades into sleep on the sofa underneath a blanket he found in the third bedroom cupboard. Her chest rises and falls almost imperceptibly, like a puppy.

'I scared you do the wrong thing.' Pim whispers.

'If I do the right thing you mean. I have to rely on you, Pim. Nobody knows about this apart from me and you. We have to keep it like that.'

She thinks hard and long. She knows that if men are capable of hurting a child like that, they would be capable of worse to cover it up.

'All I need you to do is say nothing, Pim.'

'What will you do?'

Micky knows there is only one thing he can do, and he also knows this is like a gift to him. A chance to make a difference, do the right thing.

'I'm going to take her home.'

Unsurprisingly Micky's sleep is riddled with doubts and demons, to the point where he is unsure he has even slept.

Sprawled in an armchair he surfaces from his drowse, dragged back into consciousness by what feels like a knife in his hip. He sees the girl is gone. He whirls around and looks towards the kitchen area. She has found cereal and milk and sits at the table noiselessly eating.

He walks to the fridge, downs a whole bottle of water in one. He looks at the child.

'Sa bai dee mai?' he asks.

She nods silently.

He walks to the door and her eyes follow him. He holds his palms out in a gesture of honesty and supplication, nods and smiles.

'*Song na tee.*' Two minutes.

He exits the apartment but leaves the door open so that she can still see him as he crosses the landing to Pim's front door. He tells Pim he is going out for an hour. Will she watch the kid?

Back in his place he showers and changes his clothes. He delves into his papers that he keeps in the side pocket of his suitcase which lies on the floor in the exact same spot where he dropped it over a year before. Passport, bank card, driver's license. He gulps down extra strong coffee and readies himself.

He grabs a cab and heads straight to his branch of the Siam Commercial Bank on the beach road. He asks the driver to wait.

Inside the merciful coolness he takes his numbered ticket from the machine and hangs around for an agonizing five minutes before it's his turn. He hasn't touched the original two and a half million Baht that Wrenny deposited for him all that time ago, in fact he adds to it, namely when Gow hands him his fifty grand bonuses for the runs up to the border. But now, as the immaculately turned out cashier smiles expectantly at him, he is gripped by a spooked indecision. Is he going all the way? Cash out? Burn his bridges? He is aware that if Wrenny had opened his account for him then he, or anyone else come to that, could conceivably close it. Especially with the chief of police adding his clout to the request.

'Take out two million please.' He hands over his card, account details and lays his passport on the counter. The cashier busies herself at her computer terminal and Micky turns away from her to look out of the window.

The cab is right there at the kerb and behind that is the shimmering Gulf of Thailand. Palm trees fringe the sand. He is about to run from this, and his amazing, lucrative life.

But then he thinks, *there's a fucking pedophile ring here!* And one of his bosses is front and centre with his trousers down. That utter, scumbag, slope-headed piece of shit.

He thinks of that poor kid and knows it is up to him to do this thing, no matter what it costs.

Even if it costs everything.

But he can't take her to the cops, or anyone else because he knows the colossal reach the Thai police have. And if Wrenny and Gow or whoever else come out of the woodwork and argue against what he's doing then he wants nothing more to do with them anyway. Do they know about this? Are they involved?

'Yes please, Sir.'

Micky spins around expecting to see piles of crisp one thousand notes.

'Sorry, Sir . . .'

He hears the words and goes into meltdown. He needs a drink. He needs a hit. Of anything.

'Cannot give you money without your address. Where you stay in Thailand?'

Micky clutches the counter top with his elbows, nearly goes down. Jeezus.

He picks up a pen and writes down his address.

'Thank you, Sir.'

Five minutes later he piles into the cab and directs the guy to a car hire firm on the edge of town where he has rented scooters in the past. He pays off his driver, gets the big hello from the guy there he knows and rents himself a Toyota Celica. He takes it for a week, not having a clue where he or the car will be in that time.

Back at the flat the adrenaline that has been sustaining him starts to run low, but he can't stop now. He takes a couple of minutes, sits at the kitchen table and eats some fruit. Thinks it out.

He'll take her home, then he'll call Gow and explain the situation. Gow's a good bloke. He'll say it's fair enough, no harm done. Maybe they'll find the place where the kid was 'working' and make reparations, might cost a few quid but that's as maybe.

Yeah, he reckons, worst ways he'll just avoid that filth cop and it'll all blow over.

Which is why he decides to leave his suitcase and his stuff in his bedroom. He takes a rucksack with a change of clothes, toothbrush and a few bits and of course he grabs every single Baht he has in the place but he figures he'll be back in a couple of days. He has his moody passport and his bank stuff.

And some drugs.

Maybe he'll even be back before Gow returns from Bangkok and none of this will need to be mentioned at all. But then, in contradiction of that possibility, and with a creeping doubt beginning to overtake him, he does something else. He grabs the original plastic tube he brought his heroes over in and gets to work filling it. Then he takes the framed black and white photo of the good-looking couple from next to his bed. Then, once again, Micky Targett runs.

He leaves Pattaya mid-morning on a stifling day in May two thousand and one. The good news is he's in a decent car and he knows the way to Chiang Rai. The bad news is he is totally shattered, has nearly six hundred miles in front of him and has no idea where he's actually going.

Pim had tried.

'It's a little wooden house with a blue door.'

'Jesus. That it? Is it near anything?'

Pim asks.

'It's near a field.'

Great. As he belts along the familiar motorways he starts to consider the possibility of getting stuck with the kid.

He sneaks a glance at her as she gazes in amazement at the countryside flying past. She looks like a normal child, dressed casually in jeans and a T-shirt donated by Pim's niece, but Micky can't imagine what might be in her head. Do you ever get over that?

The miles roll by but there are so many of them. Micky doesn't know if he can make it. But what's the alternative? No way can he get a room. He could pull over and try to sleep for a few minutes at the side of the road but doubts he'd be capable. His mind races, but every possibility reveals a setback laid in a trap.

So at their second pit stop just south of a town called Nakhon Sawan, Micky washes down a red Yaba with a whole bottle of Krating Daeng. He knows it will spin him out but at least he'll be spun out and awake.

They use the bathrooms, stock up on fizzy drinks, crisps and sweets. In the 7/11 Micky wonders what he looks like. What he and this child look like. Together. How sodding suspicious can you get? To the car quick where he straps her in and they get gone.

An hour later, almost to the minute, he is sucked into a tornado of a meth jag. A jangling coolness drenches him, everything moves twice as fast as he knows it really is. But he's walked this road before and can handle it. Once the initial rushes and weirdness have faded he feels good, alert and sure he can stay awake.

Then he has a brilliant idea. He was worried about being on his own in Chiang Rai but then he remembers he knows people. The knocking shop where Kovit took him that time and to where he occasionally returned. He's a good tipper and the mamasan likes him. Brilliant!

He starts to feel good about things, his doubts and fears leaving him like sweat. He reaches forward and turns on the radio and has one of those moments when it all comes together.

He has found Thai radio generally catastrophic but there are a few am rock stations that occasionally get it right. Micky recognises the tap-a-tap of the intro, the first few chords but he can't quite place it. Then comes the looping guitar and he knows. He knows providence is at work.

Yes star crossed in pleasure the streams flow on by
Yes as we're sated in leisure we watch it fly

Time can tear down a building or destroy a woman's face

Hours are like diamonds don't let them waste

Time waits for no one no favours has he
Time waits for no one and it won't wait for me

And it all becomes clear. There's a heavenly symmetry at work and Micky gets it. He gets the wholeness of life. The truth and the lies, the beauty and the ugliness, the pleasure and the pain. Man and woman. Good and bad. But most important of all is the simple right and wrong. The two most perfect halves of all. Micky knows that his sense of right and wrong was always keenly developed, he was just too weak to let his instincts govern his actions. Now, as the majesty of the guitar takes him over, and as he looks at the innocent angel sitting next to him, he understands that the strength to do the right thing has come to him.

And he will do it now.

Her feet barely touch the floor of the car but Micky can see she is tapping her toes. She senses him looking and turns her face towards him. She eats her sweets and nods her head in time to the beat. Then she smiles at him and Micky Targett's knackered heart, so used and so beaten and so stepped upon, is made whole again.

The rest of the drive is an enchantment. Of course he is both exhausted and shitfaced, but it's not all about that. The bucolic splendour of the scenery, while the light lasts, is breath-taking. The sunset will stay with him forever. Every song the radio plays is deep with soulfulness and cryptic meaning.

Then he looks down at the cherubic bundle next to him. As they hit the outskirts of Chiang Rai she soundlessly sleeps and Micky feels an almost ethereal high. But it is not from any drug, indeed he is pretty much out the other side. He feels the goodness of the world all around him. And he feels pride, pride in himself, his judgement and his courage.

By the time he finds the brothel it is around midnight. He parks outside and leaves Tikky where she is. He finds Lucky, the diminutive, smiling mamasan who greets him with a hug and a kiss. He tells her he has a young girl outside that he wants to bring in. She gets the wrong end of the stick and goes nuts.

'Lucky, no no. No boom boom. I cannot go to a hotel. Tomorrow I take her home. I want to rent a room with two beds for tonight. Okay, mai?'

'Why you bring girl here? You no like my girls?'

'Lucky please, I have money. She is the daughter of a friend. No boom boom.'

She eyes him doubtfully. 'You don't want my girl tonight?'

'No. Thank you. Only sleep. I tired. Me give you five thousand Baht to stay.'

Should have said that in the first place.

He carries the lifeless form of the girl around the side of the rambling property to the rear entrance, in through the kitchen and then along a dark corridor to a back room. Lucky snaps on the light. There is only one bed but a decent looking sofa where he lays Tik. It will have to do. He hands over five thousand.

'Who she?'

'Her name is Tikky.'

'Where she live?'

'I'm not sure. Tomorrow I take her.'

The woman backs out of the room, unsure of what to make of the mad farang.

Voices and visions inside Tikky's head torment her mercilessly and her brow furrows in response. Micky watches over her then lays down on the bed, his mind spinning with the drama of it all. He is fully aware that what he has done may be seriously bad for his health, may put him in the crosshairs of some genuinely heavy people. Fuck 'em. Apart from the two million Baht in his rucksack he is truly a man with nothing left to lose. But that isn't the reason he falls into such a profound and restful sleep.

He can smell the sweat before he senses anything else. Soon after comes a bashing, slapping sound. Then the grunt of human effort and the aura of masculinity.

Micky walks through the doors and into the gym. It's partly lit but he can tell there is only one other person in there. Over by the far wall in the shadows there's someone working the heavy bag. Except it's not so much a shadow, more a black shape, a living, dangerous thing.

Micky approaches and in the half-light sees the shirtless man for the lithe machine that he is. The crouching, bobbing and then unleashing, he's practically airborne he throws so much into the punches. Especially the left hook that lands with an almighty *whump!* leaving a crater in the side of the bag, rattling the whole rig on its chain.

The dark shape over there makes Micky feel uneasy. He's seen it before and it always scares him. Always turns his dreams into nightmares.

Micky's presence eventually disturbs the man from his efforts and he emerges from around the back of the bag and Micky sees who it is. He never knew him when he was like this, but he's seen the pictures, heard the stories. The man steadies the bag then lets go one last left with a terrible explosion of power. The whole room shudders, the ceiling plaster cracks. *Jesus,* Micky Targett thinks, *pity the poor bastard who ever stopped one of those.*

Then the man steps out of the shadow, out of the dark shape. The mop of black curls, the rock solid jawline, the cruiserweight's physique.

'You want to get changed, have a work out?' he calls.

Just so long as there's no sparring involved, Micky thinks. 'I'd like that but I can't right now.'

'Yeah, you're busy. I know. You need to be careful with what you're doing.'

'True enough.'

'All that doing the right thing . . . ,' the man shakes his head and drops of sweat scatter to the floor. '. . . not easy, is it?'

'I'm finding that out.'

'That's why some people find life difficult, they always follow the easy path. Which usually doesn't go anywhere'

Micky nods, appreciates the wisdom. Then the man takes a backwards step, back towards the gloom.

'You though,' he calls. 'You never found an easy way, did you?'

Micky suddenly feels desperately sad, aware of all the struggling. Was it a waste? Was it futile?

'But you did good.'

'Really?'

'Yeah, and it takes talent to fuck up as much as you and still come back swinging, still trying to do the right thing.'

Just when he wants to stay and talk, maybe even get his shirt off and get into it with the bloke, he starts to hear a noise. Far away and indistinct at first but then louder and more insistent. A voice, small, scared and beseeching. Soon it takes over his brain until he has his hands up to his temples trying to stop it.

'Christ, why is there always something that spoils everything?' Micky says.

'Hey, there are no such things as problems in this world, just things that good people haven't dealt with yet. That's what doing the right thing is. Now wake up and be nice to that kid. She's more scared than you'll ever be.'

The man starts to fade back into the darkness but calls out one last time before he disappears. 'You're a good boy. I'm proud of you.'

Micky looks across, wanting to talk more.

'Why you do this?'

He thinks slowly and calmly. It's a good question.

'Why you help me?'

Oh dear.

'You want to fuck me now?'

In a tumbling rush of senses and emotions, Micky looks and feels around the dark room and realizes where he is. Where he is and what he has done. It's still dark and mesmerizingly quiet. In the blackness he can see a shape highlighted by two pinpricks of wet light.

'You fuck me now,' says a mouth from below the lights, except Micky doesn't know if it's a question or an instruction.

'Tikky?'

'Why you do this?'

Micky sighs and feels his mouth glued shut by dehydration.

'I want to help you.'

'Why? Because you want to fuck me. It okay.'

She is leaning over him, her face close enough for him to smell the surgary waft of the sweets he bought her earlier. He reaches out and takes her by the shoulders, moves her to one side as he sits up.

'I don't want to fuck you,' he tells her, feeling bizarrely guilty that he is using bad language in front of a child.

'Why? You no like me.'

'Yes I like you but I am taking you to your family.'

'Why?'

Jeezus.

'You no like me.'

'I like you but you are young. I don't want people to hurt you anymore.'

He hears a pathetic sniffle and then feels her move to him, feels her arms around him. He wonders if it's wrong to hug her back but he does it anyway, feels her child's frame so tiny in his arms. He looks over her shoulder, the tears streaming from his eyes distorting his vision, distorting the world. But then, with overwhelming relief, he notices the first smudges of daylight begin to dust the room.

Outside in the street, as the Chiang Rai heat begins to build, Micky gulps coffee and considers the ridiculousness of his task. He has abducted a child, already a trafficked minor, who has been working as a prostitute. One of the country's most powerful police officers, and therefore a corrupt and uncompromising individual, will doubless feel threatened by this unexpected course of events and therefore take an active interest in recovering said infant, and very probably Micky with it. As he ponders this he hears Wrenny's portentous warning.

'Don't fuck up over there.'

They sit outside the tumbledown café Micky discovered on his first visit to Chiang Rai. His rucksack is clasped firmly between his ankles. Tik sips coke through a straw.

Slurping greedily on fearsome coffee, he ponders the good and the bad. The good is that, unless Pim tells Gow Pleasant, there is practically zero chance anyone is going to find him where he is. No one knows he is in Chiang Rai and Thailand is a big country, especially out in the sticks. He could get plenty of use out of the car because he knows the cops are so poorly organized they won't be looking for it even after the rental company reports it missing.

Then he thinks about the downside, he has no way of getting this kid where she needs to go because no one knows who she is, and all she can remember is she lives in a wooden house with a blue door.

It is a measure of how insane Micky Targett's life has become that these two aspects of his predicament will be thrown into diamond sharp clarity, and his entire existence will be changed irrevocably in the space of the coming ten minutes.

He goes to the car and rifles the glove box, pulls out the map he was hoping to find. Back at his table he spreads it out but is disappointed to see it is a standard national one, showing scant detail of the area.

As he looks it over he is aware of a shuffling figure approaching the table. He looks up to see a skinny boy.

He pushes the map across the table to show Tikky. It's a long shot, but that's all he has.

'Tikky, doo tee nee, kup,' he tells her, pointing to the map. He looks up and sees her distracted by the boy. He looks at the boy who has his sad, watery eyes trained on Micky. Right, Micky thinks, back into rural Thailand.

He looks again and thinks there is something familiar about him, then notices the crappy sign around his neck. *So* that's *where I know you from,* he thinks. *Right here all those months ago. Right at this table.*

Smiling Micky nods, reaches for his pocket. As he does he hears Tik say something in Thai. He looks up but she is speaking to the boy. It's fast and in a northern dialect so he understands nothing of it nor the boy's response.

And so it goes for several exchanges until he notices Tik's eyes are suddenly awash with emotion. She launches to her feet and a strangled yelp of passion catches in her throat. The boy has become equally animated, his eyes massive marbles of shock, his bony fingers stabbing and pointing. Micky sits there with a thousand Baht note in his hand. Then the owner of the coffee shop brings Micky a fresh mug, and she joins in as well.

Micky is bemused but unconcerned as it all looks like everyone's having a good time. Be nice if he could share the fun but hey . . .

Then the two kids embrace and they are kissing each other. Micky sees that the woman standing beside him is now gushing tears and handing out the hugs to the pair of them.

What the actual fuck?

Then, when they've all calmed down, Tikky gasps in enough breath, composes herself sufficiently to lay the righteous truth on

Micky.

'This is my brother. He take us to my family. We go now.'

In his excitement, as Micky pulls away with two screaming Thai teenagers bouncing around in the car, he gives it a little too much right boot. Over onto the other side of the road, it is only the alertness of the driver of the oncoming Nissan that saves the day. Micky heaves it to the left, waves a hand of apology out of the window and gets gone without hanging around.

But the Nissan driver notices.

Astonishingly it is only fifteen minutes later when Micky pulls the car to the end of the shitty dirt track on which it stands. The old wooden house with the blue door.

Micky doesn't know what to do. The kids go flying in and leave him outside so he thinks it best to hang back. He listens to the sounds of grief, of sadness, of disbelief and of joy. The screaming, the laughing and the crying. So much crying. Eventually the bedlam subsides and he even thinks he should just get in the car and sod off. Mission accomplished. If he gets on the motorway now and sticks his foot down he could be in Pattaya that night. Drop the car off, get back to work. Maybe no one will know.

But something tells him it's not going to be that easy. He enjoys the euphoria of the moment, knows that what he has done over the last two days or so is probably his finest hour. But it ain't over by a long way.

CHAPTER NINETEEN

It's been a while since I saw your ultraviolet smile

Back in Chiang Rai Olivier is sitting in the reception area of the inconspicuous but very amenable brothel he uses when he's in town. But far from enjoying the early morning quickie he had promised himself he is perturbed for two reasons. The first is the girl he really likes isn't due to clock on for work until the evening. The second is the prang he very nearly just had a few streets away. Not so much the accident but the driver of the car.

Wrenny told him that bloke, Micky, was based in Pattaya, but there was no mention of him being in Chiang Rai. Olivier understood he alone was to be the chosen representative up north. He was the one looking to make contacts to buy the refined smack, and he was to be the one developing the routes into Europe to smuggle it. There is a fortune to be made in Thailand at the source, and he intends to be front and centre making it. Not only that, he's been looking forward to the time he can lay some pure material on his old friends Hmed and Adid, not knowing, of course, it would be exactly the same stuff they sold him.

So he sits in the reception area of the brothel and gets on the phone. Gets Wrenny in the loop to seek assurances that Micky Targett isn't treading on his or anyone else's toes. Maybe he'll see if Paithoon knows anything too.

Gow Pleasant is in his hotel room in Bangkok when his phone rings.

'Alright, Wrenny?'

''Ello, Gow. How goes it?'

'Not bad. I'm in the Big Mango. The boat is out of the water so we've closed for a couple of days. Back tomorrow.'

'Hm, interesting. When the cats away . . .'

'How's that?'

'Micky Targett is in a car in Chiang Rai with two Thai kids. One girl, one boy. I've justt had a phone call. You know anything about that?'

'Jesus. No. I left him three days ago and he was going nowhere.'

'Well he does have a reputation for getting himself off piste now and then. Probably nothing in it, just wanted you to be aware.'

'Right. Alright I'll look into it.'

Gow places his phone on the bed and thinks. As Wrenny says it's probably nothing. He likes Micky. Has his wild side but he's got a brain, works hard and, as the Thais say, he has a *jai dee* – a good heart. Which might be the problem.

But just what is he doing up country with . . .?

His phone rings again but this time he isn't pleased to see the name on the screen. In truth he's never pleased to have to talk to him. Kun Narong holds keys to many doors, but Gow knows evil when it's at the other end of a phone line.

Micky allows himself to be dragged into the house by the gaggling family. There is the mother who, Micky guesses, is probably about forty, even though she looks twice that. There is the boy Priow who could be in his late-teens, maybe early-twenties. Leggy and ungainly. He moves slowly, talks slowly. It's as if he is damaged in some way, perhaps a birth defect or an injury. But his smile is like the sun breaking through the clouds.

There is a younger daughter, Nok. Early-teens, hair in pigtails and pretty as a picture. Her face alight with joy and disbelief.

And there is Tikky herself, and she looks at him like he is the Buddha made flesh..

There is no adult male.

So Micky is sitting on the floor of this tumbledown shack eating and drinking with the family. Newspaper is taped over a window instead of a curtain. There is no furniture. He knows that these people are unhealthy and starving but they are prepared to share all they have with him.

He feels himself breaking up.

Then his phone rings.

Outside Gow Pleasant lays it on him.

'Get that girl back here now.'

'What girl?'

'Don't fuck about, Mick, and don't lie to me. Where are you?'

'Chiang Rai.'

'And who you with?'

The hesitation tells Gow all he needs to know.

'I've just had a friend of ours on the phone. There's a girl gone missing, a very important one. Our friend is concerned.'

'Why can't you say his name?

'He needs her back. Now.'

'He tell you why?'

'Boy, this is Thailand, there is no *why* here. All that matters is keeping in with the right people.'

Micky feels it rising. A switch flips in his head and an anger, for too long suppressed, begins to rise.

'All that matters, Gow? Did you just say that? Really?'

'I told you when you showed up, on your very first night. Remember? Don't go up against a Thai. Yeah? Because you will always lose.'

'Maybe some of us don't care. Maybe some of us are better than that.'

'Fucking hell, Mick. I thought you had a brain.'

'I do, Gow and my problem is I can't stop using it.'

'So let's cut to it. You can be back here tonight. Yes or no?'

'Of course not. She's a child.'

'Then it's out of my hands. And from now on things will get very very difficult for you.'

Micky looks at the now silent phone in his hands like it is infected with the plague, and suddenly he feels the same way about his life.

Inside, as four shining, sets of eyes look happily up towards him, the enormity of his task hits home. They have to run.

'I'm sorry but there is a problem. The policeman, he wants you to go back.'

384

'No. I not go back. I stay here now.' The panic in her eyes tells its story.

'Yes I know. You cannot go back. But we cannot stay here.'

'Why?'

'They will find you here. They will come.'

She switches to Thai, explains and swaps three exchanges with her mother.

'We have to stay here.'

'Why?'

'This our home.'

Micky glances around the place. A stiff breeze and it would be gone.

'Tik they will come here, they will find you and they will take you.'

More Thai.

'We have nowhere to go. We have no money.'

Micky thinks of the two million Baht in his rucksack, knows what he has to do.

'Do you have family or friends you can go to. Maybe in one week we can come back.'

More Thai.

'My mother has sister. We go there.'

'Where?'

'Near river. Near Laos.'

About eighty miles, but over five tortuous hours later, Micky aims the Celica down yet another jungle-thick dirt track.

Tik's mother claps her hands in anticipation and directs Micky to a wooden house up on stilts. It seems in reasonable condition and Micky sags with relief as he finally turns off the engine. They all pile out and run to the house.

Micky's hip feels like someone is drilling into it. He eases himself out of the car, grabs his rucksack and joins the others.

Later that afternoon, having met auntie Chan and decided where in the two-bedroom house they are all going to sleep, Tik takes Micky for a walk through the woods. She tries to hold his hand but it freaks him out.

After ten minutes of hiking along a trail through thick woodland they come to the crest of a hill, and on the other side of the hill there is a clearing and then Micky understands why they are there. In the mid-distance, sweeping the valley that it itself created millions of years ago is a huge, brown meandering river.

'Mekong,' she tells him. 'Other side is Laos.'

Micky drinks in the gorgeous panorama, yellowed by the dipping sun. He feels a sudden and overwhelming sense of belonging. *I could live here,* he thinks. *This could be me.*

'Can sit.' She points to the grass and they both settle down.

'Mum and Auntie Chan come from Laos.'

'You ever go there?'

She shakes her head sadly. 'Only Chiang Rai and Pattaya.'

'Tikky where is your father?'

'He die last year. Yaba take him. My brother tell me today.'

Not for the first time, and he knows not for the last, Micky feels his heart squeezed just a little bit more. But with that hurt he finds another iota of strength to deal with it and the wickedness that causes it. Then she says something that makes him feel infinitesimally small.

'Other girls working with me in Pattaya.'

He breathes deep and wonders if he will ever know real peace.

But he does understand, as he sits on the grass with a child he doesn't know in a place he's never been to, that he has to give everything he can to make her life better. There and then he pledges himself because he knows that however indirectly and unknowingly, he was one of those that caused the calamities that miraculously haven't crushed her.

'Maybe we can go one day.'

She looks him in the eye, her bullshit sensor activated. 'You want?'

'I want to go everywhere. You have passport?'

'What is that?'

It's a good question and one that makes him think about his own predicament. He has a fake passport that has six years of life left on it. He can use it to get back to England, but if he is to avoid jail he'll have to stay under the radar for the rest of his life.

But he's heard a little about Laos. Coming out of hardcore communism. Opening up to tourists. Cheap. Maybe he could disappear there for a while.

'Do you want to go back to school, Tik?'

The word seems to confuse her, even unsettle her. Perhaps it's a trick question.

'I don't know. I only happy be with my family.'

As the light fades they make their way back to Auntie Chan's house and Micky is possessed by a distinct unease. He knows something is going to happen, and that thing will be in the form of a phone call. He also knows who will make that call. What he doesn't know is how Wrenny will view what he has done.

As they reach the steps up to the house the phone in his pocket warbles softly. *Getting good at this game,* he thinks. Shame it's almost certainly too late.

He motions for Tik to go inside and he checks his phone. Number withheld.

'Hello?'

There is something about the silence that fills the following two seconds of dusky Thai air that tells him both who it isn't and who it is. The silence has physical dimension. He tells himself he should have known.

'Hello, son. How you been?'

'Well well. Connie Chetkins. Nice surprise but it kind of makes sense.'

'Sense? You got any left?'

'It feels like I have. Hearing your voice at this particular time answers a few questions.'

'Oh yeah? Well I have a couple of minutes. What's on your mind? Anything at all?'

'Well yeah. We can start at that place in Pattaya, Diablos. Gow told me there are three partners. Him and Wrenny and . . .'

Micky enjoys the silence.

' . . . And you. And I can imagine you gabbed the lion's share, right?'

'An imagination can get you in trouble, son.'

'Sure there are bars and businesses in Pattaya but the money's in the runs isn't it? Drugs down from Burma and the triangle, then back the other way.'

'What about back the other way?'

'If I'm going to be driving the van don't you think I'd find out what was in it?'

More burning silence.

'Rhino horn, Elephant ivory. Tiger skins. All comes from South Africa. Got your dabs all over it, that's why your man Faf was here a while ago setting this up. Smack and Meth from up north to Bangkok and Patts and wildlife parts from you into Thailand and then shipped back up and on to China. Proper double run.'

'I've said it before, Micky, you're not as dumb as you make out.'

'And the cops and authorities are piss easy to bribe or to cut in.'

'All that has nothing to do with this call.'

'I wondered when we'd get to it.'

'You've gone and taken something that doesn't belong to you.'

'Taken? Belong? Can you hear yourself? She's a person. She's a fucking child!'

'It's a different world there, you idiot.'

'It's a different world here because scumbags make it so and people who should know better look the other way. Excuse me if I'm not that much of a cunt.'

'You've upset all the wrong people already, son. Don't add me to the list.'

'You're a father, Con. What about your Sandra? Yeah, how about that? Think back to when she was nine or ten. Some piece of shit grabs her off the street, puts her to work. So she's getting fucked all day everyday by pedo filth like your mate. Is this part of your empire? You're defending a nonce because you make money out of him?'

Micky hears a noise, looks up to see Tik and her mother on the creaking terrace of the house. He has been shouting. He holds his hand up in apology and moves along the track away from the house. The line has gone quiet and he fears he has lost the connection. Too dark to go back up the hill

'Con?'

Breathing. 'She's *how* old?'

'Nine or ten when she was snatched. You not know that?'

' . . . That I did not know.'

'That was about five years ago but she's not sure. Some life eh?'

'Where are you?'

'Sorry, mate.'

'This could fuck everything.'

'I don't care and neither should you.'

'He wants you and the girl dead.'

Been on the phone too long. Is he being tracked?

'She'll fade into the background. She doesn't want revenge but it's not her he has to worry about. If he comes after me I'll bring everything down. I liked it in Pattaya but I couldn't not help this kid, Con. Maybe you should tell him I'll take her to the papers.'

'Don't do anything stupid.'

'I don't want to but the press might like that – Hero foreigner rescues child from police pedophile ring. I'll be on the evening news, get an agent . .'

'Listen to me. . '

' . . Do shaving ads. Write my fucking memoirs.'

'Look I understa' . . .'

'Con I'm going to go. I see one person in the rear view - I'm going public.'

He cuts off the phone and goes inside for dinner.

They sense something isn't right but they know Micky has things under control. Well, they *think* he does.

On the floor around the simple yet delicious evening meal they jabber happily and Micky can't help thinking he has a new family, the tug is that strong. He thinks back to his own fractured life in Essex. His mother leaving so young, his brother a vile excuse for a son and sibling. And his dad, Rock Steady Eddie, once so strong and so proud reduced to helplessness and dependency.

Did he do enough? He still blames himself for not having the guts to reach out to Nigel and bring him to Eddie's bedside when he was asked, but he knows he is only human and he knows he can only do the best that he can and no more. He tries not to beat himself up. Then he looks at the faces around him and, his certitude absolute, knows that this time, he won't let anyone down.

Three days later he drives back to Chiang Rai town for two reasons. Firstly he needs to get to an ATM to see if his bank account is still live, and secondly he wants Tik and her mother to know they should be able to move back home. They are all to be disappointed.

At the first machine they come to he nervously feeds his card into the slot. Then he waits. In anticipation of this moment he has Tik standing next to him to translate the message that flashes across the screen.

'Closed.' She does that motion of cutting her hand across her own

389

throat. 'Finished. Card go.'

He curses himself for not emptying the account when he could. If that wasn't bad enough pulling up to the house is a million times worse. This is because the house isn't there anymore. At first he just thinks they're in the wrong place, but then he sees the scorch marks up in the surrounding trees and then he hears the wailing of Tik's mother.

They get out of the car and approach the pitiful piles of still smouldering memories that were once a family home. Micky shuffles his deck, looks for his next move. If he thought he stepped up before, he knows that now he really needs to raise his game.

'Tik, tell your mum it's okay. I can help you.'

She jabbers to her weeping mother and Micky starts to get chills just by being there. Maybe they're close by. He hustles the two of them into the car and gets gone.

Back at Chan's house Micky looks around and wonders what can be done with it. There is plenty of room to expand and build. Knock the place down and start again maybe?

He treks up through the woods to the crest of the hill, looks down upon the Mekong and across into Laos. Maybe they could run there if need be.

His phone rings.

'Yeah?'

'It's Connie.'

''Ello, mate.'

'How you doing up there?'

'Well I think the quiet might get to me after a while but I like it. Simple life, perhaps that's what I need.'

'I'd like a meet.'

'Would you now?'

'Just me.'

'What for?'

'Say goodbye. Call me sentimental.'

'I've heard weirder things. Just you?'

'You have my word.'

'I'll take that. How's nonce face?'

'Do yourself a favour and let it go.'

'Who torched the house?'

A sigh. 'He did. Not him obviously, some local goons.'

'Nice.'

'You got to stop pushing, son. I know it ain't fair but you're a long way from home and if you get away with your life on this then you've done well. I've got you and the girl a pass.'

Micky lets that settle in his head. There's a future?

'But you're a non-person, son. Stay out of sight. Even Chiang Rai town.'

'Don't leave me with a lot for doing the right thing.'

'Them's the breaks, kid. So we on?'

'Yeah. After everything it will be good to see you. When you getting over.'

'I'm already here.'

'Already where?'

'Pattaya. Got some other news for you too. An old friend of yours breezed into town yesterday. Quite a pallavar.'

'Jesus. You don't hang about, Con.'

'I've been putting out your fires, son. I'm out of Don Meung at just after noon and into Chiang Rai an hour later.'

'On your own?'

'That's what I said.'

'I'll be there.'

And he is, but the longer he waits the more he knows it's a set-up. Connie's plane shows on the board as landed but after twenty minutes there is still no sign of him. Micky shoots edgy glances over both shoulders knowing that any minute now . . .

'Hello, son.'

Big Connie Chetkins in the flesh. And alone. Then the handshake, but no pain this time. What does *that* mean?

Then they're sitting at a table over in the corner of the arrivals hall drinking bad coffee and talking and it was really nice for Micky. After all of it he can't help but concede what a solid, bona fide legend Connie Chetkins truly is, prescient cunning oozing from every pore. Okay he was involved in some foul shit but hey . . .

'So what's the plan?'

'Well, now that I know I'm not going to get killed I can set about making one. Shame someone shut down my bank account. That doesn't help.'

'That was part of the deal. You're not short are you?'

'Got the emergency stash. It'll do.'

'So?'

'First thing is to rescue whatever might be left of that kid's soul. Learn Thai. Maybe get a dog.'

'Go native eh? Colonel Kurtz.'

Micky looks him over, wonders what the catch is. Does there have to be one?

'Con, why have you come all this way?'

Connie lifts his eyebrows and shrugs and, in truth, wonders the same thing.

'Something about you that reminds me of me.' Is what he comes back with. 'You have a habit of doing the right thing even when it's obviously the wrong thing and I appreciate that. That make any sense?'

'None whatsoever.'

Connie grins. 'I spoke to Sandra last night, she says hi.'

'That's nice. How's she doing? Young James?'

'They're both good. He's got his first girlfriend.'

'Oh shut up. How old is he?'

'Sixteen.'

'Jeezus.'

'In other news Sandra's getting married. He's a plonker but he's good for her.'

Micky looks into his coffee, does the 'what might have been?' thing. They're on the beach in Mallorca.

'What shall we do, Mick?' she'd asked. 'About us.'

Where would he be now if he'd let himself fall for Sandra Chetkins?

'So you said there was an old friend of mine you saw?'

'Oh yeah, a man who bears a *big* grudge showed up in Pattaya looking for you.'

Micky can't help but think that's any number of people. 'I'm all ears.'

'Terry Farmer.'

'Get the fuck out.'

'Tracked you down and came all this way. Was going to kill you. You see what I'm saying about letting things go?'

'Fuck. My. Old. Boots.' Micky holds his fingers to his temples.

'Kind of lucky I was there, and you weren't.'

Micky gawps back at him, the word gormlessly not even covering it.

'Thank me later.'

'Christ, what happened?'

'He went a bit nuts, said he knew I was behind it all, you know, him going away all that time ago.'

'Jesus. And . . ?'

'Fortunately Gow and Wrenny were there so we slapped him a bit then called our friends at the local nick. They banged him up and told him he was looking at ten years for assault with a deadly weapon.'

'Oh my God.'

'Then we bailed him out, told him we could just as easily have left him there, gave him a grand and put him on a plane. Really, you can thank me later.'

'Holy crap, Con. Thanks. Thanks, man.'

'All part of the game, son. Probably best you're off the firm. You're just too nice. I'm sure I told you that at least once before.'

'I'm easily led.'

'It's more than that. You don't put yourself first often enough.'

So they shoot the shit for another hour or so until it's time for big Connie to get back south. Get back to the empire.

'One thing, mate,' Micky says as they stroll over to the departure gate. 'I've kind of nicked a car. You know that rental place on the outskirts of Pats we all use. Can you tell the bloke I didn't mean to do it? Gow's got his number. I'll drop it off here at the airport if that helps.'

Connie tips his head back as he guffaws. 'You're priceless, son. Always good for a laugh. I'll square it and he'll stick a claim in. Don't worry.'

They shake hands and look into each other's eyes.

'I won't see you again?' Micky asks, suddenly very sad at the prospect.

'I doubt it.'

Micky nods and then he turns and leaves.

Finding construction workers and suitable materials in rural Chiang Rai is not easy but that's not Micky's problem. He tells Tik

393

that he will pay for a new house, as big as they need it, to be built on the site of Auntie Chan's place. It's a beautiful spot and the family owns the land. At first they seem reluctant, but Micky tells them it's best if they keep away from Chiang Rai town. Then he gives Tik's mother half a million Baht in cash. It's more than she thought existed in the world, yet there it is, piled up in its multi-coloured glory in her shaking hands.

So the house gets built and there is room for Micky and he loves it, loves what he's done. He makes sure Tik and Nok go to school and delights in supplementing their English lessons. He starts to pick up some real Thai.

But he doesn't know if it can last. He needs to be doing something. Something away from the family.

One day, when he is driving back from the shops, he is distracted by a newsreader on the radio talking about New York. He can't really understand but knows there is something bad that's happened. Two planes. He takes his eyes off the road. Then he hears a loud bang against the front wing.

He gets out and sees a yellow dog thrashing at the side of the road. Panicking he scoops up the whimpering ball of mange and places it on the passenger seat, then belts to this place he's heard about. On the edge of Chiang Rai town, conceived and operated by two ex-pat Brits, Soidogs is a hospital, sanctuary and adoption service for stray dogs.

He pulls up outside a crudely built veterinary clinic. They take the dog in. While he is there Micky scopes the place out and they take *him* in as well. It's volunteering so there's no wages but it's what he's been looking for.

He continues to support the family but moves into a cheap shack he finds a couple of clicks from Soidogs. There's nothing to it but he likes that. Likes the simplicity. He tapes Sheene, Mckay and Blackmore back up onto the wall where they belong. He places the framed black and white of the good-looking couple on a chest next to his bed.

And time goes by. Years of it, but it's good and rewarding, this outlier's life of his.

He makes friends with a couple of the Burmese who help to run the place. At the end of the working week one day in early two thousand and three, or possibly two thousand and four, one of those guys asks him if he wants to have a smoke. Micky thinks he's got some ganja so goes with him to the crappy accommodation bloke where he is housed.

But it's not ganja. Micky knows he shouldn't but can see no reason *why* he shouldn't. He's not doing it because he's feeling down and wants to feel less so. It's not like it was with the smack. He finds he just likes the buzz of opium, no more no less. It fits in with his lifestyle.

Micky knows the Burmese migrant workers earn sod all and have a tough life so he starts buying the opium and dishes it out to them for free. He feels it's the least he can do. In order for this to happen the Burmese fellow introduces Micky to his supplier. It's a young Thai bloke, big lad in his mid-twenties. He's obviously making bundles because he runs a cool Yamaha R1. His name is Thanawat and Thanawat sells him the opium.

So there he is, finally content. He continues his struggle with the tonal complexities of the language but feels like he's winning that. He hangs out with his beloved dogs during the day and he reads, listens to music, smokes opium and drinks beer in the evenings.

It's not *all* he has ever wanted, but until he finds out what that is then it will definitely do.

And, watched over by his three heroes and his parents, he sleeps a perfect, guilt free sleep. Okay so he's lost a couple of back teeth and his hip digs him now and then but he has the peace he always craved.

He visits the family once or twice a week on the knackered scooter he bought for a hundred quid from one of the Burmese. He needed new wheels because he gave the Celica to Tik and he did that because she had the idea of starting up a taxi service from Chiang Rai. Using the English that Micky taught her she collects two or three travellers at a time and provides guided tours and arranges accommodation in Laos, specifically Luang Prabang, and across the north of Thailand. As she moves into her early-twenties, Micky notices she retreats less and less into the silent cave of self-preservation she fashioned for herself following her years of degradation. She has become a confident, bi-lingual, capable young businesswoman who takes care of her whole family.

Which is just as well for Micky, because he knows, and this is a familiar feeling for him, that his stash won't last forever. It is something that should bother him, but in his ongoing state of Zen enlightenment and comfort, he knows worrying achieves nothing. Something will come along.

Then, on a blazing afternoon in two thousand and eight, for his sins, something does.

Behind him he can hear the crackling growls of a couple of the dogs, suspicious of strangers and protective of their boss man. He walks to the fence, stares in disbelief at the face looking into the pen at him.

Fuck. My. Old. Boots.

Later they are sat outside a friendly little bar Micky knows, clinking bottles of cold Leo and grinning massively at each other.

'I've had a few surprises in my life,' marvels Micky with an exaggerated shake of the head, 'but this is up there. Ishy my man. Holy shit.'

'Good to see you again, Micky boy. Been a while.'

'That it has. Ten, twelve years.'

'Got to be.'

'So who's going to go first?' Micky asks.

'What, with their story?'

'Yeah.'

'Well, seeing as you live in the jungle with a pack of wild dogs I think yours will be a lot more interesting than mine.'

'Can't argue with that,' Micky says. 'First things first though. How's Kerry and the young 'un?'

And it's like turning off the light. *Please don't tell me she's dead,* Micky thinks.

'Split up, mate, and it wasn't nice.'

'Ah, *man.*'

'Took the kids, ran off back to Brighton. Cupla years ago. *And* she's hitting me for heavy maintenance.'

'Shit, sorry to hear it.'

Ishy shrugs. 'What you gonna do? Lost me job too.'

'Ah Jesus, Ish'.'

'Yeah. But there's something in the wind. Something's happening.'

'How do you mean?'

Ishmael Zamaan isn't quite sure what he means himself. The years of ridiculous growth and the advances in technology have made many people feel they are invincible. City people. Bankers. Computer geeks. Technophiles. Bonuses are still through the roof, if you're a chosen one, but the layoffs have already started for those who aren't. Like him.

But even though he fell out with the wrong people at work he knows his stuff, more than that he *knows* he knows his stuff. Which is why he has come halfway around the world. He knows something is coming. He just has a sketchy idea of what that is though. It's a long time since the man stood on a stage in blue jeans and a black rollneck and told people he could put a thousand songs on a device that would fit in their pocket. And everyone thought he was mad.

The internet.

The future.

Digital reality.

It's happening now. And more.

'There's a recession coming.'

The words blitz through Micky's nervous system and he's right back in the apartment Ishy used to share with Kerry down in Brighton. Last time around prior to *that* recession. Early-nineties, just before they got rich.

'I've heard you say that before.'

'And I was right.'

'You were.'

'And I'm right about this. In the next year or so banks will fail. The system is done. There will be new ways to buy things. Cash will soon be a thing of the past.'

He's lost Micky already, whose idea of a technical challenge is changing a fuse.

'How's the money situation, Mick?'

'I got all I need.'

'Yeah, but the future. What about your endgame?'

'What's that?'

'Endgame. What it says. Your final play. How's it going to end for you? When you're old and weak, who's going to be there for you? Who's going to wipe your arse?'

Micky thinks back to the stultifying grimness of those last few years with his dad. In spite of his recent blissful contentment it's a subject he does come to ponder. Maybe he could rely on his new family. But maybe, despite Tik's current success, they'll need to rely on him again. Fact is he has about six hundred quid's worth of Thai Baht buried in a tin behind the shack. He has no way to earn money and no prospects so to do. He is an illegal alien. He can't even travel anywhere because his passport, in the name of Phillip Paul Jackson, expired a few months back. Soon enough he won't be able to afford to stay in Thailand, and already he has no way of leaving.

'Ishy, we'll get to the how you found me in a minute. But what's the why? Why have you come?'

'I need a partner.'

'Oh yeah?'

'And you're in the middle of it here.'

'Middle of what?'

'The golden triangle.'

'You want to be a drug dealer again? I remember you telling me before you weren't very good at prison.'

The evening sun touches gently on the eyes of Ishmael Zamaan. He looks off down the dusty village street, collects his thoughts. He's not even sure of what he's been learning, reading, researching. But he knows that it will happen and he knows that when it does he will be front and centre.

'What if I told you we could sell all the drugs we could get our hands on and never have to meet any of our buyers.'

Micky doesn't want to hear about it, but Ishy has come all this way.

'Alright, I'll bite. How do they get the stuff?'

'We post it to them. We've all done that before.'

'Okay so how do we get paid? They send us a cheque? That means we have to set up a moody account which I'm sure is getting tough to do these days. Then you only get a certain amount of time. And not everyone is . . .'

'No cash, no cheques, no accounts. No banks.'

'Oh I got it, the barter system is back. I sell you a gram of coke you give me a bunch of carrots and a leg of lamb.'

'Cyber currency.'

''Scuse me?'

Ishy feels his blood loosen. He leans forward in his seat.

'I've been hearing about this bloke. Japanese. He's designing a form of payment that totally bypasses the banking system. It gets sent anonymously to your computer and that's where it stays until you want to buy something with it. No one knows about it. The revenue boys, customs, Plod. It's all under the radar.'

'A new form of money.'

'It doesn't exist yet, but it will. And soon.'

Micky drains his bottle, signals the bloke for two more.

'We set up a website advertising our stuff, people place an order, we post it and they send the money to our computer. We can even have a rating system. If we sell good stuff they give us five stars, but if the stuff is crap they can mark us down.'

Micky's mind starts to tick. He doesn't need this but he does need something.

'It'll be like Ebay for gear.'

'Like what?'

'Jesus, what are you, Amish?.'

They drink slowly, eye each other across the creaking wooden bench of a table. Micky knows nothing of what Ishy speaks, but he does know the business from the supply end. He *is* in the right place. Difficult to imagine anywhere else more epicentral to their needs. Some of the finest opium in the world is a phone call away and he knows that smack and meth aren't too far behind.

'Mate, do you think I'd come all this way if I didn't know it would work? Me and you are good for each other. Come along with me and we'll get rich like you could never imagine. Don't tell me you haven't got connections here.'

They talk for a while and make arrangements to meet the next evening. He is seeing the family tonight and can't get out of it. And he needs to get back to his little place and think. To rest and to think.

But he knows. He knows already.

As they part they shake hands and hug. Then Ishy speaks.

'At the end of it, mate. After everything, all we are left with are the choices we make.'

Micky Targett looks at his old friend and nods gravely as he snuggles into the familiar and comforting inevitability of what is happening. He is back in the drug business. He is forty-eight years old.

Micky Targett will return later in 2022 in the
concluding part of the Essex Noir trilogy

Printed in Great Britain
by Amazon